EX LIBRIS

HELEN DUNMORE

Birdcage Walk

HUTCHINSON
LONDON

1 3 5 7 9 10 8 6 4 2

Hutchinson
20 Vauxhall Bridge Road
London SW1V 2SA

Hutchinson is part of the Penguin Random House group of companies
whose addresses can be found at global.penguinrandomhouse.com.

Penguin
Random House
UK

First published by Hutchinson in 2017

www.penguin.co.uk

A CIP catalogue record for this book is available from the British Library.

ISBN 9780091959401 (Hardback)
ISBN 9780091959418 (Trade paperback)

Set in 12.5/16.5 pt Sabon LT Std
Typeset by Jouve (UK), Milton Keynes
Printed and bound by Clays Ltd, St Ives plc

Penguin Random House is committed to a sustainable future
for our business, our readers and our planet. This book is made
from Forest Stewardship Council® certified paper.

Birdcage Walk

Towards the end of the eighteenth century there was a frenetic building boom in Bristol. Builders and developers competed against one another, borrowing heavily to buy up land. Between 1789 and 1792 work began on several terraces which were to be sited spectacularly on the steep slopes of Clifton, two hundred feet above the River Avon. Among these were Royal York Crescent, said to be the longest terrace in Europe, Cornwallis Crescent and Windsor Terrace. But in 1793 war was declared between Britain and France. Bristol's housing boom collapsed, and more than fifty builders and developers went bankrupt within a few months. Hundreds of houses were left unfinished for years, in a roofless spectacle of ruin.

Prelude

If my friends hadn't decided that I should have a dog I would never have opened the gate and gone into the graveyard. I always took the paved path between the railings: Birdcage Walk, it's called, because of the pleached lime trees arching overhead on their cast-iron frame.

In late summer the rosebay willowherb grew taller than the battered headstones and monuments. Every so often the graveyard would be strimmed and the stones would show naked. The tide of green would be stemmed for a few weeks, but it could never be held back. I once saw a man doing t'ai chi in a clearing, but usually only dog-walkers ventured among the graves. The church itself had been bombed to rubble during the war. In its place there was a lawn where children were not supposed to play ball games, and some rose trees planted in honour of a forgotten royal occasion.

I liked Birdcage Walk, especially late at night, when darkness and the rustle of nocturnal creatures gave an edge to the safety of the paved path.

I was still learning to be a dog-owner. I'd never considered becoming one, but when I was left alone I soon saw how uncomfortable my solitude was for everybody. Walking on my own was no great pleasure, and we had always walked. I thought of joining a ramblers' group, but I'd never liked being organised and so the idea melted away.

Jack had belonged to a girl I'd known from babyhood, the daughter of two dear friends. Nora was moving to Australia. I took Jack on a whim, perhaps because I couldn't think what else to do. And besides, everyone was so eager to match me with the dog, and they had been very kind since I was left alone. There was no question of taking on a puppy. Jack was five years old, perfectly trained.

It didn't seem like much more than an idea until the day Nora brought Jack round, with all the paraphernalia about which I knew less than nothing. We'd had a couple of introductory sessions, of course. I'd taken Jack for a walk, feeling an entire fraud. I knew what food he liked and that he must not have it more than once a day. But this time, when Nora left, she didn't take her dog with her.

So there we were, alone together. Jack was a mongrel, or mixed breed as they say now. He was rough-haired and had a strong little body and a pointed, foxy face which at the same time expressed a willingness towards the human which you would never find in a fox.

He took to me. I let him sniff my hand and I fed him and made him walk behind me through doorways –

Nora had told me this was important – and we began to go for long walks together. Everybody talked to me. It's a cliché, I know, but it's not until you've been left alone that you realise how very few people want to pass the time of day with a solitary and no doubt rather grim middle-aged man. I entered a little world which had obviously always been there, running parallel to the one in which I lived. I talked about Jack and enquired about Rosie, Dexter, Ebony, Skye. It was pleasant, but I still liked a solitary walk from time to time.

It was one of those long, slow summer dusks and Jack and I were the only creatures on Birdcage Walk. I heaved the gate open and Jack flashed away into the dense tangle of ivy, long grass, bramble, periwinkle and wild clematis. I could just see his hindquarters quivering in ecstasy as he explored a hole where a stone had keeled over. I whistled and he came to heel in a way which still astonished me – and, if I'm honest, delighted me.

We plunged on together through the graves. Some of the inscriptions were legible, some worn away. There was a particular type of stone which flaked off in layers, taking the inscriptions with it. Whatever care had gone into choosing the words, they did not matter now. It was hard to credit that real bones lay thick in the soil, but perhaps they too had dissolved. I wasn't sure how long it took. The graves were all more than a hundred years old.

Jack vanished beneath a wild rose bush, snuffling and then barking. I called him off and he came reluctantly. His look was so urgent, so abjectly enthusiastic that I didn't have the heart to keep him back. Let him dig if he wanted. It could do no harm, after all this time. I was careful. I was not one of those who festooned the iron railings with little plastic bags of dog crap. Jack barked again. He was looking back at me, as if he wanted me to come too.

I waded through the undergrowth, lifted a thorny branch and peered at the grave where Jack was digging. It sounds fanciful, but I half believed that Jack had brought me here for a purpose. The stone leaned only slightly backwards and the inscription was deep cut. I could not read it all but a name jumped out at me: Fawkes. For some reason I was curious. I suppose I thought of Guy Fawkes, and his awful fate, and the bonfires that still burned in his name. I bent down to look more closely. Jack was flurrying up earth with his paws but otherwise doing no harm as far as I could see. He had probably found a rabbit hole. I flattened the undergrowth with my boot and knelt down. Now I saw what I had not noticed at first: there was an object carved beneath the inscription. I puzzled over it, and then I saw what it was: a quill pen, beautifully drawn in stone. A craftsman must have done this. I ran my fingers over the inscription, for most of the words were hard to read. The script was flowing and copious.

To the Beloved Memory of Julia Elizabeth Fawkes,
Wife of Augustus Gleeson,
This Stone Was Raised on 14th July 1793
In the Presence of her Many Admirers.

And underneath, immediately above the quill, was written:

Her Words Remain Our Inheritance.

The inscription struck me as unusual. No dates of birth or death were given, and although Julia Elizabeth Fawkes was clearly married to Augustus Gleeson, she had not taken his name. Of course it was the many admirers who interested me most. She was a writer, clearly, but what had she written? I had never heard of her.

I called Jack to me. He came, whining and reluctant, but this time I was firm. We were going home.

I found nothing online about either Julia Fawkes or Julia Gleeson. They had quite vanished. I tried Augustus Gleeson too, but again I drew a blank. I decided to forget about them. Whatever Julia Elizabeth Fawkes's many admirers had cherished, it had disappeared as surely as the flesh from her bones.

There it would have ended, if there had not been an Open Doors day that September. One of the houses on the list was 18 Little George Street, which had never been open to the public before. The house dated from the mid-eighteenth century, and had later become a gathering place for poets and radicals. Coleridge had stayed there. Wordsworth had visited. Shelley had declaimed a poem on the top-floor landing and then attempted to slide down the banisters. Speeches had been made and it was believed there had been a printing press in the basement. The house still belonged to the same family, the Frobishers, but it had passed to a cousin who lived in Canada and wished to sell in due course. He had recently employed an archivist to go through the many papers which were lodged there. The archivist would be on hand on Open Doors day. There was some idea, according to the Open Doors leaflet, that the house might be bought by the City Council as a museum. I doubted that. This was probably my only chance to see it.

I planned my day carefully. I would go to Redcliffe Caves in the morning, have a bite of lunch down by the water and then go to 18 Little George Street as soon as it opened at one o'clock. Jack couldn't come. He would have loved the caves, but the multiplied sound of his barking might annoy other visitors, and I doubted that he'd be allowed into Little George Street. I noted with some amusement that I was already thinking like a dog-owner, with a faint resentment that anywhere should be off limits to Jack.

It was a mistake to come early. The house was busy and the archivist was engaged with a group of local historians. I looked around. The bones of the house hadn't changed much, as far as I could see. The Frobishers had clearly been happy enough with one magnificent, outdated bathroom and a separate lavatory with a cistern which must sound like Niagara Falls when the chain was pulled. The windows all had their original glass. I liked that: it pleased me to think that Coleridge had looked out of these windows. I lingered, but the historians were tireless, and I went away.

I was halfway home when I realised what a fool I'd been. The house might never be open again. It was entirely possible that Julia Elizabeth Fawkes had visited Little George Street. She was a writer. She was well enough known then to have had 'many admirers'. Was it possible that she had left some physical mark there? I felt that I owed it to Jack to search a little farther. After all, he had made me come to the grave.

It was almost three o'clock. The local historians had gone and the archivist was drinking a cup of tea, well away from the papers which he had spread out for display over a broad polished table. He looked up somewhat guardedly as I entered the room.

'I'm sorry,' I said, 'I don't want to interrupt your break.'

'Come in, come in,' he said with an alacrity which might have been a bit forced but which I pretended to take at face value. I turned over some of the papers. They meant nothing to me, but it would be polite to dwell on them for a few minutes.

'I'm interested in a writer who may have come to the house in the late eighteenth century,' I said at last, still looking at the papers.

'What was his name?'

'Julia Elizabeth Fawkes. She was a woman,' I added stupidly.

'Julia Elizabeth Fawkes,' he repeated. 'No. I don't believe I have seen any reference to her.'

'She had another name. A married name: Gleeson.'

'Gleeson ... Gleeson ...'

'She was married to a man called Augustus Gleeson.'

'Oh,' said the archivist, suddenly all keen attention. 'The pamphleteer, I assume?'

'I have no idea.'

'Let me just check …' To my surprise, he ignored the laptop in front of him. 'I'll just have a look at the card index.' He got up, fetched a long dingy cardboard box and began to fossick about inside it. 'Gellborough … Gifford … Glanville … Ah yes, I thought so. Gleeson.'

He pulled out a card and laid it in front of me. There was nothing but a name: Gleeson, Augustus Shovell, and a sequence of letters and numbers: 2nd F L/g R/H Bc Sh 2/R/14.

'I knew I'd seen something.'

'What does it mean?'

'Second floor landing, right-hand bookcase, second shelf from the bottom, 14 items in from the right,' responded the archivist. 'It isn't my system, of course. This card index must be forty years old at least. But so far, I've found it reliable. Any matter relating to your man will be there.'

'Could we look now?'

He glanced at the door. No one was coming. The interest of the day had peaked. I heard voices downstairs, then a door shut and they were cut off.

'Why not?'

He went ahead of me up the stairs.

The bookcases were glass-fronted, and locked. The archivist brought out his keys and selected one. It turned with difficulty and he had to prise the door open with a fingernail.

'It's all waiting to be properly catalogued,' he said apologetically. 'The card index is primitive. They want a digital archive, but of course people don't realise what an undertaking that is. And if the house is sold, then the collection must go to a museum.'

'You don't think the house will become one?'

He gave me a sharp look over his shoulder. 'It's not very likely, is it?'

He was kneeling now, searching along the rows and still talking. I looked over his shoulder and saw that while there were plenty of books there were also leather-bound boxes lined up on the shelves.

'I'm afraid this chap in Canada has absolutely no idea of what's involved. He thinks I can wave a wand and everything will be online – but the place is more or less untouched and that's what makes the job rewarding . . . Ah, here we are.' The box was unlabelled. He drew it out and undid the clasp. 'Here we are indeed.' A faint whiff of oldness reached me. 'I haven't got as far as this bookcase, you understand.' He held the box and peered into it. I could see nothing.

'May I look?' I asked, and at the same time I reached out smoothly. Without waiting for his permission, I took the box. In the bottom there lay a fragment of paper with writing criss-crossed over it. Most of the sheet had been torn away. The writing was smooth and flowing. It looked as if it ought to be easy to read, but I could not decipher it. I had the feeling, suddenly, that the archivist had not known the paper was there and did not want to share the discovery with me.

'I can't make head or tail of this,' I said and, as I had hoped, he responded.

'It's part of a letter. There, that's where the seal has broken. People often crossed their letters at the time. The post was very expensive and they wanted to fill the paper as much as possible. There's a trick to reading it, and of course you have to ignore the orthographic changes. Let me see. The light's not very good here, and the ink's faded. We might take it downstairs and have a look at it under the lamp, if you're interested?' His eyes peeped at me.

'I'd like that very much,' I said.

We settled at the broad table and he drew down the lamp so that it shone clear on the paper. Every so often he scribbled down a phrase; then he pored over the document again. He turned it, read again, jotted down his notes. I sat perfectly still, waiting.

At last he said, 'There's not much in it, I'm afraid. Rather frustrating. It breaks off and then the writing across – here – seems to refer to quite a different matter. It must be written by someone who knew Augustus Gleeson well, but unfortunately there is no clue to the writer's identity. Possibly my predecessor – the person who created the card index – knew more. He must have done, to give Gleeson's full name as a reference, since it isn't given in the document itself.'

'Would you read it to me?'

'For what it's worth – but it doesn't shed any light on the lady you mentioned. This is the first part:

' . . . the Eagerness with which we read your
letter giving Assurance that you are safely come
to London. By Providence or the Act of Man
you have been preserved in health and safety.
Augustus, as you know, is staying with me at
Little George Street for the present, and the
Frobishers have been most Constant and Tender
in their Attentions to us Both. When Augustus
had read your letter he could not sit still but
must rise and walk about the room to express
his Emotion. How my Heart bounded, I
cannot . . .'

The phrases galloped across my mind. All that long-dead emotion! Hearts bounding, eagerness, walking around the room – and it was all dead and gone, and no one left to know what any of it had meant. I would not have felt it so strongly, no doubt, if I had not been left myself, like the last speaker of a lost language that no one else understood.

The archivist was looking at me. I hoped that I had not spoken aloud.

'There is a little more,' he said.

'Preserve this Letter, my dear Susannah, as we
have done with every Word you wrote to us
from France. We lodge all Correspondence with

13

the Frobishers and I most Ardently Advise you to
do the Same so that there will be a Memorial of
these Perilous Times. For months Augustus has
not picked up his pen. We can only console
ourselves that our dear Julia did not live to see
the Fate of her Unfortunate . . .

'The paper is torn just here.'

'Who was Susannah? Are her letters here too?'

'As far as I know there are none. Possibly the
Frobishers destroyed them all. Unfortunately, without
a surname—'

'Why were the times perilous?'

The archivist blinked, as if I had revealed an ignorance which forced him to reassess me. 'These were
radicals, remember. It was the time of the French
Revolution.'

I peered at the edge of the letter. 'Is that a "C"?'

'It may be. Or possibly a "D". The following letter
may be an "H", but I'm guessing now.'

'Child, perhaps?' I said. There were many such deaths
recorded in the graveyard: baby after baby, given the
same name, born and dead within the year.

'It's unlikely. We know that Augustus Gleeson had
a son, Thomas, and that he survived to adulthood.
Gleeson alludes to him in a treatise on education, and
calls him his only child. As far as we know, Gleeson
never remarried.'

For months Augustus Gleeson had not picked up his
pen. I wished that Jack were here. I would have reached

down and stroked his head, over and over, until my mind was quiet.

'There are several of his pamphlets in the City Library,' the archivist said.

'Are there?'

'He was quite well known in his day, I believe.'

'But there's none of her writing?'

'Not as far as I know.'

I touched the piece of paper. The words were faded yet they still tumbled across the paper, eager, impetuous, alive. But they weren't alive. The archivist and I were snuffling after something which no longer existed, like Jack in his hunt for imagined bones. Augustus had been left, as I had been left. But it was over for him: he was dead. They were all dead and they could no longer tell us what their words had been, before the paper had been torn across.

Even so, I touched the paper as if the heat of their lives might come off on my fingers.

1

June 1789

The night was thinning as he went down the donkey track to the quay with his tools over his shoulder. He had taken the long way round, in the dark, and was dressed as a labourer. His heavy boots were clogged with dirt. There had been rain in the night after the fine summer's day. He wore his cap pulled down over his eyes, and a neckerchief muffled the lower part of his face.

There was the boat, tied up as he had left it. It wasn't yet full tide but the water had reached the quay. It was black and oily-looking as the dawn began to spread over it.

He glanced around him. The quay steps were slippery but he went down them as fast as if they were dry, and put the spade and mattock in the bottom of the boat before covering them with canvas. It was getting light too quickly. There were ships hanging like shadows on the water, waiting for the tide. He pulled out the oars, settled them in the rowlocks, untied the mooring-rope and slid out on to the water. Before the tide could spin him round he dug in hard and pulled against it, pointing the bow across the river. There was mist on the dark meadows and on the woods beyond.

No one would notice him. He was a man on his way to work. A farm labourer or a quarryman from the stone quarries on the other side of the Gorge. He had taken a risk in leaving the oars in the boat overnight, but no one had touched them. The blades found the perfect angle and cut into the water, pulled strongly through it, released themselves, dipped again. He knew how to row, by God. He could do anything with his hands.

More and more the city sharpened itself in the light: the bulk of the Hot Well, the clutter of small boats and then the ships. But he was heading across, to the meadows. There was colour coming into everything: the brown, shining water, the run-off from his oars. She had said that the water was dirty and he had told her that it wasn't dirt but the particles of sand and mud that hung in the water and made it rich with fish. That was a long time ago now.

The city behind him was coming to life. He felt it like a prickle on the skin of his back. Men walking down the same steps he'd trod, their bundles over their shoulders. Looking out at the water. Now, quickly, he dug with his right oar and the boat shot in where he knew the mooring-post was. There were duckboards laid over the soggy land closest to the water. He stepped ashore and tied up the boat. The boards squelched as he took off the canvas, lifted out the mattock and spade and hefted them over his shoulder again. He was on his way to work.

Through the wet meadow where cows stood on the higher ground. The smell of them drifting on the last rags of mist. It was going to be hot. He walked steadily but fast, across one meadow and the next, and then he climbed over a stile that led into the woods. The quarry path was well behind him now. He thought of stone for a moment, and the houses it would build; then he turned his mind away.

The undergrowth was still wet from last night's rain. There was a rich smell with an edge to it. He was going into the old forest which had never been cut since men lived in their hill forts and watched for their enemies coming up the river. The trees had been coppiced but no more. He knew about such things. He had an interest in antiquarianism and the men knew to bring to him any object of interest that they turned up in the digging of foundations. But those hill forts had been set on the heights and he was deep in the woods, where the trees were thickest.

She hadn't wanted to come so far, but he had told her about the nightingales, and she had put on her stout boots. There were glades, he said to her, where sunlight dropped down through the tall trees and made orchids grow.

He paused, looked at the oaks on the left of the path,

the whitebeam on the right, and listened for the chink of metal on stone from the quarry. Perhaps it was still too early. He glanced behind him again. There was too much birdsong, and it muddled him, but this was the place. There was a gap in the undergrowth. He had not lied to her: there was a glade. He pushed through to it, dragging the mattock and spade. Twigs snapped at his face and he flinched.

He must have shut his eyes. When he opened them, there she was. She lay as he had left her, under a tree in the brambles and ivy. He had laid her out straight, and crossed her hands, and then he had wrapped his coat about her head. He had known that she would stiffen in a few hours, and that he would not want to see her face again. There she was. No one had come; he'd known that no one would come. It was his luck. There were no marks where he had dragged her, because he had lifted her in his arms and carried her.

This was the place. He was dry, and his heart beat hard. There would be water somewhere nearby but he could not stop to look for it now. The coat over her face was sodden with rain, and her skirts too, and her boots. There were spiders on her, and woodlice. She'd been lying there all night on her own. She could not see him now. He had pressed down her eyelids and then he had wound the coat over her face. It was a light summer coat and it moulded to her. He could not help being astonished that she was still there, even though he had placed her so carefully and marked the site in his mind so that he would be able to find it easily. He had half expected an empty glade with the first sun beginning to warm it and a cloud of gnats dancing.

He cut into the ground with his spade and carefully he sliced and lifted the sods and laid them aside. The solid sheet of limestone did not run so close to the surface here. He would be able to dig just deep enough and then when she was buried he would heap the undergrowth over her. Already he was sweating as he stripped down to his shirt and began to dig. There were lumps of stone in the soil; he took the mattock to ease them out, and then laid them aside. Earwigs ran and white grubs squirmed as the light fell on them. Flies buzzed about his head. He shut out the thought that it was she who had brought them here. It was his own sweat that drew them. The earth smelled acrid but clean too. Twice or thrice he thought he heard something and he stopped, head up, alert, sniffing the sunlit air, but it was always a woodpecker or the rustle of birds and small animals in the undergrowth. There were butterflies now, speckled ones, emerging as the air warmed. They were dancing over her. They could smell a dead thing: he knew that.

He dug and dug. He would not let his mind loose, for fear of where it might skedaddle without him. His clothes stuck to him with sweat and his head throbbed from the heat or because he had not slept. Now he was going deep and standing inside the hole he had dug, loosening more stone with the mattock. It was a fusty, crawling place he had made and fear ran over the skin of his back as he bent and lifted, bent and lifted, faster and faster now, frantic to get the job done. He did not dare to look at her. It seemed to him that she might be sitting up, unwinding the coat from about her face, and watching him out of those eyes. She would pick the twigs and dirt off her dress, and the insects. She would put the spiders aside gently. That was what she did when spiders came into the house in the autumn months: she cupped them in her hands and tipped them outside. She never minded the tickle of their legs inside her fingers.

It was deep enough now. Not as good as a sexton would have done for her, but if he laid the stones over her no fox or badger would be able to dig her up.

It was hellish work getting her into the grave. She was cold and stiff. The broken sunlight glanced over her but it could not touch her. His back burned as he knelt to pick her up, and she was heavier than she had ever been. He staggered with her to the edge of the grave. She rolled stiffly in his arms and he thought that she meant to bring him down with her. He would lose his balance and fall into the grave and she would topple in after him, pinning him there. He would never emerge.

He hated her now. She had made him hate her. He pushed and shoved until he got her in, head at one end and boots at the other. She was on her side. He had wanted to lay her on her back, looking up at the sky, but he could not turn her now. He must remove his coat from around her head, he thought, but he could not bring himself to do it. The time for that had been when she was still lying under the trees, and he had not dared.

He began to fill in the grave. Until she was covered, he put in only soil, layers of soil which still teemed with disturbed life. Once he could not see her, he began to replace the stones he had dug up. He could not stop himself from brushing away the woodlice before he laid the stones in the grave. He fitted the stones together, the smaller and the larger, as if he were building a wall. She was covered again. Nothing could touch her. She would never push the stones back like her sheets and blankets in the morning, when she sat up and reached over her shoulder to untie her hair from its night plait. Once her hair was loose she shook it out until the cloud of it hid her face.

She was hidden from him now. He shovelled in more earth and more, right up to the lip of the grave. But he knew that it would settle and leave a dip in the ground, so he carried on shovelling and then he trampled the earth flat with his boots, shovelled again, trampled again. He could not prevent himself from feeling a stab of satisfaction that the job was well done. At last he took the sods he had set aside and fitted them back over the lid of the grave. Again he trampled and smoothed. The cuts he had made would soon heal themselves in the warm dampness after rain. He pulled the ivy forward, and then he stepped back to the edge of the little glade. He squinted, to see what a stranger might see if he also wandered far from the paths and pushed his way through the undergrowth.

The grave was apparent. In the surge of early summer growth it would soon disappear, but he could not take that risk. He gathered brushwood, intertwining it with brambles and ivy and laying it artfully so it looked as if the forest was moving of itself, out into the light. Now, he thought, now you can see nothing. He stank of sweat and earth. The butterflies were still there. They were high in the column of sun-warmed air, and they were dancing.

2

March 1792

I woke up first. His arm lay across me and I shifted a little but still it lay there, heavy and full of muscle, holding me down. My head cleared and I remembered how we had fallen asleep. My eyes settled to the darkness and found objects in it: the heavy lodging-house furniture that cluttered the room even though I had cleared out as much of it as I could. It seemed to breed in the night.

There were shadows everywhere. The shutters were open and the windows stared. There was the moon in the top right-hand pane.

But the moon was inside too. It had got into the bedroom while we were sleeping. Its light walked about over the bedstead, over the chest, the basin in its stand and the blue-and-white jug. It was a restless thing and I could not lie still.

I moved my legs a little. Our skin unpeeled, thigh from thigh. I was sticky. I wanted to wash myself, but his arm held me down. There was clean water in the jug. I wanted to pour some into my hands and drink it, and then fill the basin and wash myself.

He breathed softly, steadily. He was deep asleep and would not wake until dawn. Usually he rose before me, and often he was out of the house before I stirred. Last night he had drunk off a bottle of wine and for a while he snored, but he could always sweat out his drink.

The moon was growing stronger. It slid over the sheets and touched his face. I thought he must feel it for he muttered and heaved himself on to his side, pulling the blankets with him. He was turned away from me now, towards the window, and the weight of his arm had gone.

The air washed over my body. It was cool; cold even. I did not pull the blankets back over myself. Instead I lay there and now it was not only the air washing me but the moon too. I looked down my body and saw the curves and channels of it. It looked like something that had never been touched. It was my own, even though I ached and my thighs were sore.

He did not mean to hurt me but he was a strong man and did not always know himself.

Inch by inch, I slid away from him. The bed creaked, and then was still. I listened for any catch in his breathing, but it went on evenly, just the same. I raised myself on my elbows and saw how the room was packed with shadow and everything that was ugly by day was made fantastical by the moon. I would not go back to sleep now.

I swung my legs over the side of the bed. I stood up

and the moonlight stood with me. The chill wrapped me around. I slipped past the end of the bed, went to the washstand and tipped the jug very gently, so that there would be no plash of water. The bowl filled. It was clean water and I leaned forward, scooped out a mouthful and drank. I had not known how thirsty I was until I swallowed, and then I must scoop up more water and more until it dripped over my chin and spilled in runnels down my body. I dipped both hands into the water now. This time I tipped back my head and let the water run over me. The cold made me shudder but my skin thirsted for it. Water ran over my breasts and belly and thighs. I dipped and lifted and dipped and lifted, careless of the water running over me and on to the floor. All the time the moonlight covered me too, following the stream of the water, penetrating every hollow of my body. I did not know what I felt. I knew that I was cold. I thought that there was water running over my face now and along my tongue and down the parched crevices of my throat.

There was a sound. A stifled sound, like someone trying not to cough. My heart jumped and I turned. He was lying on his side, just as before. He was still deep asleep, breathing steadily. But then I saw something glisten as the moonlight licked his face. His eyes were not quite shut. He was watching me.

A shiver flickered over my skin. I had to fight not to cover myself with my hands. He had watched me like this once before, when I was washing myself and had left the door half open behind me. I didn't know how long he had been standing there. That time I had cried out, 'Diner, you startled me!' and snatched my shift around myself, but he had come to me and pulled away the shift and stared me from from head to toe, saying:

'You are mine, Lizzie. Why should you hide yourself from me?'

I did not know enough about marriage. Perhaps it was nothing for a husband to spy on his wife's naked-ness but I felt as if he had stolen a part of me.

The moon shone while he lay as still as a fox. I would not let him guess that I had seen the glint of his eyeball. I turned back to the bowl to take up one more scoop of water, but I could not drink. His eyes were on me, drying the water, pulling away the light. I would go back to bed, and close my eyes so that I too would appear to sleep.

In the morning Diner would pull on his boots, saying, 'Lizzie, put me up some bread and fat bacon.' He would eat it with the men and he would not taste it unless I put in a handful of pickled walnuts to please him. Tomorrow we would wake and live our common day.

Our day was almost spent when the bell rang and Philo rushed to tell me that Hannah was downstairs, waiting for me in the kitchen. It was late. I knew that Hannah hadn't come to the front door because my husband might be at home and she did not want to meet him. I ran down, frightened. Hannah never visited at such an hour.

There she stood with rain dripping from her cloak on to the flags. 'Your mother's not well,' she accused me.

'What's the matter?'

'She's in bed.'

'With her writing-board, I suppose.'

There was nothing to worry about. Mammie was strong. She said herself that she never ailed. If she retreated to bed, it was in search of solitude. There were always so many visitors, and they never knew when to leave.

Hannah sniffed: her nose was red, with a drop hanging from it. 'It's rest she needs, not writing-boards.'

Sacrilege, coming from Hannah. Mammie's ideas flowed most clearly at night, with one lit candle to speed her pen while Augustus slept on beside her. There was nothing more important than that those ideas of hers should be captured and set down. Hannah had always arranged our days for that purpose. Our rooms were clean, our clothes washed and our food cooked, but even so Mammie needed the night for her work. She would wake with her mind suddenly, startlingly alive. She'd sit up in bed, reach for her writing-board, prop it against her knees, and seize on her thoughts before they vanished. Who would imagine, from the clarity of her treatises, that they sprang from a warm bed?

It was not always so warm. When I was little and money for coal was short we would stay in bed together on cold days, curled under every cloak and blanket that we owned, like porpoises under the ice. My breath smoked when I put my face up into the chill of the room, and down I dived again. But there was always Mammie beside me, working with a heavy shawl around her shoulders and fingerless gloves knitted by Hannah, which left her fingers free to write.

She didn't need those gloves any more. She had a fire in her room every day. Augustus and she lived frugally, but they were never short of what they needed.

'But, Hannah, she's not really ill, is she?'

'She's been better. She'd like to see you. Now don't fly off like that, Elizabeth, she's not as bad as that.'

I ran upstairs for my cloak and boots, while Sarah continued to scour the pots with sand, indifferently, as if she were alone in the kitchen. She didn't like Hannah.

Hannah took my left arm and walked between me and the edge of the pavement, as if I were still a child. She was so tall and stiff and perpendicular that it was like being taken in charge by a sergeant of the militia.

'Mind that puddle, Elizabeth.'

She always called me by my full name, severely. She loved me; I knew that. Hannah would beat off anything that sprang at us out of the dark. Diner called her my duenna, although that was quite wrong given how firmly Hannah believed in the liberty of women. He said that her petticoats were too short: could she not afford to buy a few more yards of flannel and make herself decent? I answered that she afforded nothing for herself, if the money saved could be given to others. Hannah would have been angry to be called a Christian, but she was more charitable than most who went to church.

The light of our lantern shivered on the wet pavement. The street where I lived was swept and clean but as we went downhill towards Mammie's lodgings the householders cared less and would not pay the scavengers. We picked our way over the dirt and I held the hem of my cloak high. Hannah was silent.

She opened the door with her own familiar key. My mother and her husband had four rooms upstairs with Hannah to care for everything as she had always done. Augustus was always from home, travelling from town to town into every wretched place that would hear his preaching on the rights of men. Tom Paine might be in Paris, but Augustus Gleeson was content to deliver his sermons to the mill-workers of Preston or the coal-miners of Radstock.

Downstairs there was a family of seamstresses, mother and three daughters. They had the best of the light in their back room and rarely left the house. We climbed the stairs; Hannah produced her second key and the door opened.

Hannah had keys to my mother's house, and I had none. I thought of that as I stepped across the threshold, took off my things and hung my cloak to dry.

'Here she is,' announced Hannah, holding open Mammie's door. I expected to see the lamp lit and Mammie sitting up in bed, wearing her spectacles, blinking at me as she rose from the depths of her work. I looked where she should have been, and saw nothing but a rounded heap under the bedclothes. A candle burned on the bedside table.

She's sleeping, I thought. But then, why waste a candle? I glanced at Hannah, thinking I should withdraw, but she gestured to me to come on. The bed took up the best part of the room and the ceiling sloped so I always had to duck my head. There was a sour smell. My mother's hair was tangled on the pillow, hiding her face from me.

'Mammie?' I said, and she stirred. She rolled over, pushing back her hair. Her mouth was gluey with sleep. I went to the washstand and wrung out a cloth and passed it to her so that she could wipe her face. Hannah pulled out the pillows and shook them into shape; then she helped my mother sit forward while she replaced the pillows to support her.

After Hannah had gone out, I fetched the hairbrush. 'Shall I brush your hair, Mammie?'

She smiled and shook her head. 'I'll do it in a minute, Lizzie. How are you, my darling?'

I sat on the bed and took her hands. The skin was dry and a little rough, as always. I picked up first her right hand and then her left, and held them to my lips. They smelled of ink.

'Are you ill, Mammie?'

'No,' she said. 'Only a little tired. And how is my girl? How is John?'

'He's asked us to call him Diner, Mammie. I wish you would remember. Or you might call him John Diner, if you prefer. He doesn't object to that.'

'But isn't it rather cumbersome, when we are by ourselves?'

'Think of it as one word, and it's shorter than Elizabeth.'

'John Diner, then. And shall I call you Mrs Tredevant?'

'Mammie,' I said, kneeling beside the bed and rubbing my cheek against hers, 'should you like me to call you Mrs Gleeson?'

She laughed. 'Very good, Lizzie.' She patted the bed covers and I sat down carefully so as not to press against her. 'Tell me, how is the building going?'

'Work will go on much better now the weather has improved. He's taking me to see the new house very soon.'

I was glad we had left the subject of my husband's name. I thought his first wife, Lucie, must have called him John. That was why he flinched at the sound of it. He heard another woman's voice, not mine.

Mammie's writing-board was on the bed, but there was no sheet of paper attached to its clips. I could barely remember a time when she wasn't working.

'How long have you been tired?' I asked her, and she answered me as gravely as if I'd been a doctor.

'About five days.'

'Five days!' And I hadn't known.

'It will soon pass. I am giving a talk in the Meeting House next Friday.'

'On what subject?'

'On hereditary privilege,' said Mammie, fumbling for her spectacles on the table without looking at them. She put them on. She was herself again, worn but eager. 'Well, my bird,' she said, 'now you're smiling. What an anxious face, when you came in.'

'I thought you were ill.' I sat down on the bed, and took her hands again. I felt as if I could never have enough of looking at her. 'Will you let me brush your hair?'

This time she let me. I took off her spectacles and brushed out her hair, all of it. It was still brown, although like her hands it was dry and not glossy any more. I thought she should rub a little almond oil into it, but she would never do that. I brushed and brushed until it had some shine, and then I plaited it so that it would be comfortable for her.

'There now,' I said. She smiled and then lay back with her eyes shut. I drew down the bed linen and slipped in beside her. I hugged her to me very gently, because I was afraid that she had a pain somewhere, and wasn't telling me. She was warm and she smelled of amber, from the scent given to her by a rich lady who had read her treatise on married women's property rights. If the gift had been lace she would never have worn it, but she couldn't resist any sweet-smelling thing. I put my face to the side of her neck and curled against her.

'Augustus will be back tomorrow,' she said. I made a sound against her neck. The Roman Emperor, home from making speeches about the rights of man.

'You must not do his work for him. You must rest,' I said. I thought of how Augustus would walk up and down the room, declaiming his next pamphlet, while my mother wrote it out in her swift, clear handwriting. And even then he would find fault. There were always things that needed to be changed, or rewritten.

'His eyes are bad,' she said. 'You know that.'

Yours will be bad too, if you write for him as well as for yourself, I thought.

'I'll come to see you tomorrow,' I said.

'There's no need, Lizzie. I'm perfectly well. Hannah shouldn't have alarmed you.'

I felt her words through her flesh and mine, as much as I heard them. 'I'll come tomorrow anyway,' I said. 'I'd like to hear how Augustus did on his travels.' She was still, and I thought perhaps she suspected my mockery, but then she said:

'I am glad you are more friendly to him now, Lizzie. He is a kind man, you know.'

'I know.' As well as all his other qualities: his ability to spew out endless pamphlets but not to write them in his own hand, his carelessness with his clothes which led to endless mending and darning, his sharing a bed with my mother in spite of his whiskery face and ginger breath, his foolishness with money which led to . . . But it had to be admitted, Augustus was kind.

'I could not love you any more, Mammie,' I said, 'if you were my own pet donkey,' and she laughed. That laugh of hers, so warm and sweet, mocking but joyous, as if she knew all the bad there was to know about the world but still loved it . . . Out of all the things I loved about her I think her laughter was what I loved the best. She laughed now because when

I was six years old, when I'd longed and longed for a donkey to ride on, that had been my declaration of love for her.

'And how is *your* husband?' she asked.

'He is well.' I hid my face against her and scrubbed my skin into hers. I shut my eyes and now I could say anything. 'Mammie, those things you told me were wrong. Now I seem to have a hard object pressing into every orifice of my body.'

I felt her breathe. 'Does he hurt you, Lizzie?'

'No. But it is firmly done.'

'Do you use the little sponge I gave you? And the vinegar?'

My mother thought I was too young to bear a child, although I was older than she had been when I was born.

'Yes.'

'And he doesn't object.'

'There is no hurry, he says. He says, "I want you to myself."'

'I suppose that is natural, Lizzie.' Her arms have come around me now and she is rocking me. Hannah would be angry if she knew. She'd say I was tiring Mammie and draining her strength, which ought to be kept for her work. 'But you had better not stay. He won't like it.'

He would not. My husband was very much against my stravaiging about the streets after dark, even though with Hannah at my side it was perfectly respectable. Nor did he like my habit of taking walks without him.

What the eye didn't see, the heart wouldn't grieve after, I thought, and carried on as before.

'He was at the house today, supervising the plasterers. They are to put our names into the ceiling.'

'So, when your visitors look up, they'll see Elizabeth Fawkes and John Diner Tredevant entwined?' More laughter bubbled in her voice.

'You are so foolish, Mammie. Of course not. Besides, I am no longer Fawkes: I have changed my name. It's to be El and Din. Eldin. Our two names, made into one. He calls the house Eldin. He thought of carving the name into the stone above the front door, but he decided not. It is to be hidden in the ceiling, just for ourselves.'

'It will be a very fine house for you both,' said Mammie, as if I were a child describing a home for her dolls.

I thought of our new house, the smallest in the terrace, built on the turn. If it was one of the grand houses we could never have had it. The new house has four large bedrooms, drawing and dining rooms, and attics for Sarah and Philo. Everything is new and smells of wood and wet plaster. The kitchen will be equipped with the latest conveniences. The garden is a raw tumble of earth and stone. We look out directly over the Gorge. Diner says it is the finest prospect in all England.

'I know,' I said.

Mammie did not really care about houses. She was content wherever she was, because she rarely looked about her except to find her pen or her writing-board. I was content, too, when I was a child, as long as Mammie's

Indian shawl spread its rich colours over my bed and there were flowers in the blue-and-white jug. Today, there were small wild daffodils that Hannah must have picked.

Augustus had not changed things much, because he was away so often. We had lived in Hoxton, Southwark, Devon and Bath before we came to Clifton. That was not long before I met Diner. Each time we moved the floors were sprinkled with water and swept, the Indian shawl spread out and the fire lit. Hannah found out the best places to buy coal and wood and candles. I rolled up my sleeves to bake bread or to skin and joint a rabbit. If it was cleaner work, such as making cakes or biscuits, I kept a book propped on the table in front of me and shook out the flour from between its pages as I read. And Mammie put on her spectacles and wrote, even as I swept under her feet. Nothing broke her concentration: she merely drew up her feet and held them there until I had passed on with the broom.

The sound of her writing is so exact in my ears that I can hear it whenever I choose: the long, steady course of her quill over the paper, the tiny pauses as she dipped it in the ink, the longer ones while she thought, the noise of writing, the friction of the pen with which she made her words and sent them out into the world. Wherever we went it was the same, until even our shifting from house to house and city to city began to seem like part of that handwriting.

I thought it would go on forever, if I thought of it at all. Those words of Mammie's might lead to Paris, or Hackney, and we would pack up and go with them. But now it seemed that Mammie and I were both roosted, I because of my husband, and she because of me.

'You had better go home now, Lizzie. Hannah will walk with you.'

I felt a pang, as I did every time Mammie said 'home' and no longer meant the place where she was. I unwound my arms from her, sat up in the bed and smoothed my hair. 'I can perfectly well go without Hannah,' I said. 'She has enough to do here, with you ill in bed.'

'I'm not ill,' said Mammie again, and there was Hannah opening the bedroom door for me to go.

3

I reached our lodgings before Diner came home. These were nothing like Mammie's four small rooms. He had taken an entire house for us, while we waited for the new house to be completed. I thought such fine lodgings were a waste of money, and there was far too much furniture. Every room was crammed with chairs and tables until you could scarcely move without bumping into them. I complained of it on the day we moved in, and began to shift and pile the furniture out of the way.

'Is that your only objection, Elizabeth?' Diner said, and he picked me up by the waist and jumped me towards the ceiling. He was in fine spirits that day.

It was past nine o'clock now and he was still absent. Sarah and Philo had gone to their attic, while I sat by the fire, in a good light, with my work. I was making a shirt for him. He didn't like to see me sewing when we were together – I should send the work out, he said – but he would change his mind when he put on the shirt. The linen was fine and I had measured him exactly. There were gussets under the arms so that he could stretch and move freely, as he had to. I sewed well and quickly, and my eyes were strong. I intended to make him half a dozen shirts, with his initials embroidered into the hems. He would pay four times as much for shirts of this quality from a tailor. We ought to have saved money, and lived in rooms.

I knew that Diner had sunk a great deal of money into the building of the terrace. The whole of his capital, I suspected, and he had borrowed many times more. The profit, he said, would come once all the houses were sold. The two large houses at each end of the terrace would have elegant columns and fine detailing in the stonework. The architect, Mr Fellingbourne, had designed the terrace so that these end houses would be more than twice the width of ours. They would not only be splendid, but they would have all the latest conveniences. A cold plunge bath was to be installed in the basement of each of the end houses, to attract the wealthiest and most discerning purchasers. But first, there must be foundations.

Work had gone on well last summer, but it had been a hard winter, with weeks of heavy rain and then weeks of frost. The labourers and stonemasons were laid off as the hours of daylight shortened. Now it was March and I still saw very little of Diner. He was on the site every day until dusk, supervising the inside work. The ironwork for the banister uprights in the end houses had been delivered, but there was a fault: they had not exactly followed the measurements for one section.

Diner had not sent to London, but had drawn the design himself and ordered the work from a Bristol ironmonger.

'It will all be put right, Lizzie,' he'd said, and I saw that he was elated rather than dejected by what had happened. There was something in him that rose to such challenges with a smile, as if it was a pleasure to him to prove he would not be defeated. The men knew that smile, and they worked the faster for it.

At dusk, when the men left work, he went to his office in Grace's Buildings. There was paperwork to be done, skilled craftsmen to be hired and brought from Bath or even London, the next order of Portland limestone for the floors. He liked to tell me what he had done each day, and I was beginning to understand how a house grew from its conception. I'd never thought, before I knew him, how much work it was to build the houses I'd lived in so carelessly. From the choice of the site to the last curlicues on the balconies, every stage must be mapped and measured precisely. And there had been a great deal of work before even the foundations were dug. The site was magnificent but it was also steep and uneven. Limestone broke just beneath the turf. Diner had to pour money into levelling the ground and building a retaining wall. Even so, he paced our lodgings when he came home at last, lit up by his enthusiasm.

'There will be no position like it, Lizzie. You will wake and see from your window a prospect that artists travel a hundred miles to paint.'

There was so much to do that he could barely bring

himself to sit down. He lived on cold beef and ham, eaten as he walked. But we would dine together every night, he said, once our house was ready.

'But how will you live here?' Mammie had asked, last time I took her to see the house. We had to scramble over rubble and jump across potholes, but Mammie never minded that. It was the rawness of it that daunted her. She had not seen the drawings, as I had. She had not heard Diner talk about the curve of the stairwell and the setting of the windows. 'This terrace is not even a quarter built. There will be nothing but noise, dust and dirt for months. You cannot live here, Lizzie.'

'The first houses are already sold,' I told her, but didn't say how few these were. Only four buyers had put down money so far. But there was a great deal of interest, and the rest would rush to buy as soon as all the roofs were on and the glory of the terrace was clear to everyone. Mammie refused to understand Diner's financial concerns, and so I could not explain to her how bold he had been – and brave too – in his speculation.

'We'll be rich, Lizzie!' he'd said, but the money was only part of it. He brought me to share his pride in the fine curve of stone that would rear itself where there had been only a scrub of grass and hawthorn. Mammie talked of the green fields that were being trampled, while Diner drew for me high pavements, mounting-blocks, retaining walls and vaulted cellars that would run out beneath the street. When the building was complete, even Mammie would see the glory of the high-slung terrace as it floated above the Gorge. And I would live in it.

Diner's face was dark when at last he came home.

'Have you eaten?' I said, putting my work aside. 'Let me make you something.'

'We have Sarah to do that,' he said.

'Sarah and Philo have gone to bed. It's past nine o'clock.'

'Then wake them, Lizzie.'

I knew he was not serious, and said I would go down to the kitchen and make something for him myself.

'I'm not hungry.'

'You will be when the food is in front of you. I'll make you buttered eggs.'

I took up a candle and he followed me downstairs. It was dark but still warm. Sarah had banked up the fire, and I broke open its crust with the poker, stirred it up and set butter in a pan to heat while I beat the eggs and salted them. Diner nipped a piece of sugar off the loaf, and held it in his mouth while he drank his wine. Once the butter was melted, I tipped in the beaten eggs and stirred until they set. The fire was too slack for toast, so I put the buttered eggs on to slices of bread. Diner ate hungrily. We sat on each side of the deal table and I thought again how well we did here in the kitchen, much better than we did upstairs. We seemed more ourselves.

He wiped his mouth and sat back in his chair. 'And how was your mother?'

I would not give him the satisfaction of seeing my surprise. I glanced at him but said nothing, and after a moment he had to disclose himself.

'You were out walking after dark again.'

'With Hannah.'

'You are not living with your mother now.'

'Of course I know that. But she was ill – tired – and so I visited her.'

'She tires herself,' he said, but gently, so that I wasn't certain that it was a criticism.

'She has so much to do,' I said. I had been hearing it all my life, from Hannah, from her friends, and lately from Augustus. My mother was the spinning jenny who span out words to clothe the ideas that burst and bubbled in their brains.

'But to what end, Lizzie? They are all talking to themselves, and nothing will remain of it but a heap of dusty papers.'

I knew that wasn't what he truly thought. He suspected and disliked the power of what came from my mother's pen. She attacked the majesty of kings, and the armies that defended the realm. Such words questioned the good order of life on which we all depended. And in my mother's case, there was mockery in the questions which gave them a subtle, disturbing power. But order would not be overturned. The French might tear down the edifices which had served them for a thousand years, but here we had more judgment.

Diner came back and back again to the subject, as if

picking a scab each time it healed. Augustus he discounted. He thought him a fool and a windbag.

'She is writing what she believes to be true,' I said.

'And do you believe it, Lizzie?' He was leaning forward now.

I could not think about it clearly with Diner looking at me.

'My mother and her friends want the world to be a better place,' I said, and heard the simpering idiocy of it as soon as I had spoken. I clenched my hands in anger. How could I so demean Mammie's plain rooms, her clear, eloquent writing, the complexity of her thought?

'And so do I,' he said, still holding me, fixing me. His brows drew together. His anger came down quickly, like bad weather. 'What can change the world for the better more than buildings of beauty and purpose? It is impossible to build without order. Your mother should have stayed longer in Paris, to see what comes of making the world a better place without setting one stone on top of another. They tear down the Bastille, but can they build it again? Augustus would not be able to put a roof on a doll's house. Does he know how to dress stone? Can he turn a lathe? Can he judge the proportions of a window and set it into a wall so that every eye that sees it will be satisfied? Can he lay a flagstone floor? No. He depends upon those who can. He is as much a guest in the world as a three-year-old child.'

'But it's more than two years since my mother and Augustus were in Paris.'

'A strange choice for a wedding journey, at such a time.'

'Augustus has many acquaintances there.' Again I heard weakness in my voice. I ought to defend my mother, even if it quickened his temper.

'I'm sure he has. And now I read that women are demanding pikes and pistols, in order to defend Paris. What does your mother think of that?'

'She does not want bloodshed.'

'Yet she writes on the abolition of privilege. Does she imagine that it will abolish itself without bloodshed? Be honest, Lizzie. No man will let me take as much as a slice of bread out of his hand without grappling me for it. Does she think that the extraordinary rights she demands for women will be freely given?'

We had had this exchange, or something like it, so often that each of us could predict the other's words. It wearied me and by the end I felt ashamed, as if I had failed. I lacked eloquence. Perhaps my mother had hoped that one day I would work at her side, as Hannah did. Hannah was past fifty now, deaf in one ear and growing old.

Next Diner would ask me about Augustus's meeting with Tom Paine. I could predict it. Once he had begun he went on scratching the sore. If he was so curious, I thought, why didn't he talk to my mother and Augustus? They would be glad of it. My mother especially. I could picture the glow in her face if he showed an interest in her work. Diner would discover how clear-minded she was, and sober too, for all her boldness of thought.

Diner knew where I had been. I thought of how he had watched me secretly in the night. But he could not watch me going about the streets. It was absurd to think of him following me. Perhaps he had come back earlier, found me not at home and questioned Sarah.

'Kings and armies do not abolish themselves,' he said, looking into the lazy fire. And then all at once his mood changed and he smiled at me. 'Come here, Lizzie. Come and sit on my knee. I have wanted you all day long.'

His arms came around me, so much stronger than my mother's. He grasped my waist and hips and pulled me against him. His voice, too, was tight.

'Do you love me, Lizzie?'

'You know that I love you.'

'But do you love me truly?'

'I do.'

'A third time, Lizzie, and let's have the truth from you. Do you love me more than anything in the world, as a wife should love her husband?'

But I was thinking of Diner watching from the shadows as I passed along the pavement with Hannah. I could not prevent a half-second's hesitation. It was enough for Diner. He pushed me off his knee as if he were sweeping a cat from his lap.

'Enough of that,' he said. 'Let's go to bed.'

He calls the house Eldin. He thought of carving the name into the stone above the front door, but he decided not. It is to be just for ourselves.

In the night I could not sleep. I heard my own voice

saying the words to my mother, like a girl newly besotted with her sweetheart and wanting the whole world to share her love. Mammie indulged me, and I think she must have warned Hannah and Augustus too, because no one spoke of the woman Diner had married before he ever met me. Lucie. They had stood up together in the church and made the same promises that Diner and I had made. I could not bear to think of it. It was not Diner who seemed sullied by that earlier contract, but myself. I was second and I would always be so. Death had put her in a place from which she could never be shifted.

Once only, before we were married, my mother broke her silence on the subject. She said, 'He is a widower, Lizzie, don't forget that.'

I kept my eyes on the pages I was checking for Augustus before they went to the printer. Much as I disliked this work, I preferred to do it rather than have Mammie tax her eyes with yet more reading and writing. 'I have not forgotten it,' I said, but she would not be put off.

'You must not try to possess all of him, Lizzie.'

'Did you say this to Augustus, before you married him?' I said, knowing it would wound her, but she refused to react.

'It would have been better if I had. You will be happy if you understand that you cannot have the past. And you have no need of it, Lizzie. Leave it alone.'

In her eagerness she had laid her hand on my arm. I twisted from her and the pages slid from my lap. They fanned down, muddling themselves on the floor. I was on my knees, putting them in order, and she could not see my face. I wondered if Augustus left the past alone, or if he tormented himself with thinking of the young and handsome man my mother had first married. My father. Did Augustus wonder how much she had loved him? And imagine the past in which he had no share? Did he glorify that past, perversely, as I could not help doing, and put a shine on to it like a May morning?

Did Augustus understand that he would never see my mother as my father had once seen her?

You have no need of it, Lizzie. Leave it alone.

I made no reply, but her words stayed with me. It was a rare piece of advice from my mother. She never spoke of Diner's first marriage again, or asked any question about his earlier life.

Diner's first wife was younger than me when he married her, after he met her in France. I don't know what he was doing there: building, I suppose. He did not tell me which part of France Lucie came from, but when I asked him he said: 'It was close to Bordeaux. A little place.'

She must have been quick in every way to have had the courage to leave her family and friends and come to England. I wished there were a drawing of her, but there was nothing. He had no locket or letter. I would have liked to know how she looked. There is no grave to visit, because she died in France, on a visit to her family. A short illness but a savage one, was all Diner ever said to me on the subject. He sent money to set up her gravestone but he has never seen it and the way things are in France I doubted that he would do so now. I found this thought comforting, although I was ashamed of it. He had not been with her when she died.

Perhaps they were not happy together, and that was why she went alone to visit her family? Perhaps they had begun to chafe against each other.

I added up these thoughts when I was alone and there was nothing else to fill my mind. I scratched at them like a sow tearing at bark to get at the smooth skin of the tree. I said nothing and then I wondered if Diner was saying nothing too, but thinking of her, as I did. Lucie means light in every language.

He has never talked to me about her, after that first explanation. He hides her from me in a place which belongs only to the two of them. When we sit by the fire together in the evenings and he raises his head from his calculations, I wonder what he sees.

4

I visited Mammie every day. Each time she was in bed but sitting up with her writing-board to hand, and so I was reassured. The weather turned again and the promise of spring vanished. We had frost at night and clear skies by day. Hannah stoked the fires, and although Mammie said that she longed for air I was not allowed to open her window.

When I knocked at the front door there would be a pause before Hannah came down the stairs to open up for me. Later it occurred to me that in that time she must have gone into my mother's room and said, 'It is Elizabeth. Let me raise you up on your pillows,' and then she would have quickly wiped my mother's temples with lavender water and smoothed back her hair.

But that is speculation. All I know is that Mammie faced the bedroom door with a smile as I came in, and although she was pale I could believe that she looked a little better each day. She laid her writing-board aside, put her pen on the table and patted the bedclothes for me to sit down. I told her how the weather was and what I had done. After a while I no longer smelled the frowsty air of her room, or the lavender water. 'And then?' she asked me. 'And then?' There was no detail of my life which was too slight or too dull for Mammie, but it seemed to me that she avoided talking about herself. I wanted to know every loaf that had been baked in her kitchen and every word she had written, as I used to do when I read her words through with Hannah before they went to the printer. I wanted it back again: the old home, the three of us with Augustus not yet thought of and Diner elsewhere, building his first houses and not thinking of me. I liked to picture him at work, where Lucie had never been. I saw his face as he spoke to the workmen, preoccupied but cheerful too, because he was succeeding. He was young then. One day, of course, we would meet: but not yet.

I laid my head against Mammie's shoulder, and stroked her arm. 'I think I'll stay with you tonight,' I said.

'No, Lizzie, you are married now.'

I thought that if my heart were taken out of my body there would be many cuts in it: sharp, distinct, each of them in a different place. Mammie was right. This was not my home any more. I had fought them all and got free of them. It had been a silent battle, mostly, full of things not said. I would have done anything then, if it had given me Diner.

'I will come again tomorrow, Mammie,' I said.

*   *   *

53

The next day was the fifth in the run of bright, cold mornings, and Diner said to me: 'We will walk over to the house today, Lizzie.' The frosts were holding up work all along the terrace, because the mortar would not set. Diner told me that was because of the lime in it. The ground was hard where foundations were still to be dug. Diner consulted the barometer night and morning and each time turned away from it in silence. A day lost meant more money to be found.

However, today he seemed in good spirits as we picked our way alongside the half-made track to the terrace. It had been churned by the builders' carts, and now the ruts were frozen. I hopped over them while Diner held my hand to steady me. My blood tingled and I wished the house were five miles distant so that we could keep on walking like this, side by side. Long ago, before the first turf was cut, Diner had said that one day the track would be a fine smooth road for us to drive down in our carriage. It was a strange thought to me: a foreign thought, and not altogether pleasing. I liked to walk. I would set out over the Downs, into the fields and woods. I liked to walk alone better than with anyone, unless it were with Diner on such a day as this.

The high pavement was still unmade. When we reached the first house of the terrace we climbed the steps and walked along the rough surface where one day there would be stone paving slabs.

'This is where you will walk each morning,' said Diner, 'from one end of the terrace to the other. That will be your promenade.'

I could not help laughing. 'But where is the sense in walking and going nowhere?'

He stopped and swept out his arm. 'Look there, Lizzie.'

We gazed out at the plunge of the Gorge. From here we could not see the river crawling in its bed, but we saw the dark curve of the trees on the other side. The forest was so thick that I never wanted to enter it. It seemed as if anything might live within it.

'That is virgin forest,' said Diner. 'It has been there since the beginning of time.'

'Perhaps there are wolves and bears, or wild men living in caves.'

He turned round. 'Never go there alone,' he said.

'I am not serious.'

'You roam too far, Lizzie.'

I was about to contest this, but the clouds were down on his face again as they were when he looked at the barometer. I wanted this to be a fine morning for us and so I pointed towards the horizon and asked, 'Are those the hills of Wales?'

'Of course.'

We stared together at the soft blue heaping of hills in the distance.

'I can see so far ... It must be fifty miles.'

'No need to go wandering, then, when it lies all before you here. You will come out of your house on a morning such as this, and walk the length of the terrace, to and fro, and see all the way into another country.'

I smiled. 'Yes,' I said, knowing that instead I would walk away in my stout boots, down into the city perhaps, or out into the fields, as I had always done. I would never confine myself to a pavement, no matter how fine the view.

'Are you cold, Lizzie?'

'Not at all.'

He took my mittened hands and rubbed them between his. 'You are cold,' he said, 'let's go in.'

The door to the house was open wide, and I could hear hammering.

'They are finishing the banisters on the attic staircase,' said Diner. He knew everything that happened in the house, just as if it were happening inside his own body. The plastering was almost done now, he'd told me.

We stepped into the hall. The floor was still raw, untiled, although everything was ordered and would be laid next week.

'Look up,' said Diner. I stared at the ceiling rose, where the chandelier would hang. Our names were woven into it in plaster: ELDIN. The script flowed as clear as Mammie's handwriting but it was so artfully done that you would think, at a first glance, that the letters were merely part of the decoration. 'Every time you enter the house, you will know that it is ours and that we are together here under our own roof.'

'Yes.' It seemed more final than a marriage, for this house would be standing long after we were dead and buried. Tears stung my eyes. I felt so alive that it was impossible to imagine we would ever be shut away in the cold ground.

'Lizzie!' said Diner. 'My Lizzie.'

'Yes.'

'I will have our names put into the tiling of this floor, too, but secretly so that no one else will be able to read them.'

'How?'

'They will be hidden within words that I have chosen.'

'What will they mean, those words?'

'I will tell you – after the tiling is finished.'

Yet the lightness of the morning had gone. The house smelled of damp plaster. Overhead, hammering and whistling continued as if others were more at home here than I was.

'It will be beautiful,' I said, but it wasn't enough. He was still waiting for some rapture that I couldn't provide. 'It is beautiful,' I said, moving into the room that he said would be our drawing room. I had never had such a room before but I could perceive its elegance, even in its present nakedness. The fireplace was in, the plasterwork complete. The windows were glazed but the shutters not yet installed. Diner had told me that the elegance was in the proportions, as a woman's beauty lies in her bones.

'Walk to the windows, Lizzie.'

I went to the window and looked out as I thought he intended me to do, but he said impatiently, 'Did you not notice?'

'Notice what?'

'The silence. There was not a squeak from the boards as you crossed them. This may be the smallest house in the terrace, but it is the best made of all.'

'It is very fine,' I said, and then remembered that those

were Mammie's words. I hoped I had not also caught her tone. I went to Diner and put my arms around him. 'It is magnificent.'

He held me back and scrutinised my face. 'Can you see how it will be?'

'Yes,' I said, but I knew that whatever his vision was, I could not share it. 'We'll have the fire lit, Diner, and you will come in and sit just there' – I pointed to a spot on the floor – 'and you will warm yourself, and then—'

'Yes,' he said eagerly. 'There will be no one else. Only ourselves, and the shutters closed.' He walked around the room, frowning. 'I thought we would wait, Lizzie, until everything was complete and the house furnished. But now I find that I cannot wait.'

He was telling me that there would be no money for the fine papers, furnishings and silk curtains he had described to me before the building began. Perhaps he was telling me that he could no longer afford the rent of the house where we were lodging. How could I let him know that I understood this, without hurting his pride? It was nothing strange to me if money was short. We hadn't always had four rooms to lodge in, when I was a child. In one house I remembered Hannah sleeping on a truckle bed beside the big bed where I cuddled with Mammie. When Augustus came into our lives he brought very little money and, worse than that, he had a saving disposition. Diner had promised that he would take me away from all those shifts; and I had been glad. I am ashamed now when I think how lightly I stepped away from the smell of Hannah's everlasting stew-pot.

He had stopped by the window and was looking out. There hung the splendour of the Gorge. That was what he wanted to give to me. I wanted to go to him but knew that I must not. If he thought that I pitied him, he would quickly come to hate me.

'I don't want to wait either,' I said, light and eager. 'Where is the sense in it? I want us to be here. We can bring what we need, and do everything as we choose, in time, when you are less busy.' He had furniture, I knew, put away in storage, although I had never seen it. A bed, some chairs and a table, a chest or two ... Surely there would be that much? I had bought linen and household equipment with the hundred pounds my grandfather left to me in his will, to be given to me on my marriage. Diner allowed me to spend it as I chose. There were sixty pounds left. I calculated quickly. We needed beds and chests for Sarah's and Philo's rooms in the attic. Those would not cost much.

Diner smiled and stretched out his hand to me, drawing me to the view. 'You shall be here very soon, Lizzie,' he told me, as if soothing the impatience of a child. I stared at the brightness of the day, and thought of my sixty pounds. I had meant to give twenty pounds to Mammie, or rather to Hannah, who would slip it away under her shawl, say nothing and use it as needed. But if Diner asked for the money I must give it to him, since it belonged to him now and not to me.

When I went to visit Mammie later that day it was Augustus who opened the door, holding it wide with a flourish that did not suit him. His big, bony forehead shone.

'My dear Elizabeth!' he exclaimed. 'You are in luck. Richard Sacks has just this moment arrived.'

'How is my mother?'

'Well. She is well.' He climbed the stairs ahead of me, and I thought again how his long legs, cased in black, were as ungainly as a schoolboy's. He knocked into things. At the turn of the stairs he stopped dead, almost causing me to bump into him. 'We are drinking tea together,' he said, turning to me and beaming as if this were something rare. 'Caroline Farquhar has sent down from London a pound of the finest tea.'

Caroline Farquhar was not my favourite among Augustus's well-wishers. She seemed to like my mother very much, and certainly she read everything that my mother wrote. But it was to Augustus that her eyes turned. I could never make it out. Caroline Farquhar was rich, widowed and far from ugly. She had no children. She might do anything she chose, but when Augustus gave one of his speeches, her lips moved too.

I had given Hannah a pound of tea only the week before. We never bought the finest quality because it cost three times as much.

'I have been drinking tea with my mother every day this week,' I said.

But Augustus, for all his lack of income, prided himself on his taste and discernment. 'Certainly that is true,' he said gravely. 'But I think you will agree, when you taste the nectar in our cups today, that we have never before drunk tea.' He lifted one hand, as he did when explaining a point of philosophy. 'And very likely this is not only true of our subjective judgments. It may be that there is a platonic ideal of tea in comparison with which all our previous experience must be considered merely as a shadow – a foreshadowing—'

'Hold on to the rail,' I said sharply, for he had wobbled in his discourse and I thought he might fall on top of me.

The little parlour seemed crammed. Augustus's legs were stretched out before him, while Richard Sacks, who was a heavy man, sat square and rocked back and forth as he spoke, until the joints of the chair creaked. Hannah, very upright, knitted and listened. Mammie sat back from the fire, her hands idle. I drew my chair close to hers, took her hand in mine and chafed it.

'You're cold, Mammie. Come closer to the fire,' I whispered, but she shook her head. She was far away, as she knew how to be. She had absented herself even from me. I wondered if she did the same when she lay in bed with Augustus, because I could not think of any other solution to the mystery of how she bore with him. And especially now that I was not a girl any longer and knew what marriage meant. My mother might have lived in peace with me and Hannah, and yet she had chosen Augustus.

'I'm not cold, Lizzie.'

Hannah raised her head and looked over at us attentively, as if she were trying to make out what we were saying. I saw my mother shake her head minutely in response. She and Hannah had had almost a language of gestures and silences between them when I was a child, to pass those messages which were not for me. I had never challenged them. I liked the feeling that Mammie and Hannah were there to manage things, and I was safe with my book or my doll. But not now.

'What is it?' I whispered. 'What does Hannah mean?'

'Nothing, Lizzie. Hush.'

Hannah had dropped her eyes, but now Augustus was looking over at my mother. 'Julia,' he said fondly, 'do not tire yourself. You have been sitting with us an hour or more. Do you not think, Hannah, that she should rest?'

'She will please herself, I dare say, as you have done,' snapped Hannah. Richard Sacks coughed and rubbed his hands along his broad thighs. He knew. Hannah and Augustus knew. All of them were skirting something which was invisible only to me.

'Mammie,' I said aloud, 'let me take you to your room,' and I put my hand under her elbow, almost forcing her to rise. She gave way to me and we went out of the room without speaking to anyone.

I shut the door. It was chilly in the bedroom, with the fire down to a few red coals. Now we were standing face-to-face, I saw how pale she still was, blotched under the eyes. Her breath was sour. All at once it came to me, as if the truth had travelled from her body into mine.

'Mammie,' I said, 'you are never going to have another child.'

She looked at me steadily, and nodded. There was no smile on her face or mine.

'How could you?'

'It happened, Lizzie.'

'What about the sponge? What about those extraordinary methods of self-control you described to me? Could Augustus not practise them?' I almost said: *As Diner does.*

There was silence between us, until I broke it.

'But, Mammie, you are almost forty. How can you have a child?' Safely, I meant, but did not dare to say it in case those words, once spoken, might begin to work on her.

'Lizzie,' she said, 'Lizzie, Lizzie, Lizzie.'

'Hannah knows,' I said, 'Augustus knows. Even Richard Sacks knows. No doubt Augustus has already communicated the intelligence to Caroline Farquhar and that is why she sent the tea. Only I was to remain in ignorance, it seems.'

'Augustus had no business to speak to Richard about this matter.'

'But he did. He blabs. He is like a child, and you all indulge him.'

None of this was what I wanted to say to her. We stood apart, and then I saw her shiver.

'You aren't well, Mammie. Lie down while I make up the fire.'

I wrapped the clothes about her and went to kneel by the fire and coax it up with fresh small pieces of coal and the bellows. Soon the flames grew and I laid more coal before returning to the bed.

'You must keep warm,' I said to her. 'Mammie, were you ill like this before I was born?'

'I don't think so. I can't remember. It was such a long time ago, Lizzie. Now don't look like that; it is not the end of the world. Hannah will look after the baby, as she did with you.'

The baby. It was the first time I'd thought of there being a baby. All I had seen at first was the risk to Mammie. I knew nothing of babies, although of course I saw them often enough, red-faced and squirming inside other women's shawls.

'And you'll keep on writing,' I said, 'as you did with me.'

'I was not eighteen when you were born, Lizzie. I had scarcely begun to think, let alone write.'

And three years later, my father had died. His parents had not wanted him to marry Mammie, and they liked her even less after my father died and she began to write. Once, when she spoke of them, I suddenly real-ised: those people she is talking about are my grand-parents. Since they had never visited me or sent me a letter, the thought seemed unreal, but I had to admit that the hundred pounds my grandfather had left to me was solid enough.

There was one portrait of my father, a miniature which my mother kept in a small ivory box, and gave to me when she married Augustus. He looked very young, and, as even Hannah allowed, very handsome.

'Hannah will look after everything,' I said.

'I suppose so,' said Mammie wearily. 'She is angry with me.'

'Why?'

She sketched her own body with her hands. 'The baby. She says it will hinder my work.'

'She should be angry with Augustus.'

'Yes, she is that too.'

'But you said Hannah will take care of the baby.'

'Perhaps it is too great a burden to load on to her now. She is not a young woman, as she was when you were born.'

And you are not young either, I thought. 'I can help you,' I said.

She laughed. I was lying on the pillow beside hers, where I supposed Augustus sometimes lay. She turned and rubbed the back of her hand along my cheek. 'Of course you will not, my darling.'

She was right. I had offered because I knew nothing of what a baby meant. Hannah and Mammie had cherished me but they had also made me strong. They did not let me understand that I had any limitation. They had brought me up to believe that in mind and spirit I was the equal of any creature on earth. I could read and cook and sew and pack our belongings into boxes for the carter to take us from lodging to lodging, and I could walk as far and fast as any boy.

'Why should it hinder your work, Mammie? Between Hannah and you and me, there are three pairs of hands. Surely no baby can require more than one at a time. Or you can put it to a wet-nurse,' I added, although I knew she did not believe in wet-nurses.

'Don't think about it any more, Lizzie. I'll keep on writing, Augustus will continue to travel the length and breadth of Britain, and Richard Sacks will sit and drink tea with us.'

'But probably not tea of the quality we had today.'

Mammie laughed. 'Oh Lizzie, you do me good. I'm tired, that's all it is. My head is in a fog, and I cannot think straight.'

I thought of Augustus and Richard Sacks in the parlour, conversing as eagerly as ever. They would talk on all day and half the night, drinking up Caroline Farquhar's tea while my mother lay here too sick and tired to think. I looked over at the fire and saw that the coal-bucket was almost empty. I picked it up, and the brass tongs, and marched into the parlour. Hannah was no longer there: she must have gone into the kitchen. Yes, as I thought, the parlour coal-bucket was full. Augustus must have got up and filled it. I knelt down and began to transfer the coal from the parlour bucket to my mother's, piece by piece, choosing the largest and finest lumps. The talk between Augustus and Richard Sacks died away.

'What are you doing, Elizabeth? We shall have no fire.'

'Then you must go walking with Mr Sacks. The exercise will heat you, and do you good.'

They made no reply but I could sense them glancing at each other over my head. I had transferred all the coal that was worth having now, leaving only a little slack in the bottom of the bucket. I got up, and faced Augustus.

'You might eat your dinner in a tavern tonight, to

save Hannah work. She has a great deal to do, while my mother is ill.'

'Has Julia spoken to you of our expectations?' Augustus asked me. I thought how silly his face was, like a sheep's. His mouth was forever opening and closing, like a sheep's in pasture. His white bony fore-head gleamed like the sheep's skull I had found in the summer, when I was wandering on the Downs.

'Indeed she has,' I said briskly. I was not going to let him guess at my fear, or my anger. It was done now. Mammie, not I, was going to have a child.

5

It was some weeks after we moved into the new house that the floor was tiled. As he had promised, Diner had words tiled into it, but so subtly that I could only read them because he told me where they could be found. They read: 'Out of the strong came forth sweetness.' I was taken aback, because I'd thought from what he had said earlier that he was going to place our names there, hidden within the design of the floor. But he told me that he had changed his mind and instead had placed there part of a riddle first asked by Samson in the Bible.

The Bible is a book I know less well than many others. I could not imagine that a riddle out of the Bible would have much to do with our marriage.

'You must know who Samson is, Lizzie,' said Diner.

I remembered that Delilah had cut off his hair while he slept, which sapped his strength so that he could be captured.

'Samson was on his way to marry a Philistine woman when he killed a lion with his bare hands. He returned later to the carcass, only to find that a swarm of bees had made its home there. He took out the honey and made a riddle: "Out of the eater came forth meat, and out of the strong came forth sweetness."'

'Well, I suppose that riddle might be hard to guess,' I said. 'Who would think of a man killing a lion with his bare hands? Let alone digging honey out of the lion's belly, when it ought to have been swarming with flies and maggots. If it were not in the Bible, it would be hard to credit.'

'You speak very freely, Lizzie.'

'It is what I was brought up to do. I can sew you a fine shirt, but I cannot embroider a text for you.'

'Is that another riddle?'

'You know it is not.' If he wanted a quarrel, I was ready for it. It seemed to me that Diner was talking to me as if I were a child. *You speak very freely.* It made me indignant, as if he had laid hands on me. I think he saw it, because next time he spoke his voice had changed.

'You are right, Lizzie, it should have been impossible for them to guess the answer to the riddle. Samson made the solving of it into a bet with the Philistines, and none succeeded. But then for seven nights the Philistine woman whom he had married wept and told him he did not love her because he would not confide in her the answer to the riddle. She persisted until on the last night she coaxed the secret of the riddle out

69

of Samson and then she told it to her people. Consequently, Samson did not win his bet.'

'Was that before Delilah, or after?' I asked.

'It was before.'

'So he did not learn much from his experience.'

'She betrayed him,' said Diner, 'as he knew she would.'

'What do you mean?'

'He knew the woman would betray him, and yet he still told her.'

'And this is the story you have put into the tiles on our floor?'

Diner laughed and put his arms around me, lifting me to him. 'It is the story of the honey that you are to me, Lizzie.'

'From a lion's carcass? Are you Samson then?'

He held me away from him. His face was heavy. 'Whatever strength I have, Lizzie, I swear it is all for you. Whatever sweetness there is in my life, it comes from you. I know that you will not betray me.'

'Of course I will not,' I said, making light of it although it chilled me that he should think of betrayal. 'I will never coax any of your riddles out of you, or cut off your hair while you are sleeping.' I smoothed back a lock of it. 'You shall keep it all, I promise. Tell me, Diner, did you learn your texts well when you were a boy?'

'I would have been thrashed until blood ran, if I had not known them by heart and been ready to answer any question on them.' His tone was calm, as if this was the order of things.

'There will be none of that with our children,' I said.

'Our children? What spirits are you conjuring now, Lizzie?'

'Invisible ones, except to me.'

'Do you think of them often?' he asked, almost jealously, as if I were keeping something from him.

'Of course,' I said.

He folded me to him again. I felt him quiver, as he did sometimes, as if from weakness, but I knew it was not weakness. The quiver came from him holding back his own strength. I thought of my mother's writing, and that nowhere in her pamphlets did she write that the muscles in a man's arms could hold a woman still whether she wanted or no. I wanted Diner to hold me, but his story of the lion and the honey did not please me. I would keep my thoughts hidden, and not look closely at the tiles.

That night I woke to the coldness of Diner's body as he slid into bed beside me. He was cold all along the length of him, and I shifted away without meaning any harm. He pulled me to him.

'Lizzie,' he said, and his voice was hoarse, as if he had been shouting at the men. But it was the deep middle of the night. I tried to raise myself to look at him, but of course I could see nothing. Besides, he was holding me too tightly.

'Are you ill?' I asked. I thought it might be the shivering fit that takes hold before a fever.

'No,' he said. 'Hold me, Lizzie.'

Perhaps he had had a nightmare, and had got up to walk it out of his head but found that it only settled more deeply there.

'It's all right,' I said, and I wriggled myself deep into his arms. He was shaking now. Surely it was the prelude to a fever. What should I do? Hannah used to sponge my hands and arms, to cool me. But he was still cold and stiff all over, not like his warm living self. It was as if something had got hold of him and was tossing him between its teeth. I heard his teeth chatter and now I was shaking too, not from fear but from the tremors passing through him into me. I held him tighter.

'It's all right,' I said again. 'You're ill, that's all it is. I'll look after you.'

I felt a tenderness for him that I had never felt before. I clasped him as close as I could, thinking that the shivers would run out of him into me and then away into the night. I would still him and then he would sleep. But he was shaking worse than ever and the clacking of his teeth was so loud in my ear that I was afraid he would bite his tongue through. Perhaps he could not breathe. The thought flashed through me of shouting for Philo but I rejected it. Diner would not want Philo or anyone to see him like this. I pressed my face against his and spoke softly into his ear so that he would hear me.

'You're safe,' I said. 'Don't be frightened. It will pass soon. It's me, I'm here, it's Lizzie.'

I am not sure whether he heard me or not but after

a while the shaking grew less. Some shudders still went through him but his body began to relax. He grew warmer. I felt a wetness between his skin and mine: he was drenched in sweat. I realised that I was rocking him, very gently, and that his grip on me had loosened. I was holding him now.

He went down into sleep without a word. It was best, I thought. He had sweated as people sweat when a fever breaks, but I had not felt heat in his skin. What was this sickness? I lay awake for a long time. I had eased myself away from him so that I would not get cramp in my arm where he lay on it, but we were still close. Usually, at night, he would turn away from me and fling his limbs wide on the bed as if he were running in his sleep. But tonight he lay curled, still, his face turned to mine.

I thought: *Out of the strong came forth sweetness*, and now I was glad that he had put those words into the tiles of the floor. I thought that I understood them. He had said that I was honey to him, and it made me glad, but at the same time I was uneasy. I did not like it that a tale of death, rottenness and betrayal had entered our house almost as soon as we were in it.

In the morning I woke and Diner was by the bed, standing there and looking down on me. He was up; he was dressed; he had been out; he had set the men to work. He was himself again, or it seemed.

I sat up, leaning on my elbows. 'Are you well this morning?'

He frowned. 'Of course I am well. Why do you ask?'

'You shook last night as if you had the ague.'

'Ague! Lizzie, I shall begin to think you are like Delilah and wish to weaken me. I never had a fever in my life.'

I lay back on my pillow. I did not want to argue with him. 'Will you be late?'

He did not reply but merely nodded and was gone. I threw the bedclothes aside and hurried to dress myself. I would not think about it now.

Throughout May and June the work went on well. All day and into the long light evenings our house was full of the sounds of building. Diner drove the men hard. Sixteen houses at least must be finished before the winter, and they would sell for sure, he said. Buyers would see the terrace as he saw it. Even the dullest spirit would be seized with the desire to live here. The terrace would become the talk of the city and everyone would crave to possess a part of it. Once those houses were sold there would be enough money to complete the terrace, and then the profits would come tumbling in.

I knew we could not afford another winter like the last, with Diner's capital sunk in the ground and money bleeding from him week after week. I understood his business better now. I listened, and paid attention to figures and conversations. Sometimes I called for him with Philo at my side when he stayed late at Grace's Buildings, and if he was in the mood for it he would show me drawings and calculations. Sometimes we missed him, and later he would tell me that he had walked the streets for hours, working out his plans.

He was lit up all through those weeks of early summer. He could see the stone curve of the terrace shaping itself according to his vision and he did not care how hard he drove the men. Every day there were a dozen difficulties to be overcome. A delivery not made, or made late so that a day's progress hung suspended; a workman drunk and falling from a scaffold; accidents, illnesses, orders mislaid; a crate of tiles dropped in transit and cracked: all these things multiplied by many more and always the cost of it, the surging cost of the build which was in Diner's head from the instant he woke until the time when he began to run again in his sleep.

I lived in the dust of it. These were the clearest, sunniest days of the year and mostly I rose early, before the men arrived for work. God knows they came early enough. Mortar set easily and men whistled as if they liked their work. The young ones did, perhaps, but there were older men whose bodies were already worn and twisted by digging and shovelling and working out in rain and cold with only a length of sacking over their shoulders. Every day they must get up at dawn and haul bricks and stone until their backs broke, if they wanted to live. Their faces were cracked with lines where sweat and dust lodged as the day went on. They worked harder, I saw, whenever Diner was near, because he had no tolerance for any man who could not press himself on through the day as he did.

Sometimes I glanced at the young men who swung themselves from the scaffold with such limberness that it seemed impossible they would ever grow old and struggle to haul barrows of cut stone. There was one called Abel who would play tricks, pretending to fall and then grasping the bar at the last moment, when the foreman's eye was elsewhere and Diner not to be seen. The others would look up and laugh and egg him on, and they would whistle out a warning too, on a note that I came to know, which meant that the foreman had been spotted. I took care that they never saw me watching. They did not trust me, and why should they have done? For all they knew, Diner had told me to report to him everything that I saw. Perhaps they believed it was why he had brought his wife to live in the middle of a building site.

It was a different matter for the skilled craftsmen. They had a trade and they guarded it jealously. Their skill was built into their hands and nobody could take it from them. The labourers had only their bodies. I came to see what it meant to be a carpenter or a stone-mason, and how they could parlay with Diner while the labourers must take whatever was going. They were rough but none of them troubled me: Diner could quell any man, and they all needed the work.

Suddenly furniture appeared, and curtains. I had come to like our house empty, with echoes that travelled from room to room, and the beauty of proportion which he had taught me seen naked, as it were. There was something else I loved about it, although it took me a while to understand what that was: Diner and I were encamped in the house together, with a few things around us that belonged to us, and because this was the way I had always lived it was dear and familiar to me. I was not at ease in a settled home with everything in its place. I preferred to think that at any moment we might whisk up our bits of furniture, put them on a cart and go somewhere we hadn't even thought of yet. Of course I never said this to Diner. He spoke of our house as if it was built to last us a thousand years.

'Some furnishings will arrive tomorrow,' said Diner.

'What furnishings?'

'A rug or two for the drawing room. Some little tables. Various things, Lizzie.'

The things were not new or beautiful, but there were plenty of them. They came on a cart and two men shuffled them into the rooms. The rugs smelled fusty. There were pictures to hang on the walls, and a curious marble statue, half woman and half tree, which was placed in the hall. One by one the things filled the rooms, and our house began to look like a place where anyone might live. For me, its beauty was dimmed. When I asked Diner where all this furniture had come from, he said that a friend had accommodated him. He had many such friends, for whom he had once done favours. It was the way the world worked, he told me.

I straightened a mirror and wondered where it had hung before, and whose face it had shown. A friend, Diner said. I wondered what friend it was, and where these furnishings had been before they came here. Diner had furniture when he lived with Lucie. Had he stored it while he was in lodgings, with every penny sunk into the building of the terrace?

I gazed into the mirror. There was my own familiar face, which I never liked to look at too long. What other face had gazed here? I thought of Lucie, whom Diner had never described to me.

A little later I understood the logic of this sudden furbishing. Diner began to bring prospective buyers to our house. As he had said before, there would be no finer workmanship anywhere along the terrace even though our house was the smallest. It was comical, in a way, to see how these buyers were drawn into the house and how they looked around and barely noticed me even when I was sitting in the window, sewing. Diner would say: 'This is my wife, Elizabeth,' and I would stand and we would be introduced. Some of them understood that the rooms were beautiful: I could see it in their eyes. They looked past the furnishings into the exquisite spaces that Diner had made. Others needed Diner to tell them about the cost of the marble fireplaces, the quality of the mahogany banisters and the convenience of the mews which would be built behind the gardens. But at some point every one of them would walk to the windows that looked out on to the Gorge and fall silent. Sometimes, if a man had come with his wife, they would look at each other and I would see the eagerness in their faces even though they tried to conceal it for fear of raising the price. Diner would always say to them that this house was by far the least significant in the terrace, and they liked that. They could imagine even greater splendour within the bare roofless shells that might one day be their homes. He would describe to them how the pavement would be finished, and the road below with its mounting-blocks where the carriages would come round.

Week after week, the buyers came. Some of them came twice, or three times, but each time, when it came to putting down their money, they would sheer off. They were skittish as colts, Diner said, but he would have them. It was the times. The unrest in France caused men to hold their money close. He would break them. I saw that he did not doubt himself: the fine weather and the steady pace of the building had brought his confidence almost to exhilaration. He smiled at me as he spoke, as if we were at one in our ambitions. Perhaps we were.

As each day began I would prepare the house carefully, putting flowers into the drawing room and wiping away the dust that settled every hour because of the building work. Philo could not keep up with it. I laid the scene and then I took up my work and sat in the window as leisurely as any lady. I thought of Mammie, and how she would laugh. I pushed away the knowledge that she would be disappointed too, to see me idle my time away in no better cause than putting on a show to catch a wealthy buyer. I smoothed the piece of embroidery which I brought out at these times rather than plain sewing. I would play my part.

I wondered if any of the men had known Lucie. Not the labourers, probably, who were hired from season to season, but there were carpenters and masons who had worked for Diner over the years. They would have seen her. They might have spoken to her. When they saw me, perhaps they compared me to her. I wished that I could look inside their heads, and see what they saw.

6

I had not meant to tell Mammie about Diner's illness. There was no other name I could find for the sweats and shaking that racked him, even though he denied that he had ever had a fever. Some nights he was perfectly well, and I almost forgot it, and then, for no reason, I would wake and find him clutching me as tremors took hold of him. I could not think of another reason for such shaking, apart from fear, and Diner was not afraid of anyone

Mammie had a way of drawing words out of me, even when I was determined to remain silent. I had already told her that Sarah had left, and although I did not give the reason she understood instantly that there was not enough money. We were sitting together, with Mammie reading aloud to me while I sewed a set of caps for the baby. Hannah and I had sewn the nightgowns already and worked a shawl. Hannah had written a list of what would be needed, and we were fulfilling it steadily. Mammie was reading from Bartram's *Travels*. Caroline

Farquhar had lent us the book, which she had had from a friend lately returned from Philadelphia, and she sent it with a letter full of such extravagant praise for its author that I was almost dissuaded from opening it. But even my dislike for Caroline could not stop me relishing the book, once we had begun. *Travels Through North & South Carolina, Georgia, East & West Florida, the Cherokee Country, the Extensive Territories of the Muscogulges, or Creek Confederacy, and the Country of the Chactaws; Containing an Account of the Soil and Natural Productions of Those Regions, Together with Observations on the Manners of the Indians.*

I liked wonders, but not improbable ones. Mr Bartram's book was full of wonders, all described with such coolness and accuracy that I could believe in every one of them. I preferred the passages about hawks, alligators and rattlesnakes, while Mammie liked to learn about the society of the Indians. That afternoon she had found a passage which combined the two.

'Here you are, Lizzie, there is something for you in this, but you will have to be patient while he meets an Indian king. He is travelling with the trader we read about earlier.

'Our chief trader in answer informed them, that the re-establishment of friendship and trade was the chief object of his visit, and that he was happy to find his old friends of Talahasochte in the same good disposition, as they ever were towards him and the white people; that it was his wish to trade with them, and that he was now come to collect his pack-horses to bring them goods. The king and the chiefs having been already acquainted with my business and pursuits amongst them, received me very kindly; the king in particular complimented me, saying that I was as one of his own children or people, and should be protected accordingly, while I remained with them, adding, "Our whole country is before you, where you may range about at pleasure, gather physic plants and flowers, and every other production:" thus the treaty terminated friendlily and peaceably.

'Next day early in the morning we left the town and the river, in order to fix our encampment in the forests about twelve miles from the river; our companions with the pack-horses went a head to the place of rendezvous, and our chief conducted me another way to show me a very curious place, called the Alligator-Hole, which was lately formed by an extraordinary eruption or jet of water. It is one of those vast circular sinks, which we beheld almost every where about us as we traversed these forests, after we left the Alachua savanna. This remarkable one is on the verge of a spacious meadow, the surface of the ground round about uneven by means of gentle rising knolls: some detached groups of rocks and large spreading live oaks shade it on every side: it is about sixty yards over, and the surface of the water six or seven feet below the rim of the funnel or bason: the water is transparent, cool, and pleasant to drink, and well stored with fish; a very large alligator at present is lord or chief; many have been killed here, but the throne is never long vacant, the vast neighbouring ponds so abound with them.'

'How I should love to see an alligator king,' I said.

'I would rather see the King of the Siminole and all his chiefs,' said Mammie. 'What a man he must be. See him stretch out his arm as he says to Bartram: "Our whole country is before you, where you may range about at pleasure." Do you think that our own King would be as magnanimous, Lizzie?'

I laughed. 'Farmer George has no alligators. He is a dull fellow.'

'It must be a fine thing,' said Mammie, 'to gather new physic plants and learn their use. Bartram is taking specimens and seeds wherever he goes, and they will be sent back to London for examination. He hopes to propagate many new species here.'

'I'm glad to hear it,' I said, 'otherwise one might almost think, from his description, that he was travelling for enjoyment.'

'But imagine how many diseases may be cured one day, by such plants.'

The word 'disease' stuck to my mind like a burr. Perhaps Diner was really ill, and I had been hiding it even from myself. Sweats – chills – shaking: even if it was not ague, there were many serious diseases which began in such a way—

'What is it, Lizzie?'

I thought of passing it off, but I had hidden too much from her lately. 'I'm afraid that Diner isn't well,' I said. She listened with an eagerness which meant more to me than any speech as I told her about his symptoms.

'I feel sure it is nothing,' she said firmly. 'He looked as well and strong as ever when I saw him last Sunday.'

'But then why should it happen?'

'Perhaps he has bad dreams. One can wake in a sweat from a nightmare.'

I had thought of that already, but it hadn't convinced me. Diner lived in the daylight world of building, land and money. His imagination went into stone. I couldn't believe him plagued by nightmares like a character from one of Mrs Radcliffe's novels.

'You might ask him whether anybody else in his family was troubled by such symptoms. His father, perhaps.'

'How can I ask him that? He is not even aware of what happens. In the morning he remembers nothing of it.' And besides, Diner rarely spoke of his family, and when he did it was to recall instances of such brutality in his childhood that I quickly changed the conversation.

'Perhaps he needs to be told,' said Mammie in the gentle voice she used for her most determined ideas. The vertical crease in her forehead deepened. She looked older because of her pregnancy, and it frightened me. I knew that she also looked older because she was anxious for me, and had been anxious ever since Diner and I had married, although she tried to conceal it. He was not the man she had imagined for me, if she'd imagined anyone at all. A spurt of anger set me back. She had had two husbands. Did she think that another Augustus would satisfy me? Or was I to become a second Hannah Rougemont, the handmaid of a woman whose brain ran faster than her pen? My mother knew I was not like her. My words would not kindle a milk pudding.

I wished I had said nothing about Diner's illness. These two would never understand each other. I was the only link between them and each of them tugged on it hard in the hope that the other would let go.

'I expect it is only because he works so late,' I said. 'His mind is full of the building work. No wonder it disturbs his sleep.'

'I don't want it to disturb yours, Lizzie.' She stroked my cheek. 'Look at the shadows under your eyes. You must tell him. Sometimes, once a man knows where his nightmares come from, they stop.'

I wondered if she might be talking about my father. But no, more likely it was Augustus. I could not begin to imagine what dreams he might have, and the thought of my mother comforting him as I tried to comfort Diner made me shift away from her. My mother's hand dropped, but her eyes stayed on me. My irritation melted. No one, I thought suddenly, would ever look at me like that, except for Mammie, because to her every good thing, every moment of happiness that came to me meant more than if it came to herself. Even Diner, who loved me, could be jealous of a cherry tree in blossom because I looked up into its branches, or of a child skipping in the street because I smiled at her. He told me once that he liked my grave face. If I smiled too much, people would misunderstand it. I laughed at him and he said no more then.

'How do you know so much?' I asked her, and I took her hand and pressed it to my lips. The taste of her skin went deep inside me, as if it belonged there. She smiled and protested:

'Why, what's all this, Lizzie? Are you nuzzling your old pet donkey?'

'I must finish these caps,' I said. 'Your baby would have to be wrapped in newspaper if it were left to you and Augustus.'

'Hannah has been sewing too,' said my mother slyly.

'You're fortunate, then, that you have the pair of us at your service.'

'I'm sorry, my darling. I am a poor example to you. My brain is so clouded that I can scarcely think.'

She had said that too often lately. She was dissatisfied with everything she wrote and the week before there had been a fierce argument with Hannah because Mammie had torn up the text of a pamphlet after Hannah had copied it out fair for the printer.

'As soon as the baby is born, your mind will be as it was,' I said quickly. I hated to hear her doubt herself.

'I can say nothing new. Others can write better. Why should people listen to me?'

If she began to think like that, then the whole foundation of our life would crumble. Why had she ever written? Of course most people would not heed what she wrote. They would mock it, or denounce it, or ignore it. They would attack her morals and her reputation; but she was used to that. To write about injustice and the rights of men and women was to invite ridicule, but she had written on those subjects indefatigably for years. Her writing had no flamboyance, but the clarity of her arguments made its own persuasion among those who were prepared to be persuaded.

When I was a child and sat under the table to listen I believed that crowds would march behind her with banners while the sky flared with gold. A child must hope that its parents are invincible, I suppose. But I had admitted to myself some time ago that the number of those who followed her would remain few. I had less belief than my mother had, or Hannah, or Augustus, or any of them. I had had that faith once, but somewhere I had lost it even though I still lived by its pattern.

Now it seemed that in France, everything my mother and her friends had long talked about was coming true. Human beings really were capable of uniting to defeat tyranny and injustice. A new order could be created, based on the rights of man. And woman too. I was the one who had been mistaken. Everything they had dreamed of and written about was coming to pass, not two hundred miles from London. They read aloud the precious letters from Mammie's old friend Susannah Quinton, who was in Paris now, in the thick of it. She had taken part in fraternal marches behind a liberty bonnet. She had watched food riots from a high window, and written the scene so vividly 'that I can believe I am there myself,' said Augustus solemnly, as he folded the letter again after reading it. I wondered why Mammie had not read it aloud to us, since Susannah was her friend: a true friend, who gave Hannah Rougemont a length of fine blue wool to make a warm dress for me, the winter I was seven. Friends such as Caroline Farquhar rarely did anything so useful. They thought we could live on fine tea and ink, I suppose. And now here was Mammie looking tired and old.

'The trouble is, Mammie, this hot weather doesn't suit you. We should have a picnic in the cool of the evening, as they do in the Royal Parks of France. You and Augustus can come, and Hannah, and Diner will join us. We'll have some of Gresham's ham, cut fine, and Philo can make milk bread. They were selling raspberries very cheap in the market, Philo said. You know how much you like raspberries and cream. Shall I arrange it?'

'Yes, Lizzie, do,' said Mammie, but I saw that it was to please me that she agreed, and not in any hope of pleasure for herself.

We had our picnic the next day. Philo and I worked together in the kitchen to prepare the food. It was another dry, hot afternoon but the ham lay cool on a marble slab as I cut fine shavings from it, rosy and translucent. Philo had bought fresh salads and the raspberries, and she had spied a tray of small custard tarts with cinnamon which the baker was selling cheap because of the hot weather. She had baked milk bread into twists and these were almost cool on the racks. We packed up the baskets, adding a small bottle of blackcurrant cordial. Philo wrapped our plates and glasses into a cloth that would later serve for spreading out on the grass.

'I never been on a picnic before,' she said, and her eyes shone in her sharp face. 'Only et my dinner out in the field when I was a littl'un scaring the crows.'

The baskets would be heavy but we were not going far: only a little way uphill across the sheep pasture where Augustus, Hannah and my mother would meet us. They were to bring a blanket for us to sit on, and bottles of soda water. Diner said that if he finished work in time, he would join us. We would eat our dinner when the heat of the day was over.

'Is the bread cool enough now?'

She picked up a loaf, tapped the bottom, sniffed its golden crust. Her sallow face flushed with excitement. 'A man come upon a young girl down by the quays last night. They were crying it in the market.'

'What happened?'

'He got more'n he bargained for, didn't he? She fought like a hellcat and he was took up with stripes all down his face and like to've lost an eye. But she lost her treasure. Only thirteen, taken a supper down where her brother was working late.'

'Poor girl.'

'I wunt go down there past six o'clock at night, no matter what, once the men've been drinking.'

'No, you mustn't, Philo.' She was small for fourteen

and it made me shiver to think how easily she could be overpowered. Maybe her speed was her protection. She swerved and scuttled through the streets and missed nothing. Philo had started off scaring the crows when she was four years old and more scared than they were. But she flapped her arms bravely and came home with her halfpenny. It made her laugh to think of it. She ran errands and minded babies and later she learned cooking in the house of an apothecary's widow, who gave her bed and board. Philo had risen at four o'clock and worked until she fell into her bed already sleeping and slept so deep that it seemed only a moment until it was morning again. The widow had taught her everything she knew.

'If we didn't forget the blessed salt!' she cried now, and as she reached over the table for it I saw how her hem barely covered her boots.

'Philo,' I said, 'stand up straight a minute.'

She did so.

'Your skirt is shorter,' I said.

'Must've shrunk in the wash.'

'No, it's you. You're growing. Give it to me tonight and I'll let out the hem.'

She was taller and the pinched shallowness of her face was filling out. Her clothes were skimpy on her. How had I not noticed? Her feet must be growing too.

'Do your boots pinch, Philo?'

She shrugged and looked down at her feet as if they had nothing to do with her.

'I shall buy you another pair.' I'd make her a dress

for the winter, too, because I doubted that anything she'd been wearing six months ago would fit her. I calculated quickly how much it would cost. I would not tell Diner.

The light slanted golden and long shadows sloped across the turf. We had spread out an old blanket, and the smell of crushed grass and thyme rose whenever we moved. My mother could not sit on the ground in her condition, so Augustus had brought a bentwood chair for her, and a cushion for her back. He had carried the soda water too, slung into a deep pouch across his back, and so he had walked laden like a pack-pony, not caring who saw him as he went through the streets. For once I felt softer towards him.

Augustus lowered himself to the ground beside my mother's chair, his long legs folding up like a spider's. What could it be like to touch them? His legs were so thin. I wondered if they were hairy, too. How was it that he could have the face of a sheep and the body of a spider, and how could it be that my mother had chosen him out of all the men she might have chosen? The one thing I knew for certain about my father was that he was a handsome man.

Was my mother beautiful, or was she not? I could never tell. I watched her covertly. She was wearing a brown linen bonnet that I thought hideous but liked too, because she had had it so long that it seemed a part of her. As if she felt my gaze, she untied the strings and took it off. The breeze ruffled the damp hair on her forehead. Golden light filled the cracks and creases of her skin like water, and made them smooth. Augustus picked up her bonnet from the grass and laid it on his lap. He did not care how foolish he looked, any more than she cared that the bonnet was ugly. They were a pair, I thought suddenly. I saw that it might be possible for her to love a man who made himself look a fool for her sake.

I saw her flinch a little and then smile, as if something had happened that she must hide. I went over to her and knelt beside her chair, on the other side from Augustus. 'Are you all right, Mammie? Are you enjoying our picnic?'

She took my hand and held it between hers. 'This child kicks so strongly,' she said.

'Did I?'

She shook her head. 'It was such a long time ago. I can barely remember.'

You look so old, I thought. You are too old to be having this child.

'What are you thinking of, Lizzie?'

'I am thinking of Diner. If he doesn't come soon, there will be nothing left to eat.'

'You could put some aside for him.'

'I suppose so. But he said he would come.'

I leaned my head against her chair, and closed my eyes to feel the sun. Diner was never foolish, I thought. Would he carry a chair through the streets for me? No. If I were swollen with his child, he would think I should stay at home. Or perhaps that I could walk up and down the pavement until I had had my fill of exercise.

When I was with my mother I could not help seeing Diner through a darker glass. When I stepped out of our house the world changed a little and I saw things differently. I allowed myself to think how Mammie would frown in disapproval if his face hardened with anger against me, or if she saw him push me away when I offended him. She had never seen such things or heard of them: I had made sure of that.

A minute later I was ashamed of my disloyalty to Diner, and half afraid that he would be able to trace it in me, like a slug's trail. But why did he not come? There might not be another evening as beautiful as this. Already the evening breeze was beginning to grow cooler.

'Do you want your shawl, Julia?' asked Augustus.

'No, I am perfectly warm,' my mother answered quickly, and I knew that she understood how much I wanted Diner to arrive before the picnic was over.

I watched Philo picking daisies and scabious to make a posy. The daisies were shutting already. Philo's long shadow bent to the earth and straightened, almost touching the hawthorn bush behind us. Augustus began to talk about the beneficial impulses stirred by Nature in the human heart, but there was no need to listen to him. Hannah sat upright with her legs sticking straight out in front of her and worked the hem of a dress for the baby. I took the end of the loaf and the thickest piece of ham that remained, and set them aside for Diner. The raspberries were bruised by their journey in the basket and his portion was bleeding juice.

Still he did not come. Before long the evening would melt into dusk, and he would never have come. The others were beginning to look about them as if they thought it was time to go home. Hannah folded her work. Philo hung a daisy chain around her neck. She had a lapful of flowers now to make her posy, but Hannah shook her head and gestured for her to pack up the remains of the picnic. Only Mammie sat still, her eyes closed and her lips smiling. I wondered what she was thinking of.

'Should I clear the cloth?' Philo whispered to me.

I knew she had no more inclination to go back indoors than I had. 'No. Leave it for now.'

'We should go back, Julia,' said Augustus. 'The dew is not wholesome for you.'

My mother opened her eyes. 'We could sit here all night and not catch cold,' she said. Her smile flickered with conspiracy. 'There's no need to go yet.'

'Cutpurses are out on the Downs after dark,' said Hannah.

'Not here, surely. We are within sight of houses.'

'Well, Julia, you may sit on your chair as long as you like,' said Augustus, 'although once it becomes dark I shall begin to think of my bed.'

'You'll stay with me, won't you, Lizzie?' asked my mother.

'Of course.'

Philo tied her posy with a long thread of grass, and bit off the ends. She grubbed up a piece of turf, sprinkled it with soda water and wrapped it around the stems. The blue of the scabious glowed as Philo offered the posy to my mother.

'Why, Philo, thank you.' Her fingers touched the flowers gently, getting to know them. She lifted the posy and smelled it. Philo had placed a sprig of two of wild thyme in among the flowers.

It was only when I looked away that I saw it was growing dark, although the turf still breathed out the smell of the day that was over. Our faces glimmered in the dusk. Even the birds were settling and their song had sunk to chirrups. As if something had been agreed without words, Hannah clambered to her feet and began to help Philo pack away the plates and glasses. Augustus handed my mother her shawl, and gave her his arm to rise. She stood, leaning on him a little, but looking away towards the Gorge where darkness was thickening.

'I have never been to the other side,' she said, as if to herself.

'Then I shall take you,' said Augustus with a ponderous gallantry I would have mocked on any other night. He bent towards her and I saw tenderness on his face. For once he did not look so very much like a sheep. 'We shall hire a boatman, and he can row us down the Gorge as far as the sea, if you would like it.'

'He'd need to be a strong boatman,' said Hannah.

'Lizzie must come with us. Will you come, Lizzie?' asked my mother.

'Where must she come?' asked another voice. He had come up behind us, from above. I had been looking for him to appear from the other direction. I jumped, in spite of myself and even though I knew his voice almost instantly. But Mammie answered calmly:

'We were talking of a trip across the river, and now Augustus suggests that we should hire a boat and go down the Gorge.'

'Lizzie doesn't like the water,' said Diner, and I flushed because I had told him privately that I hated the brown eddies where the river's current met the incoming tide. Even when we walked safely on the path of the Portway I was afraid of falling into the brown surge, to be sucked down, carried off and lodged deep in the mud. I could not swim and I doubted if anyone could swim in that water. The tide rose as much as forty feet, covering the mudbanks and drowning the water-meadows.

'I would come with you, Mammie,' I said.

'Thank you, my bird.' Her voice was so warm as it came across to me in the dusk that it reminded me of how she used to say goodnight to me, long ago. She would carry a candle and I would glimpse her face as she turned, shading it, and then closed the door almost silently, as if I might be already asleep. And I would turn on to my side and sleep instantly, as if she had released me from the daylight world.

Diner frowned. He never liked the way my mother had so many sweet names for me, and I for her. I made myself busy unwrapping his bread and ham from its napkin. I laid a few leaves of salad over the meat, and salted it. The leaves were limp with the day's heat, and the edges of the ham had dried. Diner took the food, peered at it, and then wrapped it up again.

'Aren't you hungry?'

'No,' he said. 'I see I am too late for the picnic.' His voice sounded aggrieved, as if he suspected us of pleasures which had stopped at the instant of his arrival.

'There's mustard,' I said. 'Philo has it. I wish you had come earlier.'

'I could not come earlier. But take my arm, Lizzie. Let Philo carry the baskets home – they won't weigh much, since they are empty. You and I shall walk a little, along the Gorge.'

His coming broke up the picnic. Augustus hooked the chair over one arm and supported my mother on his right. Hannah walked on her other side with the cushion and a basket of empty bottles and Philo followed after. They melted into the dusk so quickly that it was as if they had never been here. The grass was flattened, that was all, and it would soon spring up again. I slipped the bread-and-ham into the pocket of my skirt.

We walked along the sheep-track that skirted the Gorge. It was still visible where the turf was rubbed away and the pale stone caught what light there was. Diner walked between me and the slope that dropped away to the crags. Once we stirred a dark bundle by the path and it ran away bleating.

'A wolf will have it,' said Diner.

'You know there are no wolves here.'

He laughed. 'Perhaps they come across the water at night.'

'Wolves don't swim.'

'Who knows?' He had picked up a stick and now he shied it into the darkness. I heard the whistle of its flight.

'Did the work go well today?'

'Well enough. And your picnic?'

'I wish you had been there. Be careful, Diner, you are going too near the edge.'

'Don't you trust me?' He folded his hands around my arm. 'You are perfectly safe. My eyes are used to the dark.'

On our left the slope was steep. The sheep still grazed on it, but below was the sheer drop of the limestone crags, down to the Portway hundreds of feet below. If you fell you might slide, clutching at plants which could not take your weight. They would be ripped from their roots and you would slide again, unable to help yourself, digging your hands and feet into the thin soil that would not hold you. There would be the edge, a last scrabble and then the plunge into darkness. My heart was beating so hard that I was afraid Diner would feel it and think me a fool and a coward. We walked on and I wondered how long I would have to walk before I could safely say that it was time to go home.

'You know where you are now,' he murmured. 'This is the place we came for you to pick those yellow flowers.'

'Yes.' I remembered. I hadn't been afraid then. It had been a bright April morning and I had known Diner for perhaps two months. I thought of nothing but him from the moment I woke until I slept again. At night, he inhabited my dreams. It seemed long ago. If I met now the Lizzie of those days, I would not be able to slip myself into her skin.

Yes, we had gone walking on the Downs and I had picked wallflowers among the rocks. Diner had braced himself and gripped my right hand so that I could lean out and pick the flowers with my left. How had I dared to do that?

'You believe me, don't you, Lizzie?'

'Of course I do.' I spoke too quickly and I could hear the thinness of my voice. It was cool now and the air was sweet but I could not taste it.

'What's the matter?'

'Nothing. Can you really see your way, Diner? I cannot.'

'We are almost there.'

He stopped, took my hand, and laid it on something cool. A rail. A wooden rail. Yes, I knew where I was now. After I'd picked the flowers we had wandered on, and Diner had kept hold of my hand. The sun had been so bright that it prickled my eyes. Diner had told me that a famous painter had come here to paint the views and this rail had been erected for him so he could lash his easel to it in bad weather. Otherwise, when the wind was fierce, he might have been blown over the crags.

I remembered how we'd looked west across the forest, and then south over the dirty smoke of the city and to the hills beyond. It had been so light then that the landscape had seemed to run with it, as if light could become

water and wash over everything. I had not been frightened of anything then.

'You know where you are?' asked Diner.

'Yes.' I knew that if I turned my head to the right,
the hills of Wales were there in the dark. Lights glimmered here and there and the sight of them made this
place seem lonelier than ever. But why was I lonely
when Diner was here with me?

I gripped the rail.

'Let your eyes grow used to the dark,' said Diner.

The dark swelled before me, enormous, breathing
from every shadow. It crisped the hair on my head and
I knew that I was afraid. I did not want to grow used
to the dark.

7

'A Gentleman, arrived in town on Tuesday morning, who left Paris on Friday noon, relates: "That at the time he came away, all was tumult and confusion – the shops were shut up – the King had been dethroned – several of the King's party in the Assembly had been put to death, and others were in custody expecting the same fate. The mob had attacked the Palace, in which were the Royal Family, defended by the National Guard and Swiss Body Guard. It is reported, that one hundred and fifty of the guard had been killed in the conflict, but it was not known if the King or any of the Family had been hurt ... It is said, six of the Assembly were beheaded, and 21 in custody."'

Caledonian Mercury, August 1792

Diner placed both fists on the table, one on either side of the newspaper. His head was down like a bull's, challenging me. 'Now you see what comes of it,' he said.

I was silent. Earlier I had been at my mother's while Augustus paced the room, reading newspaper columns aloud to us as if we were incapable of absorbing them without his intervention. His hand shook and the paper rattled. It was not the same newspaper as the one Diner had brought into the house. 'A tyrant has been swept from his bloody throne. Those who resisted were punished. Six of the Assembly were beheaded,' Augustus said.

Their heads were separated from their bodies. I knew that there was now a machine sanctioned to carry out such executions. I tried to think how it would be to wait for the falling of the blade. I could not stop myself from reaching up to touch the stem of my own neck. It was warm, and strongly joined. There, the pulse beat under my thumb.

'Were they killed by the guillotine?' I asked.

Augustus had glanced back through the columns. 'It does not say.'

'Have you nothing to say, Lizzie?' Diner demanded now.

'Where did you get that newspaper, Diner? It is Scottish.'

'From John Macleod at Grace's Buildings. You think that only your friends are concerned with these matters, Lizzie? You are very composed. But perhaps what I read was not news to you.'

'Augustus read an account to us earlier.'

'Did he throw his cap into the air, and cheer, and caper about the room?'

'He read it, and we were silent.'

'But surely this is what he has worked for all these years. His good friend Tom Paine must be rejoicing.'

'Tom Paine may wish for kings to be taken down from their thrones, but I am sure he does not want it to involve such butchery.'

'Your mother—'

'Diner!'

'She writes on the abolition of hereditary privilege. Isn't that so? And now hereditary privilege has been dethroned. She must be satisfied. When you get what you want, Lizzie, are you not satisfied?'

His question caught me unawares. If he had not been sitting so close to me, I could have answered it calmly.

I had wanted him, and I had had him. I had wanted him so much. I had craved the touch of him. When we had barely met I longed to press myself against his clean linen and smell him. And then we were going to be married and I would rub my face against his and know that soon we would be licensed to be alone together, naked. It seemed the most preposterous and wonderful thing I could ever have imagined. How I had wanted it. Everything else had fallen away to a distance, even Mammie. I'd watched her mouth move as she warned me that there was more to marriage than what I was feeling now, and I had thought: You know nothing. You are old and you have forgotten.

She had run away with my father before they were even married. Well, I say 'run': they did not go far. However, a cottage in the country twenty miles out of London was far enough to end their reputations. My father threw away his family on an impulse which it seems he came to regret, even though he died when he was only twenty-five. Perhaps he'd thought they would soften and accept my mother, but they never did. He wrote letters which were never answered. Perhaps he looked into my cradle and saw his burden lying there in flesh and blood, rather than anything he could love. Hannah would say only: 'Your father was the handsomest man I ever saw,' which was a curious remark coming from her. When had Hannah ever noticed a man's beauty? I plied her with questions but she would never say more. Mammie said once: 'He could not believe that there would be no money. There had always been money.'

Diner had no family, and he depended on nobody. His money was made with his own hands. There was no one whom our marriage could offend. I had wanted him and I had had him, and here he was, so close to me now that I could not breathe right. It seemed that the more we were joined, the less I knew him. I was not that eager, greedy girl any more. I had not been afraid when I stood with him on the edge of the Gorge, in the dark. I had had no reason to be afraid, but my skin had prickled, just as it was prickling now.

'Are you satisfied, Lizzie? Is your mother satisfied with the pulling down of the King?' Diner demanded again. He spoke too loud; he thrust his face at mine.

My mother had risen when the newspaper reading was over. Her body was thickened by pregnancy but her face was thin and there were new lines cut into it. 'So many deaths, Augustus,' she had said.

But Augustus had answered, 'It was necessary. If the King had succeeded in his escape last year, he would have gathered an army to restore his position and crush the Revolution. He is in league with foreign powers to overthrow the sovereign will of the people. The people understood their duty to their fellow men, those living now and those yet to be born.' He glanced at his desk as if he would have dearly liked to write down his words, but thought better of it, bowed his head and stood reverently, as if he were in church. His eyes were almost shut. 'There have been kings in France for a thousand years, and now they are no more,' he intoned, and after that Hannah had also risen to her feet and opened her mouth for this first time:

'Amen,' she said.

My mother had looked from Hannah to Augustus. '*Frenchmen,*' she said, '*we are free. Frenchmen, we are brothers.* Do you remember those words? That was only two years ago, and now here are a hundred and fifty men killed, and who knows how many others beside.'

'The Guard refused to yield the King to the will of the people,' said Augustus. Hannah said nothing but her nose flushed red, as it did when she was angry.

'They were not tried and found guilty of any crime,' said my mother. 'They were killed by a mob. The same mob that flocks to any hanging. You know it, Augustus.'

What would Diner have said if he had been there with us? I thought now. What would he have made of that moment, of Hannah's tall, raw body in its narrow petticoats, of Mammie's words or the way that Augustus looked like a satisfied sheep while he spoke of slaughter?

Mammie had left the room, and I went after her, closing the door on Hannah and Augustus. I could see that she did not want to talk, even to me. Her face was set. She would have thrown on her cloak and walked out over the fields for hours, but she had shooting pains in her legs from the weight of the child growing inside her. She could barely walk comfortably to the end of the street. Each time I looked at her I felt a shiver of relief that my body was still my own, and that Diner never spoke of a child.

'Go home, Lizzie,' she had said. 'They will talk of this for hours, and I know you will not want to hear it, any more than I do.'

'I wonder if Susannah was there.'

'It would have been very dangerous for her. A mob will seize on anything. They might have thought her an English spy.'

'Even with a cockade in her hat?'

'I hope she was not there. I shall write and urge her to come home.'

'Augustus won't like that. No more letters for him to read aloud.'

'That's enough, Lizzie. I shall write to her now.'

I knew that the parlour would soon be boiling over with friends, and the newspaper worn out with greasy fingers. The talk would rise and rise, and it would not end until long after Mammie had finished her letter and fallen into sleep. We had found such friends in every town and country, wherever we travelled. We found a society, a club, a family. We knew one another instantly, by signs and tones of voice, by words used in special senses, by handshakes, brotherhood and the smell of wet ink. While I played on the floor with my doll, quick, passionate speech spun itself into the tobacco smoke above my head. Mammie's voice talking of liberty was my lullaby.

'If your mother and Augustus had been in Paris, would they have rushed to the Tuileries with the mob?' asked Diner.

'You know very well that my mother would do no such thing. As for Augustus, I doubt that he would pick up a pike to kill a fellow creature. Think of what it must have been like.'

'You are right, Lizzie. Your mother, Augustus and all those others who stood around your cradle are not the kind who wield the pike and cut their fellow men to pieces. Instead, they set loose those who will do the work for them.'

I was angry, but would not let him see it. He might say what he liked about Augustus, but I had to turn his words away from my mother. 'Surely those six members of the Assembly must have been killed by the guillotine,' I said.

Diner's eyes were fixed on mine. I could feel his anger, like heat. 'All it takes, then, is the pulling of a lever.'

I had not been able to stop thinking about this. There would be no bleeding in the instant after the blade fell.

The tissues would be shocked and still. But before you could blink the veins would spread and pump out their blood on to the ground. If the head were still living, would it see that? Was it possible for a human head to glare in terror as it was held aloft? I touched my own neck again. I tried to think of how those instants of execution might pass. At one moment, you would be standing there. Probably you would be bound. You would be yourself. The wind would blow your hair and the noises of the city would surge in your ears. Your blood would beat fast and it would seem that your stomach was in your mouth with terror. Every thought you had ever had would be there, coiled inside your head.

I could not explain it even to myself, that a man might set in motion such a lever and put an end to the world that lived inside another's head. It seemed so monstrous and yet it could be done so easily. It made killing as simple as pouring a cup of water. There was no danger to the killer, or necessity to wrestle with a fellow creature who would fight for his life as hard as you fought to extinguish it.

'And yet, it is such a step,' I said slowly. 'Once you have taken one life, why not any number? What is to protect you from evil then?'

Diner moved back from me. He looked down at his hands, and turned them over. 'You are a strange girl, Lizzie,' he said.

'No. Everyone must think so, who considers it at all. Think of it, Diner. To kill another human being is like crossing a river by a bridge which is then swept away behind you. You can never go back again.'

He was very pale. It flashed across me that he might be ill, that one of his shaking fits might begin. I put my hand on his sleeve. 'Did the men finish distempering the plasterwork in the drawing room of number seven?' I asked. I was merely parroting back to him what he had told me that morning of the work scheduled for the day, but when I showed such interest it always pleased him. Not this time, however. He was sunk in thought. I touched his hand, to bring him back to me, and he raised his head.

'God knows what will happen now,' he said. He looked for once utterly confounded.

'What do you mean?'

'In France, of course.'

'The representatives of the people will restore order, I suppose. They cannot continue like this,' I said.

'So you believe that?'

'How can anyone know? It's beyond us,' I said, meaning not only that the confusion unleashed in France was beyond our understanding, but also that it was beyond us in other ways that made us safe. There was the sea between us and France. There was a different language and other customs. They were not us, no matter how much Augustus spoke as if people much like him were lighting a fuse in Paris that would spark to London and set us ablaze with liberty. Augustus talked constantly about the human condition and yet seemed to know so little about it that he did not even understand how my mother longed to walk freely in the fields and could not.

'It will come close enough,' said Diner. Later I understood that he had already guessed most of the consequences that there would be for him, once the King of France was off his throne. He knew that the kings of Europe would not stand for that, for fear that the same thing might happen to them. They were right to be afraid. If one king can be seized hold of like a common thief and taken where he does not wish to go, then where does that leave the system of majesty which keeps us all kneeling? What the people of France did today, the people of Spain or England might dream of doing tomorrow.

My husband had foresight. It was in his bones: he knew how to lay his plans and how to work until the image that burned on his brain grew into a great façade of stone. He could discuss the mixing of lime mortar or the tuck-pointing of a façade so surely that the men deferred to him, but he also had vision. He saw the crowned heads of Europe coming together and deciding on war. He glanced down the corridors of the future and saw disaster, but he looked away again. He pretended that he was like the rest of us, who saw nothing yet. And so he sat there at the table and shrugged, and at last he took my hand. He held it for a long time in silence, and I sat still and thought that while we were together, nothing could harm us.

Sarah had left some weeks ago. She had seen which way the wind was blowing, she said, and had found herself a better place. Philo and I did the work of the house together now. I changed my dress and sat in the drawing room only when the buyers came. The high pavement was still not paved. Diner feared it would discourage buyers that they had to pick their way through the dirt, but the cost of the stone to pave it would be immense. This work – and much else besides – could not be done until more houses were completed and sold. The building went on from morning to night, but there were never enough hours.

I had given Hannah the twenty pounds. Instantly and without a word, she tucked it into her skirt. Mammie would never have allowed me to give it to her. Out of what I had left, I'd bought a bed and chest for the attics, and a chair for Philo, so that she might sit in peace there if she liked. I still had enough to buy food and coals, and pay Philo her wages. We had been in the house for four months now, and we lived mostly in the kitchen.

I was glad to sit with Diner's hand around mine. He still slept badly, and often I would wake to find him absent. If I got up, wrapped my cloak around me and searched for him, I might find him at the kitchen table, covering a sheet of paper with his calculations. The lines crossed and recrossed so that no one but he could read them. On other nights, the house was empty of him. I thought of him walking the city streets, beating out figures in his head.

The summer days were passing quickly. All too soon winter would halt the work again, and the men would have to be laid off. One buyer had withdrawn from a house that Diner had believed was safely sold. He had chosen to buy in Bath instead. There were only three houses finished and taken, and not by the fine families Diner had envisaged. One was a widow who kept a lodging house, with every room instantly crammed and earning money. A man who had made his fortune from the pits at Radstock bought the second house in the terrace, but did not live in it. It would be worth good money one day, once the terrace was complete, he explained to Diner, but for now he expected to buy at a substantial discount. He understood Diner's situation most precisely, and got what he wanted. Diner could not bear to look at him when he came to take possession of his property. The third house contained a family from London with two children in a consumption, who had been advised by their doctor to take daily treatments at the Hot Well. They had money. The father lived in London. I saw only the mother, the servants and two little boys who never played or ran. We had been in the house four months and it seemed that I had spent years picking my way over rutted mud.

I had never known how a single house was built before I met Diner, let alone a terrace. I'd thought that houses rose in order, and were roofed and finished all at once. What I learned, as Diner's terrace grew, was that houses might be like teeth erupting in an infant's mouth, with pain and trouble. They might look more ugly at first than the smooth gum that was there before them.

I was used to living snugly, in rooms wrapped around by other rooms, warmed by neighbouring fires in back-to-back fireplaces. Now I had no neighbours. There were only the three houses finished at the northern end of the terrace. On either side of our house, on the turn, there were the shells of houses, unroofed and without floors. They looked like ruins, although they were the opposite. At night, when Philo was asleep and Diner out, I felt like an inhabitant of Rome after the barbarians had taken the stones of the temples to wall their fields. I could not understand why Diner did not come home. What could he be doing in Grace's Buildings, night after night?

Before I married, Mammie had asked me how my husband made his money. 'He is not an architect, Lizzie. He is not a mason or a carpenter. You say that he builds houses, but what is it that he does?'

I would have explained it all to you, Mammie, if I'd been able. I now understand that he has some capital, although no one ever knows how much. Even I must not know that. With this money he borrows more, until he can buy the piece of land he wants. Once the land is secure he lets it lie, until he is ready to build or until others are ready to believe that this piece of land is as valuable as he knows it to be. The prospectus he writes for his buildings is like a message from the angels and taken down by man. You could not read it and be unmoved. Your heart would be stirred by the desire to live on exactly the spot that John Diner Tredevant had chosen. You would see yourself walking on the high pavement and looking out from the airy rooms into the billowing spaces of the Gorge. You would be on fire with the longing to open one of those doors and call it your own.

He borrows more money to buy wood and stone, marble and cast iron, glass and glazed tiles. He does not buy all this at once, because the cost would be overwhelming, but his suppliers know that they can extend credit to him. Once the houses are sold they will have their money. They supplied him before when he was building Canford Square and Little Morton Row. He made a handsome profit then and everyone knows it. A terrace looped along the slope above the Gorge may seem fanciful to some, but men like my husband are not fanciful, and they are not deterred.

Neither are the men who flock to be hired. He hires skilled men and day-labourers, and men to oversee them. He rolls his gold out so thin so that it will cover a whole field. Mammie, I should have told you that the gold would roll so thin that one day no one would be able to see it. But I didn't know that then.

It was late again, almost ten o'clock. Philo was asleep, worn out after washing day. The house above me felt heavy, like a weight pressing me down. I wished that Diner would come home, but he did not. I was restless and so I climbed the kitchen stairs into the emptiness of the house, and then crossed the hall into the drawing room. The shutters were open. The black windows showed my candle guttering as I moved. I set it down, but still the light of my single candle prevented me from seeing into the night. I blew it out, and waited for my eyesight to settle.

The sky glimmered a little and I thought that the moon must be rising, although I could not yet see it. It would be a quarter-moon tonight. The Gorge showed as a greater darkness. I touched the glass, spreading out my fingers. It was a cool evening for August, and the glass was cold. From here I could see no lights from the far end of the terrace. Everything was still and lifeless. There were pools of rainwater gathered on the unmade pavement. I heard a fox bark.

It was too dark for me to see into the forest on the other side of the Gorge, and I was glad of it. Owls would be hunting now. I thought again of bears, and wolves, and strange creatures that were half-man and half-beast, sheltering from human eyes in limestone caves. I remembered how Diner had told me that long ago there were men encamped on the highest part of the Downs. They built their fortifications where they could spy their enemies stealing out of the woods. There were such forts on both sides of the water, and they guarded the river.

Diner told me that there would have been encircling walls beneath the bulge in the turf that the sheep now grazed. The shape of the houses built by those long-ago inhabitants might still be visible, if you knew where to look.

My eyes were quite used to the dark by now. I supposed that if anyone were outside they might see the pale disc of my face floating against the glass, and think I was a ghost. My dress would not show at all. I wondered if I should stay within the house, or go outside. Tonight, the one seemed as chill and strange as the other. Only Philo, heavily asleep, made the house human. Sometimes I would tiptoe up the wooden attic stairs and stand outside her little room, to hear her. When she lay on her back, she snored. She did not like sleeping alone up there, and I could not blame her. She missed Sarah's company at night, even though otherwise she was glad to be rid of her.

My face made no reflection on the glass. The dark outside, it seemed, was equal to that within. This house could not be haunted, because no one before me had sat at this window and looked out, waiting. Lucie had never lived here. She did not know this window and the glass did not know her reflection. There was no reason for me to feel uneasy, oppressed, as if I did not belong here and someone else was taking my place.

At that moment, my eye caught movement outside. There was someone there. I moved very cautiously backwards, so that my face would be hidden. A shape showed in the faint moonlight. I breathed sharply, in terror of seeing a woman, and then I knew him. It was his shape: I could not mistake it. Diner. He stepped over one puddle and another, and then stood still. In a moment he would come into the house. I would light the candle quickly so that he would not guess that I'd been sitting in the dark, foolishly. He would say, 'Well, Lizzie! Have you been waiting up for me?'

But he did not. He turned towards me, but I am sure he did not see me. The moonlight lay faint and blue and in it I saw his face. It was not distinct: I could not see any feature. He looked up, and seemed to be scanning along the terrace, searching for something in the jagged, half-built outline. It seemed as if his eyes passed over me and my heart thudded again.

His hands were clasped behind his back and he stood for a long time, unmoving. It gained on me that he was not looking at the terrace. There was something else, something I could not see.

At last he moved. He stepped away to the edge of the pavement, and disappeared. He was climbing down the steps that led to the track which was not yet a road. He would be hidden from me by the height of the pavement, and then he would reappear.

Sure enough, he did. He was on the turf now, and walking towards the edge of the Gorge. Moonlight showed the clear outline of his body as he moved. He looked smaller than I had ever imagined him. I must not blink in case the Gorge swallowed him as I might swallow the night air in my breath. But even though I watched and kept on watching, he vanished.

8

'From the London *Times*, Monday the tenth of September 1792.'

How I wished Augustus would not read the newspaper aloud. It had become a regular ceremony, now that Susannah Quinton had left Paris and there were no more letters. He hated the London *Times* and read it only to disbelieve its reports, but there was no denying the reach of its correspondents. By the time the newspaper came to us it was already well handled, and once we had read it we passed it on.

'We have very good authority for the detail that follows. Many of the facts have been related to us by a gentleman who was an eye-witness to them, and left Paris on Tuesday—and other channels of information furnish us with the news of Paris up to last Thursday noon—These facts stand not in need of exaggeration. It is impossible to add to a cup of iniquity already filled to the brim.

'When Mr. Lindsay left Paris on Wednesday, the MASSACRE continued without abatement. The city had been a scene of bloodshed and violence without intermission since Sunday noon, and although it is difficult and indeed impossible to ascertain with any precision the number that had fallen victims to the fury of the mob during these three days, we believe the account will not be exaggerated when we state it at TWELVE THOUSAND PERSONS—(We state it as a fact, which we derive from the best information, that during the Massacre on the 2d instant, from SIX to EIGHT THOUSAND Persons perished) . . .

'When the mob went to the prison *de la Force*, where the Royal attendants were chiefly confined, the Princess DE LAMBALLE went down on her knees to implore a suspension of her fate for 24 hours. This was at first granted, until a second mob more ferocious than the first, forced her apartments, and decapitated her. The circumstances which attended her death were such as makes humanity shudder, and which decency forbids us to repeat:—Previous to her death, the mob offered her every insult. Her thighs were cut across, and her bowels and heart torn from her, and for two days her mangled body was dragged through the streets.

'It is said, though this report seems dubious, that every Lady and state prisoner was murdered, with only two exceptions—Madame de TOURZELLE, and Madame de SAINT BRICE, who were saved by the

Commissioners of the National Assembly, the latter being pregnant. The heads and bodies of the Princess and other Ladies—those of the principal Clergy and Gentlemen—among whom we learn the names of the Cardinal de la ROCHEFAUCOULT, the Archbishop of ARLES, M. BOTIN, Vicar of St. Ferrol, &c. have been since particularly marked as trophies of *victory* and *justice*!!! Their trunkless heads and mangled bodies were carried about the streets on pikes in regular cavalcade. At the *Palais Royal*, the procession stopped, and these lifeless victims were made the mockery of the mob.

'Are these "the Rights of Man"? Is this the LIBERTY of Human Nature? The most savage four footed tyrants that range the unexplored desarts of Africa, in point of tenderness, rise superior to these two legged Parisian animals.—Common Brutes do not prey upon each other.

'The number of Clergy found in the Carmelite Convent was about 220. They were handed out of the prison door two by two into the *Rue Vaugerard*, where their throats were cut. Their bodies were fixed on pikes and exhibited to the wretched victims who were next to suffer. The mangled bodies of others are piled against the houses in the streets; and in the quarters of Paris near to which the prisons are, the carcases lie scattered in hundreds, diffusing pestilence all around.

'The streets of Paris, strewed with the carcases of the mangled victims, are become so familiar to the sight, that they are passed by and trod on without any particular notice. The mob think no more of killing a fellow-creature, who is not even an object of suspicion, than wanton boys would of killing a cat or a dog. We have it from a Gentleman who has been but too often an eye witness to the fact.'

'Very good authority! A gentleman who has been an eye-witness, indeed! I don't believe a word of it,' declared Caroline, and her glance swept the room for approval.

'How I wish Susannah had not left Paris,' said Augustus. 'We should have had a more accurate account. The *Times* gentleman is a very convenient fellow; he always sees and hears exactly what is required of him. I cannot believe that anyone above the age of ten would be taken in by these fabrications. Carcasses of mangled victims! Mr Lindsay has been reading too much Mrs Radcliffe.'

'His language is highly coloured, certainly,' said Hannah.

'And he is rather too fond of exclamation marks,' said Augustus, and smiled. 'How is your mother, Lizzie?'

'She is sleeping.'

'But she is better?'

'Yes, much better.'

I had passed the previous night in a chair beside her bed. She had been violently sick, and Augustus had sent for me even though Hannah had tried to persuade him that it was not necessary. Fortunately, Diner had not been at home when Augustus's message came. He would not have liked my being called away, but as it was I moved swiftly, leaving a note for him and telling Philo to grill lamb chops when he returned.

Mammie was much better this morning. I would be able to go home soon, and leave her to rest. It was a cream cheese she'd eaten that had made her so ill. She had no pains now.

'I wish we were back in London,' said Augustus. 'The London Corresponding Society meets regularly at the Crown and Anchor now. We have so many friends there.'

'We have friends enough here,' I said, alarmed. Diner would not leave Bristol. But Hannah said:

'We are needed here, Augustus. This is where we are called to work.' She spoke with such certainty that for the moment he was silenced. Hannah nodded at me. If she could have winked (she never could) I think she would have done so. My heart filled with affection for her: Hannah, whom I mocked too often in my mind. She understood that it was impossible Mammie and I should ever live apart.

A few days earlier Diner had asked me to draw a design for the garden. I knew very little about such things, because we had always lived in rooms, but I was flattered that he asked me. He thought that if we laid and planted a flower garden in the latest style, it would please the buyers. I did not mention that behind our house lay a mess of rubble: he knew that as well as I did, and we both knew how unlikely it was that he would call the men off the building work to shift rubble, bring in soil and landscape our small plot into a flower garden. And besides, it was already September and flowers were dying.

I drew as if there were a team of men waiting to fulfil my plan. I know now that I drew plants that could never possibly live in the soil of Bristol, which was full of lime, and I drew plants that needed shade where there was none. Diner was as ignorant as I was, and the plan pleased us both.

'Draw in as much detail as you can, Lizzie. Next year you shall have your garden. Spring is the best time for planting.'

He touched my heart then, because he wanted to think of our future and not the precarious day-to-day we were living now. If no one bought the houses ... It made me sick to think of it. I could go back and live in rooms easily enough, but not Diner. There could be no more public humiliation than for a man to begin a magnificent terrace and be forced to abandon it, or sell the houses at a knockdown price to anyone who would have them. That was not going to happen to him.

I walked home through the sunshine, thinking of green things overhanging the walls and how I would push the plants into the soil. There would be nobody to see me grubbing in the dirt, except Philo, who would be happy to do the same. She liked to be outdoors far more than she liked to be in the house. I supposed that the taste came from her bird-scaring days. She had worn a sack over her shoulders against the rain, she said, and once she got over her fear of the birds she had been happy, running, flapping her arms and shouting as loud as she wanted.

It was late in the evening when we heard a banging on the door. Philo was in bed, so Diner went to open it. The rain was streaming down and there was a boy of about ten, out of breath with running. He took off his cap and handed me a much-folded note which had been tucked into it to keep dry.

'Dear Lizzie, Your mother finds herself very much indisposed this evening. Yr Affte Friend, Hannah Rougemont.'

I ran back into the hall to find my cloak.

'Where are you going?'

'To my mother. Ask the boy to wait while I get my boots. He can go back with me.'

'Lizzie, calm yourself. Your mother is having her baby, that's all.'

It was early, surely? It was barely six months since she had told me she was pregnant. Could it really be the baby already?

'If she is indisposed, isn't that the obvious cause? But it's no reason for you to rush to her bedside. It's late, Lizzie. You must break this habit of roaming out in the dark and rain.'

'Hannah would not have sent this boy if she hadn't wanted me to come.'

'Hannah is an old maid. Tomorrow will do very well.'

Diner gave the boy a penny and was about to send him on his way when I slipped past to the door.

'I will come back straight away if there's no need of me.'

'I have need of you, Lizzie. You are my wife.'

The boy twisted his cap in his hand and looked at neither of us.

'Come with me then,' I said to Diner.

'I will not.' He folded his arms and stared at me angrily, but did not put out his hand to prevent me. I pulled open the door, letting in a gust of night, and was gone before he could call me back.

At my mother's lodgings, all was darkness and confusion. Shadows swarmed on the walls as I lifted my candle. The wind blew the flame flat: the wind had got into the house behind me. There was my mother on the dark bed. I saw her face, white and glistening. I lifted the candle high and came close and I saw it was sweat that made her skin shine. Behind me the door banged.

'The door to the street was left open!' shouted someone behind me.

A woman pushed past me. The midwife Hannah had got. She had her cuffs rolled to her elbows and she was carrying a dish.

'Mammie?' I said. 'It's me. It's Lizzie,' and I was glad I had come.

Her head turned on the pillow as I set my candle down on the little table by the bed. I could not see her eyes. They ought to have more candles. As I thought this, in came Hannah with a candlestick in either hand.

The flames blew sideways as she carried them to the mantelpiece and planted one on each end.

'I shall need more than that,' said the midwife, who was crouched at the end of the bed, looking under my mother's skirts. My mother moaned and thrashed from side to side as if she were trying to get away from the probing hands. Hannah went out and the door slammed again, shaking everything.

'You're doing nicely, my dear,' said the midwife, sitting back and showing her teeth.

My mother looked at me but did not see me.

'Mammie!'

'Don't be bothering her,' said the midwife. 'If the Pope of Rome came in the room now she wouldn't look at him.'

The pain washed away. My mother lay limp on the bed and I took her hand.

'It's not so bad,' she muttered.

'You're going strong, my lover,' said the midwife loudly, as if my mother were deaf. I waited for the smile that ought to have curled my mother's lips but it did not come. She lay there like someone drowned at the bottom of a pool. A spasm went over her and she clutched my hand and then pushed it away.

'Get Hannah,' she said and her head snapped from side to side on the pillow.

'It's a rough old night out there, I dare say,' said the midwife, and she went to the window, lifted the curtain and peered out as if what was happening in the street interested her more than what was happening in the bed. Mammie could not be so bad, for the midwife to turn her back on her like this.

'Yes, it's raining hard,' I answered. My mother twisted herself and then reared up as if she too wanted to get as far as she could from that bed. The midwife glanced round and hurried to her.

'Go down now,' she said. 'Get yourself down and rest, my girl, you need your strength.'

'It's coming again,' said my mother and she sounded wild, but the midwife took no notice except to press her down.

'I'll get Hannah,' I said. I was suddenly afraid like a child and glad of a reason to leave the room.

Hannah was hanging out the baby clothes we had made on a rack before the fire. There was a dress, a cap and wrappings. There was a clean nightdress of my mother's too. The fire was built up high and the flames blew from the wind dancing down the chimney.

'She wants you,' I said, and Hannah got up from her knees. At the same time a noise came from the bedroom. A cry, quickly smothered, and then a groan.

'She's hurt herself!' I said before I could help it. I wanted to run to her and drag away whatever was hurting her.

'No,' said Hannah, unfolding the baby's shawl and lifting it to her cheek to feel for damp. 'It's not so bad. She'll be like this until the morning, and then it will be over. That's how it was with you.'

Hannah had no child. What did she know? But she had been with my mother then and all had been well.

After I was born my mother was as strong as ever. It would be the same again.

'Where's Augustus?'

'He went out. Now, Lizzie, boil up more water and we'll have tea.'

It seemed incredible to me that Hannah could even think of tea, and that she could be so leisurely about going in to my mother, but it comforted me too, just as the midwife stepping to the window and looking out at the weather had done. Things were not so bad. The midwife expected it to be like this and so did Hannah. They were not frightened.

Now Hannah was gone and I filled the kettle and swung it out over the fire. There was a faint smell of crisping cotton. Perhaps Hannah had put the rack too close. I moved it away a little and the cap fell to the floor. I snatched it up and examined it, but there wasn't a speck of dirt on it. It was so small. It would not be worn until that battle in the next room was over. There was a towel, folded, on the chair. Hannah had got everything ready. On the other side of the fireplace there was the cradle on its stand, and the bedding was spread out too. Outside the wind was punching at the walls and I heard rain spatter hard on the glass. I had put my cloak on the back of the door to dry. I heard my mother's groans, rapid, protesting, mounting, and then they fell away. She did not cry out this time. I lifted the kettle from the fire and splashed water on to the tea-leaves.

I don't know how many times I set the kettle to boil

as the night went on just as Hannah and the midwife said it would. I had never guessed it would take so long. Hour after hour and still the midwife seemed satisfied when she came out to take a cup of tea or visit the privy in the yard.

'She's doing nicely,' was all she said, and Hannah cut slices from the loaf and gave her bread and cheese to keep her strength up. She munched and swallowed and even asked if we had such a thing as a pickled onion, while Hannah sat with my mother. We had not, but I rummaged at the back of the cupboard and found a jar of Hannah's preserved plums. The midwife ate heartily, and then she wiped her hands on her apron and went back into my mother's room.

Hannah gave me bands of flannel to hem, because she said we could never have enough of them, and so I sat by the fire and worked. We were reckless with candles. I sewed flannel after flannel, made tea, cooked gruel for my mother – 'to keep her strength up,' the midwife said – but she took a couple of spoonfuls and then vomited it. Even with the fire burning I was cold. I found myself yawning, but I was pitched to every sound that came from my mother's room. She did not want me to go in, Hannah said. She poked at the fire, rearranged the baby clothes, spread the bedding for the cradle closer to the fire. Suddenly I saw that the candle flames were growing paler. Light was seeping around the curtains.

'It's morning, Hannah!'

It was morning. Grey and rainy, but the storm was

gone. Leaves were dashed down all over the pavement and I saw a boy dart down the street with his coat over his head. I knew him: it was the boy from last night. It seemed a hundred years ago, and I wondered who he was and where he was going now. Perhaps it was another message about another birth? I pulled back the curtains and then went from candle to candle, blowing them out.

'Your mother wants you,' said the midwife, appearing at the door.

My mother was sitting bolt upright in bed. Her eyes were bright and her face flushed. 'It isn't hurting now, my darling, that's all over, he'll be here soon.' Her voice was hoarse and rapid but she looked well, I thought, better than she had looked all night. 'And you've been here all night, Lizzie, and now it's morning. You must eat something. Mustn't she eat something?'

'Be quiet now,' said the midwife. 'Don't be exciting yourself or she'll have to go out again. Let me take a look at you.' Without warning she whipped up the sheet and my mother's nightdress. 'Lift your legs for me. That's right.'

I saw the white edge of my mother's thigh and the hand of the midwife grasping, her bent head between my mother's legs. I looked away.

'You're almost there. You're nearly there now, my darling.'

My mother's face contorted. She seized hold of my hand and squeezed it. 'Go away now, Lizzie,' she said, gripping me so tight I could not move.

'Don't push,' shouted the midwife. 'Hold on now. In a minute now you can push. I'll tell yer when.'

My mother heaved herself up, dragging on me. I put my arms around her shoulders to support her but she flung me off. I stepped back and the midwife jerked her head towards the door.

'You don't want to be here now,' she said. 'Get that other one.'

Hannah brushed past me and shut the door on me. I went over to the fire and tried to warm myself. My legs were shaking. I put my hands up over my ears and pressed them hard so that I heard my own blood sing. The little baby clothes must be as dry as bones by now. I thought: She believes it's a boy. I had never thought of it being anything but a girl. Surely this could not go on any longer? I pressed hard on my ears. 'Come on now,' I said. 'Come on now come on now come on now,' over and over although I could only hear the words inside my head. But they blocked out everything.

The door opened and Hannah rushed into the room with something in her arms which made a thin, pulsing cry. She seized a warm flannel square from the rack and wrapped up the baby before I could see it, then she thrust it into my arms and rushed back into the bedroom.

Its face was tight as a ball, streaked with blood and white grease. Its mouth opened and the pulse of its cry filled my ears and the whole room. I gripped the bundle and sat on the stool close to the fire to keep it warm. I got my arms around it more comfortably and held it closer, rocking it. The sound dwindled. On the next shriek the baby gave a convulsive yawn. Its eyes closed. It was asleep.

I found that I was smiling. Such a strange little thing. Even asleep it looked fierce, as if it had set its mind on that one thing only. I touched the skin of its cheek with my lips. Yes, it was warm. It was so light in my arms. It had streaks of dark hair too. No eyelashes. Little tight-shut eyes. A quiver went over its face and I rocked it again until it settled.

Time passed. There was nothing to be frightened of now, I told myself. The night was over. The baby was born.

9

The door from the stairway opened and there was Augustus, rumpled and pale from lack of sleep. His legs scissored across the floor towards me.

'Well? How is Julia?'

It might have been fear which made him speak so loudly. 'Hush,' I said. 'The baby's asleep. Hannah and Mrs Rowe are with my mother.'

'All's well?'

'I think so.' I wanted to shake his complacency, but could not find the words. 'It took all night. The baby has only just been born.'

'The baby,' he said, and came close. He stared down at the bud of a face and put out a finger tentatively, as if to touch it, but his hand fell to his side. 'And Julia is well?'

'I think so.'

'I meant to have come back earlier. The pot-boy woke me, sweeping around my legs. I stayed awake until three but I must have fallen asleep over the fire. A good boy.

He found me a new loaf and a slice of cold bacon.' He told me this artlessly, as if I ought to be interested. I thought of my mother and what her night had been.

'So you stayed awake until three,' I said. 'Did you play cards to pass the time?'

'A little. Dr Stamps kept me company until two in the morning. Is it a boy?'

I realised I did not know. I had not even thought about it. The baby had been thrust into my arms and I had held it almost as long as it had been alive. I tucked the flannel in more closely around it and breathed in the baby's smell. It smelled of bread, and faintly of blood. Was it warm enough? Should I dress it in the clothes Hannah had draped over the clothes horse? The baby stirred in my arms and uttered a wheezing sigh.

'Hannah will tell us,' I said. I thought suddenly: It is his child.

'Do you want to hold the baby, Augustus?' I asked, hoping that he would not, and he seemed not to hear. He went to the door and stood irresolute. All was quiet, as if my mother's cries and groans had never been. They would be washing her, I thought, and straightening the bed so that she could sleep in peace after her labour. I was as stunned as if I had been walking through a storm all night. It was calm now, but everything was changed. Here was this little creature in my arms, who had come into the house without passing through any door except the gateway of my mother's body. Its small face was shut tight, as if it did not want to be in the world yet.

But Augustus was no longer thinking about the baby.

'I shall go in to her,' he murmured. It was his right; I knew that. He turned the door-handle noiselessly, listened again, and crossed the narrow corridor to my mother's room. I heard her door open, Hannah's voice raised, and then he was back in the kitchen, paler than ever. He looked very ill. He stumbled to a chair, sat down and planted his head in his hands.

'Augustus?'

'I am sorry, Lizzie,' came his muffled voice, 'I have never been able to endure the sight of blood.'

'Blood!'

'Hannah sent me away.'

She won't send me away, I thought, as I went to the door.

There was a heap of blood-soaked linen on the floor and there was Hannah, kneeling at the foot of the bed. For a moment I thought she was praying and a pang of terror went through me. Hannah never prayed. But then I saw she had books in her hands. And there was Mrs Rowe, hard at it too, her bare forearms bulging as she heaved at the bedstead to lift it. I dared to look at my mother. Her eyes were closed and her body jerked as the bed moved. It looked as if they were torturing her.

Hannah turned and saw me. 'Quick, help us with this. Put the child down.'

I laid the baby down where it could not roll and heaved alongside the midwife until the end of the bed was lifted from the floor. Hannah crawled between us and laid books under the bedposts. We lowered the bed again and the bed-end was raised so that my mother's head lay lower than her feet. They had taken away her pillows. Mrs Rowe went to her and felt the pulse at the side of her neck. What she found seemed to satisfy her, for she stepped back.

'She's lost a fair deal of blood, but she's doing bravely now.'

Hannah bundled together the stained linen with clumsy hands, her lips trembling like an old woman's. To see Hannah overset like this frightened me more than ever. I could not move to take my mother's hand or comfort her. Even the air of the room seemed shaken, as if some dreadful act of violence had been committed.

'The child came easy enough,' said Mrs Rowe. 'A fine boy. The afterbirth was where the trouble lay, but it's come out clean now.' And to me, with a cool stare as if to gauge what I would be good for, 'You'll need to burn this mattress, once she's fit to be moved.'

I saw Hannah's blue-ware basin by the side of the bed. There was something large and meaty in it, like a great piece of liver. The midwife bent over it, examining it closely, and then she covered it with a cloth. 'We shall have to watch her,' she said, 'but I'd stake my life there'll be no further trouble.'

Her words were more reassuring than her face, which was streaked with sweat and dried blood, as if she had been working in a slaughterhouse. Easy enough, I thought. If that was easy, then what in God's name was difficult? My own body was clenching itself. I picked up the baby and rocked it, soothing us both. The baby was a boy. I had never thought of its being anything other than a girl.

'We shall need plenty of hot water, Lizzie,' said Hannah, putting both fists to the base of her spine and pressing as she did when she had backache. She was trying to recover herself but her face was haggard. There was something piteous in it that I had never seen before, as if she were looking to me to help her.

'It's all right, Hannah, I'll see to it,' I said. I had taken for granted Hannah's mania for order, and that she would always work like a horse. But now I saw that she was an old woman, and I had never noticed it before today.

She was right; we'd have to wash everything. I could send for Philo to help and we'd do the work together. Or better, I'd tell Philo to take the washing home, where we had a proper wash-house. All the linen would fly in the air as if there had never been any blood. The rain had stopped now and the sun was chasing clouds over the sky.

'You must rest, Hannah, you've been up all night.'

There was still the butcher-shop smell in my throat, making me gag. I tucked the baby close, went to the window and undid the catch.

'For the love of God, do you want to kill us all?' cried Mrs Rowe.

I bent over the baby, to hide my face. There were red marks on his cheeks, like minute strawberries. A fine boy, Mrs Rowe had said, but he felt so light, as if he might vanish away again as suddenly as he had come. I wondered if my mother had seen him yet. She was so deeply asleep, as if she might never wake again. Her shocked, still face was a thousand miles from us, in another world.

'I have an errand now,' said Mrs Rowe. 'I'll be back directly,' and she nodded at Hannah as if it had been agreed between them. I went into the kitchen and told Augustus to call in a boy from the street and give him a penny to fetch Philo. He went clattering down the stairs and I heard him calling, then in a few minutes he was back, rubbing his hands as if he had done great things.

'The room is clean now,' said Hannah, coming in with the laundry ready in its sack. 'You can come in.' Her voice was always level when she spoke to Augustus and she was never angry with him as she was with me and Mammie.

'Will you come in with me, Lizzie?' said Augustus. 'I think Julia would like to see the child.' I rose and followed him. As we entered my mother's room I saw Augustus glance at the books propping up the bed, notice that they were his and hesitate as if he would have liked to stoop and read the titles. My mother's eyes were still closed. She was white and sunken, but I had got a grip on my fear. The bleeding was stopped. It had left her weak and besides the night had exhausted her. Of course she wouldn't be awake. There were good reasons why she should look like that.

'When she wakes, she will be more herself,' said

Hannah. Augustus stood there, looking down at my mother. I could not read him.

'Julia,' he said, very quietly. He kept his back to me. My mother's hand lay on the covers but he did not touch it. I thought it was no wonder. It was his touching that had brought her to this. 'Julia, we have a son.'

I stepped back. He had not held the baby, but it was his. Augustus was the father and here they were, the three of them: mother, father and child, even if it was I who held the baby and not my mother.

Hannah came forward. She did not exactly displace Augustus, but she wiped my mother's face with lavender water, and he moved aside.

'I have to watch her closely, until Mrs Rowe comes back,' said Hannah.

'What has she gone for? Where has she gone?' asked Augustus sharply.

'To the cook-shop, to fetch herself a steak and kidney pudding.'

'Any of us could have done that. She ought to have remained here, with Julia. I suppose she will fetch herself a pint of porter with it. I told Julia that she ought to have a man-midwife, but she would not listen to me.'

'Mrs Rowe has been on her feet all night,' said Hannah. 'I told her I would send a boy to the cook-shop, but she wanted the air. She'll be back directly.'

'I'm sure she ought not to think so much of her stomach, in her situation.'

I thought what a hypocrite he was, when he'd no doubt had a good hot dinner before settling down to play cards, and then his new bread and cold bacon in the morning. He still had his back to us. He reached out and patted the pillow beside my mother's head, but still he did not touch her. He turned then and I saw that his eyes were bleared.

'My poor Julia,' he said. 'Come, Lizzie, we must let her rest. Hannah will stay with your mother.'

I did not want to leave her, but there was the baby. He was Augustus's son but that could not shake the tenderness that flooded my body. I crooked my elbow high to shield the baby from the draught as we passed through the corridor into the kitchen. He should be kept close to the fire to keep warm. He must be hungry, but I had no idea what to give him. I had heard of babies drinking goat's milk and taking arrowroot, but this baby was so small. My mother had said she would nurse the child herself, as she had suckled me. My father had been horrified; he had wanted me sent out to a wet-nurse. But she had got her way and now fashion had caught up with her. All the fine ladies liked to be painted with their babies at the breast.

She looked so ill. I could not see how she was going to feed this baby and I knew next to nothing about how to look after it. Hannah was too old for it: that was suddenly, startlingly clear. We were all like stopped clocks without Mammie to set us going. The bare sight of her lying there, shut in on herself and bled of all her strength, made me feel helpless, abandoned, as if I were a child again.

I was not a child. I was responsible for the baby until

Mammie could take him. There was no time to indulge any other feeling. I must find out how to get milk for him, and how to feed him, how he should be clothed and how he should sleep.

But Augustus clapped his hands together. 'The child must be sent to a wet-nurse. Hannah must make some enquiries, and find a clean, decent woman in one of the cottages at Westbury.' He was full of purpose now, happy with it, and I was silent. What if my mother came to herself and found the baby gone? She would look so wild – she would think that it had died and be frightened . . .

'I think we should wait,' I told him. 'The baby is fast asleep. I will make enquiries about food for him. We can wait until my mother wakes and tells us what she wants to do.'

'A clean, decent woman. There must be a suitable creature. A child of nature, unconfined – I would wish my son to share the upbringing of Rousseau.'

'But Rousseau hated wet-nursing.' This at least I knew, because my mother's views on the subject were formed by Rousseau's *Émile*, which she had read aloud to me until I yawned.

'The great philosopher's mother died when he was nine days old. His genius was fed by his wet-nurse.' And Augustus beamed on me with the kindliness he always felt when he bested anyone in an argument. I wanted to protest but I could not be bothered to enter into an argument about Rousseau.

'She looks very bad,' I said instead. The baby was

making little sounds, more creaks than cries, but I was afraid they would grow stronger. If he began to scream he might never stop. I began to walk up and down the kitchen, rocking him.

'She will be much better when she wakes,' said Augustus, as if he knew. But he did not. He had turned pale at the sight of blood, and left the room. I doubted if he had ever held a baby before. He knew nothing except how to hand the work over to someone else.

The door opened. It was Maria Rowe, smelling of meat pies, fresh air and something else besides ... Augustus was right, she had had a nip for sure. She tugged off her cloak and threw it on a chair by the fire.

'Now, let's be having you,' she said, reaching for the baby. She didn't care tuppence about him catching cold now, but stripped off the flannel to examine him closely. The stump of the cord must be dressed, she said. The baby must be given sugar-water. The baby's face contorted and flushed purple and it began to shriek, but she took no notice and did not attempt any comfort. She set it on a flannel in her lap where it rolled help-lessly. Its arms and legs flew out and its hands snatched the air. She seized it between her hands and lifted it high so that it drew up its legs, screamed and voided a thin stream of blackish tarry stuff on to the flannel.

'A fine boy,' she said, laughing at him.

I wanted to snatch the baby from her. His whole body was purple now and he was screaming steadily, without tears. His sex was wrinkled and too big, surely, for his tiny body. He had a barrel chest and skinny, dwindling legs. What if he were to turn out like Augustus? But the midwife seemed to think that everything was as it ought to be. She wiped him down with a damp cloth, dressed the cord stump with an ointment she whipped out of her pocket and then wrapped him up again with bands of clean flannel, trussing him over and over until he looked like a caterpillar gone into a cocoon.

'There you are, my fine gentleman, that's you taken care of for the present,' she said, and sure enough his cries began to calm as soon as he felt himself bound. She held him out to me like a parcel. 'I must go in to your mother. Do you know how to make sugar-water?'

'I'm not sure.'

She huffed impatiently. 'Isn't there such a thing as a loaf of sugar in the house? You'd think nobody knew there'd be a baby coming into it.'

'There's sugar in the cupboard. What must I do?'

'Scrape a little off the loaf and mix it in warm water. He'll sleep once he has something in his stomach.'

And then what? I wanted to ask, but I was ashamed of my ignorance. I laid the baby in its cradle and tucked its shawl around it. 'Sit here, Augustus, and rock the cradle. With your foot, like this,' I said.

Augustus rocked vigorously, but the baby did not settle. He would take the sugar-water and then sleep: that was what the midwife had said. I got it ready in a little cup, dissolving the sugar in hot water and then adding cold. Would he take it from a spoon? The salt spoon was the smallest we had: perhaps he would drink from that. I picked him up again and tucked him firmly into the crook of my left arm. By this time he was crying furiously again and the noise made me clumsy. I worked the spoon past his gums and tipped it until the water ran into his mouth.

'You are choking him!' shouted Augustus as the baby sputtered and went purple. I lifted him quickly, held him over my shoulder and patted his back as I had seen mothers do. I was sweating and my heart beat fast.

'He's got to feed,' I said. 'Go away if you don't like it.'

This time I put a very little sugar-water in the spoon, no more than a big drop, and tipped it over the baby's mouth, but just as I thought it was going in he writhed so that the drop fell on his nose. I wiped it away and then I thought: Perhaps he will take it from my finger. I dipped my little finger in the cup and held it between his lips as his mouth opened for the next shriek. His gums closed around my finger, sucking furiously. He kept on sucking when the drop was surely gone and I had to pull my finger loose. Instantly, he started to cry again. Another drop, another rage of sucking, another fit of screaming. He was sweating too, hot with the passion for his food. But soon we were in a rhythm and he was no longer crying but instead smacking his lips blindly at the air until the next drop came. I went on until I thought he had had enough. I did not want to make him sick. He was sleepy now but he still sucked at my finger and every time I tried to take it out of his mouth he began to whimper. I wouldn't fight with him. I'd let him suck until he slept.

Augustus was watching us. 'How do you know what to do, Lizzie? Have you seen it done?'

'Ssh. He's dropping off.'

I knew nothing. It was the baby who had taught me what to do.

'"The earliest education is most important and without a doubt is woman's work,"' observed Augustus, and I could not help smiling.

'I am not educating him, Augustus, merely giving him some sugar-water.'

'You did not recognise that I was quoting Rousseau?'

'Rousseau was not at the forefront of my mind,' I said. Augustus was so absurd and yet . . . he was smiling too. He bent forward and dabbed gingerly at the baby's cheek with his finger.

'He is almost asleep. You have done well with him, Lizzie.'

Hannah came in then. She spoke to me, and not to Augustus. Her mouth was no longer trembling and she had combed her hair back into her cap. But her head nodded faintly, like the head of an old woman.

'Your mother is awake now, Lizzie,' she said. 'She would like to see you.'

10

The baby is to be called Thomas, after Tom Paine. My mother is too weak to draw him to her breast, but he lies against her, wrapped in his cocoon.

'Lizzie,' she says. 'My Lizzie.' She writhes a little and I lift up the baby for fear he should roll off the bed. This time she does not notice, or protest. 'I'm very ill,' she says.

'It's all right, Mammie. I'm here.'

'Where's the baby?'

'He's here. Look, in my arms, quite safe.'

'I don't mean that baby, I mean the other baby,' she says quickly, irritably. 'Hannah must look for it.'

'She will,' I say, as soothingly as I know how. My heart is so stilled by fear that it seems hardly to beat.

'Oh Lizzie, it's coming,' she says, and her voice tightens with terror.

'Hush, Mammie, it's all over. You've had the baby.' But instantly Hannah is there, on the other side of the bed, with the hartshorn. My mother breathes deeply and sighs. Now Hannah is measuring out laudanum, dropping it on to Mammie's tongue.

'Swallow, Julia, swallow.'

I see my mother's gorge rise, and then she swallows. 'Better,' she says. After a while, with her eyes still shut, 'I thought I was dying.'

'Hush, Julia. You'll frighten Elizabeth.'

Thomas stirs and creaks in my arms. The smell in the room is appalling. It hits you as soon as you come over the threshold. It is a smell of rottenness.

The first day after Thomas was born, we thought all was well. Augustus sent for the doctor, who examined her carefully and prescribed an ointment of white wine, flour and honey to be applied to her breasts, as she still intended to nurse the baby. On the third morning she awoke with a headache. She shook and could not get warm no matter how many clothes we piled on the bed. By evening she was burning hot. Milk fever, said the doctor, and urged us to apply the ointment more freely. By the next day her stomach was swollen and the smell had begun to fill the room.

'Take it away, it hurts my head,' said Mammie in a low, rapid voice. She was flushed almost purple along her cheekbones. Hannah held her wrist and counted her pulse. When she looked at me I flinched from the fear in her face.

'Take the baby into the kitchen, Elizabeth,' said Hannah.

Mammie had not let us take the baby before; we had

had to steal him away when she was asleep. She wanted him beside her even though the doctor frowned on it. I put Thomas into his cradle and called for Augustus to rock him. There was no answer so I went to look. He was in the parlour, keeled sideways in his chair, asleep. He had been up all night so I could not blame him.

'Augustus.'

He woke with a jerk. His eyes widened, focused, saw me. 'Julia—'

'Nothing's happened. But come and rock the baby before he cries. I must go back to her.'

She was pushing the covers off her distended stomach, where the pain was. Hannah was carrying away more soiled cloths. I sat by the bedside, took a piece of wet flannel and sponged her face, her neck, her wrists and forearms. There were dark red blotches on her wrists and knuckles. They had come since the morning and they were spreading.

Sponging seemed to comfort her. Gently, I pulled the bedclothes over her again so that she would not catch cold. It was very hot in the room with the fire lit and the windows tight shut, but the doctor said it would be dangerous to let the air in on her.

'Lizzie,' she said, opening her eyes, 'I don't like these rooms. I don't think we should stay here. Shall we go back to Hoxton? You liked it there. You remember the little apple tree in the yard? But don't climb so high, it won't take your weight.' She was trying to heave herself up in the bed, but she was too weak.

'Yes, I remember. There was one apple and I picked it for you but you cut it up and we all had a share.'

'Yes. Yes. We must go back there. Tell Hannah. What are we doing here, Lizzie? I cannot remember.'

'Looking after you, Mammie. You are not well.'

'Don't be frightened, Lizzie, I'll be perfectly well in the morning.'

She lapsed into sleep.

'Is the doctor coming again, Hannah?' I whispered.

She nodded. We both knew that my mother was worse, even in the last two hours.

'What can he do?'

'I don't know, Elizabeth.'

'He must do something!'

He had bled her twice. He said it would reduce the inflammation in her blood.

'She cannot be bled again,' said Hannah. 'He spoke of purging her but now he says that with such a flux coming from her, it will do no good.'

'But she can't go on like this.'

'No,' said Hannah, and now I heard it in her voice: that my mother would not go on. That there would be an end to it. We could not get back to where we had been safe.

The blotches are coming thick and dark. I push up the sleeve of my mother's nightgown and see that there are purplish patches on her elbows now. Her mouth has fallen open and her breathing is short and harsh.

'Mammie,' I whisper, but she does not stir her head towards me. It has come so fast.

'Let her rest,' says Hannah.

An hour passes, and another. The doctor comes, lifts her wrist to take her pulse, touches the blotches on her skin, says she must take more laudanum. Augustus appears at the bedroom door and steps to my mother's side.

'Julia,' he says peremptorily, 'Julia!' just as if she has slept too late in the morning. She rouses, looks up at him in dark confusion and then falls back into a stupor.

Later I wash her temples with orange-flower water. She feels it: she opens her eyes. She knows Hannah, and she knows me. I see her eyes following me as I squeeze out the cloth. Hannah is there again with the laudanum. She sinks into sleep once more but she is restless, as if she has dreams that alarm her, and she pushes feebly at the bedclothes.

'I'm here, Mammie,' I say. 'It's me, Lizzie. Don't be frightened.' As the words come out of my mouth I remember how she has so often said them to me in the dark of the night, when I woke in fear.

'Elizabeth,' says Hannah sharply, 'look at her hands.'

I do not know what to look for. The blotches on her skin are the same. Her fingers pluck at the edge of the sheet. Her mouth is open again, her nose prominent. The softness of her cheeks has fallen away. Her breath snores and catches.

'The way she's pulling at the sheet, it means she's going,' says Hannah. 'Shall I bring Augustus?'

'No,' I say.

*   *   *

I sit with her until she dies, and then Hannah and I wash away the blood and filth from her body with clean water. I sponge her with lavender water so that she will smell sweet. The midwife has come back and she knows how to bind my mother's jaw, stop up all the orifices of her body and then lay her out on the bed with her arms folded across her breasts. But she cannot stop the milk that still leaks from them.

We call Augustus then. He stumbles, gives a great cry and throws himself down on his knees beside the bed, sobbing. I watch him from far away with cold amazement, thinking: So you did love her.

I did not cry and my hands did not tremble as I helped to wash her and lay her out. The midwife pressed down Mammie's eyelids firmly, with her thumbs. You must never touch people's eyes: Mammie told me that when I was little. It seems so long since she spoke that I cannot remember what her last words were.

11

'No, Augustus, Thomas is not thriving.'

Caroline Farquhar kept her stare on me. 'Really, Elizabeth,' she said, 'I think Mr Gleeson has a father's feeling, and knows better than you how his son does.'

She might say what she liked on the subject: I would not answer her. She might call him Mr Gleeson, but she did not fool me. I knew that in her heart he was her own Augustus.

Caroline Farquhar had arrived post-haste after my mother's death, to apply the balm of consolation to the wounded soul of a great man. She wanted to closet herself with Augustus and decide every detail of what should be done with my mother's papers. I was too young and Hannah too old.

'And besides,' she had said, 'I am so very great an admirer of your mother's genius! There is no one – always excepting of course Mr Gleeson – who more perfectly understands it. You mourn her in the flesh, my dear Elizabeth, but we mourn her in the spirit.'

The feathers in her hat had swept over me as she passed by. She barely noticed Thomas. Any baby must be an encumbrance, and one who reminded Augustus of his dead wife could not be tolerated. The sooner the baby was out of the house and placed with a decent woman in some village not too close by, the better.

'Julia's legacy must be safeguarded,' she had declared. 'Not one precious word must be lost to the generations yet to come.' Like Augustus, she had a way of looking as if her phrases pleased her, and ought to be recorded.

Augustus could not see Caroline for what she was. He did not perceive her as a woman: she was a useful appendage, like an umbrella. He did not see that she had grasped him by the handle and intended to have him. I wished he would open his eyes. Once Caroline Farquhar possessed Augustus, her interest in my mother's work would blow away like smoke.

Augustus realised none of it, any more that the sheep understands the slaughter until its throat is bare to the knife. He thought that Caroline had come to support all of us out of the goodness of her heart. She was staying with the Frobishers in Little George Street, but she was at Augustus's lodgings all day long. He believed Caroline was a true radical, because she told him so. She had escaped from the prison of her position. He did not see that she made sure the way was left open behind her, and that she could return to her privileges any time she chose. She would never burn the bridge behind her, as my parents had done.

Caroline Farquhar possessed a great deal of money

but very little beauty, and so Augustus could not imagine that she might set her cap at him. Like many ugly men, he prized beauty and believed that he merited its possession. He had his own vanities, innocent as they were. Now, because I told him that Thomas was not thriving, his feathers were ruffled.

'I am sure Thomas does well with Mrs Platt,' he said. 'She had references from the Milward family, who spoke of her as a most excellent and conscientious wet-nurse.'

'And who most conveniently left Bristol for Exeter, so that we were unable to speak to them about this excellence and conscience of hers,' I said. 'When did you last see Thomas, Augustus?'

'You know very well that I have been in Bruton and Frome these past two weeks, visiting the silk mills.'

He was huffy now. He did not want his work slighted: those endless journeys of his; the gathering of information that he would prose into his pamphlets. Caroline never slighted him. I could hardly believe she was sincere, but he believed it. Caroline, with her maid, had accompanied him on his tour of the mills. I wondered what the silk-throwers of Bruton had made of them. Augustus was accustomed to walking thirty miles, but Caroline's feet barely touched the ground. She and her maid would put up at the best inn, and she would open her blue, blank eyes at the sight of hardships she was sure that she would never share.

I thought of the skin around Mammie's eyes, creased and tender. I thought of her only a very little at a time. Instead, I thought of Thomas.

'Really, Elizabeth, you take rather too much upon yourself,' said Caroline. 'Mr Gleeson has done everything to ensure the child's welfare.' She turned to Augustus, as if the conversation was closed. 'We must continue with the draft of your article,' she said to him in a low, private tone.

To do justice to Augustus, I think he scarcely noticed whether Caroline was with him or not. He worked on, buzzing like a fly at a window through which he would never be able to escape. He did not seem to notice his own misery, and could do nothing to ease it. He still looked up when the door opened, as if he expected to see my mother come in, untying the strings of her bonnet. I saw her too, in a flash that hurt my eyes. I saw her fingers find the knot in the strings and loosen it, deftly, rapidly, as she did everything. She was not dragging with pregnancy now: she was herself again.

'Lizzie,' she said, 'Lizzie, tell me, how has Thomas been?'

She had been out and now she was back. I had taken care of the baby for her. The light went and she disappeared.

'I went down as far as Evercreech, to the Albion Silk Mill,' went on Augustus.

'And I have been here,' I said. 'I visited Thomas this morning. Mrs Platt did not expect me and he was lying in his dirt. He was crying with hunger, but she was out visiting a neighbour. She had left a girl of eight to watch him. The child told me that she often earns her halfpenny that way.'

I did not tell him how many times I had walked out to the village, with the excuse of a fine cream cheese for Mrs Platt, a rattle for Thomas, a cotton quilt for his cradle.

'I hope you did not quarrel with Mrs Platt, Lizzie.'

'Of course not. I would never quarrel with a woman who has sole charge of Thomas. She has only to say that he suffered a fit and died of it, and there will be no gainsaying her. I was extremely civil and agreed with her that a child of that age must cry to exercise its lungs. When she said she needed a further allowance for porter to strengthen her milk, I said I would discuss it with you and visit her again tomorrow with your answer.'

'I am paying her very good wages already!' exclaimed Augustus.

'Of course you are. There can be no question of paying more. Thomas must be fetched away immediately, before harm comes to him.'

'But what would we do with him here?'

'You would not need to do anything, Augustus. You must go on with your article. I can look after him. He is almost three months old now,' I said, exaggerating Thomas's nine weeks of age. 'He can be fed from a pap boat. I have spoken to Mr Orchard and he says Thomas will do very well on pap. He is a good apothecary and will oversee everything.'

'Hannah might care for him, I suppose,' said Augustus slowly.

'No. Hannah is too old. She cannot be expected to care for Thomas now.'

'My dear Elizabeth, you can scarcely make your husband a present of a three-months' child,' broke in Caroline. She could not help herself, although it would have been better policy to hide her dislike of me.

'That is a point,' said Augustus. 'That is a point, indeed. What do you say to it, Lizzie?'

'I have already spoken to Diner,' I said. It was a lie, but it would soon become the truth.

'Have the child here!' said Diner. He stood up, and strode around the table without looking at me. As he turned, he struck the table's surface with the flat of his hand. My throat tightened. My voice did not want to emerge, but I thought of Thomas in the cradle at Mrs Platt's. When I'd unwrapped him there were crusts of filth on his scrawny thighs. I could not be silent.

'Only for a little while,' I said, 'until his health is restored, and then Augustus will have a nurse for him. If he stays with that Platt woman, he will die.'

'Lizzie, you must know that many infants have the strength to come into the world but not to remain in it.'

'Thomas is all I have left of my mother.'

Diner walked around the table again, head down. He went more slowly now and his hands were loose at his sides. After a while he lifted his head, looked at me and said, 'You have a soft heart, Lizzie. Too soft, perhaps.'

'I am not as soft as you believe,' I said. 'I was firm when you asked me to marry you. My mother did not want it. Augustus did not want it. None of my friends knew or understood you then.'

'They would have liked to see you married to Richard Sacks, perhaps,' said Diner, and amusement glinted in his eye.

'Good God, I would not touch such a man.'

'But you touched me.'

'Yes.'

'You were my girl.'

'Yes.'

'And are you mine now, Lizzie, above all others?'

I pushed away Mammie's shadow. 'Yes,' I said. 'You know that I am. And Thomas is part of me. When I see him suffer I must fight for him.'

'Fight?'

'Yes. I will not let him die because of that woman's greed and idleness.'

He stared at me, measuring me. 'Would you fight for me, Lizzie?'

'Your enemy will be my enemy.'

He smiled. 'Now I see that I was right to twist our names together into the ceiling. You are part of me. I suppose we must have the child. But mind, Lizzie, not for long. Once he is thriving, he must return to his father.'

I smiled too. He reached out and tipped up my chin to gaze more closely into my eyes.

'Stay like that,' he said.

And so now Thomas was in the house. He was asleep in his cradle in the attic beside Philo, so that she could rock him when he woke. He was her charge, and he must not disturb Diner. He was a good baby and usually he slept on until it was light. I had the double task of making sure that Thomas was well fed and cared for, and making it appear to Diner that there was no baby in the house.

I would never have thought that something as small as Thomas could make so much work. We seemed to be forever feeding him, cleaning him, hushing him when he cried, and all the while food must be bought and cooked, the house cleaned, the washing done. Each night I fell into bed, exhausted, but when Diner reached for me I turned to him as if gladly. He must not feel a change, even though I longed for sleep above anything. Afterwards I slept in a fury of dreaming. The dreams left their taint behind. I woke with my heart beating fast and my nightgown stuck to my body. It was always dark. I was always afraid that something had happened in the night, and Thomas was dead. Diner lay still at my side. His nights had grown quieter, while mine were full of tumult.

I had succeeded. I'd brought Thomas into the house, where he would be safe. Sometimes, at night, I would steal upstairs and into Philo's room. The boards did not creak as I tiptoed across the floor, put my hand into the cradle and felt the heat of Thomas.

'Where's the baby, Lizzie?' I heard Mammie say.

'He's here with me,' I answered. 'Don't be frightened, Mammie. Go back to sleep now.'

'Thank you, my bird,' she said. 'My lovely girl.'

I waited and waited, until I felt her presence leave us. Slowly it withdrew, like the tide slipping down the banks. I waited until there was nothing. Warmth rose from Thomas. He stirred and snuffled in his sleep and I rocked the cradle gently until he settled again. Philo snored. The smell of the baby was sour and sweet, milk and urine and the smell like bread where sweat would gather on the plumes of his hair and damp them down.

Diner did not want me to bear a child. He withdrew from me and voided his spunk on the sheets. I tucked Thomas's shawl around his feet and left him with Philo.

The days passed. Thomas needed careful feeding, I said to Diner, after his neglect by Mrs Platt. Philo was a sensible girl and able to do everything under my supervision. It would not be so long before the baby was well enough to go home to his father. I kept this thought in Diner's mind because I know how finely the balance hung. He tolerated Thomas now, but he might soon resent him.

'You will be worn out, Lizzie,' he accused me one night when he came home to find me fallen asleep at the kitchen table.

'I would not choose to have Thomas here, if he were well,' I said quickly. 'But sit down now. You have not had a glass of wine.'

I poured it and gave it to him, with the nip of sugar he always held in his mouth while he drank.

Every morning, as soon as Diner had left the house, I took Thomas from Philo. I mixed goat's milk with arrowroot and a little sugar, as Mr Orchard had directed, and I fed Thomas from the pap boat with a spoon. He ate eagerly, snuffling for more, heating himself until a dew of sweat stood on the bridge of his nose. Day by day, the wrinkles on his legs filled out with flesh. He was smooth-skinned now. He cried lustily for his food, and I could not push the pap into his mouth fast enough to satisfy him. His flailing fists knocked the spoon out of my hand. I held him close while he nuzzled and butted at me, as if he expected to find milk from my breast. My breasts ached and I thought: This is how I would feel, if he were my own.

Once I locked the bedroom door, unbuttoned the bodice of my dress and then untied the ribbons of my camisole. I unwrapped Thomas's shawl and held him against my naked breast. He was sleepy after his pap but he turned into me and began to nuzzle me with his lips. I cupped his head with my hand. For a moment I did not know who I was. I looked at my hand and thought it was lined and stained with ink.

I was careful not to inflame Diner's suspicions by signs of tenderness for the baby. Instead, I cleared away the feeding things, rattles and cradle as evening came on, and gave Thomas back to Philo as soon as I heard the door. I did not speak of the baby to Diner unless he asked. You would rarely have guessed, from our conversation, that Thomas was in the house.

I had no tears for Mammie. She still came to me in flashes, as if she were working so hard on one of her pamphlets that she barely had time to eat or speak. I was quite used to that. Sometimes I thought I heard her in the next room, writing. The quill flowed across the paper with a steady, frictional, familiar sound, and then there was a pause while she dipped the nib into her inkwell. She would be silent, thinking, and then the quill would begin its journey again over the white paper. If I listened I could never hear it, but if I paid no attention, the sound might come to me.

I held Thomas in my arms, and fed him, and kissed the hollow at the nape of his neck before I laid him back in his cradle. I washed and aired the pap boat. The goat we had hired for his milk was tethered on the Downs and the milk brought to us fresh each morning. Augustus gave me a few shillings, sheepishly, and I paid for the rest out of what I still had from my grandfather's money. Diner never asked about it. Philo would run out with the blue jug to be filled with milk. She brought it in, warm and frothing, covered the jug with muslin and placed it in the larder.

November gave way to December. The weather was cold, with such drenching rains that some days I never left the house. Diner's boots were heavy with mud and his cape soaked. When I heard him come in I would run to him and lift the sodden cloth from his shoulders. I would make him sit on the oak chair in the hall and take off his boots for him. I would never have thought of doing such things before Thomas came. Diner sat there, wet and weary all through. He looked as if he would have liked never to stir again, but the next day he would be up again long before it was light, and go out again into the raw morning.

We ate in the kitchen. He only wanted plain food, and

besides money was short. He was happy with a bowl of broth, a chunk of bread, cheese or ham. But there must be sugar. Always he needed a piece of sugar curled from the loaf, to hold in his mouth while he drank his wine. He drank more wine than he used to. When he was warm and softened he would reach out, touch my hair and smile. One night he said: 'This is as I thought it would be.'

I could not see into his thoughts. I was almost afraid to look into them, in case I found Lucie there. Perhaps he was trying to remake with me the life he had loved so much with her. I wondered if she had knelt to take off his boots, and if she had looked up at him and smiled as he cupped her cheek or ruffled her hair. They had loved each other and Diner had had no need or thought of me then.

Late one evening Thomas woke with a cry so sharp it speared its way through the house all the way down to the kitchen. Diner gave no sign that he had heard it. I made an excuse and ran up to Philo's room, but there was no sound and when I peeped through the door I saw her and the baby sleeping. In the morning Philo was red with excitement.

'His tooth's cut!'

Surely it was too early for that? I felt inside his mouth and she was right. The ridge of a tooth had erupted from his upper gum.

Philo laughed and said, 'He'll be up and walking by Christmas.'

One day the sun shone and I wrapped Thomas in his shawl and went to see Hannah. She had been ill with rheumatism and I thought, when I saw her, that she had aged ten years since my mother died. Even so, she hauled herself to her feet, cracked the crust of the fire and set the kettle to boil. I noticed a printed sheet by her chair, and picked it up.

'Read it, Elizabeth. It is written by Tom Paine.'

'Did he send it to Augustus?'

'He sent it to London and it was printed there for friends to distribute. A copy was sent to Augustus. It is Tom's address to the National Convention in Paris, calling for the trial of Louis Capet.'

'You mean, the King?'

'Louis Capet, a citizen who used to go by the title of king,' Hannah corrected me. 'Read it. I suppose that they translated it into French for the Convention, but this is Tom's own good plain English.'

Augustus must have swelled with pride. His old friend, now a member of the National Convention in Paris, advising it on the fate of the King of France: it was all beyond his wildest dreams. My mother would have calmed him. She never let Augustus float beyond himself, as he was apt to do.

I tucked Thomas into the crook of my arm, and began to read:

The despots of Europe have formed alliances to preserve their respective authority, and to perpetuate the oppression of peoples. This is the end they proposed to themselves in their invasion of French territory. They dread the effect of the

French Revolution in the bosom of their own coun-
tries; and in hopes of preventing it, they are come
to attempt the destruction of this revolution before
it should attain its perfect maturity. Their attempt
has not been attended with success. France has
already vanquished their armies; but it remains for
her to sound the particulars of the conspiracy, to
discover, to expose to the eyes of the world, those
despots who had the infamy to take part in it; and
the world expects from her that act of justice.

These are my motives for demanding that Louis
XVI be judged; and it is in this sole point of view
that his trial appears to me of sufficient importance
to receive the attention of the Republic.

'He does not call him Capet. He calls him Louis XVI,'
I said.

'Tom has a wonderful way with words,' said Hannah.

'Do you think that his words will be translated into
deeds, as well as into French?'

Hannah looked at me severely. 'They must be,' she
said. 'It is as he says: an act of justice.'

I looked down at Thomas, fast asleep. He would
remember none of this. As for me, I did not care tuppence
for the King of France or for Tom Paine either, although
it was heresy to say so. I had grown to detest this
shadow-boxing with great events. We were far away
from Paris. We could influence nothing. Where was the
sense in all these words and the eager reading of them,
the passing on of intelligence and the taking up of

attitudes? How could Hannah pretend to feel so strongly? It was like trying to touch naked flesh with heavy gloves.

'Julia said to Tom once—' said Hannah.

'I must go. He will be hungry.'

'You are always going, Elizabeth. You no sooner come than you go again.'

These weeks had seamed her face with grief. She wanted to talk to me of Mammie, to make her come alive again between us. But I would not mourn Mammie with Hannah or with anyone. In this I was not soft, as Diner said: I was hard. It was all gone, all of it, the life we had lived. It could never be brought back and so it was better not to remember it. Mammie would come to me, or not, as she chose.

I had folded up her Indian shawl, pretending that I wanted it for my bedroom. I had wrapped it in paper, tied it with string, and put it in a box at the foot of my bed.

'I am sorry, Elizabeth,' said Hannah. 'I should not have troubled you with Tom Paine.'

Her nose was red: poor Hannah. She was on her dignity, gathering it about her because she had asked something of me and I had refused her.

'I am sorry too, Hannah. I'm only tired, and worried about Thomas. Philo thinks he is getting another tooth. He has one already, did I tell you?'

'You had your first tooth at three months,' she said, easier now that we were back on familiar ground. 'We neither of us realised you were cutting it, but one day you cried and I looked into your mouth and said to Julia, "Why, this child has a tooth already, and another coming!"'

Only Hannah remembered. Only Hannah knew what we had been, the three of us.

'I dare say it will be the same with Thomas,' I said.

'Julia said it was a wonder you had not bitten her.' She smiled, and then her face quivered. 'I never told you, Elizabeth, how your mother grew while she was carrying you.'

'What do you mean?'

'I had her height measured on the door-frame, a mark for every year. Of course, when she left, we never saw those marks again.' My mother had taken Hannah with her, who had been with her as governess since she was twelve. Her parents would not have kept Hannah in the house anyway. They said that she had corrupted their daughter and pandered for my father. 'But later, when they married and we all found lodgings, I made another mark to show her present height. We didn't think any more of it; she was past growing, I thought. But one day she went through the door holding you, and I saw that the top of her head was well past the mark.'

'Perhaps she was wearing thicker shoes.'

'I am not a fool, Elizabeth. I measured her against the mark in her stockinged feet, and she had grown two inches.'

'And so all the time that I was growing, she was growing too.'

'Yes.' After a while she added, 'And she was writing,

too. She wrote a page shortly before your birth, and gave it to me to keep.'

'Was it ever printed?'

'No. It was only a few sentences. She scored out the rest and then recopied what she wanted to keep, and gave it to me.'

'Have you still got it?'

'Of course. I would never destroy a word of hers, unless she wished it.'

I took a breath. I could not harden myself against this. 'Would you show me, Hannah?'

Hannah's hands fidgeted together. She had got into this habit, like an old woman. She seemed reluctant and I wished I had not asked her.

'I will show you,' she said at last. 'But remember that she was younger then than you are now.'

She went to her own chest, a small wooden chest very like a sailor's, which held all her personal possessions apart from her clothes. I had never seen inside it, not even in my young and curious days. I had not dared to touch it.

'Help me down, Elizabeth.'

She could not kneel without assistance, and once she had searched deep in the layers of her possessions and come up with a black-bound book, she needed me to help her stand again. The book was a prayer book. Hannah tapped it apologetically.

'I had it in my childhood and even though I have quite thrown off superstition, I have never brought myself to travel without it.'

She opened the book, and took out a folded sheet of paper, and unfolded it. I saw my mother's writing. It was more spiky than it had become later, and the ink was brown with keeping.

'Cheap ink,' said Hannah, 'but written in her own hand. Read it, Elizabeth.'

I took the paper. There was very little written on it.

But I know One Thing, that I have my own
Spirit and it is the Equal of any Man's and in
this I might say: I have my little Horse and I will
ride it even if in truth it is a Donkey and a poor
slow Thing.

I knew instantly that she had written it in case she died of my birth. She had wanted to leave proof that the path she had taken was the one she had chosen, and she had not thrown away her life at sixteen. She had been poor then and rejected by my father's family and her own. Many of her friends refused to meet her, even after her marriage. She had plunged into a new world and she did not yet know the depth of it.

I wondered if she had read that paper to me long ago, when I was a child too young to understand it, and I had remembered her words in some part of me when I hugged her and said: 'I could not love you any more, Mammie, if you were my own pet donkey.'

Hannah took back the paper and folded it so that it fell back into the same creases. She put it back into the prayer book, closed it and snapped the clasp, but made no move to put the book away. Her hands were fidgeting again as they caressed the worn black leather. Her eyes were filmed and inward and for now there was no place for me in her grief. All she wanted was to sit there with the book in her lap.

'I must go,' I said. 'But come and see us, Hannah. He is never in until past eight in the evening. And then you can see Thomas too.'

She sighed, and I noticed the faint trembling of her head on her neck.

'It's better if you come here, Elizabeth.'

I had realised a while ago that it was not only Hannah's visits that Diner disliked. He did not want any friend of mine to come to the house. Susannah Quinton had paid a visit some weeks earlier. She wanted to see Mammie's grave, although we had not yet set up a stone. It was necessary to wait, and besides, I dreaded the discussion there would be over the words that should be cut into it. I had always liked Susannah. She had round, brown, startled eyes, more startled than ever since she had been in Paris, and she had good sense. She did not care a fig for Caroline Farquhar. Susannah would wink at me behind Caroline's back when she prated of 'the people' while bullying her maid over the washing of her lace. Susannah gave Hannah a guinea towards her mourning, although she could ill afford it.

Diner did not like Susannah. He said nothing amiss when she came to the house, but the hour passed awkwardly and he did not leave me alone with her.

After that I made sure to see her elsewhere. I questioned her closely about what she had seen in France, and it was nothing like the newspaper reports which Augustus read out. She had left a great deal out of her letters, she said, for fear that they might be read before they left the country. Often she was in confusion as events raged around her. Only afterwards would she understand that she had been present at some significant moment which would be described and redescribed endlessly by those who had not been there. She had brought with her several copies of *Le Père Duchesne*, which she had sewed into the lining of her petticoats. I could not read French well but Susannah translated for me. The language was very different from that of Susannah's letters. 'Je suis le véritable Père Duchesne, foutre!' I listened to the text and thought I would not like to be denounced by Père Duchesne, but Susannah was passionate in her support of the pamphlets.

'Père Duchesne represents the common people! You can have no idea of how they have been abused and oppressed by their rulers. Listen: is this not magnificent?

'Je me fous des menaces, et elles ne m'empêcheront pas de dire la vérité; tant qu'il me restera un souffle, je défendrai les droits du peuple et ma répub-lique, foutre. Ma vie n'est point à moi, elle est à ma patrie, et je serai trop heureux si ma mort pouvait être utile à la sans-culotterie qui, malgré les assassins et les empoisonneurs, sera toujours la plus forte.'

'You go too fast, Susannah. I can barely follow.'

The truth was that I could not follow at all, but Susannah persisted in thinking my French far better than it was.

'Well, let me see ... "I don't give a ..." Hmm ... he is very blunt, Lizzie. "... for threats, and they won't stop me telling the truth; as long as I have breath in my body I shall defend the rights of the people and my republic ..." Hmmm, hmmm. "... My life does not belong to me at all, but to my country, and I'll be only too happy if my death can be useful to the sansculottes" – you know, Lizzie, the revolutionary party – "which in spite of murderers and poisoners, will always prove the strongest."'

'Yes, that is very fine,' I said. 'But it sounded better when you spoke in French.'

'Absolutely! French has become the language of liberty and struggle!'

Susannah hugged me warmly when she left. 'Dear Lizzie! It does me so much good to see you. Your eyes, you know, are so exactly your mother's.'

'But you love me for myself.'

'Lizzie! How can you say that? Of course I do.' Susannah opened her own round brown eyes very wide; then she caught me to her again. 'We are living through such times that those yet to be born will look back in wonder.'

'That is what Augustus says.'

'Yes. But all the same – and I hope you will not misunderstand me ...' She dropped her voice almost to a whisper. 'I am glad to be home for a while.'

'Will you stay? I wish you would.'

'No, I must go back. You cannot understand until you go there. I am a witness to history, Lizzie.'

'As long as you are only a witness. But you are English. What if Père Duchesne took it into his head to denounce you?'

'He would never do that,' said Susannah confidently. 'I am on the side of the people. I have no wealth, no position, no privileges to protect. I too defend the rights of the people and of the Republic.'

'Promise me that you will not be only too happy to make yourself useful to the sans-culottes by dying. Leave that to Père Duchesne.'

'Lizzie, if only I could take you to Paris! You would not be so cynical then.'

I saw Susannah several times during her stay, but I never mentioned it to Diner. There was no need for him to hear of her, any more than he needed to hear Thomas's cries. His eyes watched and followed me, but I told myself that he could not see everything.

12

The trial of the King of France began. Everyone in England called it that, although he was king no longer. In France, at the trial, they called him by his first name: Louis. He was Louis Capet now, a man like any other. It was what we had always believed to be the truth: that all men were equal and none should set himself up above another on the grounds of birth. The divine right of kings was no more than a justification for unfettered tyranny.

Even so, I could not quite believe that it had all come about.

'Louis, la nation française vous accuse. L'assemblée nationale a décrété, le 3 décembre, que vous seriez jugé par elle; le 6 décembre, elle a décrété que vous seriez traduit à sa barre. On va vous lire l'acte énonciatif des délits qui vous sont imputés . . . Vous pouvez vous asseoir.'

We had eaten, but Diner did not want me to clear the table yet. He read the passage aloud to me in French, and then translated it. He had spent a good deal of time in France and he could translate as rapidly as he read. I wondered if he and Lucie had spoken French together. But of course they had. It was an intimacy beyond bearing, that they had shared not only their lives but a language too, and one that I barely spoke. I forgot about what Diner was saying as I pictured them together, talking in low impassioned tones and then laughing at some private joke.

'Lizzie, you are not listening.'

'I am sorry. Please read it again.'

'Louis, the French nation accuses you, the National Convention has decreed, on the 3rd December, that you will be judged by it; on the 6th December the Convention has decreed that you will be brought to its bar. The list of the crimes of which you have been accused will be read to you ... You may be seated.'

'It is very curious,' I said, 'to think of the common people giving the King permission to sit or stand.'

'They will kill him,' said Diner. The words fell between us like stones. I had not yet thought such a death possible.

'Surely not. Augustus believes that they will send him into exile.'

'Then he's even more of a fool than I thought. They cannot leave the King alive. If he is imprisoned his existence will be a rallying-point. If he is exiled he will not go quietly. He will call on every crowned head in Europe to raise an army and restore his kingdom. Those who have brought him to trial know that, and they also know what will happen to them if the King's armies take back France. No man will vote for his own torture and execution, Lizzie. They will kill him, and then you will see what comes of it. These French will ruin us all.'

He spoke with anger and with impatience, as if he saw too clearly what lay ahead and was weary of waiting for it.

'They cannot ruin you,' I said. 'They are hundreds of miles away and even the most eager of the sans-culottes will scarcely make their way to London, let alone Bristol.'

I must have smiled at the thought of them arriving in our city with banners and tricolour cockades. I did not mean to mock him, but Diner looked at me as if I were his enemy and said: 'You find all this amusing, Lizzie? You think nothing of the kind can happen here, even though it is what everyone you know has been working towards for years? The mob in Bristol would gather in an instant. You have not seen a riot, I think. I have. Perhaps you should learn to build something, and then watch while others destroy it.'

His hands clenched, and for an instant I was afraid. My skin prickled, even though I knew there was no reason for it. You are a fool, I told myself. You have no cause for fear. He will not hurt you.

'But, Diner, we are in England here. Whether they kill the King of France or let him live, it will be all the same to us.'

This was heresy. Augustus would have lectured me roundly on the links that tied each one of us to our brother men, our fellows in the struggle for liberty, wherever they might be. We were bound to one another. What happened across the Channel was not obscure to us, since the cause of radicalism in England hung on the fate of France. The success or failure of the revolutionary forces was our success or failure too. I had heard it all so many times and had acquiesced with my lips, but in my heart I could not feel it. It seemed to me that there was a self-interest hidden in the core of all of us, which cooled us when we contemplated any fate which did not touch us directly. Or perhaps I was cold-blooded, as Caroline Farquhar had once accused me. I chose ignorance, she said. I chose passivity. She herself, I think, was all fire and air in her own opinion.

'You cannot be so ignorant, Lizzie,' said Diner. 'Do you really think that the storm in France will not blow my hat off?'

'I suppose, if they kill the King . . .' I was thinking aloud, remembering Hannah's stories of Garrick playing Macbeth. She had never tired of telling me how Garrick had looked as he held up the dagger after killing Duncan. To witness it had been one of the great moments of her life. 'If they kill the King, then perhaps blood will have blood,' I said now.

'Why do you say that?' he asked, with a pounce of anger that frightened me again. But I was determined to say out my piece.

'I was thinking of *Macbeth*. Hannah used to recite those speeches to me so often that I have them by heart still:

'It will have blood, they say; blood will have blood:
Stones have been known to move and trees to speak.

'Macbeth fears that the man he has killed will come back and revenge himself. You know the play; you know how Banquo returns after his death.'

Diner turned away from me, towards the fire which bubbled peacefully in the grate. 'I am tired,' he said. His hand hung down beside his chair, and I took it up and kissed it.

'Don't think of such things now,' I said.

He turned his head slowly and smiled at me. 'What should I think of, Lizzie?'

'Tell me what you have done today.'

'Strong and Wishart have left.'

They were his two best stonemasons.

'Is the work finished?' I asked, but I knew that it was not.

'No. They say that they have worked for too long on the promise of pay. They are short-sighted – they should know that I will reward them handsomely once the houses are sold – but there is no more arguing with them. I have stretched that rope too far. Don't wrinkle up your brow, Lizzie. I prefer it smooth. There.' And he stretched out and passed his hand across my fore-head so firmly that it was an order, not a caress. 'They will come back to me.'

I could not help blinking. His fingers seemed to feel their way into my mind. 'Those buyers who came last week – the lady with the cough,' I said quickly, to distract him, 'have they visited again?'

'They have been to Grace's Buildings twice.'

'Then perhaps—'

'They are wasting my time. She looks as if one more winter will carry her off. Her husband is indulging a sick fancy.'

I had been sure of them. She had walked about, talking about what furniture she would put in this room or that, and how she would make a morning room from one of the bedrooms because it caught the early sun. She was so animated, clinging to her husband's arm and laughing when there was no cause for laughter.

'Are your clients always like this?' I asked him. 'I cannot make it out. Her husband had money, surely, unless he was flashing the gentleman. He must know whether or not he wants to buy.'

'He is not going to buy a house for her to die in.'

'They talked of the future all the time they were here.'

'He must know she has no future.'

It was December now. She would not survive the winter. She would be gone next year and the house unsold. The thought of it chilled me through, even though I scarcely knew the woman. It was the dead of the year too, when hope had shrunk down.

'So many people have come to see the houses,' I said. I knew Diner would not let himself give way. 'Why does it take so long? Why do they come so often, and talk and talk, and never decide? Is it always like this?'

'They are fearful,' said Diner. 'They wonder why others have not bought before them, if the terrace will be everything that I say. There is no reason in any of it. I could have sold each house in Canford Square twice over, and still had them coming for more. These houses here are twice as fine – three times – and then there is the situation: it will never be matched again. The whole of the Gorge open before them . . .' He clenched his fists again, and then slowly relaxed them. 'They do not see it. They refuse to see it.'

'They will see it.'

'You think so, Lizzie? I'm not so sure. They look at the empty houses and the ones not yet built. They ask me questions that I cannot easily answer. But I will have them. They need to believe that a better and luckier man will snatch at the chance of buying, if they do not. They must be brought to fear that more than they fear any other loss.'

He had won so many times. He still believed that things would turn and he would get the better of these shilly-shally skinflints. But he was anxious now. He had laid off men before, plenty of times, but he would never have chosen to lose two skilled masons who had both worked with him for years. Whatever he said, he knew that they would quickly find other work and be engaged when he needed them again.

'There is a certain point, Lizzie: I cannot exactly explain it to you, but once I have brought a buyer to that point, I know I can tip him over. I am a wrestler and I use my opponent's momentum to make him fall. But if he will not come to the point, then I am powerless. I cannot very well lift the money out of his purse. That is, unless you are willing to come into the business as my accomplice, and lift his handkerchief and purse from his pocket.'

I was glad to see him smile at last. 'I might be willing. I am quick with my hands,' I said.

'You are, I know.' He took my hand between his, ran his lips over it and gently bit the cushion of flesh at the base of my thumb. 'But what should I do if you were transported?'

'You'd come with me. They must need houses there.'

'Felons are not very likely to pay me for my work.'

'But think how cheap we could live.'

'You would dislike the company, Lizzie. Australia is not America: there is no society there. Only a wilderness which is no doubt as full of savage animals as the menagerie at Exeter 'Change.'

'But I would have your company.'

It struck me, suddenly, how little there was to hold me here, if we could take Thomas with us. Hannah would remain with Augustus, growing old. Augustus would be himself, whatever happened. He was an unchangeable creature.

I could step out of this life, and find another. It seemed suddenly as easy a thing as opening a door to walk through it. I would not be leaving safety behind, because there seemed to be no safety anywhere. Since the day Mammie died I had barely kept my footing. The life we'd had was gone. There was nothing left of it and nothing in its place but this: Diner nipping the flesh at the base of my thumb with his teeth. I would never see Mammie look up and smile as I came into the room and say, 'How's my girl?' I was not her girl and never would be again. No one would ever look at me with such tenderness, simply because I existed. I did not know who I was. I felt safe only when Thomas was in my arms.

Perhaps we really could begin our lives again? Diner was right: Australia would not do, but America might. They were building there. We heard of new towns and cities rising where there had been wilderness only a few years earlier. Diner's skill would be much in demand.

No one would know that Thomas was not our child, I told myself. There would be other children later. In America they had already had their revolution and cast off the yoke of the King. The sky had not fallen.

Diner's lips moved over my palm and I shivered.

'Let us go upstairs, Lizzie,' he said.

That night I lost myself. I forgot everything except the dark place where we clung together. We were one creature, made out of sweat and salt and all the juices of our bodies. This time he did not pull out of me but came inside me, shuddering, and I did not push him away.

Afterwards, when he was asleep, I came to myself. His weight on my arm began to be heavy, and very gently I shifted myself to ease it free. He murmured but did not stir. I lay awake for a long time. I was not falling now but floating free. My thoughts of a hut in the wilderness seemed childish now. I remembered Mammie's voice, reading of the Indian chiefs and the wonders they revealed to Bartram. Her voice was low and clear and easy. I could still hear it yet I would never hear it again. Thomas would never know it. These days I had to remind myself that he was her child. He would miss her without ever knowing what it was that he missed. I vowed that if I had a child of my own, it would make no difference to my love for Thomas. For once I felt no anxiety about him. He was safe and sound, upstairs with Philo. There was no need for me to steal upstairs to be sure that he was still alive. Every day he grew stronger. I loved to kiss the creases of his neck and his soft feet that had never yet trodden on the ground. Philo blew raspberries on his back and we laughed together over his laughter.

Caroline Farquhar wanted to write great things on Mammie's tombstone. *The Matchless Eloquence of Her Instrument Was Ever Tuned to the Delight and Benefit of Her Fellow Creatures.* Hannah pursed up her face and remarked privately to me later that it made my mother sound like an opera singer. Augustus stared about him with a clouded look and said, 'Excellent.

What you propose is excellent, Caroline,' but without doing more than glance over the words. It came to me that he could not bear to think of it, and in the dark and quiet my heart softened to him. Caroline Farquhar would go back to London. When my mother's tombstone was set, it would have none of Caroline's words on it. It would have her own name on it, and her dates of birth and death.

Augustus would agree. He would not want fancy carving, when it came to it.

America was another pipe dream. I saw clearly now that it was not so easy to step out of the life which held us. No matter how far we went, we would take with us not only our selves but all the ghosts of our lives.

Besides, Augustus would not willingly part with Thomas, and Diner did not want children with me.

13

Diner woke me. I did not know what had hit me but then I came to myself and knew that it was his hand, flung out, striking me across the face. It was not a heavy blow, but enough to startle me out of sleep. I rubbed my cheek. He was shifting from side to side as if trying to dodge an opponent. I remembered what he had said to me about wrestling, how he would bring his opponent down by getting him off balance. He was wrestling now, with something I could not see.

The blow went through and through me. He groaned in his sleep and then said something, a word I could not make out. I was afraid he might strike out again and I sat up carefully so that he would not feel the movement and eased myself to the very edge of the bed.

He was asleep, I told myself. He did not know what he was doing. But he had hit me. Where was he in his mind, to forget that I was sleeping beside him?

My skin smarted. I sat and listened until he lay still

and his breathing deepened. It was no lighter now than it had been when I went to bed. There was so much dark at this time of the year, lying over the earth like a lid. It lifted for a few hours and then closed down over us again. One day it would close down forever. Here was I and here was Diner: two lumps of flesh that were alive now and would soon, inevitably, be as cold and unresponsive as—

I was not going to think of that. Her body had been stiff within hours, all the warmth fled. Her eyes solid when I touched the cold lids. No impulse towards me.

I did not know what breath meant until she died. It was everything that gave quickness and life: it was thought, feeling, animation. Without it there was nothing.

It was only time that lay between me and that day when life went out of her and she was still warm but utterly absent. She was warm when I bathed and washed her, and helped the midwife to stop up the orifices of her body. I could do this for her at least. Trapped air wheezed out of her as we turned her. It sounded for an instant like life but it was death. She would never take another breath.

I worked so fearlessly that the midwife praised me for it, but I knew she thought me unfeeling.

Time could not distance me from it. Every moment was distinct. Even her hair had no warmth in it when I combed it out. It was rough and matted from her struggle towards death. The shine was gone, with the scent that had always clung to it. It was dead stuff, and I could not bring myself to cut a lock to remember her by, although the midwife urged me to do so.

Augustus cut a lock of hair, tied it with a black thread and put it away in a box.

I could not kiss her lips or cheek but I kissed her forehead and felt the resistance of her flesh. The lines in it were slack. I fetched rosewater and rubbed it into her temples, behind her ears, over her breast. I had rubbed her with orange-flower water while she was alive. She would smell sweet, at least. But even so there had been a smell from her body that the rosewater could not mask. She smelled of meat that had been kept too long. I flinched at the smell and at my own betrayal of her in noticing it. A good daughter – the daughter Mammie deserved – she would have known nothing but the purity of love and grief.

For the first time tears had pushed behind my eyelids. I dabbed the inside of her wrists. I had never touched her there before without feeling for the jump of her pulse.

And now I was alone, with my husband beside me. I must not think about it. I would get up. I would put food into my mouth, chew and swallow it, wash my face, twist my hair into its knot. I would do all these things, day after day, even though all the time there was an end appointed for them which I did not know. My pulse might as well cease now, I thought as I lay in the darkness, since one day it was bound to do so. My blood would be still and thick in my veins. There were so many years to get through and for the moment even Thomas could not rouse me to feeling. He would do as well without me. Better, perhaps.

Mammie was out there in the dark and cold. No one would ever bring her in, to warm and dry and cherish her. There was rain seeping through the earth and into her coffin. Water gets everywhere. It finds a way, no matter how tight the carpenter dovetails his joints. When rain spattered on the windows I could never run to open the door for her, take off her cloak to dry it by the fire, kneel to take off her boots. She was part of the cold darkness. She would never come in. And here I was, still putting food into my mouth and swallowing it.

I lay bound, as heavy as if I too had the weight of six feet of earth above me.

Diner stirred. He spoke thickly, indistinctly, and I again could not catch what he said, but then he repeated it and my brain made out the word: *Lucie*.

He was dreaming of her, as I was thinking of Mammie. In his dream the earth had lifted from her coffin. She had risen and come to him. She did not stink of the grave; she was not streaked with filth and suckered with worms. She was herself again and come to find him. They were talking together in their own strange, sweet language, questions and answers tumbling out of them. When they broke off at last she glanced at me without curiosity and with a certain disdain, as if she had expected to discover him with a creature such as me. But now she had come back, all that could be put aside. She chattered to him softly as she smoothed out the covers and prepared herself to slide in beside him.

I got up out of the bed. I did not dare look behind me as I snatched up my clothes from the heap where I had thrown them down the night before. They smelled of my own body and I held them close. My feet found the path to the door and I squeezed the handle so that it opened noiselessly, then I went up through the house like a ghost.

There was no sound from Philo's attic. I longed to lift Thomas, to hold his warm damp heaviness and snuff the smell of his skin. I must not do it, I thought. I must leave him alone. He would be frightened. He would cry and I would not be able to comfort him. I must leave him to Philo.

I dressed myself blindly, felt my way down to the kitchen, broke open the fire and lit a candle. I would not go out looking like a wild creature. I smoothed my hair and knotted it, took water from the barrel, dipped a cloth and wiped my face.

I must eat or I would be weak. I chewed a piece of bread but could not swallow it and spat it out into the fire. There was milk in the jug, more than enough for Thomas, and so I drank a little. The kitchen hung about me, so strange that I could not believe I had ever set foot there before. It was beginning to frighten me. I must get out, I thought. Where can I go?

There was only one place. I would go there and perhaps Hannah would be as she was before, crisp and capable, scolding me but making me at home. I knocked against the dresser as I blundered to the passage and the garden door. There would be a bruise and Diner would ask me about it when he scrutinised my body, inch by inch, as he so often did. I drew back the bolt stealthily, as if he were breathing behind me, and slipped out. The garden door was bolted too, but it gave way easily. It opened on to the lane behind the houses, where Philo threw the ashes. I lifted my skirts high, out of the dirt.

I slipped through the streets silently. When I passed another living creature we went by like shadows, not guessing at each other's business. It was dark but I knew from the stir of the wind that it was almost morning. There were people waking. The yellowness of a candle sprang up in an upstairs window as I went by. Soon the men would be at work on the terrace: those who remained. But there was frost on the ground and the earth was hard. Diner would not like that. I slid on a frozen puddle and went down, cracking my knee, and then I realised that I was running. I must not run though the streets like a madwoman, I thought. Hannah must not see me like this.

I reached the house, looked up and sure enough, there was a light. Hannah must be stirring already. I tried the main door but it was locked. I did not want to pull the bell and so I thought: I will make Hannah come to the window.

I stepped back and crossed the street until I could see the kitchen window clearly. Candlelight bloomed yellow. Hannah was there for sure, but Augustus would be still fast asleep. He was never an early riser.

'Hannah,' I said, not loud enough for her to hear, willing her to hear me. 'Hannah.'

I would bring her to the window. I would make her come to me. I thought of her and the threads that had bound the three of us close. I thought of her rising from the fire, and coming over to the window to look out, without knowing why she did so.

'Hannah,' I urged her again. 'Hannah, come to the window.'

She did not come. I saw that the street was not fully dark any more: the black was thinning into grey. It was no longer night, but morning, and Hannah could not hear me. I had tried to touch her mind, but it resisted.

I went back to the door and jangled the bell until I heard the sleepy slur of feet over the floor. It was one of the girls downstairs, with her hair down her back, yawning her night-breath into my face, and cross too, at being woken. I brushed past her protests and went up the stairs in the dark. I knew the way well enough. I knocked on the outer door, at first gently and then hard, because Hannah was awake. I knew it. There were sounds from inside. Footsteps, scuffling; quick low voices that I could not quite make out. Why didn't anyone come? I rapped again, loudly, to frighten them. I would rouse the house if I had to. After a moment's silence I heard footsteps approaching the door.

'Who is it?'

'It's me, Lizzie. Open the door.'

'Lizzie! Wait. Wait a minute.'

The bolt did not slide. Instead there were footsteps going away, another silence and then I thought I heard a door shut. The footsteps came back, the bolt slid, the key turned and then the handle. There was Hannah, blinking at me as she held up her candle.

'You made me wait long enough,' I said, and stepped inside.

'Good gracious, child! Whatever are you doing here at this time?'

Hannah looked old, crumpled, unwelcoming: it was all quite different from how I had pictured it.

'I saw your light,' I said. 'I knew you were up.'

'It's far too early. The household's still asleep.'

The household! Who did she mean: Augustus? Caroline Farquhar? Had Caroline come back? *It's far too early.* Hannah spoke as if I were a visitor who should call at the proper hours. I was shocked, and angry too. There she stood, blocking the kitchen door, but behind her I could see the glow of the fire. I realised that I was very cold. I had not put on my boots and the frost had struck through my thin shoes.

'Why have you come here, Lizzie?' It was an old woman's voice, querulous, complaining.

'To see you,' I said. 'Or so I intended. Let me warm myself and I'll be off again, since it's clear enough that I'm not welcome.'

Hannah took no notice of my anger. She answered

as if I were still a noisy girl at home: 'Hush, Lizzie, don't speak so loud. You'll wake Augustus.'

She shut the door to the staircase and shooed me before her into the kitchen. But as I crossed the passage, I looked along to the door of Mammie's room. There was a light in there too. Augustus wasn't sleeping: Hannah had lied.

'Good morning, Augustus!' I said loudly.

'Don't disturb him!' said Hannah, so sharply that if I had not known her and Augustus I'd have thought she was afraid.

'Why has he a candle burning, if he is asleep?'

'He has bad dreams,' said Hannah. She had hold of me by the sleeve, tugging me into the kitchen. 'Sit down by the fire, Lizzie, and I'll make you some tea.' She shut the kitchen door firmly. We never did that.

I sat down and listened like a fox while I warmed my hands. Yes, here they came again: muffled sounds, footsteps, voices. There was someone else there and Hannah didn't want me to know it. She and Augustus had secrets together. It went through me like a knife that Augustus had found another woman already, and the two of them were wallowing in my mother's bed.

Hannah had her back to me as she measured out the tea. I stood up swiftly and silently, went over to the door and eased the handle open. She turned at the draught but I was already through to the passage. I saw a flicker of movement at the bedroom door. Someone had been about to come out, but had gone in again on hearing me. The door was ajar. I ran to it and pushed it wide. There was the bed, tumbled, with the clothes slipping to the floor. Augustus stood in the middle of the room, fully dressed.

'Where is she?' I asked. He did not seem surprised to see me: he must have heard my voice.

'Why, Lizzie, what do you mean?'

'You know what I mean. There was someone in here with you. Where has she gone?'

A strange look came on to his face. I saw that he understood me. I turned to search but he put out his hand.

'No, Lizzie,' he said. 'Wait.' He took hold of my wrist and looked into my face as if he were sorry for me. 'It is not what you think. Not at all.'

'Then what is it? I know that you have someone here and you are hiding her from me.'

His eyes scanned me. 'Did you come here alone?'

'Of course.'

'Your husband does not know that you have come here? No one knows?'

'Diner knows nothing. He's still asleep.'

'Can I trust you, Lizzie?'

'What do you mean? What are you saying? *Trust me?* Leave hold of me, Augustus. I promise you, I will find her.' I began to pull away. I was sure that he would not use force, and I was right. I shook him off and he did not try to hold me. Instead he folded his arms and said quietly:

'You may come out now, Will.'

A hand came out from under the bed, and then a foot. The bedclothes slithered as a figure crawled out and levered itself to its feet.

'It is all right,' said Augustus. 'Lizzie, don't be frightened. Mr Forrest is a friend of ours.'

'He must be a very intimate friend, to be hiding under my mother's bed.'

The young man smiled. He was dusty: he glanced down at his clothes and noticed it, but refrained from brushing himself clean. He was tawny, with very bright hazel eyes and a white skin like a girl's. He appeared not in the least embarrassed.

'Lizzie is our dear Julia's daughter,' explained Augustus. I thought he would have done better to explain the young man to me, but he did not, and the young man did not seem to think it necessary either. I saw how uneasy Augustus was. He was trying to think what was to be done.

'Why were you hiding under the bed?' I asked. A stain of colour flowed into the young man's white face, but he smiled and his eyes sparkled.

'I was practising,' he said.

'For what?'

'In case you had been someone else. Someone very much less welcome.'

I saw him glance at Augustus, a look that meant the same as those words Augustus had said: *Can I trust you, Lizzie?* But who were they to doubt me?

'This is Augustus's house, not mine,' I said. 'He may do as he chooses. You have no need to explain yourself to me. But my mother has not been dead three months, and she died in that bed.'

I had not intended to say it. I always kept my feelings well hidden from Augustus. He could think me cold if he liked.

It was the young man who made me speak: Will Forrest. I said his eyes were very bright, but when I looked close at him – I could not help doing so – I saw that it was not exactly brightness. They were soft, and full, and brilliant all at once. I could not easily look into them. He was not very tall: three inches taller than me, perhaps, as we stood almost face-to-face. His skin was as fine as a girl's but there was something about him so utterly unfeminine that it drove the comparison away. Now he was brushing off the dust.

'You must think me very strange,' he said.

'Yes.'

'Mr Forrest is on his way to the colony of Virginia,' broke in Augustus. 'He will take ship from Devon. He is taking his leave of his friends along the way.'

'I see,' I said. Will Forrest remained silent and smiling. There was something between them, as palpable as smoke in a room. They were not going to tell me. If Mammie had been there she would have known everything, and I would have known everything through her, but now I was cast out.

'Mr Forrest will not see much of the New World under my mother's bed,' I said. 'Do you take me for a spy, Augustus? I shall go home.'

'And you will say nothing?' He could not help himself.

'Of course I will say nothing.'

'She deserves better than that,' said Will Forrest. 'Miss Lizzie – Miss Elizabeth—'

'Mrs Tredevant,' I said.

'Oh – you are married. I had not thought of that.'

'You had no need to think anything. You had never clapped eyes on me until two minutes ago.'

'Of course, you are right. It seemed that I had known you for longer.' He held out his hand, as frankly as a brother, and I took it. The skin was soft but the hand itself was strong. He held mine for a moment and then very quickly – almost as if shyly – he put it to his lips and just as quickly gave it back to me. But I knew already that he was not shy.

'Mrs Elizabeth Tredevant,' he said. It sounded like the name of another woman, older than me, guarded, respectable, over-ready to take offence or to guide others into the pattern of right behaviour. He drew out each syllable and then seemed to throw the name away as if he also knew that it was not really mine. He went on, 'I have written a poem, and consequently I am likely to be taken up for sedition. What Mr Gleeson said to you is true: I intend to take ship, but not to the New World. This old one interests me too much. I am going to the Highlands of Scotland. I shall set sail for Glasgow and then travel on to Oban and thence by fishing-boat to a small town ... After that, if I walk north for thirty miles or so I shall reach a place where I can be forgotten in less than a fortnight.'

'The Highlands.' Mammie had travelled there once. She

told me of clouds smoking over mountaintops, of islands like a handful of flung and shining pebbles, of cliffs so high you could barely see to the foam beneath, of girls walking ten miles with creels of fish on their heads. 'They say it is very beautiful. I should like to go there.'

'Connoch is the nearest town to my friend's cottage. You would not call it a town, Miss Lizzie – it is a straggle of a street merely, no more than a fishing village. Boats come and go, and I shall be rowed in late at night when it is dark. No one will notice me. There's a house where I may stay safely overnight and in the morning I shall take the road north. It is a track scarcely wide enough for a loaded donkey. It goes over the moor, and then it follows the brow of the sea-cliff for miles. After that I must go inland a little and cross a glen which is always dark even on the most brilliant morning. My friend Alexander says there was a great slaughter there centuries ago and the land has not forgotten it. You may see eagles there. You climb again to the pass and after you have gone through it the land opens out again, very bare and desolate. He has advised me to buy a leather water-bottle and fill it wherever I can. At last, when you have given up hope of anything but walking over the edge of the world, you come to the sea again. The path dips down the side of the mountain to a bay where there are four cottages. Two are empty, in one there is a blind old woman who lives alone, and then my friend lives in the fourth, closest to the water. He has a boat, and catches fish. He makes his fire of peat turves. He grows potatoes in a bed of rotted seaweed and they come out as clean as eggs. He is making a new translation of Virgil: the fourth Georgic. It will be very fine.'

'Does he live alone?'

'Yes. He has a wife and two daughters in Glasgow, but they have not accompanied him.'

'You speak as if you have seen it all.'

'No, I have never been there. I have not even written to Alexander for months. My letters are intercepted, you know. I think he may be angry at my silence, but as soon as I see him I shall explain everything.'

'Are you quite certain that he is still there?' I thought of Will walking over the mountains with his pack on his back and his leather water-bottle, his feet dusty and blistered. What if he came to the cottage and there was no smoke from the chimney, only a door hanging open?

Will smiled. 'Of course he will be there. He'll make me a bracken bed, if he has no mattress for me. He is the most generous of men. I shall bring enough oatcake in my pack that I shall not be a burden to him. I shall catch fish and pick mussels off the rocks, and dig his potato beds for him. In the evenings Alexander shall play his flute. He plays very well, Miss Lizzie, you would like to hear him.'

'But winter is coming. Won't you be lonely?'

'I shall miss London. I am a Cockney, you know. I need the stir and dirt and bustle of it around me. But I would rather bounce on the waves in a cockleshell with a fish-hook in my hands than sit still inside a prison.'

'Your friend will be glad to see you. It will make a change from having only one old woman to talk to.'

'The sunsets, he says, are the longest and most exquisite he has ever seen. He climbs out over the rocks to the westernmost point and sits with his back against a boulder, watching them. The old woman, I believe, scarcely speaks English.'

'One might tire of sunsets.' I spoke dryly but I longed to see it all. Will Forrest had a way of speaking which kindled the words and made everything leap into being. I could see it too: the rough track and the eagles soaring.

'There is a mark on your face,' said Will. His colour deepened.

'Where?'

He pointed. 'Just there, on your cheek.'

'Oh! I expect it is from when I was making up the fire.' I rubbed hard, to wipe off the smut.

'I think it is a bruise,' said Will.

'Oh yes. I knocked against the dresser in the dark. I had forgotten.' I felt the heat rise in my own face. He was looking at me so closely, and yet it was entirely different from Diner's scrutiny.

'It is nothing much,' he said. 'It is only where the light catches it.'

'You must take more care, Lizzie,' broke in Augustus, and we both turned. We had quite forgotten him.

But Augustus was not accustomed to being forgotten. He cleared his throat, clapped his hands and said, 'You must sleep, Will. You have not closed your eyes all night, and you have had your clothes on these past three days at least. Lizzie and I will leave you now. Hannah will bring your breakfast and then you will rest. Give me your boots. I will take them to be mended.'

Will did not protest. It was true: he looked very tired. His face was pinched and pale now that the colour had receded. His hair stood up where he had run his hands through it. I wanted to settle it with my own fingers.

'Goodbye, Mr Forrest,' I said, and perhaps he thought I was still hostile, for he nodded to me as if we were acquaintances who had met by chance in the street.

14

I sat by the kitchen fire in silence while Hannah prepared a plate of bread and ham and clattered pots on the shelf until she found the mustard. She had blown out the candle: it was full morning. Diner would be wondering where I was. I knew that I should leave, but I did not stir. I put my hand stealthily to my cheek, where Will Forrest had seen the bruise.

Augustus came in with Will Forrest's boots in his hand and his coat over his arm. He put the boots by the door.

'Give me the coat, Augustus,' I said. 'I will brush it.'

The hem was clagged with mud and the whole coat stained and spattered. There was a tear in the sleeve. Perhaps he had scrambled through a hedge while he walked those forty miles westward. It was an expensive coat but worn and shabby, and I wondered again about who Will Forrest was and how he lived. I took a stiff brush from the drawer.

'I will go down and brush this in the yard,' I said.

'No,' said Hannah. 'The girls downstairs will know it is not Augustus's coat. They are full of gossip.' She spread out a drawsheet over the floor. 'Brush it over this, Lizzie, and I will shake out the sheet after.'

Hannah was preparing spiced ale so that Will Forrest would sleep well. She was more animated than I had seen her for weeks. Thomas did not rouse her as this young man had done. I brushed and brushed at the coat until all the loose dry mud was out of it, and then I sponged the stains. I hung it up behind the door while Hannah bundled the drawsheet together.

The ale was mixed and now Hannah heated the poker in the fire as she did at Christmas. When it was red-hot she plunged it into the pewter mug full of ale. It hissed and steamed and a smell of nutmeg filled the kitchen. She put the mug on to a tray with the food, and said, 'I'll take this in to him now.'

When the door closed after her, Augustus said, not looking at me, 'You will say nothing of all this, I know, Lizzie.' But I thought that he was not quite certain of me, and my temper rose. I would tease him a little.

'A woman can have no secrets from her husband, you know, Augustus.'

He turned to stare at me. He did not recall that he had said this to me himself not many months before. Now he was in a quandary. He would have to reveal his true opinion of my husband, if he were to prevent me from betraying Will Forrest to him. I watched him think it out, with his mouth slightly ajar.

'How can you be so sure they won't come here looking for him?' I asked.

Augustus hesitated. 'They think he has gone north already,' he said at last. 'He took the mail to York several days ago, and he believes that he was followed to Lombard Street by a spy. He made sure to state his destination clearly and then he left the mail at the second post, doubled back, walked forty miles until he was west of London and then took the mail to Bath, and so onward to Bristol.'

'Did they not think it strange that a man who had paid his fare to York should get off the mail so soon?'

'He said he was ill with a putrid sore throat. He was muffled to the eyes and spoke hoarsely, so I dare say they were glad to get rid of him.'

'But what can it have cost? Mail to York, and then to Bristol? He must be a rich man.' Such extravagance was a rare thing in our company. If we had to travel farther than we could walk, we chose the slowest and cheapest conveyance.

'He has many friends, amongst whom I am proud to count myself,' said Augustus in his best style. I smiled to myself: there was no one in the room besides myself to admire his phrases.

'I have never heard you speak his name before today. I have never heard you read from his poems.'

'Lizzie,' he said, with the air of one who has long ago uncovered a secret, 'you are not fond of poetry.'

It was true that I was not fond of poetry when Augustus read it aloud to us.

'So tell me, Augustus. Why was I to be kept in the dark? Do you think I would blab?'

Augustus gazed at me. He did not resemble a sheep at that moment: it was a long, truthful, penetrating gaze. 'You mock me, Lizzie,' he said at last. 'How am I to know what you truly believe? You are married to a man who thinks of little but money, property and advancement. You cannot help it. You are part of him. You become like him.'

'I am myself, Augustus. I am not a thing to be passed from hand to hand. Have you forgotten that I am my mother's daughter?'

Augustus stared at me. 'Why, Lizzie—'

'And besides, Diner does more than *think*. He acts. He makes his mark. He wants to build rather than to destroy. Is that so very wrong?'

Augustus looked at his knuckles. 'Julia always insisted that you were the same as you had ever been, and nothing would change you.' He paused, as if unwilling to continue; then he looked at me and said: 'But I see changes.'

It pierced me, to think of Mammie and Augustus discussing me. She had defended me as if I needed defending. I wanted to slam Augustus's argument back in his teeth but I could not. Diner was no friend to radicalism. He feared and detested it. It might be part of my history but he only humoured it as a quirk of my upbringing which would be smoothed out now that I was married to him and knew better. He was sure, he said, that I was no true radical. I was like an English child who had grown up speaking German because she lived in Germany. But as soon as she came home the language would fall away from her like the shell from a ripe chestnut.

Diner always treated Mammie with respect, was polite but reticent with Hannah and Augustus, and never wished to meet any of their friends. Only when he was alone with me did he blaze out against the ruin he believed that radicalism would bring. And where was I? Caught somewhere between them all, perhaps . . . And I was lazy. I knew it. I rarely wanted to think my thoughts to their conclusions.

Augustus was right: I did mock him, and I never mocked Diner.

'I am bound to change,' I said. 'I am not the child I was when you came to live with us.'

'He builds houses,' said Augustus. 'But we wish to build a society free from oppression, want and misery.'

I could not bring myself to argue any more. A deep weariness had overtaken me. It seemed as if every word we spoke was like mud, clodding our boots, sucking us deep into the mire.

'I believe in the truth of your intentions, Augustus,' I said.

'Thank you, Lizzie,' he said quietly, and then was silent for a while. I longed to leave. I wanted to go back to the house, scoop Thomas out of his cradle and walk with the soft damp weight of him in my arms, up and down the room until all my thoughts had dissolved. But I would go back to Diner, and he would ask where I had been. What would I say if he asked how I came by the mark on my face?

Augustus had not yet finished. He stood with bowed head and hands clasped behind his back, in the way that had brought out in Mammie a certain smile I could not remember without pain, it was so humorous, so tender. She had loved him and I had never wanted her to love him. My heart was always swollen with jealousy. I was so used to this condition that I did not believe anything else was possible.

'Your mother was a very remarkable woman,' he said at last.

I could not reply. He angered me too much. I could not bear it that he spoke of her in the past tense, as if her life were something finished and agreed upon. It was not finished. She had been torn out of her life. She had wanted to live. If she had not become pregnant—

But then there would be no Thomas, and it was his existence that held me now. The bubbles of milk at his mouth. The way he would smile, open-mouthed, and his head would wobble as his eyes followed me around the room. I was a miser and Thomas was my treasure; mine, although Augustus had a right to him. I would never give Thomas up.

Augustus did not seem troubled by my silence. He went on: 'You cannot imagine, Lizzie, what it must have been for your mother to leave everything behind and live as she did. What a fire burned through her!'

'It is you who cannot imagine,' I answered him. 'You talk about fire. You stand at the blaze and marvel as you warm your hands. But that fire was my hearth, Augustus, from the day I was born. I knew nothing else. I was not introduced to any other way of thinking, until I met Diner. You say that he thinks of little but property, money and advancement. You are mistaken. You and he are a pair, although you will never see it. Diner dismisses you. He says you are impractical in your ideas and ineffectual in your acts. You reduce him. You claim his only motive is a pocketful of gold. You are both convinced, and you are both mistaken. I am so tired of conviction, Augustus. I wish that you would allow yourself a little uncertainty.'

'Why, Lizzie,' he exclaimed. 'Lizzie!' I could not tell if he was reproving me, or was again surprised that I should speak to him so directly. For once I had said what I meant. And when he continued it was not what I expected. 'I have never heard you say so much to me before,' he said, almost as if it pleased him.

'There is too much talking. You are all forever talking. When you are not writing, that is.'

'Where would the world be, if we did not communicate?'

He looked as if he would like to settle to an argument, so I said quickly, 'It is not my business. I am not talking about the world. But all these words! All these reams of paper! What does it achieve?'

'I hope you will never scorn your mother's writing.'

'I will never read it,' I said. I had flown beyond myself now, and was talking to him as if we were naked before the angels. 'I will never read it, because I cannot bear to hear her voice trapped in those pamphlets when her body is coffined six feet deep.'

'You must not think like that, Lizzie,' said Augustus, and he made a movement towards me, quick and warm. He almost took my hand and then we both collected ourselves. 'You must never think of her in such a way.'

I had never heard him speak in that tone to me before. It was possible – I knew nothing about it – but it was possible that this was how a father might speak to his child.

'She is alive in you,' said Augustus, and I thought he looked at me fixedly, as if he almost saw my mother there. 'She is alive in all of us. Her memory—'

Memory. What was that to set against the worms? I sighed. I had not meant to sigh so deep, but my body betrayed me.

'You may be sure that I shall say nothing of Mr Forrest,' I said as I left the room.

It was full daylight as I walked home and the streets were busy. Diner would be up and out. He would have missed me and been angry at my absence, but I would have until evening to think what to say to him.

Or so I thought, until I rounded a corner and almost collided with him. He took me by the upper arms. If I had pulled away I think it would have hurt me, but I did not move. I said, 'I am glad to see you. Hannah sent for me because she was unwell, and I am just on my way back to the house.'

'Why do you say "to the house"?' he asked me, frowning. 'Why do you not say: *I am on my way home*?'

'It was only a matter of words,' I said. 'It has no significance.'

'Words always have significance. You should know that. Hannah is old and her ailments will increase. You cannot go running to her whenever she calls on you.'

'She has done so much for me.'

'And what have I done for you, Lizzie?'

'You are holding me too tight,' I said.

He stared at his hands as if he had not realised that they were gripping my arms, and we were standing in a public street. He released me. I wanted to rub the place where his fingers had bruised me, but I would not do so. I thought of Thomas in his cradle in the attic.

'Everything,' I said.

'What do you mean?'

'You have done everything for me.'

'And yet it is not enough for you. You go running to Hannah as if—'

'What?'

'No matter,' he said, and I saw how angry he was. He was jealous of Hannah, a sick old woman, because she held a small part of my affections. He had not seen Will Forrest crawl out from under my mother's bed and smile as if we were two conspirators. If he knew of that – but he never would—

'Let us go home then,' I said.

He shook his head. 'I have business in Corn Street.' Even I knew what that meant. He needed to raise more money. The backing that he had was not enough unless the houses sold quickly. 'You understand me, Lizzie?'

'I think so.'

'It is this damned uncertainty!' he burst out. 'There is no reason in it. It is uncertainty which is killing the market. If there is war with France – no one knows, and so no one will act. Forsyth withdrew his interest this morning.'

Mr Forsyth's interest had not been very welcome at first. He wanted to buy a pair of houses at the price of one and a half. It was speculation and it would rob Diner of almost all his profit. But it would cover costs. I had rarely seen Diner so angry as he was the evening he decided that he must accept the terms. And now even that fish had slipped out of the net.

'I am sorry,' I said.

He looked at me closely. 'Yes, I believe you are,' he said. 'You have dirt on your face, Lizzie.' He rubbed my cheek with his finger. 'What's this? It will not come off.'

'I bumped into the chest in the dark.'

'Poor Lizzie.' He fingered the bruise. 'Let us go home.'

A woman who was hurrying past stopped suddenly, looked at Diner and then looked again. She hesitated. Diner could not see her, for she was behind him. She reached out and plucked at his sleeve.

'Mr Tredevant, sir.'

He felt her touch and swung round. 'What is it?'

'You don't know me, sir, but I'm a dressmaker at Jacob's Well. Everyone around there knows me: Mrs Iles is my name. I made a dress for your wife.'

He looked at me. 'What is all this, Lizzie?'

'I mean, for Mrs Tredevant. The grey silk.'

My stomach clenched. Lucie, she meant. Lucie had ordered the dress.

'And then she died, sir, and she never had it.'

I felt rather than saw the shock go through Diner as he grasped her meaning. He drew in his breath sharply but when he spoke he was perfectly rational: 'Do you want money?'

'No, sir, she brought the silk to me and when the dress was made I sent her a bill for my work and she paid that too. A girl came with the money but she wouldn't take the bill back again although I signed it. Your wife never had the dress. I had no direction for her, you see, sir, or I would have sent it. You may ask anyone for my character. And then I heard that she was dead in France and you had moved. I put the dress away.'

'You could have found my direction. I am well enough known in the city,' said Diner. There was no expression in his voice.

'I kept the dress very safe, sir. It has been more and more on my mind that you ought to have it. I made enquiries and got a description of you, and I have been looking out ever since.'

I believed what she said. Mrs Iles was a small creature, fastidious in her dress but pale and blinking with overwork. She must be honest. She could easily have sold the dress and said nothing. 'You must take it, sir. I live at Jacob's Well. You may come for it now if you choose.'

Diner had turned away and was already striding down the street. His feelings must have overpowered him. Mrs Iles looked after him, and then at me. I should go. I should leave this, but I could not. It was Lucie's dress and I must see it.

'I will come,' I said quickly. 'Where do you live?'

'Beside the surgeon's. I have a room on the top floor.'

I nodded and hurried after Diner.

15

I did not go for the dress that day, nor for many days after although the thought of it possessed me. Diner never spoke of the conversation with Mrs Iles, and I was busy with Thomas, who had developed a fever and would not take his food.

'It's his teeth,' Philo kept saying, but I did not believe her. I asked Mr Orchard for his advice, and he gave me a draught which put Thomas to sleep for eight hours. He lay still and hot and flushed and it frightened me because he was so unlike himself. I never gave him laudanum again. I thought he would be safer awake and crying. Instead I bathed his arms and temples with tepid water, as Hannah used to do for me when I had a fever, and walked him up and down to soothe him. He was not so very ill, but it was enough to alarm me. His head flopped on to my shoulder and he cried whenever I put him down. That night I did not go to bed.

'Augustus can have his child back now, if he is going to cause you so much trouble,' said Diner.

'It's no trouble. He will be better in the morning.'

I sat with the baby in the kitchen, by a low fire, and thought of the grey dress and the woman who had never worn it. It would have been shaped to her body and would fit no other. It was of no use to anyone now. Still, I wanted to have it. To spread it out, and see what her shape had been. If Diner found out, I would say that silk was valuable and I did not want to waste it.

The dressmaker was the first person I had met who had known Lucie, apart from Diner himself. I longed to talk to her. It was unjustifiable, of course. Mammie would have been ashamed to see me spy on my own husband. She would never have stooped to such a thing.

I had two secrets now: the dress, and Will Forrest. Thomas stirred and mewed in his sleep. 'Hush,' I said, shifting his weight, feeling his forehead and the back of his neck. I thought he was a little cooler. 'Hush, hush, my darling.'

He was all mine in the sleeping house. A baby might die so easily, between one day and the next. Thomas must be watched closely. He must not think of escaping us.

Yes, he was a little cooler. He was sucking in his sleep. He must be thirsty, I thought, and I dipped my finger into the pitcher of water at my side and held it to his lips. He sucked, and I gave him more. There was one candle burning, and by its light I saw his eyes open a little and search for me. There I was. His face blossomed; he smiled.

'Here I am,' I said to him. 'Go back to sleep now.

You're getting better, Thomas. Soon you'll be quite well again. Hush now, hush, go to sleep.'

One day, I thought, Diner and I will have a child. Diner might say what he liked now about wanting me alone, but the time would come. The thought of it disturbed me. It seemed disloyal to Thomas and I did not want him to guess that I had any idea of another child. I could not imagine what this other baby might be like. I could see only Thomas.

Five days later the baby was perfectly well and eating more strongly than ever. Philo complained that he had scarcely finished one feed before he was screaming for another. He was making up for what he'd missed, and neither of us minded the work. Philo ran for extra milk: the goat was kept in a shed now that it was winter.

'I shall take Thomas out tomorrow,' I said. 'The air will do him good. It has turned so much milder. You wouldn't believe it was close to Christmas.'

'A green Christmas means a full churchyard,' said Philo, and then caught herself. 'What am I saying?'

'He'll be perfectly warm wrapped in my shawl.'

It was one of those days when December is like spring. There was no breath of wind and the sun was soft. There was even a babble of birdsong as I went down the footpath past the Lower Crescent and eastward to Jacob's Well through the green fields. Smoke hung over the city. The tide was out and boats lay keeled on the mud. Beyond, the hills shone. They looked like a land of magic, although I knew that if I walked that far they would dissolve into ordinary plough and pasture.

I had borrowed Philo's shawl and tied Thomas into it. Diner would not like me going out in shawl and pattens like a servant girl, but I would be home long before he returned. No one took notice of me, dressed as I was. I might cross the city from end to end, as long as I looked out for myself. Diner had gone to Corn Street again and after that he had work to do at Grace's Buildings.

I might sell the silk and give him the money without saying where I'd got it. Or else I could use it to buy things for Thomas. Lucie would not mind that.

I walked along the footpaths, fast and free, and no one troubled me.

I had to ask for the surgeon's house. It was a mean place, and the house beside it was meaner still. The windows were so narrow that I wondered how she could see to sew in there. But I lifted the knocker and let it fall.

'You'll need to knock louder than that, my lover,' said a young man carrying a ladder, 'if it's Mrs Iles you want. She's right up top.'

I banged the knocker down, stepped back and saw a face come to the window. It was the dressmaker.

She had her chair arranged so that every drop of light from the window would fall on her work.

'I suppose you spend a great deal on candles,' I said. 'They are expensive.'

Her work was laid on the table before her: dark green woollen stuff – for a child's dress, I thought. I drew back the shawl from Thomas's head and she came close and peeped at him.

'How old is he?'

'Three months. He was born in September.'

'He's a fine child, and looks like to live,' she said. Her voice was harsh, and deeper than her small frame suggested. I untied the shawl and laid Thomas down on the sofa she must have put there for ladies to sit on while they made their orders. He was fast asleep. Mrs Iles sank down beside him.

'Will you show me the dress?' I asked, but she was bent over Thomas and did not hear me. I asked again and this time she turned.

'It is packed away in paper. If you will wait . . .' She hesitated and I saw that she was not quite sure of me now. Yesterday, when she saw me with Diner, she had thought me a lady. She was doubtful now. It was her business to know to a halfpenny what Philo's shawl was worth. I held out my hand, with Diner's ring on it, so that she would see it and be reassured. Instead she stared as if transfixed.

'You understand that I am Mr Tredevant's wife.'

Her mouth opened. 'Yes,' she said. 'Yes. I've been paid. I don't want any money. You can take the dress now.'

She hurried to the cupboard and fetched out a parcel. 'You will want to see it,' she babbled. 'You've not been cheated. I can account for every yard of the silk.' She was unpacking it, shaking out the folds. The grey silk rushed to the floor and spread out in the shape of a woman.

I stood up. The dress was as tall as I was and the silk rippled as it might ripple when its wearer walked in it. The grey was very light, almost silvery in colour.

'With her colouring, being so fair . . .'

This dress had been fitted on Lucie. She had been in this room. Mrs Iles had seen her, touched her, measured her, spoken to her. If I asked Mrs Iles about how Lucie looked or walked or talked, she would be able to answer; but how could I ask? I was afraid of the answers. Fair meant light-skinned and light-haired, but it also meant, perhaps, that Lucie was beautiful. If only Diner would speak of her, but he never did.

. . . being so fair.

Suddenly I understood that Mrs Iles had stared at my ring because she recognised it. Lucie must have worn it. No, more than that: it had been Lucie's ring, before it was mine. My heart beat hard but I did not know what I thought or felt. Lucie had gone to France and left her ring behind; and yet it had been given to her by Diner. Perhaps they had quarrelled. Perhaps she'd had no intention of returning.

No, I thought, you are inventing what suits you. More likely, Lucie would not wear a valuable ring on a long journey and she had left it at home for safe-keeping.

Mrs Iles lifted the dress higher. Bobbing her head ingratiatingly, she approached me with it. Before I could stop her she had held it against me.

'You are almost the same size. An inch or so taller

perhaps. I never forget a measurement. It can be altered for you within a day.'

'No,' I said. 'I am not going to wear it.' I drew back, as if she might sew me into it before I could stop her. But she took no notice of my refusal.

'A tuck *here* and *there*. Your arms are longer than hers. I can let it out, or inset a lace cuff . . .' Her fingers were coming after me, prodding me as she measured me by touch. I pulled myself free.

'It was a mistake. I should not have come here. Dispose of the dress in any way you choose.'

Mrs Iles stepped back, clucking sorrowfully. She gathered the dress back into her own arms and stroked the silk as if it had been a child's head. 'Such beautiful stuff,' she said. 'Such a cruel waste.'

'You can sell it, I suppose.'

'I'll fetch you the bill.' She laid the dress over her work table and scrabbled in a drawer. There it was, signed and dated, marked as paid. A second piece of paper fell to the floor and Mrs Iles scooped it up. 'Ah dear! The note she sent me. She wanted to know when it would be finished. She had an engagement and wanted to wear it – but I told her I was going as fast as I could, with all the work I had on hand. And then I heard no more.'

'May I see it?'

She did not respond, so I reached out and took it. The writing was fast and flowing. 'I hope not retard with the dress I need by <u>the Friday next</u> if you please. Lucie Tredevant.'

'So she paid you before it was delivered.'

'She paid for the dress when she was measured. She wanted it so.'

Strange creature, I thought. If she was so eager to have her dress, did she not realise that Mrs Iles might work more quickly if she had not already received her money?

'The dress was ready for her by the Wednesday. I would have sent it round but I had no direction for her. I expected her all that day and the next but she never came.'

Whatever the engagement was, Lucie had not kept it, but had gone to France instead. It began to look more and more as if there had been a quarrel. I was not merely imagining what I wanted to imagine. Lucie had gone away in haste and perhaps in anger. It was possible that she had not meant to return.

'I will keep the note,' I said. 'And the bill. Dispose of the dress.'

I pushed it away, to make myself clear, and she began to fold it again. I watched her fingers touch the silk tenderly and I thought: She won't sell it. She will put it back in the drawer and keep it.

'It is quite certain that she is dead?' asked Mrs Iles in the same loud, flat voice, as if she were asking about a bill.

'Good God! What do you think I am? She has been dead these three years and more.' I snatched up Thomas and wrapped him into the shawl again.

'I meant no offence,' said Mrs Iles. Her voice ruminated. 'I've known women do many things, but I'll never understand why she didn't come to fetch her dress. This is Spitalfields silk. But never a word nor a note. If she was going on such a journey, why, it was only a step out of her way to call in. I am always here. She was a milliner, you know, back in France. She chose this pattern out of a book she'd borrowed. It was a pleasure to deal with her.'

'The silk must have been very expensive.'

'She had it as a present.'

Diner would have given it to her, I thought. That silvery waterfall of Spitalfields silk: God knows what it would have cost. It drew me. I could not leave without touching it. I put out a finger and stroked the silk. Mrs Iles stood back and watched me with her hands folded meekly in front of her.

It sent a shiver through my flesh. How soft it was. The sheen was like the bloom on grapes, which might be rubbed away by careless handling. Lucie had touched it too, like this. She had thought of how she would wear it and be beautiful in it. We were not alike, because I would never wear such a dress. For the first time I felt no jealousy towards her. This was her dress, shaped to her body, and she had never worn it. She had died instead and had been put away six feet deep in the French soil. She was rotted and her shroud was a rag.

Thomas stirred against me. His mouth opened and then his eyes. He was hungry and he would cry all the way home if I did not hurry. He was lusty and impatient too, with no idea of waiting for anything. I could not help smiling, in spite of myself. Before Thomas, I had never realised how peremptory a baby would be or how strongly the current of life flowed in its small body. It swept everything else aside.

'A fine child,' said Mrs Iles. 'You are fortunate.'

'He is not mine. He is my brother.'

'Very fortunate. A child is a great blessing. She would have found it so.'

The woman was either deaf or pretending to be so. 'He is not mine!' I repeated, and the words came out too loud.

'I asked if she had children. She said not yet, but she had hopes. You are thinner than she. See where the ring slips on you.'

I twisted my ring back so the stone caught the light. It would always work its way towards my palm. Diner said he would have it altered for me but I did not want to part with it. Mrs Iles had noticed everything: it was her profession. She would easily read the swelling of breasts or belly. She would know so much that I did not dare to ask her. I thought of Lucie standing in the light with the dress flowing down her, and I turned my thoughts away.

'Sell the dress,' I said, and turned to the door.

16

I almost walked by without recognising him. There was nothing of him to be seen under a broad-brimmed hat and a long, heavy coat with its collar turned up. But the familiarity of the hat caught my attention. I knew it, surely. I turned, and the man turned too, looking back at me.

Of course. It was Will Forrest, hidden under Augustus's hat. And wearing Augustus's coat too, the one in which he tramped the length and breadth of England even when there was snow on the ground. What would he do without his coat? The thought of it made me feel an odd pang of tenderness for Augustus. He would be like a snail without its shell.

Mr Forrest looked at me, did not know me, looked again. I'd forgotten that I was also disguised, in Philo's shawl. I pulled back a fold so that he saw my face, and asked, 'Why are you out in the street? You should not take such a risk.'

'A man cannot stay indoors like a caged parrot.'

There were his eyes, full of light and humour.

'There will be nothing to smile about if you are caught,' I said, thinking of Hannah and Augustus and what might come to them if Mr Forrest were traced to their lodgings.

'I shan't be caught. I shall walk up to the Downs, take the air, smoke my pipe, and all anyone will see is a perambulating chimney. I am scarcely a man at all. Perhaps you will accompany me?'

'Does Augustus know you are out?'

'He was not at home himself. Fortunately he left his coat behind: he said the day was too mild for him to wear it. It houses me completely. I may as well be indoors, for all that can be seen of me.'

It was true that there was no trace of his red hair and under the hat his skin might have been dark or pale.

'You should keep your collar turned up,' I said. 'I thought that you would be in the Highlands by now.' I was already falling into step beside him. As I did so I pulled the shawl forward around my face again. Thomas squawked. For a moment I had forgotten his hunger. 'Oh no, he is crying. I cannot come with you.'

'What have you got there?'

'A baby. What did you think?'

'A cat, perhaps. I've known girls to be very fond of cats.'

'But not to the extent of walking in the streets with a cat in a shawl. I must go. He is about to scream.'

He peered at me. 'I can see nothing. Are you certain it is a baby you have there? Is it yours?'

I could scarcely feed Thomas fast enough when I got home. I was making the pap thicker now, on Mr Orchard's instructions, and between mouthfuls I offered him sips of warm milk from his own cup. Philo knelt on the floor beside me. The baby's greed made her laugh and she rocked on her heels like the child she was. She liked nothing better than to watch Thomas with his pap.

'You going give your Philo a little smiley, bab? No, you thinks of nought but your stomach till 'tis cram-full. I never seen such a greedy-guts. Look at you there, mambling like a pig in clover.' She pinched his cheek and he kicked in ecstasy as the spoon came to his lips. 'Shall I mix some more?'

'You'd better. But is it good for him to eat so much, Philo?'

'Course it is.'

She couldn't wait to get her hands on him again. 'I'll change him,' she said when the baby's appetite was sated. She stripped off his clothes and kissed his thighs, his knees, his feet, caring nothing for the sour ammoniac smell that came from his napkin. 'I could eat you up, I could.'

'Philo . . . can I leave him with you, just for an hour or so?'

'Course you can! Me'n Thomas'll make the bread, won't we, bab? I prop him up, see, in that chair, and he watches me.'

'Mind he doesn't slip down. He rolled right over this morning.'

'You won't slip down, will you, not the way your Philo'll cuddy you up. You'll be good as gold till that bread's in the oven and my floor's scrubbed. Then we'll have us a little kick on the bed, shall us? Shall us?'

Her sharp little face was soft as she heaved him up into her arms. She was still scrawny, Philo, although she had enough to eat now. It couldn't make up for what she'd missed. Mammie used to say that from the look of her Philo must have been half starved in her infancy. Her teeth were bad and she'd had two pulled since she'd been with me. Often her face swelled up with the toothache, and an east wind made her cry when the pain was bad.

'You need a new shawl, Philo. There is not enough warmth in this one for winter.'

She glanced up at me. I thought I would never forget that look: sceptical, pitying, because I talked of things that neither I nor anyone else would change.

'I'll buy you another,' I said. 'There are three cold months still to come.'

She turned away, saying nothing. I saw that she did not really believe me. I ought to have said nothing until I had the shawl in my hand ready to give her. I would buy her one second-hand that had no holes in it and would be thicker and better than what she had.

'Make sure you don't lay him down flat after all that food,' I said instead, but she still pretended not to hear. She was vain enough in her way, Philo. She thought she knew better than anyone when it came to Thomas. But I could trust her. She would lug Thomas about for hours sooner than let his stomach gripe him. 'I'm off now,' I said. 'I shan't be long.'

I don't know what Philo thought of me going out a second time with her shawl over my head. She was very quick. I'd asked her to call me Lizzie when we were alone together, but she never once made the mistake of calling me so before Diner. If Diner came home early and asked where I was she would say, 'Miz Tre'vant's gone up Miz Rougemont's,' in a way that made him complain that she was an imbecile.

I wore my stout boots. Pattens were all very well for the paved streets, but I was going over the fields. It was mizzling and although it was only two o'clock the light was already fading. The wind had changed, blowing colder as I hurried on to the Downs. Very likely he had turned already and gone home, I told myself, but I did not believe it. He was a poet. If the wind howled and the rain drenched him, so much the better. He could scarcely hope for a thunderstorm at this time of the year, but he would go to the highest point where he might gaze outwards at the weather blowing in from the west against the chasm of the Gorge. He would want to see everything. He would watch the boats beating their way upriver, and the white posts that glimmered through the dusk, marking the towpath far below. He might catch sight of a peregrine folding its wings for a dive. He would stand and face the immensity of dark, leafless forest opposite. I followed the footpath, climbing swiftly as the rain blew in my face.

I had not been mistaken. He stood with his back to me and did not hear me as I approached across the grass. A sheep ran away, baaing; he still did not turn. I came so close that I could see how the heavy wool of Augustus's coat was beaded all over with drops of rain. I smelled tobacco smoke. He was indeed as black and straight as a chimney and quite unrecognisable. I slowed my steps, wondering how long he had been standing there and what his thoughts were. Perhaps he was composing. I ought not to disturb him.

I moved into his sightline without speaking. Philo's shawl was rain-wet and its colours darkened. He might not even know me. I went to the wooden railing that looked over the Gorge, and stared down on the drifts of rain that shuddered as the wind took them. I thought I could smell the sea, far off as it was. I leaned forward and peered to my right, where Wales lay.

A hand came on my shoulder and grasped it tight. I swung round.

'It's you again,' he said. 'I thought it was. But for a moment I doubted myself. I feared that you were a girl in trouble, come to cast herself away. That shawl is a very common pattern.'

'I am only looking at the rain.'

'Yes,' he said quickly. 'It is beautiful. And yet there is no one besides ourselves to admire it. People think a great deal of sunsets and sunrises, but this is what I like better: a winter's day, all the tints suppressed, wind and sky and rain. Your shawl is all over raindrops: aren't you cold?'

'A little.'

'And here I am so handsomely set up inside your stepfather's coat. Perhaps we should make an exchange.'

'Philo's shawl would not cover you.'

'Who is Philo?'

'The servant girl.'

'Who does she love?'

'No one, I hope, apart from baby Thomas.'

'Because *philo*, you know, is Greek for love. *Philo-anthropia* – φιλανθρωπια – philanthropy: love of humanity. *Anthropos*, you know, does not indicate the male sex.'

'I have never learned Greek, Mr Forrest.'

'I beg your pardon. I am a fool. I like to talk about words.'

'So do most of the people I know.'

'But not you?'

'No. Most of the time I would rather scrub a floor.'

'But you do not do so, I think. I am told that you are married to a man who makes his fortune from speculative building.'

'There are no fortunes to be made nowadays. Philo and I do all the work of the house.'

He took hold of my hand, as he had done before, and scrutinised it, turning it over. I saw how red my knuckles were. There was a brown, healing burn on the back of my hand.

'I divine that you are telling the truth,' he said. 'A few days in gloves, an application of white lead and vinegar and all these marks will be gone.'

'And then where will be your powers of divination?' I asked him.

He swung out his arm and hurled his pipe over the edge of the gorge. We watched it turn and tumble until it disappeared.

'I am glad I came out,' he said. 'I have smoked myself back into my senses. I wonder why it is that women do not smoke?'

'They do in the rookeries of St Giles.'

'What do you know about St Giles?'

'I have been there with my mother. I was ten or eleven, I think.'

'Strange choice of promenade.'

'No one molested us. I used to think that her cloak was magical, and when it spread around us both nothing could hurt us.'

'I should like to have such a cloak. She must have been a very remarkable woman.'

'That is what everyone says.'

'But you don't agree?'

'No. It sets her apart. She never thought herself remarkable.'

'She was too modest, perhaps.'

'She could not have lived in any other way.'

'You must miss her very much.'

Another shiver of rain crossed the vastness of the gorge. I stared outwards so as not to look at him. 'I am not yet sure that I can live without her,' I said, and as I had hoped and trusted, he made no reply.

Darkness was thickening in the abyss beneath me, grain by grain. I blinked and could no longer see the hills of Wales. He was right: it was more beautiful than summer, or at least, it suited my mood better. *The tints suppressed* ...

'Would you write about such a scene in your poems?' I asked.

'Perhaps. Does anyone live in that forest?'

'I believe not. Men work the stone quarries, but they go home at night.'

'I would not want to sleep there. God knows what comes out of those trees, after dark.'

'I must go home,' I said. Diner had had me followed once and an old shawl would not throw him off if he decided to track me again. 'You should go back, too. Even in that coat, it is better for you not to be out. Why have you not already left for the Highlands?'

'My ship has gone to Oporto instead, with a cargo of fifteen thousand empty bottles. They are promiscuous in their favours, these sea captains. He was to have taken me to Glasgow. Meanwhile Augustus believes I should stay where I am. I shall lie low enough, you may be sure of it. I would not risk his safety and Hannah's. You are soaked through, Mrs Tredevant. You should go home and scrub a floor to warm yourself.'

'You may call me Lizzie. You may also turn your hand to housework yourself, if you like. Hannah is old and rheumatic. She will do everything for you, because for her a poet who may be taken up for sedition is like Charles Edward to the Scots. But you must not let her exhaust herself.'

'Aha! I am ahead of you there. I swept out the kitchen this morning and laid the fire. I am an early riser. I write for two hours, lay the fire, eat my plate of porridge and it is still only seven o'clock. I am a passable cook, too, although so far I have not managed to persuade Hannah to let me cook the dinner. If she likes she may sit with her feet up like Queen Charlotte and I shall do everything. Although it must be admitted that Queen Charlotte had fifteen good reasons to sit on a sofa.'

'You are very unlike most of Augustus's friends.'

'I see that you have the wrong idea about poets. We are makers, you know. We do not sit about admiring words. We must seize hold of them and chisel at them until they do what we want. Or what the poem wants, perhaps – but that is another question. I am so glad to have met you, Miss Lizzie. I have been lonely.'

His eyes shone at me through the dusk and I did not believe a word of it. Such a man would never be alone, unless he chose.

17

Diner was home before me. I did not know it at first, because the house was dark and still. I left my boots to dry, hung up Philo's shawl, and then climbed the stairs to the attic. I paused outside the door and heard them: Philo's voice running up and down like a singer trying her scales, and Thomas's fat, convulsive laughter. They'd be lolling on the bed together, babbling nonsense, entirely happy. My eyes stung and I leaned against the wall. I would not disturb them. I went downstairs again, through the house that seemed tonight like a sketch of itself and not the real thing, as if at any moment the walls might dissolve away and leave us all to wake on a bare hillside.

He was in the drawing room, sitting by the unlit fire, immobile. One candle burned on the hearth. It was a kitchen candle in a rough holder that did not belong here. Much of the furniture had gone now, vanished as suddenly as it had appeared, as if it was no longer worthwhile to keep up appearances. There were no more buyers to impress. The sofa remained. It was our own: it had been a poor battered thing when Diner had picked it up, but I had stuffed its cavities with wool and stitched a cover out of a pair of old red curtains from Mrs Clumber's shop. I sat down.

'Is that you, Lizzie?' he asked, without turning his head.

'Of course. Shall I light the fire?'

'I'm not cold.'

It was damp and dreary enough outside, but I too was still warm from the walk home. He raised his head and I forced myself to hold his gaze steadily. I felt as if my conversation with Will was printed across my brow.

'Where have you been, Lizzie?'

'To market, and then to Mr Orchard's.'

'I have told you before that you must not be out in the dark unaccompanied.'

'It gets dark so early now.'

'All the more reason,' he said. 'But you do not listen, do you, Lizzie? You think that you know best. I tell you that your wanderings will get you into trouble. Are you listening to me now?'

'Yes.'

'Come here.'

I stepped to him reluctantly. He took both my hands and pulled me towards him. The light from the kitchen candle fell on me and left him in shadow.

'This is your house, Lizzie,' he said. 'I built it for you. And yet you are restless, as if you were still living in lodgings. What will it take to make you content?' He shook my wrists, not hard but so that I could feel the strength in his hands.

'I am content,' I said.

'Truly?'

'Indeed, I am.'

He was still gazing at me, but I could not see into his eyes. I looked straight ahead, letting the light of the candle dazzle me. At last, his fingers relaxed.

'Did I ever tell you, Lizzie, about the first house I built?'

'I don't think so.'

'It was at Horace Row. The building was complete and the cottages tenanted, but there was a scrap of land left. A poor piece. A triangle. They had miscalculated and could not complete the row, or so they thought. I looked at it closely and thought otherwise. You know where it is, down by the docks?'

'I think I do.'

'A row of cottages built for dock-workers. But better than many, even so. I did not have the money to purchase the land. I walked past it again and again and I calculated how it could be done.'

'A triangular house, you mean?'

'Almost. From the front it would look much the same as the others in the row, although it would be narrower. I would set the windows a little closer, and one of them would not be a window at all, but a painted sham, made to match. I saw how I could fit the design to the shape of the land and deceive the eye so that the row would look complete.'

He was relaxing now. He looked away to the side of him, as if he could still see that triangular house, the first he had made.

'So how did you get the land?' I asked. I would draw him on to safer ground, and keep him there.

'I went to the landlord with a proposition. By then I knew to a penny the rents he was getting from the row. I calculated exactly. If he would come in with me, I would bear the cost of building. He would not part with capital, and I had not expected it. We came to an agreement that I would have an interest in the completed building and the rent would be divided between us. He did not understand how much better off he would have been if he had paid me a fixed sum.'

'But how did you raise the money for the building?'

'I borrowed it, Lizzie, against the signed agreement for future rents. Two families live in each of those cottages. I called in favours – I had been in the trade for some years by then – and I built the best part of that house myself. When it was all done and the first tenants had moved in, the landlord tried to cheat me. My share of the rent was late on the first quarter day, and later the second. He told me that the tenants had not paid. It did not take me long to dissuade him from that course. When a man tries to hook your bread out of your mouth, you must close your teeth upon him. I had no further trouble. There you have it, Lizzie: the story of how your husband became a man of property. I borrowed again, and built again. My stock grew until the time that I could buy my own piece of land to build upon, and make my own profit. The rent from that cottage still comes to me on the nail.'

He spoke quietly, as if all this had happened long ago, and to another man.

'You are only thirty-six,' I said.

'I am no longer that young man who walked up and down Horace Row, making his calculations. I could not do it again. A man can do such things only once in his life, Lizzie. He can work until he convinces himself that he does not need sleep or food like other men. He cannot do them twice.'

'You will not have to.'

We were at ease now and my fear had ebbed away entirely. I lifted the candle to the mantelpiece so that I could see his face. What I noticed was the shabbiness of his shirt. It even had a tear in the sleeve. Now I looked closely, he was dishevelled all over. His hair not groomed, his face unshaven.

'You must have a better shirt than that. Wait.' I went out with the candle. It was quite dark now and shadows bulged and shrank on the walls as I went up to our bedroom. We still had the deal press where I kept our clean linen, and there was my sewing. I picked up one of his new shirts. I smoothed it over my arm, took the candle again and went downstairs to where Diner was sitting in the dark.

'We must have more light than this,' I said briskly. 'But first, please try on your new shirt.'

He looked up at me in surprise. 'What's this, Lizzie?'

'You know I was sewing new shirts for you, and here

is one of them.' I did not say that they should have all been finished months ago, but I'd had so much sewing to do for Thomas. 'Take off that old thing, it is only fit for rags.' I would sell it to Mrs Clumber. It might be worn but the linen was good.

He stood up obediently, unbuttoned the neck of his shirt, pulled it over his head and handed it to me. His hair was wild now. He looked quite unlike the Diner who was so measured, dark and stern, who walked with purpose and spoke because he had something to say. He was lost tonight. I folded his old shirt carefully. He did not like anything to be treated carelessly: we were alike in that. The new shirt had been laid away in paper and was uncreased. I shook it out and held it against him.

'I think it will be a good fit.'

He put it on, and I buttoned the small buttons at the chest and cuffs.

'Lift your arms,' I said, and watched how the shape held. 'How does it feel?'

He straightened his back and moved his shoulders. 'Good,' he said. 'Very good.'

'You will have half a dozen.'

'Very good, Lizzie.'

I saw that he was moved, and I said, 'You have given me so much.'

He gave an odd bark of laughter. 'So much! My poor Lizzie, you have no idea of our situation.'

'I think I have.'

'They will take the clothes from our backs, I warn you.'

'You mean, your creditors?'

'But I will fox them yet. I will not sit quiet and let them strip me of everything I have worked for all these years.'

'I know you will not.'

There was a tap at the door. It could only be Philo and I would have to answer her. I went over to the door quickly and opened it a little so that she would not see Diner standing there in his new shirt.

'What is it, Philo?'

She leaned against the door-jamb, clutching Thomas, who was wide awake and staring. A candlestick wobbled in her other hand. 'I got the bellyache so bad, I got to lie down.' Her face was covered with a sheen of sweat. She looked awful.

'Give Thomas to me. Come along, Philo, I'm taking you upstairs.'

The smell in the attic was terrible where she had voided her guts in the chamber pot. 'I'll clear this,' I said. 'Get into bed.'

I did not dare put Thomas down because I knew he would scream. I tucked him under one arm, took the chamber pot in my other hand and made my way down to the kitchen. We ought to have more light. We ought to have sconces on the walls. It was not safe, feeling my way in all this darkness. At the drawing-room door I made up my mind, set down the pot and opened the door. Diner was sitting by the cold fire again.

'You must hold Thomas,' I said to him. 'Philo is taken

ill. I must take care of her, but I shan't be long. If he cries, walk him up and down.'

I settled the baby on to him. Diner did not speak and Thomas stared up unblinkingly at the new face as I hurried from the room before he could cry.

The kitchen fire still glowed. I went out by the back door, threw the filth into the privy and cast a shovelful of ash after it. I swilled the pot with water from the pump and went back upstairs to Philo.

She lay on the bed holding her stomach and moaning.

'But you were all right when I came in,' I said to her. 'You were laughing with Thomas. When did this start?'

'I got to use the pot,' she said. I helped her out of bed and held her skirt clear while she voided herself again. 'I et pig cheek,' she muttered when she was lying flat again. 'Leave the pot.'

'Poor Philo.' The slops were half liquid and the smell made me gag. I fetched her another pot from our room and emptied the filth again. There was no sound from the drawing room. A third time Philo clambered out of bed, trembling all over, and voided herself. Afterwards she lay flat, exhausted, while I sponged her face. I fetched her clean water and she sipped a little then said: 'Thomas.'

'He's with Diner.'

'God alive.'

I sat beside her for a while. I thought she was asleep until she began to writhe and moan again, clutching her stomach. This time she vomited. Again I carried it away; again I listened at the drawing-room door and there was still no sound from Thomas.

'It's all out now,' said Philo, without opening her eyes, when I came back with the clean pot. I picked up her hand. It was clammy and it flopped back on the blanket when I released it. She lay still, no longer moaning. I sponged her face and hands again, and then thought of the lavender water in my room. There was a little left. I ran down for it.

'This will make you feel better,' I said. I bent over Philo and dabbed her temples with the lavender water, then her wrists. Philo's nostrils dilated. She loved any scent: she always sniffed when I had rubbed rosewater into my hair.

'No one ever done that for me,' she muttered, and then she was asleep. I waited for a while, but she was right. It was all out of her now, whether it was the pig's cheek she'd eaten that had made her ill, or something else. The pot was by her bed and she had water. I could leave her.

'He cried,' said Diner when I came back into the drawing room. 'I walked up and down with him.'

Thomas was fast asleep, sprawled face down across Diner's lap with his shawl spread over him. Diner did not know how to gather him close, as a woman would, but nevertheless he had soothed him.

'I'm afraid he has rumpled the shirt you made me,' he said.

'No matter, I can iron it. Philo is asleep now. We must have the cradle in our room tonight, Diner.'

He smiled faintly. 'Do you think I am going to put the child out in the rain?'

'Of course not! You got him to sleep as well as I could have done.'

'He twitches like a puppy. I suppose he dreams.'

'He dreams of food,' I said, and smiled because I was so glad that for once Thomas did not have to be hidden away in the attic like a secret. But I had gone too far.

'I did not want him here, Lizzie,' said Diner, without anger but with a seriousness that I could not ignore. 'He must go back to Augustus.'

'But not now,' I said. 'Not yet.' I lifted the baby to me. He shuddered at the change, but did not wake. Diner was looking straight at me.

'It is you I want for my wife, Lizzie,' he said. 'Not a creature broken down by childbearing.' He spoke as if he could see that woman in front of him, and I wondered who she was. It seemed as if anything could be said or thought, with Thomas in my lap, the cold hearth and the light of one candle burning down. I knew that his parents had died of the putrid fever before he was ten, and that he had travelled from the north of England to Cornwall, to be taken in by an uncle.

'Had you brothers and sisters?' I asked.

'There were eight of us.'

'Where did they all go?'

'Three died with my parents. The others went to relations. We were scattered and I have not seen any of them since I left Lancashire. They will have taken other names, as I took my uncle's.'

'But you could find them.'

'They would no longer be my brothers and sisters, even if I found them. They would be strangers now.'

He spoke so definitely that I did not like to pursue it, in spite of my curiosity. It occurred to me that we were now having the conversations we should have had long ago, before we married. My mother had not pressed him for information. It was a point of honour with her: that I was independent and should make my own decisions on my own grounds. I suppose she wanted to do the opposite of what her own parents had done, but it struck me now that there might have been a compromise. Diner had seen his parents die, and three of his siblings. He had left his home and all that he knew. We had been ignorant of this, because we were too scrupulous to ask.

'Do you know, Lizzie,' he said, 'I cannot remember their names. Only Bessie. And I can see her outline, but not her face. It is the same with all of them.'

'It is natural, I suppose, after so long,' I said carefully, although my heart was squeezed in my breast. I did not like to ask him if Bessie had been one of the three who died.

'I used to wonder, when I was working in my uncle's yard, why I had lived and they had not. But there is no reason in any of it.'

Thomas was fast asleep and his warm damp heaviness pressed into me. He smelled of new bread, and salt, and milk. He anchored me. As long as I held him I could not float away into the darkness.

After a while Diner stirred and said, as if continuing a conversation he had been having with me in the silence: 'You would never think evil of me, would you, Lizzie?'

'No.'

'Or be afraid of me?'

A pause came, longer than I intended. The truth was that there were moments when I feared him. I had feared him tonight, when he seized my wrists and held them tight. It was not something I thought about or wished to feel: indeed, I tried not to think of it. But my body prickled and would not settle.

'Of course I would never think evil of you,' I said. I could not stop thinking of Lucie's dress, and how she had ordered it, paid for it but gone to France without collecting it or leaving any message with Mrs Iles. And she had left her ring behind. She had twisted her ring on her finger, as I did now, and never thought that one day it would go to another woman.

A little later we went up to Philo's attic and Diner lifted the cradle from beside her bed without disturbing her. He carried it downstairs and set it up in the slip of a room that was to be our dressing room one day, when it was fitted out. There was no door, so I would be able to hear Thomas perfectly, but he would be out of sight. One day we would do this for our own baby, I thought, in spite of what Diner had said. I could have a child without growing haggard and losing my hair. I could have a child without dying. But Diner did not want a child. He would be jealous of any child from my body, even though it would be his own child too.

'It's only for tonight,' said Diner. He caught me to him and held me in a grip that stilled me.

'Yes,' I said, 'only for tonight,' and I rubbed my face against his neck and felt his pulse jump under my lips.

18

Philo was not well enough to work for several days, and so I had a great deal to do. Thomas came everywhere with me as I went to market, cooked and did as much cleaning as I could. I washed Thomas's linen, but there was no time for the rest.

I was glad of the work. It stilled the rushing of my thoughts, and if Thomas would not settle in his cradle I tied him into my shawl and carried him with me. He was quite content then, and never cried. The thought of having to live without him frightened me. Diner would change his mind, I told myself again. Thomas would become ours, as he had already become mine. He would be the eldest of our children.

When I went to bed I fell asleep almost at once. Diner was never home until very late. He would come in silently, while I was sleeping, and sometimes I would rouse later to hear him moving about. I think that he slept very little during those days. The less progress that could be made on the terrace, the more hours he spent at Grace's Buildings. I no longer wondered what he was doing because I knew that he, like me, was busying himself furiously in order not to think about the fears that rose up as soon as we were still.

One day as I hurried home in the winter gloom I saw our terrace without knowing it, in the way that sometimes you may see a dear friend in the street before recognising her, and discover features that familiarity blots out at once. My house stood among roofless ruins. The terrace was not rising to perfection. It was falling away. The scale of Diner's dream came to me as if for the first time, and I saw the scale of the failure too. Who would buy here now? Who would look at this place and desire it?

The news from France darkened. I thought of how Augustus and Hannah had greeted the early days of Revolution like children waking to a June morning of brilliant sunshine. It had not lasted. Clouds had come, a sharp wind and rain. Even Hannah, though she still approved of everything that was done, had lost her appetite for it. 'None of us has ever lived through such times,' she said, but not in triumph now. I thought I detected in her voice a certain apprehension, as if she did not know how to measure the forces that had now been unleashed. But the people could not be wrong. Their instincts would show them the true path from oppression to liberty.

It was Will Forrest whom Hannah cared for now, when she was not thinking of Mammie. Perhaps the two of them were bound together in her mind and to cook for Will or wash his linen was not so very distinct from doing it for Mammie. To the rest of the living world around her she had become indifferent. A few days earlier I'd seen her walking slowly through the market, and she was not the Hannah I knew, but an old woman. Her lips were moving and her brow was knitted with anxiety, as if there was something she must remember and she could not, no matter how many times she repeated it. She did not notice me. My brisk, raw-boned, upright Hannah with her scoldings and her passions had vanished, and it felt as if a tree had fallen, letting in such a flood of sky that my eyes could not bear it. I hurried away without greeting her. When I reached the cheese stall I turned and she was staring after me. I didn't think that she had recognised me, but a wash of shame made my skin burn in spite of the chill of the morning.

By Thursday Philo was still weak but able to take care of Thomas again. I took him upstairs to her and turned to the neglected housework. Dust from the building came in everywhere, gritting underfoot. It was a bright morning, and the low winter sun shone in and showed up the dirt. Even though the house was new it seemed to breathe out dust through its pores every night, no matter how hard Philo or I had worked the day before.

I rolled up my sleeves and wrapped myself in an apron. Augustus and Hannah said that I was getting

thin but I had never felt stronger. It was good to act
and not to think. I stoked up the range, filled the boiler
and began to sweep. As soon as the water was hot I
would scrub the scullery and kitchen floors.

I was scouring the deal table with lye when there
was a ring on the upstairs bell. I was not expecting
any visitor. Perhaps, after all this time, it was another
of those prospective purchasers who would never buy
but liked to linger over their refusals? I was sick of
them. It seemed that they did it to provoke us, and
we were helpless to force them into action. I would
ignore the bell. Besides, it would not help if a buyer
found me scrubbing out my own kitchen. We must
look prosperous and confident, never desperate to sell
at all costs. Diner had impressed that upon me. The bell
didn't ring again, and so I crossed to the window to
glimpse the caller leaving. The area window darkened,
and before I could step back the figure of a middle-aged
woman in a travelling cloak came down the steps. She
was looking in. She had seen me. There was nothing
for it: I wiped my hands on my apron and went to open
the door.

'Je cherche Monsieur Tredevant,' she said, without
any greeting to me. She took me for a servant, naturally
enough, dressed as I was and with my hair bundled into
an old cap.

I recognised her language although she spoke too
quick for me. I knew the word *Monsieur*. I scrabbled
through my mind for the French which Hannah had
struggled to teach me. 'Il est ...' What was 'out' in

French? I could not remember, so I waved at the distance beyond us. 'Il est . . . out,' I said.

Her black eyes fixed me impatiently. Clearly she thought me a fool as well. 'Je suis la parraine de Lucie, sa femme,' she said.

The name of Lucie went through me, but the rest of it meant nothing and I could not answer. The woman clicked her tongue in exasperation.

'Your master wife. I am *parraine*,' she said loudly, in the way one speaks to a foreigner. She pushed her face into mine and I became indignant. We were in England. It was for her to speak English. How should I know what she meant? I had never paid attention in Hannah's French classes, and she had given up when I was thirteen. But by chance I seized upon the word I needed.

'Lucie . . . morte,' I said.

She rolled her eyes at me in angry scorn. 'Ah bon, vous parlez donc français,' she said, as if I had been trying to deceive her, and off she rattled at top speed: 'Bien sûr qu'elle est morte, c'est pour ça que je suis venue ici. Je suis de Bordeaux, et depuis très longtemps une amie de la famille Ribault, mais j'ai dû quitter la France. Oui, j'ai dû quitter mon pays à cause de ces ordures qui haïssent les gens honnêtes. Bourgeoise! Moi, je suis propriétaire d'une petite chapellerie, ou bien je l'étais jusqu'à ce que ces diables aient rendu impossible le travail des gens honnêtes. Et si je suis bourgeoise, j'en suis fière. C'est la bourgeoisie qui soutient la société.' She glared at me but I could not imagine why. Her words reminded me of the speeches that Augustus liked to make as he walked about the room, only in the case of this woman I could not grasp more than one word out of ten. 'Je suis arrivée à Bath il y a quelques semaines, et tout à coup je me suis rendue compte que Bristol n'est pas trop loin de Bath. Et puisque le père de Lucie ne peut pas venir voir le tombeau de sa fille . . . Son pauvre père, il m'a dit plusieurs fois: *Si jamais tu arrives en Angleterre, ma chère Armande, tu vas visiter le tombeau où repose notre mignonne. Tu vas y placer quelques fleurs.* Et voilà ce que je vais faire!'

She flung back her head at me in a sort of triumph. 'Le tombeau!' she almost shouted. 'Le tombeau de Lucie! Il faut absolument que je le visite!'

The language slipped past me and made no sense. Besides, I did not want to hear her. She was talking about Lucie. She was connected to Lucie, to Lucie's family.

She was sweating. There were beads of moisture on her upper lip and I smelled her emotion. I could not dismiss her: she was real. She was a middle-aged woman, heated and distressed. She had searched the streets of a strange city in a strange country, and she would not give up now.

'You are a friend of Lucie,' I said slowly, hoping that she would understand. She threw up her hands.

'Lucie! Yaise! Lucie. Where . . . ?' and she broke into a furious pantomime, crossing her arms over her breast, closing her eyes then snapping them open again to glare at me. '*Where?*'

How I wished that Diner would come. He would understand her perfectly. It seemed that this woman did not even know that Lucie was dead, if she was asking where she was. And yet of course she must know, since Lucie had died at home, in France. I must have misunderstood.

I heard a sound from upstairs. A heavy door, closing. The front door. It must be Diner, because Philo would have come down the outside steps. It was Diner, as if my need of him had brought him home.

'Wait!' I said, and hurried to the kitchen stairs. I picked up my skirts, looked back at her, gestured again: 'Wait!' and ran to fetch him.

He was in the hall, taking off his coat.

'I am so glad you are back.' I went behind him and helped to draw his arms out of the sleeves. He liked such attentions, and besides now he could not see my face. 'There's a woman downstairs, a strange woman. It is something about Lucie.'

'Lucie!'

'Yes. She is French, I think. She's speaking French. You know how poorly I understand it.'

'My God,' he said, but quietly and as if to himself, and turned to face me. 'She is looking for me, you say.' His pupils contracted. He looked inwards, barely seeing me. I waited, but he said nothing more and did not move.

'She's waiting downstairs.'

'She spoke to you? She asked you questions? What did you say?'

'I am sorry. It was so stupid – I could not follow her. You know I don't speak French; or only a very little. I was cleaning the kitchen. She thought I was a servant.'

He had lost his colour. Even to hear Lucie's name distressed him.

'You had better go down,' I said. 'I don't want her to come up here.'

'No.' He reached for his coat again. 'I will see her. I may have to go out again directly, Lizzie.'

I went to the top of the kitchen stairs. I could hear them talking, her voice sharp and high, his deeper. I could make out enough to know that they were speaking French, and that I could not follow any of it. Their conversation sounded familiar, as if they knew each other. I pictured the woman, her black eyes snapping, the smell of her sweat, the dark shadow of hair on her upper lip.

After what seemed a long time, I heard the area door open and close. I ran through to the drawing room and peered out of the window. I could see them making their way along the rough terrace that would one day be paved. They were close together. She was holding his arm and they were still talking. It seemed to me in that instant that he was disappearing from me forever, into his own past.

An hour later, he was home again. I asked no questions, but for once he was expansive.

'A strange business,' he said, pulling off his boots.

'She is a friend of Lucie's family. I knew her, of course. She had a little millinery shop where Lucie first learned her craft. She is staying in Bath, but she intends to set up in London.'

'Why did she come here? Does she want your help?'

'No.' He looked at me directly. 'She wanted to see the place where Lucie lived. I suppose it is very natural.'

'So you showed her?' I realised that I did not even know myself where Diner had lived with Lucie.

'Yes.'

Everything was explained. It was sad, and unsurprising, yet I could hardly bear it. First Lucie's dress, and now this.

'I suppose if it had not been for the Revolution,' I said, 'she would never have come to England.'

'A great many things would have been different. She has had to leave her home and now she must make a new life in London. I don't doubt her capacity for it, but she will have neither the time nor the money to be visiting here. We shan't see her again, Lizzie. Don't let it trouble you.'

'I wish I had paid more attention in Hannah's French classes. I could barely understand a word she said.'

'I should not care if I never heard another word of French,' he said, and he came over to me and took me in his arms. I felt then what I had not seen: he was trembling slightly. His arms went round me and held me close. 'It is you I love, Lizzie. Only you.'

'But you were happy with Lucie,' I said into his

shoulder. I had never dared to say such a thing before and I had to force the words out of my tightened throat.

'At first,' he said. 'We were not so well suited, as time went on. There, Lizzie. Does that satisfy you?' He pushed me away from him to look down into my face.

'She is dead,' I said.

'You are serious,' he said, touching my cheek. 'I like that in you. Lucie was always smiling.'

'She was happy with you, I suppose.'

'One may smile too often,' he said, and then shook his head a little, pulling me to him so that I no longer saw his face.

Later that day I took Thomas to see Hannah. He needed the air, and I wrapped him up against the cold. Mammie had always taken me out regardless of the weather. She believed a child should grow up stirring and hardy and that there was no difference in this respect between girls and boys. I would trot along beside her, holding her hand, while we walked for miles together. Mammie had no family to disapprove of her, and neither had I now. I would follow her pattern in bringing up Thomas.

It did not do to think of her. I could feel the exact pressure of her fingers around mine, and feel the swish of her skirts. I could hear my own footsteps too, as my stout little boots clumped over the cobbles beside her.

Ten times a day it stopped me like a bolt into my chest: that she was no longer here. That she would never be here. That I might walk and walk and yet I would never again come home to her. I had left her to marry Diner but I had never thought that she might leave me so soon. If I had known it, what would I have done? I did not want to think about it. She had brought me up to work and to walk freely and to know my own mind and now here I was in a world that wanted those qualities very little. Diner loved me but he kept half his life apart from me.

Will Forrest was sitting on a stood beside Hannah, helping her to wind her wool.

'I am knitting a coat for Thomas,' she said. She looked more cheerful than I had seen her for a long time. The pair of them were cosy together, sitting by the fire. I wondered if Will would ever leave. He seemed a fixture here.

'How is Augustus?' I asked.

'He has gone to Bath with Caroline Farquhar. He is to address a meeting there.'

'Hannah,' I said, 'what does *parraine* mean in French?'

'It means godmother. You should know that, Lizzie, if you had attended to your lessons at all.'

Lucie's godmother . . . Diner must have known that, and yet he'd called her a family friend. And that other word, the one she had repeated so vehemently: could I remember it correctly?

'What about *tombeau*, Hannah? What does that mean?'

'Your pronunciation has improved, I will say. Perhaps you should take up your study again.'

'I am only repeating what someone said to me. What does it mean?'

'Tomb. The words are very similar, Lizzie. If you think about it, you will be able to make them out.'

I kept my voice as level as I could. 'Yes,' I said. 'I expect I will.'

She had been asking about Lucie's tomb. Perhaps she wanted to tell Diner what they had done, what stone they had chosen, what words. More likely, she wanted him to pay for it. It was expensive to set up a stone, and perhaps they had chosen an elaborate memorial? Diner would not have wanted to tell me about it.

'How long am I to stand here like a lay-figure?' asked Will Forrest, holding out his hands with the skein of wool between them.

'Have a little patience,' chided Hannah, as if he had been her son. He was so very much at home. 'And, Lizzie, please keep that child from dribbling over my wool.'

Will's eyes slid sideways to me and he pulled a comical face. Why should I think of Lucie, who was dead and gone? I would not.

'I should like to read some of your poems,' I said.

'Should you really? People very often say that without meaning it, so I am on my guard. You are under no poetry-obligation to me, Miss Lizzie.'

'I mean it,' I said. 'As long as you do not get Augustus to read it aloud. I prefer to read to myself.'

'Augustus has been very good to me,' he said with sudden seriousness. Colour rose in his white cheeks: it fascinated me that a man should be so fair, and show every feeling. 'He is a good man.'

'I know,' I said, and in that moment I did know it. All my irritations with Augustus fell away and I saw only his kindness and dogged persistence in what he believed to be right. 'But even so,' I whispered, trusting to Hannah's deafness, 'do you not think, Mr Forrest, that for all his fine qualities Augustus does in some respects resemble that valuable creature, the sheep?'

A spurt of laughter escaped him. 'You should not make such jokes while I am winding wool,' he whispered back. I could not help laughing, too.

'Shall we venture upon another chimney perambulation, Miss Lizzie?' he asked. For a moment I could not think what he meant. My mind was too much distracted. But as soon as I realised, I knew I would go. Hannah had not heard a word. I said nothing, but gave the slightest of nods.

'Tomorrow, then,' he murmured. 'At two o'clock in the same place.'

I had no excuse; I knew my stupidity as soon as I agreed.

I went home with Thomas, fed him and laid him in his cradle to sleep. Philo was up and stirring, but there was no sign of Diner. I had not expected him to be at home. I must prepare our dinner, make bread, order coals and candles, clear out the grate in the drawing room, riddle the range, enquire about setting up a drying rack in the kitchen because I was sure we could not afford the washerwoman for more than another month – there was so much to do that I could not think where to begin. It will be easier when Philo can work again, I told myself, but for a moment my spirit quailed. It would go on and on like this, with Diner always absent, or seizing me fiercely to himself at night, driving himself into me until I wanted to cry out with pain, and then barely speaking to me the next morning. Thomas would always cry and want feeding and the house would grow dirty as soon as I had finished cleaning. How could it not, when every time we stepped out of the house we brought in mud from the unmade road and pavement? After the heavy rain of the autumn we were living in a swamp, a quagmire, not a street. The potholes bubbled with reddish-brown water.

I went over to the glass in the hall. Soon, no doubt, that too would be gone. My sour weariness did not show on my face: instead, it was a blank. I tried a smile.

'*There*, that's better,' Mammie would say when she knelt down to wipe the tears from my face after a fall. She'd smile, and I'd believe her and stop crying. I would come to her with a bloody knee or a friend's spite and she would change the weather for me.

Lucie was always smiling. I would have thought any man would be pleased to see his wife smile, since it showed that she was happy. But he had not said it with any pleasure. A week ago I would have been glad to hear him speak critically of Lucie, but now I was uneasy and did not know why. I felt as if I were blind, feeling my way into a labyrinth by a thread. I'd asked him if they were happy, and he'd replied: *At first.*

The truth was that when I first met Diner I had been so mad to have him that I had seen nothing else and would have listened to no one. Mammie had let me have my way, because of her belief in my freedom.

I leaned forward until my breath misted the glass.

'Are you happy now?' I whispered.

19

I was determined to buy Philo's shawl, and see the doubt fade from her face when she saw it. The next morning I hurried to Mrs Clumber's with Thomas tied close to me. I never entered her shop without a pang of distaste. It smelled musty and there was dirt in her fingernails as she picked over the clothes.

'I am an honest woman and I run an honest business,' she often said, forgetting that honest people rarely find it necessary to insist upon the fact. She cheated me, as she cheated everyone, but her stock was good. Some genius forewarned her of death or ruin and she would be first at the house, offering to relieve its bewildered inhabitants of gowns and shawls at the fairest price in the city.

Thomas had fallen asleep. I looked down at his perfect eyelids, the line of them so delicate that they seemed sealed, not closed. He stirred and his face shivered, then back he went into sleep again. I wondered what babies dreamed of, I wondered what he saw in his dream.

'Put him down here,' said Mrs Clumber, and she gestured at a pile of old nightshirts.

'He isn't heavy.'

'Please yourself.'

She had bricked up two downstairs windows to save tax, and the third was small and dirty. She did not clean it, I think, because she did not want her customers to see too much. The shawls were piled by the counter. I started to search through them, but she pressed in and picked out three with a practised flick of the hands. What hands they were. Quick and strong, without an instant's hesitation in them. She would make an excellent pickpocket. She spread the three shawls over her counter, and her eyes glinted at me sidelong.

'I see you like the blue,' she said. I hadn't done more than glance at it, but she was right. The shade was delicate as mist, and I liked it very well. But I thought it might seem dull to Philo. She was drawn to colour like a bee, although the only bright thing she owned was a knot of scarlet ribbon I had given her, to pin to her hat on Sundays.

'Or the brown is very serviceable,' Mrs Clumber went on, and held out a fold for me to feel. It was good, thick wool and not too much worn, but it was rough to the touch. I would not want to wear it.

'Serviceable indeed,' I said. 'How much?'

'Five and six,' she said. I allowed my eyes to widen but said nothing. I lifted the shawl again, to feel the weight of it. It smelled as if an animal had slept on it.

Still holding it, I bent my head so she would not see my eyes slide to the third shawl. It was green and purple, boldly checked. The colours of those heather hills Mammie had described to me, from her visit to the Highlands of Scotland.

'The brown is priced too high,' I said. 'Are there others you have not yet shown me?'

She bent to rummage through the pile and quickly I reached to feel the texture of the third shawl. It was much finer than the brown, soft and dense. It lacked weight but I thought it would be just as warm.

Mrs Clumber pulled up an armful of drab broadcloth. I looked with interest, asked her to spread it out fully, felt the fabric between thumb and finger and enquired about the price. There was a hole where the moth had been at it.

'This one is a very nice quality of article, and fresh in today.'

Fresh, indeed. It had been stripped off the back of a dying woman for sure.

'Yes, it is good cloth.'

'Superfine broadcloth. You won't find better.'

'Well, I will call in another day,' I said, half turning to go.

'You have not looked at this one,' she said, shaking out the green and purple shawl. 'I had it from a Scottish lady.'

'Too bright for a servant,' I said indifferently. 'Such colours may do very well in Scotland.'

She frowned. 'The blue, then. You liked the blue.'

'For myself perhaps, but I am not in need of a shawl.'

She was pushing the green and purple shawl away, as if she wanted to get rid of it. Very likely she'd had it on her hands for some time. How Philo would love those colours.

'I can offer you this at a very moderate price,' she said.

'It would have to be moderate indeed to tempt me.'

'Five shillings.'

'Too much for a servant's shawl. Surely there is another in that pile which you have not shown me?'

She glanced at the heap of shawls. For once, her true opinion showed on her face. There was nothing there for which she'd given more than ninepence.

'Four and six-three,' she said. 'I can't go lower.'

'It is not worth more than four shillings. I should have to have it dyed before she could wear it.'

'Call it four and thrippence and have done.'

I kept my face hesitant, as if I thought she was cheating me. We were there now. She would not go lower, although I doubted that she had paid a quarter of that, in some job lot of loss. I caught my lower lip between my teeth.

'The girl must have something to wear, I suppose,' I said. Mrs Clumber took my money, tied the shawl with string and bundled it into my arms. I took it reluctantly, as if I was already thinking better of the bargain.

'I may have some shirts for you soon,' I said to encourage her. God knew we'd all be buying our clothes from Ma Clumber if the times didn't improve.

*   *   *

I hurried home, eager to give the shawl to Philo, picturing her face when she saw it. But I was wrong. When I held it out, her face remained blank. I cut the string and the shawl spilled out of my hands.

'Take it, Philo, spread it out,' I said. 'Let me see how it looks on you.'

The soft material glowed on Philo's lap. The purple was true heather and the green was like a field with dew on it. Such colours! Philo fingered the shawl, head bent, but she did not say a word.

'Do you not like it?' I asked foolishly.

Philo's fingers tightened. She said nothing and suddenly I felt ashamed. She did not trust me – and why should she? She would not show any liking for fear the shawl would be taken from her. It was what she had learned from earliest childhood and she would not easily unlearn it, quick as she was. How sharp her face was! She had lost weight with her illness. I smiled as if the matter was finished and began to untie my own shawl. Thomas was warm and damp and still fast asleep.

'Well,' I said, 'I must go out soon. Are you well enough to look after Thomas?'

'Course I am.'

'He'll want his pap when he wakes. Remember not to let him gobble, or he'll get a bellyache.'

She nodded. 'He's always a good boy for me,' she said proudly.

'I know. You're very good with him, Philo.'

She nodded as if it was no more than her due.

'I can always have the shawl dyed brown, if you don't like the colours,' I said casually.

'No!' she exclaimed, and her fingers gripped the folds. 'I never had such colour.'

'It will suit you, I think. Go and put it on upstairs, look in the glass in the drawing room before Thomas wakes.'

Her waxen face flushed as she gathered the shawl to her and went. How shabby her gown was, too. She ought to have a new one, but that would cost six shillings or more. It would have to wait. I listened and thought I heard her feet tapping up and down, up and down, as she paraded before the looking glass.

It was bright now, cold and windless. I thought of Will Forrest and his afternoon walk. Would he really steal Augustus's coat again? Yes, I thought he would. I pictured him buttoning the coat to his chin and putting on that absurdly wide hat. He would open the front door to look up and down the street. He would hurry along with his hat pulled over his face, and glance behind him to see if he was followed. Nothing could be more obvious. He would go to the same place. He would not wait for me, precisely, but he would linger.

When Philo came down she had taken off the shawl and put it away. She said nothing of how she had liked her reflection, but she hung about me. I gave her Thomas and busied myself with clearing the pots from the side of the sink.

'Did you buy it thinking of me?' she asked hoarsely, to my back.

'Yes,' I said, rattling the pots.

'Go careful, miss, you'll chip 'em!'

'*Lizzie*, remember,' I said. 'There's no one here but ourselves.'

'I forget,' she said.

'We shall need more milk for Thomas's pap. Can you fetch it?'

'I'll take the bab, case he wakes up and you're working.'

'If you're sure it won't be too much for you.'

She glanced at me with scorn. Too much! What kind of a soft thing did I think she was?

'I'll get my shawl,' she said, and clattered off up the kitchen stairs. When she came down again the shawl was bundled around her and folds hung to her heels. Her thin face poked out warily.

'Philo, take it off a moment. Let me show you how to arrange it.'

She looked at me suspiciously but let me double it and tie the ends behind.

'There, and now you can easily hold Thomas and keep your hands free. You look lovely, Philo. I knew it would suit you.'

She ducked her head and smiled.

20

I waited a few minutes after they had gone and then I fetched Philo's old shawl, folded it over my head so that my face was hidden, and went up the area steps. It was such a beautiful afternoon. I breathed the cold air deeply and watched my breath fan out in puffs of white. There were two men working a pulley outside the end house, lifting slabs of Portland stone. They were the only sign of life along the terrace today. They called out to me, as they would have done to any servant girl huddling in her shawl. I hurried on to the Downs.

Yes, he was there. In streaming rain the heavy coat and wide hat had been fair protection against the weather, but today it looked like a disguise. The rain had hidden us and now the brilliance of the day distinguished every feature.

'You should not stand here, Mr Forrest,' I said. 'You are so ... so exposed. And how has Augustus let you have his coat again?'

Will Forrest laughed. 'He has borrowed mine,' he said. 'It's a fair exchange.'

Unscrupulous man, I thought. You knew Augustus would not refuse you.

'Come with me, Miss Lizzie. I have found a wonderful place where we can sit and talk. I have so much to tell you.'

He led me to the edge of the path and glanced around. There was no one coming. 'See there? The sheep have made a way. It's perfectly safe; I have tried it.'

'It doesn't look safe.'

'Follow me. You're not afraid of the height? Good. Put your feet exactly where I put mine. Hold on to this whitebeam: here.'

Below us birds sailed in the abyss of the Gorge. It was steep, but he was right: it was not impossible. We were on a little path, sheltered by rocks and wind-blown shrubs.

'Take my hand here. We go this way.'

I took it and with my other hand lifted my skirts so as not to stumble. The path was very narrow and although the slope to my left was not as sheer as further along the Gorge, I did not think I would be able to stop myself if I fell. Ahead of us a shoulder of rock jutted out, narrowing the path. Will let go of my hand and edged himself around the rock, leaning into it and treading carefully over the rough surface. It was not so very narrow perhaps.

'Shall I come back and fetch you?' he asked.

'No.' It was only a few yards, and the path was quite

safe, as long as I did not look down or stumble. I had never minded heights before. I tucked up my skirt so as not to trip over the hem, and began. He was ahead of me, holding out his hand. How far was it? Fifteen feet, no more. But I saw out of the corner of my eye a bird plunge down the vault of air to my left. A peregrine. I could not stop watching it or tell if it was the bird falling or the air around me. I leaned in to the wall and clung, sick and dizzy, unable to move.

'Lizzie! Lizzie! Look at me!'

I opened my eyes.

'No, look at me. Nothing else. You are very close to me now. Lean in to the rock, as you were. Move your left foot, Lizzie. Just a little step. And now another. Good. One more. You are almost here. Close to the rock. No, don't look round. Only at me. Another step, Lizzie. One more.'

His hand caught mine. He pulled me into him and held me close, turning me, pushing me ahead of him on to the broad place where the path opened out. It was safe now. We stopped and I turned to face him.

'If you had fallen!' he exclaimed, and I understood that he was seeing it as if it had truly happened. My body tumbling over and over into the Gorge as the bird fell. He heard the cry I had not given.

'It was the falcon,' I said. 'I should have been all right, but when it dived—'

'I should never have brought you this way.'

I disengaged myself from him.

'We shall go back a different way,' he said. 'Not so close to the edge. You will do very well, Lizzie.'

I thought: If there was an easier way, why didn't he show it to me the first time? But I could not be angry. I was overcome by relief that there would be no return around that shoulder of rock. He, too, was recovering his usual spirits. The colour was back in his face and his eyes no longer saw me spinning down and down into the gulf below us.

'And now, look where we are,' he said, as if he had brought the place into being. On our right was a shallow cave hollowed from the limestone and garlanded with ivy and old man's beard. A tongue of smooth turf lay in front of it.

'We will sit in the cave's mouth,' he said. 'We shall be able to see everything, and no one will see us except the peregrine. You might live in Clifton all your life and never know that this cave was here, but I have been exploring, and the other day I found it. Look, we can sit down together.' He bent and brushed the surface of the turf. 'It's perfectly dry.'

I tucked my shawl around me and sat just in front of the little cave. It was not much more than an impression in the rock, but it sheltered us. Anyone looking down from above would see nothing. He settled himself beside me. The winter sun was low in the sky and full on us. In this hidden spot, it felt warm. I pushed back my shawl and let the warmth spread over my face.

'A bird in its nest must feel like this,' he said. 'Safe, and secret.'

His presence was insistent: he would not let me forget him. He had crushed me to him in his relief and I had yielded, but it was nothing like Diner's grip and it neither frightened me nor disturbed me. I ought not to be here with him, I thought, and yet I too felt safe. The sun was so sweet and I was drowsy. Even the bare ground was not cold, because the sun had been on it. I closed my eyes and watched motes move across the veined red.

'Wake up, Miss Lizzie,' he said, 'I must talk with you.'

'About what?'

'You must be wondering why I am not in Scotland yet.'

'A little.'

'My plan has changed. I am to go into Somerset, to a place a thirty-mile walk from here. Mr Gleeson has friends there.'

I noticed he did not name the place.

'When?' I asked.

'It is not decided. Next week, perhaps.'

'I see.'

'You could visit me, Miss Lizzie.'

'You forget that I am not Miss Lizzie, since I have a husband.'

'He seems a most absent husband to me.'

'I assure you, he is not.'

We were not looking at each other, but staring ahead into the glister of light. The air hung blue in the depth of the Gorge, and the forest opposite was as black as smoke.

'Look at these little flowers,' said Will. 'What do you think they are? Surely they should not be blooming in December?'

'They are squills, I think.'

It was Diner who had shown them to me. Autumn squill, he'd said. He told me that there were many rare plants in the Gorge, some of them found nowhere else. He knew their names exactly. He could draw them, as he drew rough plans for his buildings before the architect worked on them. All at once I saw his fingers: quick, nervous, purposeful.

'I am very fond of children,' said Will Forrest, turning to look me full in the face.

'I dare say,' I said. 'It's easy enough to be fond of children when you have none. Let me give you Thomas for a day and you will see how much poetry you write.'

'You are mocking me again, Miss Lizzie.'

'Again?'

'Yes. You look so grave but I am not deceived. I would take care of Thomas, you know.'

'For an afternoon?'

'For life.'

His fair skin glowed in the afternoon light. He knew nothing, I told myself. He was ingenuous and a poet. He had money and he had never scrubbed a floor in his life.

'If you came with me into Somerset, I would take care of you both.'

I sighed. Here we were, sitting in a rock cradle slung

above the Gorge. For the moment we were free and accountable to no one, or so he thought. It was Scotland of a kind, although we had not tramped miles across the moors to find it. There, across the Gorge, lay the county of Somerset. He would cross by the Rownham ferry at Hot Wells and walk away with his knapsack into another life, without me, because what he was suggesting was only fit for this moment, this place.

'Look, another peregrine,' he said, and pointed. It hung, balancing, drifting.

'Perhaps the same one,' I said.

'We will take a cottage. We could keep a goat, and grow vegetables. Philo could come with us to look after Thomas.'

'And we would all live on air, I suppose.'

'I have money,' he said, as if it was a natural condition, like his red hair.

'I am married. You and I have spoken together perhaps three times, or is it four?'

'You know we would be happy,' he said.

'How can you say that?'

'It is true. I know it. You are not happy here. You look after Thomas, and grieve for your mother. What reason is there for you to stay?'

'I cannot argue with you.'

'No,' he said passionately. He had pulled off his hat and now he ran his hand through his hair until it stuck up around his head. 'You cannot. You have no argument to set against mine.'

He is beautiful, I thought, watching his fine fair skin where the flush came and went as if all his feelings were turned into colour. His tawny eyes were narrowed against the sun, but they seemed to squeeze out their own light. He was all aflame with whatever burned in his mind, and for the moment I was part of it. He had seen my fall in the same light, and so he had caught me to him. But it was a fantasy, not a reality. Perhaps he was tired of being alone. Augustus had told me his age, and he was older than I'd imagined. Perhaps he thought my presence would lend sweetness to this vision of life in a Somerset cottage. If so, he did not know me. I had not been brought up to be the answer to any man's question.

'But what if I also wish to write, like my mother?' I asked.

'You do not,' he said, with such certainty that I was silenced. My mother had said: *In time my Lizzie will discover what it is that she was born to do.* Her faith in me was a flame that might flatten when the wind blew on it but would not be quenched.

A wave of desolation swept through me. How was I to live in a world where no one had faith in me? Diner mistrusted me. If he could see me now he would think himself justified in following me and watching what I did. Only Thomas smiled at me with utter trust, and waved his arms when he saw me, but then he did the same to Philo and would have done so to anyone who fed and cherished him. Will Forrest wanted me to go with him but he did not know me.

'You are everything I need,' said Will, and he smiled as if that must be enough for me.

So I am to stir the pot, while you write the sonnets, I thought. We are to be stuck down the bottom of a Somerset lane in the winter mud, with the only sounds the scratch of your pen and Thomas howling.

'Don't be offended, Lizzie,' he said. 'I would not wish it on anyone.'

'What?'

'The desire to write,' he answered. 'If I am to be truthful with you, I am only myself in poetry. It is my native language and I talk any other with difficulty.'

'But we are talking now,' I said.

'I know!' he said, and delight leaped across his face. 'I knew as soon as I saw you, Lizzie, that I could be alone with you and it would be the same as being alone with myself.'

I smiled. 'It is very hard to work out whether or not that is a compliment.'

'You may be sure that it is.'

He was a puzzling creature. He seemed very little like a man and yet he was one, indisputably. I felt it. He talked with such intimacy and yet I still had no idea what he saw when he looked at me, or what he really thought of when he thought of me.

'You would be disappointed in a week, if I were fool enough to come into Somerset,' I said.

He was not listening. 'At night,' he said, 'we shall sit by the light of the fire, with Thomas in his cradle beside us. We'll rise at dawn and walk for miles until we know all the country around us. I shall compose out loud as I walk: you will not mind that, Lizzie? Do you know the stars? I know them all. I shall teach Thomas the constellations, and I tell you, he will be happy. He will never be shut away out of the light to drudge at his letters. He will learn more than would ever be beaten into him at school. We will plant apple trees, quince, medlar and mulberry. We will keep bees and Thomas will learn from their society. And if we tire of it, Lizzie . . .'

'If we tire of it?'

'We shall come to Bristol in disguise, and go to the play.'

The sun fell on us and I could not help smiling. If I yielded, if I went down into Somerset with Will Forrest, I need never untangle the knots that made up my life. I could cut them through in one afternoon and not think of them again. Once I had left him, Diner would never pursue me. I would be dead to him. I would never again have to feel the anguish that seized me when I saw him lose his grip upon all that he had built. I would not feel him thrash in the bed beside me, or catch me a blow across the face. I would never see him defeated or learn what that defeat would do to him. I would no longer be afraid.

I let my thoughts run on, because I knew that this was a story told for comfort, as a child tells such stories in the dark. For Will it was a story born of loneliness and it would fade soon enough. I could not blame him for discounting my husband, whom he had never seen.

He could not know that I was bound to Diner by a thousand threads.

'You will do well in Somerset,' I said. 'You are one of those creatures who is loved wherever he goes.'

I spoke in the tone which says: *I am going to blow out your candle now, and you must go to sleep.*

'But not by you, Miss Lizzie,' he said, and he laughed, not from any amusement but in surprise perhaps that I resisted him. 'You prefer your husband, although you are never with him.'

'Even so,' I said, 'I am necessary to my husband, and he is necessary to me.'

The sun was moving off the rock-face. I had the strangest wish that Diner could see me now, and know that I had not betrayed him.

'Your pride, Miss Lizzie, will be your downfall,' said Will Forrest, and he dug his fingers into the turf. 'Go back to your house then, and see what happiness you find there.'

'It has nothing to do with happiness.'

'It is true that marriage seems often to have little to do with happiness. But who am I to judge? I have never been married.'

I could not reply.

Suddenly his attention was arrested. He peered down close, and his voice changed. 'Look here,' he said, lifting a handful of turf to show me. 'It is like a garden in miniature. Those specks: see, they are flowers.'

'I wish you had not dug it up,' I said. 'Your garden will die.'

'Not so.' He stooped, and carefully fitted the turf back into the spot from which he had lifted it. The skirts of Augustus's coat impeded him, and he switched them aside impatiently. 'It will rain tonight. The wound will heal as if it had never been.'

'When I first met you,' I said, 'I thought you were very young, but now I think you must be older than I am.'

'Yes, I am old enough.' He pulled off his hat and bent his head towards me. 'Can you see a grey hair?'

I peered. 'No, I think not.'

'But I am lined. Tell me the truth: I am lined, am I not?'

'Very lined.'

'And I have lost several teeth, which is why I smile with my mouth closed. I expect you have noticed.'

'No, I had not noticed.'

He laughed, and I saw that his teeth were good, with only a single chip on the front.

'Do you ever tell the truth?' I asked him.

'Only in poetry. That is why I write poems, in order to discover what I truly think and feel.' He sighed. 'You and I should have met long ago, Lizzie, when I still had my teeth and before you learned to be so proud.'

His eyes gleamed. I could not tell if he was really angry with me, or laughing at me. Either way, I discovered I did not mind.

'But surely Augustus does not advise you to bury yourself in Somerset? He must see it as a temporary measure. You cannot be a radical in a potato patch.'

'I am a poet. You call me a radical but I could never do what Augustus does. I see doubly, and he sees singly.'

'You were radical enough for them to threaten you with imprisonment for sedition.'

'Yes. I cannot explain it. I am not a man of action, Lizzie. I wear Augustus's coat but it does not fit me.'

'You might go to Paris. Your gifts would be welcome there.'

'You think so! I'll tell you a secret, Lizzie. I cannot bear the sight of blood. If you were to rip your finger on a briar I would turn sick and faint, and you would have to bind it up yourself to get the wound out of my sight. Is that not contemptible?'

I thought of Mammie, the sodden cloths, the iron smell of the blood. The mattress taken off to be burned.

'No,' I said, 'it is not contemptible. But sometimes blood cannot be avoided.'

'There are many who say that. They will sow the field with blood and bring up a harvest of liberty. These are the words they use.' He was silent for a moment. 'I saw a man stabbed once.' He hesitated again. 'He was my friend. We had been drinking together all evening and we thought ourselves immortal. We staggered home together and we were fools enough to go through the park. We were attacked. I gave them everything, instantly, but Gregory resisted. He had a watch given to him by his father. It happened so fast I do not remember a word being said. There was not even a cry. I heard a grunt and it did not sound like a noise a man could make. Then the thieves were gone and Gregory was on the ground. Very likely they did not mean to kill him. I lifted our lantern: it was still burning. He looked at me but I could do nothing for him. I pressed my fist into the wound in his stomach. There was dark stuff coming out of his mouth and I thought it was wine and then I knew that it was blood. I cried out for help and no one came. His eyes were still open but he died. I will not go to Paris. I will be happy in a potato patch, in the right company. I will rise early, walk, dig, write. I like to be alone.'

'I am sorry,' I said.

'I did nothing for him.'

'You could not have done.'

'He was drunk. He scarcely knew where he was going. I was leading the way.'

'You were both drunk. Such things can happen anywhere, in the street or in a doorway.'

'Yes. But it was I who said we might hear a nightingale if we went home through the park. I did not know how much blood there was until I looked at myself in the glass, and then I threw away all my clothes. I will not go to Paris. Won't you come with me into Somerset, Lizzie?'

'You said you liked to be alone.'

'I could be alone with you. With you I would lose nothing. Look at us now! We are part of each other's solitude. You do not pry into my heart.'

I thought of Diner and how we had dissolved into each other on those early nights, so that there was nothing I did not know of him, or he of me. Or so I had believed. I shivered: we had been sitting too long.

'We must go back,' I said. 'It gets cold when the sun is off the rocks. But we must not been seen together.'

'I'll go with you as far as the path, in case you stumble.'

'You said you knew an easier way.'

'Even so, you might stumble.'

'We must hurry,' I said. 'It will be dark soon.'

21

Philo was on the front steps, looking out. As soon as she saw me she began to run towards me, and I ran too, quickened by fear.

'Where's Thomas? What's wrong?'

She was blotched with crying and incoherent.

'Was it Augustus? Did Augustus come and take the baby?'

She shook her head.

'Philo, for God's sake. Tell me what's happened.'

It came out clotted with sobs. 'The babby was crying. I was walking him up and down like I always do. I swear to God I never leave him crying. Mr Tredevant – he come in. He says – he says —' Philo's mouth squared and she bawled like a baby. I took her by the shoulders and shook her.

'Philo!'

'He goes and shouts right in my face, *'F you can't stop that damned caterwauling I'll stop it for you.* I couldn't hold on to Thomas. I had to let him take him.'

I saw it. Thomas, beside himself, purple and flailing. Diner, black with rage, plucking him out of Philo's arms.

'Where's he gone?'

'I don't know.'

'Did he take him out? Did he wrap him up?'

Philo nodded helplessly. 'I couldn't stop him.'

I realised that I was digging my fingers into Philo's shoulders and I released her, stepped back and saw the men who'd been working the pulley along the terrace. They had stopped work and were staring at us.

'Get inside, Philo. Quick.'

I stripped off the old shawl and wrapped myself in my cloak. 'You stay here. If he comes back with Thomas, don't say a word. Take the baby upstairs and keep him quiet till I come back. He may have taken Thomas for a walk, to calm him. I shall go and find them. It's all right, Philo, Thomas will be back directly.'

I heard myself gabbling, and Philo's face showed she did not believe me. When had Diner ever dreamed of taking Thomas for a walk? Hot panic swelled in me but I forced it down. I must think clearly. It was my own folly that had caused this: if I had not gone to meet Will Forrest then Philo would not have been alone with Thomas. While we were playing with words, Thomas had been taken away. But I would find him and bring him back and then for once I would confront Diner.

I ran even though people stared after me, all the way to Grace's Buildings. There was a pair of heavy oak doors which were usually kept locked, with a small entry cut into the right-hand one, tall enough to fit a stooping man. Diner had told me once that the doors were made to withstand war, siege and riot. Heavy bolts and iron bars ran across them, and the doorway could be easily defended. Perhaps he had meant to tell me that one day he would lock me out.

I twisted the handle. It gave, the latch went up, I pushed it open and stepped in. Light from the glass dome high above fell into the hall like snow-light. Everything was quiet. Curving flights of stone steps led upwards, floor above floor to the dome. Diner's rooms were on the second floor.

A door opened and a man I did not know came out, stopped, stared at me. I could not reach the stairs without brushing past him.

'I am here to see Mr Tredevant.'

He stared again, bowed, and made way. I felt him watching me as I ascended. I stepped as lightly as I could but the stairwell echoed. The stairs turned, and turned again. I was on the second landing, and there was the door to Diner's office. I tiptoed to it and put my ear to the wood. There was no sound. If Thomas was there, he must have cried himself out. Noiselessly, I turned the handle. The door gave way easily, and with a push it was open.

He was where I had seen him a dozen times before, bent over his desk with a heap of papers in front of him. But everything else was different. The room was more or less dismantled, with bare shelves and boxes of papers on the floor. My God, I thought, he is packing up. Things were far worse than I'd known. The curtains were gone from the windows, the drawings of Canford Square and Horace Row from the walls. Even the Chinese rug had disappeared. I saw it all in an instant, and that there was no sign of Thomas.

Diner did not look up. He was so immersed in what he was doing that he had not sensed the opening of the door. I stepped forward.

'Diner,' I said.

His heard jerked up. He had expected me. Of course he had. His eyes narrowed, watching me.

'Lizzie.'

'Where is Thomas?'

'I have a question for you first,' he said. A muscle jumped under his cheekbone. 'Where have you been this afternoon?'

'Walking,' I said, looking straight at him. 'You know I love to walk over the Downs.'

'I have told you more than once, Lizzie, that now you are my wife this must cease.' He dropped his voice as he spoke the last words, chill and separate.

'Where is Thomas?' I asked again.

'He is where he should be, with his father.'

Such a wave of anger went through me that I had to clench my fists so as not to spring at him.

'With Augustus, I suppose you mean,' I said.

'Of course.' He glanced down at the papers in front of him, as if he was waiting for me to go away so that he could get on with his work. But I knew him too well:

this was playacting. He was as angry as I was, and his air of bland preoccupation was meant to taunt me.

'I will fetch him home, then,' I said. 'It is time for his feed.'

Slowly, Diner stood up. His fists went down on the desk, supporting his weight. 'You will not,' he said, even more quietly.

'Then tell me what has changed. You agreed to have Thomas with us.'

'Where were you this afternoon?'

'I told you. I was walking by the Gorge.'

'Alone?'

He knew. I could tell it immediately. He had followed me or had me followed, or perhaps some well-wisher had given him the information. I must answer him now or he would crush me.

'I went alone,' I said. 'You may ask Philo, or anyone. But by chance I met an acquaintance.'

'Who was that?'

'A friend of Augustus. I met him once, when I went to visit Hannah. He has been staying with them for a while but now he has gone into Somerset.'

'Gone, has he?'

'I believe so. We exchanged greetings and he told me that he was on his way to the south of the county.'

'I believed you were at home, caring for Thomas.'

'I am almost always at home.'

'Almost!' he cried out, and then immediately dropped his voice again. 'I suppose a man might say that he is almost always honest, or almost always sober. Have you other such friends whom you meet by chance when you happen to go out walking?'

He got up from his desk and came towards me. My flesh shrank but I held my ground and he stopped, at arm's length. I must be bold, and speak out.

'If you don't believe me, say so. If you think I am giving you the slip and meeting another man by design, then accuse me and let me defend myself. I have nothing to be ashamed of and I will not be attacked as if I had.'

His face tightened. I could not read him now, or guess what he might do. But when he spoke, it was calmly.

'You have changed very much, Lizzie, since the day I married you,' he said.

We faced each other. He looked worn, and older. I thought of the many times he had lifted me in his arms and held me to his breast. All night we had found a thousand reasons not to separate, as if our bodies were no longer whole unless they were entwined. Only when morning strengthened at the windows and boys whistled in the street had we allowed ourselves to become two again.

'I have not changed,' I said, meaning it, although as the words echoed through the bare room they sounded hollow. Diner watched my face for a long time, as if from a long way off. At last he reached out. His hand came towards my face but I did not flinch. He lifted a lock of hair that had come loose on my forehead. He stroked it back, glancing around at his office, the scattered papers and the marks on the wall where the drawings had been.

'You may as well fetch the child,' he said. 'It makes no odds now.'

I ran down the flights of stone steps to the door. This time I could not open it and I wrestled with it, sweating, frantic, until I saw that it was quite simple. While I was upstairs, someone had slipped the bolt across at the top. The man who had seen me had done it, perhaps, to keep out other importunate wives.

I came out into the clatter of the street. There were sober knots of sober men discussing their business, and boys threading in and out of them with messages. They all looked at me a little too long, as if I should not be there. I drew my cloak around me and pulled up the hood as I set off for Augustus's lodgings. Thomas was quite safe there. Hannah would rouse herself to comfort him, and Augustus would look on awkwardly, full of good intentions. I found myself smiling, and then I wondered if Diner had seen Will Forrest when he went to the lodgings. If he had he would know my lie. But no, if he knew that I had lied to him he would have confronted me with it. More likely Will had hidden himself in the bedroom as soon as he heard the door. Diner could not very well have arrived silently with a crying baby in his arms.

He did not trust me. If I had changed, so had he. I thought of Lucie's dress: the waterfall of silk that she had never worn. For the first time I did not wish Lucie out of existence. I wished that she were here, now, and that I could question her.

*　　*　　*

And there indeed was Thomas, fast asleep in a nest of shawl on Hannah's bed. Hannah had put a coral beside him. There was no sign of Will Forrest and I did not like to ask.

'He's been chewing on the coral, just as you used to do,' she said.

'Is that the same one I had?'

'It bears the marks of your teeth, Elizabeth. I put it away in my chest, and now it's come in handy.'

I was touched to think of Hannah's keeping my teething coral all these years, when she could never have thought it would really *come in handy*. She looked more alive that I'd seen her since Mammie's death, and she could not keep the reason to herself.

'I am going into Somerset for a month or so, Elizabeth.'

'Somerset!'

'A friend of mine has taken a cottage there and he wants me to keep house for a while, until he is settled. Augustus says he can very well spare me.'

'You need not keep secrets from me, Hannah. You mean Mr Forrest, I suppose.'

'Yes,' she said, and smiled with such satisfaction that I felt an absurd pang of jealousy. I did not know whether I was jealous of Hannah, or of Will Forrest, but I did not want them to go away together without me.

'He is very lucky to have you, Hannah,' I said, 'but you must make sure to come back again. We shall miss you too much.'

Thomas was stirring, champing and sucking at the

air, and would scream with hunger as soon as he woke. I must get him home.

'Where is Augustus?' I asked, picking up the baby and folding his shawl around him tightly. Thomas always liked to be held secure.

'He is in his room, working, but he wanted to speak to you, Elizabeth. I think I might venture to disturb him.'

'Not now. I must get back. I will speak to him another time.'

'There was something very particular that he wanted to say to you. You have time enough, surely.' She cast an expert glance at Thomas. 'The child is settling again. He will sleep for another half-hour or so.'

'I'm sure it can wait until tomorrow.' I bent to kiss her cheek. As always, the softness of her skin surprised me. 'Thank you, Hannah.'

'I hope you know what you are doing, Elizabeth. There is no necessity for Thomas to go back with you. Augustus is quite willing to engage another nurse and I believe that Caroline Farquhar has offered to pay for one.'

'She would be willing to pay for anything, as long as it kept Thomas far away in some cottage out of sight.'

Hannah stood up. 'You have always done as you wanted, Elizabeth.'

I was stung. 'I am looking after my mother's child. My own half-brother. I don't see that there is anything so very wilful in that.'

'On the face of it, no,' said Hannah, with all her old dryness. She was coming back to herself. She was going to have her own world again, taking care of Will Forrest and his writing as she had taken care of Mammie's for so long.

'So when do you go, Hannah?'

'Very soon. Augustus is arranging it all.'

'What about your rheumatism?'

'I am well enough.'

It was true that she moved more freely today than I had seen her move since Mammie's death. My eyes blurred. Surely I could not want to cry, because Hannah was going into Somerset for a month – it was more than absurd, when I had Thomas safe in my arms.

But I did not get away without seeing Augustus. His door opened as I came out of the kitchen, and there he was, blocking my way. He looked rumpled and astonished to find that the daily world was still here: it was his working look.

'Ah, there you are,' he said. 'Come in here, Lizzie, I need to talk to you.'

I followed him. There was no fire but the door to the kitchen was open and the room was not too cold. Augustus closed the door.

'I see that you have Thomas,' he said.

'Yes.' I was not going to have any argument on the point. 'He is coming home with me now.'

'Are you sure that is wise, Lizzie?'

'Why do you say that?'

'Your husband was here, as you know. I spoke to him. I formed a strong impression that he did not want to have Thomas in his house. And, you know, I cannot have my child living where he is not welcome.'

My child. It was the truth, but it stung.

'Diner has agreed to it,' I said. 'What happened today means nothing. Diner and I had argued earlier and he was angry. He regrets it already, Augustus. Indeed, it was he who told me to come here. Thomas is well cared for with me.'

'You do not need to defend yourself, Lizzie. Thomas will do very well with a nurse now.'

'But, Augustus, you saw yourself how malnourished Thomas was when he came back from the wet-nurse. No matter how often I visited Mrs Platt, no matter that she was well paid for her trouble, it made no difference to her carelessness. She left him hungry, to cry in the care of a child while she went visiting. She let him lie in his dirt until his skin was raw. She had no more conscience over Thomas than a farmer has over a litter of piglets. Less, probably, since at least the farmer hopes to sell a fat pig at a good price.'

'Yes. Yes, you are right, of course. Mrs Platt was not well chosen. But there are other nurses.'

'If Thomas has to chop and change he will never thrive. Mammie, I know, would want him to be with me.'

Augustus peered at me. 'You think so?'

'Yes.'

'I think she would not have wanted you to be burdened with a child that is not your own.'

'Thomas is no burden,' I said, looking down at the baby who slept now, peacefully, as if to prove the truth of my words. He had put on weight and I loved his warm, packed solidity. He felt as if he meant to stay with us. My arms tightened around him. I wanted to press my lips to his forehead, to breathe in the smell of him, but instead I looked up at Augustus.

'Diner was angry because Thomas cried and I was not at home,' I said. I spoke softly, and the effort of doing so made me realise how sharp I was with Augustus as a rule. 'He resented my absence and he is not used to babies. But it will not happen again.'

Augustus nodded, as he did when someone made a particularly acute point in a debate but he had not yet decided whether to agree or to oppose.

'Thomas will be always with me or Philo,' I said. 'Mrs Platt left him with a child while she went gallivanting. You cannot know what any wet-nurse is doing unless you have her in the house and watch her constantly. The baby has no voice to tell you.'

'It is true that your mother intended to keep the baby with her.'

I did not say anything. I could sense his thoughts swaying this way and that. How much better it would be for him if his work was not interrupted. He would not in conscience be able to leave Thomas with a nurse now, unless he visited him often.

'Let us try again for a month,' he said at last, 'and then I believe we had agreed that it would be time for Thomas to come home.'

Home, I thought. There was little chance of that, if Caroline Farquhar had any say in the matter. Thomas would always be an outsider. But Augustus had assumed his authority as father, and God knows, even if Thomas had been my own, my wishes would have counted for nothing against that authority. Augustus was alive to the baby's existence now in a way that he had not been before. Thomas looked more of a person, perhaps. He no longer had the crumpled, dangling legs and pulsing head of the newborn. I'd seen how gingerly Augustus touched him then, and how quick he was to hand him back. *My child*, Augustus called him. He meant to claim him. Up until now I had only thought of Thomas as Mammie's child, with Augustus's parenthood as something which could be set aside. He was her baby. He had come out of her body and had killed her in doing so.

And yet I could never blame Thomas for Mammie's death. I remembered it all too well. He had been forced towards birth by a pressure nothing could have withstood. I heard again Mammie's cries cutting through the rooms. She could not resist either. Death had been as strong as birth and it had swept her away. It was so simple and yet it had taken me so long to understand even a part of it. I still felt under my fingers the hardness of her dead flesh. I felt in my arms the damp, living solidity of the baby who had come out of that flesh. Like me, I thought. It went through me like a dart that we were indeed truly brother and sister.

'I have rarely seen a man angrier than John Diner was today,' said Augustus. He looked at me penetratingly, and now his face was not sheep-like at all. I wondered, suddenly, what Diner had said in his anger.

'You must be careful, Lizzie,' he said. 'You must not rouse such anger against yourself.'

I would have liked to resent his words, but I could not. I thought, oddly: Augustus is my stepfather. We had never used the word. Augustus had never claimed me in any way as a daughter. Nevertheless it was the fact, and now, with Mammie's death between us, we were bound more strongly than we had been when she was alive.

'I am very careful,' I said.

22

January 1793

I slept poorly, waking again and again to feel for Diner beside me and find him absent. At last I fell into a heavy sleep and did not wake until past six, when I heard the door close downstairs. I lay still, pretending to sleep on, while Diner came in, pulled off his clothes and lay down. Almost at once he fell asleep, as still as a stone.

When I went downstairs, I found his coat in a heap in the hall and his boots by the kitchen door. I picked them up, scraped off the mud and brushed his coat while Philo clattered around the kitchen with Thomas tied into an old cotton shawl of mine, to keep him from crying.

There was a rip in the lining of Diner's coat, and I mended it. It was consoling to make the stitches very small and the mend almost invisible. I did not want to wonder where he had been tramping.

I was cooking mutton stew with carrots and pearl barley for his dinner. I knew he liked it. We owed too much money at the butcher's for me to order there any longer, and I went instead to the market stalls. The stew bubbled gently. We would eat together, at the kitchen table, and I told myself that we would be content together. He seemed to have accepted Thomas back into the house, and the days had passed calmly. Soon the bad, cold, inactive months would be over. It was January already; only February, and perhaps March, and building could begin again. I did not dare to think of how the men would be paid.

I heard his feet on the stairs. He must have found his boots, for they clumped heavily on each step. I wondered if he'd noticed that I had cleaned them.

'There you are,' I said, and I went over to him, but he did not reach out for me. I looked down and wiped my hands on my apron. I must smell of the kitchen. Very likely there was a smear of grease on my cheek.

'Lizzie,' he said. He looked around, as if he were confused.

'Come to the fire,' I said. 'I'm sure you are cold.'

The kitchen was warm, and I also kept a small fire burning in the attic grate, where Philo was with Thomas. We brought in wood for the fires, but it was never enough.

'They have killed the King,' he said.

I was slow with lack of sleep. 'What, Farmer George?'

'Lizzie, you cannot be as stupid as you pretend. They have cut off the head of the King of France,' and he took his hand from behind his back. He was holding the newspaper. 'Sit down, Lizzie. I will read the account to you.'

'By an express which arrived yesterday morning from Messrs. *Fector* and Co. at Dover, we learn the following particulars of the King's execution:

'At six o'clock on Monday morning, the KING went to take a farewell of the QUEEN and ROYAL FAMILY. After staying with them some time, and taking a very affectionate farewell of them, the KING descended from the tower of the Temple, and entered the Mayor's carriage, with his confessor and two Members of the Municipality, and passed slowly along the Boulevards which led from the Temple to the place of execution. All women were prohibited from appearing in the streets, and all persons from being seen at their windows. A strong guard cleared the procession.

'The greatest tranquillity prevailed in every street through which the procession passed. About half past nine, the King arrived at the place of execution, which was in the *Place de Louis XV*, between the pedestal which formerly supported the statue of his grandfather, and the promenade of the Elysian Fields. LOUIS mounted the scaffold with composure, and that modest intrepidity peculiar to oppressed inno-cence, the trumpets sounding and drums beating during the whole time. He made a sign of wishing to harangue the multitude, when the drums ceased, and Louis spoke these few words. *I die innocent; I pardon my enemies; I only sanctioned upon compulsion the Civil Constitution of the Clergy.* He was proceeding, but the beating of the drums drowned his voice. His executioners then laid hold of him, and an instant after, his head was separated from his body; this was about a quarter past ten o'clock.

'After the execution, the people threw their hats up in the air, and cried out *Vive la Nation!* Some of them endeavoured to seize the body, but it was removed by a strong guard to the Temple, and the lifeless remains of the King were exempted from those outrages which his Majesty had experienced during his life.'

Diner ceased reading and folded the newspaper. He'd bought the London *Times*, I thought, even though we had so little money. And so it was all over. I looked out of the area window and could just see the hard, white January sky. The ground, too, would be as hard as bone. I wondered if they had buried the King, or what they had done with his body.

'Augustus was right,' I said. 'He was sure that they would kill the King.'

'He will be satisfied, then, since his prophecy has been fulfilled.' Diner stood up and began to pace the room, flinging his body forward, turning, pacing, turning again at the same spot and pacing back. A grin, fixed and curious, lit up his face. I could not hear Thomas but I knew he would be grizzling up in the attic, and that Philo would be trying to soothe him. Why did nature give children teeth with so much trouble? I clung to the thought of Thomas.

'It is my turn to prophesy,' said Diner, 'and I think I will be as successful as Augustus. We shall have war.

France wants war: we saw that against Prussia and Austria. Now we shall go to it.'

'They will not fight here,' I said, thinking of Thomas upstairs. 'It will all be far away.'

'You think so. Come, Lizzie, I want to show you something.' He smiled, and held out his hand. He looked very ill. 'Let us go and look at the cellars.'

These vaulted cellars were his pride. They ran out under the pavement, and were fine rooms in themselves. They were barrel-vaulted and a man could stand upright in the centre. The walls were brick-lined. There were shelves for a wine cellar, although we had no fine vintages laid down. Preserves could be stored in brick alcoves, hams hung and cheeses ripened. Every precaution had been taken so that rats and other vermin could be kept out, or, if they got in, could be trapped easily. Philo did not like to go down there, and besides, we lived from day to day on what we bought in the market, often at the end of the day when things were cheap. There was not money enough for the kind of housekeeping these cellars allowed.

We went out across the area, Diner first, carrying a candle, and I behind him. He unlocked the cellar door and pushed it open, then stood aside to let me go first. There were steps down, because of the slope of the hillside. I heard him lock the door behind us. Cold came up to meet us as we descended. There was another door ahead, close-fitting and sealed at the base to keep out the rats. I knew how a rat could seem to melt its bones to squeeze into the narrowest space.

I moved aside, Diner turned the key and there we were.

'Close the door behind you, Lizzie. We will not trouble to lock this one, since there are only ourselves down here and the outer door is locked so that no one can get in from the street.'

What street? I thought. There was only raw mud and stones, and how could there be any passers-by? And yet he had shut us in here. I was uneasy but I would not show it.

'Have you got the key safe?' My voice piped thinly and I wished I had not asked.

'Of course.'

He lifted the candle high and spun shadows around the vault. This was the first cellar, and another door led to the second. It was all as well built as the house itself but even so I thought that I could smell the earth pressing in upon the bricks.

'We are under the pavement,' he told me, and I knew that in his mind he was seeing the finished pavement with its fine stone slabs, and not the rutted earth which really existed. 'Imagine these walls, Lizzie, lined with enough stores to keep a household fed for a year.' He moved close to the wall and examined the work. 'This will last for two hundred years,' he said. 'It is sound work. Look how well the bricks are laid. I had to stand over the men here. They would have skimped the work, calculating that what lay underground would never be seen, but they were under my eye and so they did not dare. Look, Lizzie, the mortar is perfect. Come, let us go further in.'

'It is cold down here.'

'My foolish Lizzie, you should have put on your shawl. Come here, let me warm you.'

He drew me close. He held me tightly but he was not warm himself, and I shivered.

'We must go back,' I said, but he did not answer. I listened and thought I could hear the earth settling around us, but Diner noticed nothing. He ran his hand over the bricks as a man might run his hand over the flank of a fine horse.

'Yes,' he said, 'this will stand in two hundred years.' He leaned forward, and to my astonishment he laid his cheek against the wall and closed his eyes. 'I built this,' he said.

I stepped forward and took the candle out of his hand. 'It is well built, Diner,' I said.

'Shall we not stay here, Lizzie? Is this not a fine house for us? I think I shall sleep well here,' he said. 'I do not sleep well at nights. Perhaps you have noticed.'

'You did not come home last night.'

'No. I walked. I don't know where.'

'I would have walked with you if you had asked me.'

'Would you? I think I could not ask you to do that. Hold the candle steady.'

'I cannot. The cold makes me tremble.'

'Don't you know that we are under the earth? It is always cold here. We must get used to it.'

'No,' I said, as firmly as I dared. 'I shall be under the earth long enough, but for now I prefer the sun. Or the fire, in winter. Come back with me into the house.'

I spoke as if I had the key in my hand. I turned with the candle and moved to the door without looking to see if he followed. Sure enough, I saw his shadow stir on the wall. There was the faintest chink of metal, and then he held up the bunch of keys and scrutinised it.

'We did not lock the inner door,' I said, and we passed through it together.

At the second door he stopped, and fumbled.

'Pass the key, Diner. I have the candle here.'

I did not look at him but held out my hand as if I had no expectation of refusal. He put the bunch on my palm, with one key separated from the others. It fitted the lock. It turned easily. The door opened and we stepped out into the area. Cold swept across us and whiteness glared. For a second I thought we had died and come into another world.

'It is snowing,' said Diner.

Flakes fell on my sleeve and clung there. One touched the candle flame, making it sizzle. I crossed to the kitchen door with snow squeaking under my boots. How quickly it had covered the ground; or perhaps we had been underground for longer than I'd thought. I was chilled but I did not want to go indoors. The tender, dazzling snow-light was wonderful after the coffin air of the vaults.

'Come, Lizzie,' said Diner. He took my arm in his grasp. 'You are chilled. You must come inside.'

I remembered how I had believed we were more ourselves in the kitchen than anywhere else in the house, but today I could not feel it. Even my thoughts were prisoned. We came in, the door shut behind us and Diner pushed the bolt across. He took hold of my shoulders and turned me to him. My throat tightened.

'Lizzie, do you truly love me?'

'You know that I do.'

I thought he would take his questioning further, as he had done before, but this time he did not. His eyes searched my face. I wished I knew what he was looking for, or if he would be satisfied. When he took me in his arms he was shuddering as if the cold had pursued him into the house.

'You must not leave me,' he said into my hair.

'You must not think of that. I am here, with you.'

'If I could sleep at night, my thoughts would not be in such disorder. I can never tire myself enough to sleep.'

'Not even if you walk all night?'

'My thoughts grow strong with exercise. They are perverse. I have the devil in me sometimes, Lizzie. Do you feel it?'

'There is no such thing. The devil is a tale for children.'

'You learned that at your mother's knee, I suppose, where other children learn their catechism. All the same I cannot separate myself from the idea that there is something moving within me which is not myself. Sometimes I seem to hear its breath – but in the vaults it is quiet. Didn't you feel that, Lizzie? Shall we go there again?'

'Not now, Diner.'

I would not go there again, ever. I felt the breath of something cold at my ear and at the back of my neck.

'Another time, then,' he said, as if it was a promise

between us, and then he pulled away from me suddenly. His voice changed: he was the old, authoritative Diner again. 'I have work to do, Lizzie. We cannot be maundering here. I must go to the Exchange. And there is the order of Portland stone for the staircases – they want their money on the nail, but they shall not have it. I will beat them yet, Lizzie!'

His eyes glittered with purpose but they glanced aside and did not quite meet mine. The look of illness was wiped away as if a hand had passed over him, but I was not reassured. Diner looked more strange now than he had done when he laid his face against the cellar wall.

'I have made mutton stew,' I said.

'It will take more than mutton stew to keep us out of the debtors' rooms at Newgate,' he said. 'I am going now, Lizzie.'

'When will you be back?'

'I cannot say. Keep some food for me. My credit is used up at the chophouses.' He laughed, as if I should laugh with him, and went up the stairs to find his coat.

I let him go, although afterwards I thought I should not have done. He had asked me if I perceived a devil in him and I had not answered him. He had said he felt breath within him that was not his own. But then, whose could it be?

23

There was only one person whom I wanted to see. She would look up as I came in, and give me her smile.

'Well, Lizzie! It's much too long since I have seen you. Where have you been? Come here and let me look at you.'

I would kneel by her desk. She would brush back my hair and scrutinise my face.

'You're pale. You haven't been sleeping. How are you, my treasure?'

There was so much I wanted to tell her, but I could not speak. I gazed into her face. Lines pulled tight over her cheekbones, but her look was what it had always been. Warm, curious, searching, as if there was nothing in me that she did not want to know or hope to love.

'My girl,' she said, and she stretched out her hand and laughed.

'Am I so comical?' I asked.

She stretched her hand towards me but she was receding. I could not see her face any more, only her hand, stained with ink, and then even this vanished.

But this time my imaginings left me cold. This was not my real mother but a doll of my brain who moved and spoke as I chose, and could never surprise me. I had married Diner but I had not moved beyond her. I had stayed where I had always been, sitting by her skirts, repeating her phrases. Her friends used to praise me because I played for hours with a flock of sheep carved from wood. I made a sheepfold for them and tended them, but sometimes I would put a barrier at the entrance and one lamb would remain outside, bleating pitifully, until I relented and let him in. I could lose myself in such games because my mother was there, working, talking not to me but to her companion, as close to me as if she held me in her arms.

And yet I would often wake and find her absent, and there would be Hannah telling me that Mammie had had to go to Hampstead, or the Highlands of Scotland, or even once to Italy for more than three months. She could not take me with her because I'd had a putrid fever and it was not safe for me travel. The water in Italy was dirty. I would be better at home with Hannah. When she returned I was angry and would not look at her. Every time she smiled at me I turned my head away, and talked to Hannah, or my doll. I must have thawed to her slowly, I suppose. I remember how she gave me a piece of fine lace to make a doll's coverlet, and I tore it and pretended that the cat that lived in the rooms opposite us had stolen in and ripped it with its claws.

Hannah scolded me. She always saw through me.

Well, they were not here, either of them. I went

upstairs, and gave directions to Philo not to take Thomas outside. The room was warm and he was fast asleep with his backside humped into the air. He had formed the habit of rolling over like that and neither Philo nor I knew whether it was good for him or not. I bent over the cradle and heard him snuffling into his sheet. His cheek was red where he had pressed his cheek into a fold of his blanket. The curdy, intimate scent he brewed filled the cradle. I wanted to lift him and kiss him but of course I could not disturb him.

Philo was quite well again. I was teaching her plain sewing and she had taken to it eagerly. I picked up the nightdress she was hemming for Thomas, examined it, and gave it back to her.

'That is very good, Philo. See if you can finish both nightdresses this afternoon. I'll be back later, before it's dark. Keep the fire well built.'

'You're never going out in this.'

The snow had stopped, although the sky was heavy and yellow with another fall to come.

'Only for a while. Don't you like the snow, Philo? Don't you think it's beautiful?'

She shook her head vigorously. She snipped a fresh piece of thread with her needle between her lips, and when she could speak, she said, 'I like it by the fire.'

Of course she did. She must have starved with the cold often enough when she was a child, and learned to dread snow and ice. It was never the barefoot, ragged children who shrieked with delight as they ran out into a snowy morning.

'Make sure he doesn't cry.'

She nodded importantly, and bent to her sewing again.

I wrapped myself in my cloak, put on my boots and took a basket so that if I met anyone it would look as if I was going to the shops. But I chose another direction, towards St Andrew's, the new church. Augustus had paid a fine sum for Mammie's grave-plot, but her stone could not be set for another three months. The sexton said that the earth must settle.

I had not been there since her burial. When I was a child and I used to frighten myself sometimes by imagining Mammie's death, I always saw myself visiting her grave daily to plant flowers and water them with my tears. The reality, now that it had come, was that I avoided it. I would walk a long way round so as not to pass the church, let alone go into the graveyard. There had been burials there for centuries, but most of the older graves were lost in long grass and willowherb. The new part, close to the splendid stone church, was well tended but not as beautiful. Augustus had bought the plot on the border between old and new. He had chosen it so that Mammie's grave would be shaded by a lime tree in summer.

I paused at the end of our terrace, and looked back. Snow hid the rawness of construction but it could not hide the gaps. Foundations were heaped with snow. Roofless houses gaped. Diner's terrace looked like a centuries-old ruin. There were footprints over the high pavement – still unpaved – but these were half filled with snow that had fallen after those who had made the marks had walked away. No one was working now; nothing moved down the length of the terrace. From our chimney and a couple of others, smoke rose straight up, dirty against the yellow sky.

A pair of crows flapped across the depth of the Gorge, cawing. I shaded my eyes to follow them and then I heard their low, hoarse cry. They were ravens, not crows. Diner had taught me the difference, and how to look for the shape of the bird in flight in order to know it. He had picked out sparrowhawk, kestrel and buzzard, and shown me the ledges on the limestone cliffs where peregrines nested. I would look and see nothing, and then he would take my arm, point it in the right direction and make me follow the line of my finger until I saw the bird. He would show me the sparrowhawk drifting high up, waiting for prey. It expended no effort unless it had to, Diner said. It used the currents of the air as mariners use the currents of the sea.

The ravens vanished into the forest on the other side of the Gorge. I thought of the people who had lived in their hilltop forts on either side of the river, and how they would have drawn close to their fires in winter, huddled together, telling stories and waiting for spring to come while their bellies growled with hunger.

It was too cold to stand still for long. I turned my back on the terrace and picked my way onward, making tracks in the new whiteness. There were boys out in the streets, hurling snowballs. One ball whizzed past my head and I bent down, scooped up a handful of snow, packed it tight and hurled it back. The boys had not expected it: they scattered, whooping, to find fresh ammunition while I picked up my skirts and ran on through the snow.

The lych-gate was open. Someone must have come here after the snow had stopped falling, because there were crisp-edged footprints on the path ahead of me. I walked around the bulk of the new church towards the place where Mammie lay, and the footprints walked ahead of me. Two sets of prints, side by side, and then in single file where the path grew narrow. I found myself following them as they crossed the graveyard, until they led away from Mammie's grave. I saw two muffled figures in the distance but I turned away from them. I had not come here to find company.

There was the mound of Mammie's grave ahead of me. I had memorised the name on the gravestone next to her, so I would always find it easily. There was the lime tree, pollarded since September, its stumpy branches full of snow. When we had buried her the earth had been dark but today light poured upwards from the snowy ground. Even though there was no sun, I had to blink against the intensity of it.

Snow lay over her like a blanket. There was no trace of the raw grave I had last seen. If it had not been for the letters cut into the stone of the next-door grave I would not have recognised this place.

She was quite safe. Nothing could touch her; nothing could disturb her. There was nothing to be done here. Another time I could bring a root of pansies and plant it, or I could clip the grass if it grew too long over her. But for now the snow had taken care of everything, and made it beautiful. I believed that she was there, not lying on her back with her hands folded as I had seen her put into her coffin, but curled on her side under the snow where nothing stirred. She did not know that I was here. Even if she had known it, she would not have roused herself. She was far away, locked in a sleep that would never be interrupted.

I wondered if Augustus came here, and if he did, what he saw.

A sound from the other side of the graveyard made me turn. They were voices, low but clear in the still air. I could not make out the words. Now I recognised the woman: she was muffled to the chin but I had registered that shape and face too clearly to forget it. She was Lucie's godmother. She stood at the shoulder of a younger man who was sitting on something – a stool perhaps – and sketching with quick, firm strokes. They were beside another grave which, like Mammie's, was not yet marked by a stone.

Diner had said Lucie's godmother was leaving Bath for London soon, but here she was in Clifton. I could not think what she was doing in this graveyard. Perhaps she or the young man had family connections here. I hesitated.

She looked up. I saw that she did not recognise me, because the last time she had seen me in my apron she had taken me for a servant and now I wore my cloak with the hood pulled up. I could have left the graveyard without speaking to them, but instead I drew my hood more closely around my face and waited with my hands clasped, looking down, until it seemed that their attention had left me. I glanced cautiously to the side, and saw that they had gone back to their work: the young man sketching, the older woman watching and occasionally putting out her hand as if to indicate something to him. I would wait a little longer. It was cold, but not intolerably so, and with my cloak wrapped closely around me I was warm enough.

Yes, they were deep in their work now. I stepped carefully through the snow, my head bowed. I stopped as if to read another gravestone, and went in between the trees until I was behind the pair of them. Their breath smoked white. She chafed her gloved fingers and said something which sounded like a complaint. They did not seem to notice as I drew closer, passing behind them.

His hand went quickly across the paper, but as I watched more closely I saw a certain nervous hesitation just before each stroke of the pencil. His fingers paused as if a vibration ran between his brain and his hand each time he made a mark. She spoke to him but he never looked at her; he only inclined his head, and drew on. The paper was pinned to a board and tilted towards me. I could see the drawing clearly enough each time his hand moved away. His subject was the grave a little to the right of him; he must have chosen the angle so that he could include the stone angel which belonged to a neighbouring grave. He had drawn it very beautifully, reducing the over-ornate stonework to purer lines. But it was background: in the foreground was an unmarked grave, like my mother's, with a rose bush growing at its head. The bush was leafless. One dark-red hip still clung to a thorny twig which was bowed down by snow. Perhaps the family had not wanted a stone, but had preferred roses. He was drawing the bush now. I watched as his pencil conjured up the pallor of the ground and the depth of the snow. It would be a fine drawing. Someone would treasure it and frame it. The air was so still that I could hear the sound of his pencil, and his breathing. The woman stretched out her hand and pointed to an immature birch tree which was growing some ten yards off. He looked at it too, considered, shook his head.

It was then that the woman turned, as if she had felt my eyes on her. I could not help meeting her gaze, and now, even with my hood, she knew me. She exclaimed aloud in French, and prodded her companion to draw his attention to me. She spoke hurriedly to him, much too fast for me to make it out. I stepped forward, and walked towards them.

'Bonjour,' I said. She was silent, but her eyes snapped at the young man, urging him on.

'Good-day,' he said, and I knew from his accent that he was also French.

'It is a very cold day for drawing,' I said.

'And cold for you also,' he said rather pointedly.

'I am here to visit my mother's grave.'

'Ah, I understand. Then it is not so strange. Excuse me, I must explain this to Madame Bisset.'

He did so, too rapidly for me to follow. Nor could I understand the volley of words she let loose in reply, but I knew that they were angry words and meant for me, not for her companion.

'What does she say?' I asked.

'She says that it is strange that your husband has not set a stone on the grave, after so long. She says – that perhaps you have discouraged him.'

'I don't understand you. You are mistaken. My husband has nothing to do with the grave, and the reason that there is no stone is because it is not yet six months since her death. She died in September.'

'You mean your mother?'

'Yes.'

'Madame Bisset does not concern herself with that. She is talking of Lucie's grave.'

'Lucie's!' I stepped back. I could not believe it: was he mocking me? Had they decided to punish me, because I was married to Diner and Lucie was dead?

'Yes.' His face was clear and open as he pointed to the snowy mound that he had been drawing. 'This one is Lucie's. Your husband came to this place and he showed it to Madame Bisset. But surely you knew this. You know the graveyard well. You live here in this city, while we are strangers.'

Whiteness dazzled in my eyes. His words were bright flecks in it but they too jumped and danced until I could make no sense out of them.

'Surely you know this,' he said again. His sallow face was impatient now, as if I were pretending stupidity.

I forced down my thoughts.

'You draw very well,' I said, in a voice which surprised me by its calmness. 'And you also speak English very well.'

'I am here since – for three years, already,' he said. 'I live in Bath. Many of us live there.'

'You mean émigrés?'

'I think that "exiles" is your English word,' he said.

'And you are drawing this for Madame Bisset?'

'No, it will be for the father of Lucie, Monsieur Ribault, if we can arrange a way to send it to him safely. He is an old man and will never be able to visit his daughter's grave.'

I saw that the task had affected him. He was one of those ugly men who cling to a spirit of chivalry that more handsome men can afford to dispense with, and besides he was an artist and he would sit here in the snow until the drawing was done to his own satisfaction. I stared at the grave. What this man said was inconceivable. Lucie had fallen ill in France. She had been buried in France, by her family. I remembered every word Diner had said. I could not be mistaken. He had told me this, and he had told Lucie's godmother that she lay here in an unmarked grave.

'And Madame Bisset is really her godmother?' I asked. It seemed as if all truths were collapsing around me.

'Why do you ask such a question?'

'No reason. I did not mean to offend you.'

'You should go home, madame, and ask your

husband why he does not raise a gravestone to the memory of his wife. Although, for myself' – he paused, holding out his pencil before him and squinting at it as if to make a measurement – 'for myself I prefer the rose tree.'

'So do I,' I said.

All this while Madame Bisset had stood silent. I glanced at her face and thought that it was impassive but then I looked again. It was not so. She was possessed by an anger which would not express itself on her features, but would be implacable. She hated Diner; she hated me. She believed ill of us both, and if she could, she would do us harm. She did not know that we were now entirely separate, as the head is separated from the trunk when the blade of the guillotine cleaves it. A moment before the stroke the body was entire, speaking, breathing, trusting to its own wholeness. But now, although the eyes still stare and the limbs twitch, there is no connection. The creature is dead.

'But you see how I draw the angel, as if it is hers,' said the young man.

'Yes, I see it all. I must go now.'

I took a last look at the drawing. Madame Bisset had loved Lucie, that was clear. She had been bold in coming to our house, bold in questioning Diner and bold in bringing this young artist here so that there would be a memorial to Lucie on paper if not in stone. Her father would be consoled by an image which was a lie. It was because of Lucie that we were all standing here, and even though she was dead and we were alive I understood now that she was stronger than all of us.

I walked away. It was very cold and I wanted to be at home but I could not think where to go. My legs shook. My hands had begun to shake too and I thrust them deep into my cloak and clenched them to keep them still. I must not think of anything. And yet something within me had resounded when the young man spoke of Lucie's grave, just as a bell resounds when it is struck, even after years of dumbness. Lucie had not died in France. Diner had lied to me. I had not known any of this before the moment when the young man spoke, but it seemed now that I had known it all.

24

I went home, because of Thomas.

'He's been a good boy,' said Philo fondly. 'He et all his pobs and then straight back to sleep. That blessed tooth is through.'

'Good. Has Mr Tredevant been home?'

'No, he ent been home.'

He might come home any moment. I must be quick.

'Philo, I find I must go to see Mr Gleeson. I may be some time, so I will take Thomas with me.'

'You're never taking him out in this! It'll be dark soon, and with the snow—'

'He'll be wrapped up to the eyes and I'll carry him inside my cloak.'

'What if you slip down and fall on top of him?'

'I won't do that. Hurry, Philo. Put his pap boat in a basket for me, with some of his milk in the blue can, but make sure you cover it tightly. And put in half a dozen clouts and a pilcher. He'll need a spare gown – a cap—'

'You're never going to take him away?'

'Don't be frightened. I'm not taking him away from you, but if it comes on to snow again then I may need to stay longer at Mr Gleeson's than I intend.'

'I can come!'

'No, you stay here for now. If Mr Tredevant comes home, tell him I am at my stepfather's house because he asked to see Thomas. He will understand that the snow has kept me there. Make his dinner and do the work of the house as usual. If he needs me he will easily find me. Now be quick.'

She did not like it but she saw that there was no changing my mind. I could not explain it all to her. I thought of nothing but that I must get Thomas out of the house, now, before Diner came home.

'I'll put on his pudden cap,' she said, 'that we were keeping till he starts to crawl. He'll be warm in that.'

'It will wake him if you do. Put in it the basket, and I'll change him when we get there.' When the basket was filled we lifted Thomas, deep in sleep, limp and warm. He mewed and shuddered all over at the change of temperature, but did not wake as we wrapped him quickly in his warmest blanket. I tied him into my shawl, and wrapped my cloak over us both. Philo watched us over the banister until we were out of sight.

It was beginning to snow again, very lightly. As I walked I felt as if I were following in my own footsteps, a second self going after the first. I trod carefully, because the weight of the basket and the baby would have taken me over if I began to slide. These were old boots, but they had nails knocked into the heels and they held me secure.

Augustus would be surprised to see me. I had made such a point of taking the baby home with me, and insisting that Diner's anger had been a passing thing. I had meant it then: I had seen no threat. I had understood nothing. Now I clutched Thomas to me, not daring to hurry in case I fell. Whatever happened, Thomas must not be hurt.

As I walked the light thickened and the snow came down more heavily. I looked up and saw it whirl against a lighted window, but snow fell in my eyes and blurred them. It was not far now. I wondered where Diner was. In my mind an endless line of footprints unrolled, leading farther and farther away from me.

There was the kitchen window, full of warm, ruddy firelight. They had not yet lit a candle. I picked my way to the door and knocked loudly.

It was Augustus who came down. 'Why, Lizzie, are you out in all this snow?' he asked, a question to which there could be no sensible answer. Instead, I stepped inside and pulled back my hood. Snow fell on the floor and Augustus stooped to gather it before it melted.

'Our neighbours downstairs complain terribly if we allow water to pool on the floor,' he said.

'Let me take off my cloak.' I put down the basket and, as I untied my cloak, Augustus saw Thomas wrapped in my shawl.

'Is it not rather cold for him to be out?' he asked mildly. 'But you know best, I am sure.'

A change of tone indeed. Perhaps he had had time to think about the reality of having Thomas to live with him. A moment later the true cause came out: 'Caroline Farquhar is here, Lizzie. She will be pleased to see you.'

Augustus carried my basket and I walked up the stairs behind him. It was so good to feel again all the old, familiar annoyances: Caroline Farquhar; Augustus's long, black legs ascending the stairs ahead of me; the thin, out-of-tune singing of the seamstresses who lived downstairs: they were all here, just as they had always been. Nothing had changed so very much. Augustus had greeted me just as usual and had not seen that everything in me had changed.

'You are out of breath,' he remarked as we reached the top of the stairs.

'Am I? Perhaps it is the cold.'

It was dread that I had swallowed down, filling my stomach, squeezing the air from my lungs. Caroline Farquhar was here and so there could be no conversation with Augustus, even if I had known what to say. A rose tree; a white mound of an unmarked grave; an ugly young man who drew beautifully. How could I give him those things and expect him to make sense of them, when I could hardly do so myself? If I made a tale of them it would sound less credible than one of Mrs Radcliffe's more lurid fancies.

'Ah, Caroline,' said Augustus, opening the door to the parlour. 'Here is Lizzie come through the snow to see us.'

There were four candles burning in the parlour. Very likely Caroline had brought them with her, because they were fine wax candles and not what we usually had. The fire was hot and my mother's tea-things stood on the table beside Caroline.

'Good God!' she said. 'You have brought the baby.'

'I suppose she could not very well leave him,' said Augustus.

'But it is so cold. Surely it cannot be good for an infant to be out in such cold.'

I put my hand close to Thomas's sleeping face. 'He is quite warm.'

'Sit here, Lizzie, close to the fire. Caroline is telling me the news from London. She says that there are many wearing crêpe bands for the death of the King of France.'

'They are even carrying effigies of our dear friend Tom Paine through the streets,' said Caroline, stretching her eyes wide. 'They read nothing but the penny broad-sides which call the King a martyr. Of course every crowned head in Europe is now feeling its own neck in fear, and the press is directed accordingly. They are out in force, you may believe! Kemble closed the Haymarket on account of the execution. They have expelled the French Ambassador and war is expected at any moment.'

'We are very fortunate to have your first-hand account,' said Augustus.

'Did you see the effigies?' I asked. I was curious as to what such a thing might look like.

Caroline hesitated. 'Not with my own eyes,' she said at last, 'but I obtained a close description from someone who saw it pass by him not fifty feet away. It had been shot through with bullets.'

'We are certainly fortunate,' I said. 'In France they do not trouble to shoot at effigies.'

Caroline gave me a sharp look, and said no more. Augustus unfolded a sheet of paper. 'I have a very different account here,' he said, 'from one who is daily witness to events in Paris. He says that there is no such hatred and madness as our press pretends. The King's trial was carried out with all due process. Votes were taken in the proper form. Many preferred him to be punished with imprisonment, since they did not wish to make a martyr out of a vain, luxurious man who had ruled foolishly, has plotted against his own country with her enemies and would not hesitate to plot again and bring ruin upon France.'

'But such wishes for clemency did not prevail,' I said.

'No.' Augustus sighed, and folded up his letter again. It came to me that he did not want me to see the signature. He did not fully trust me, then.

My own self-possession disturbed me. The Lizzie who had glanced behind her, out in the snowy street, seemed to have vanished. Each word and gesture came to me with absolute clarity. I saw Augustus and Caroline more vividly than I had ever seen them.

'He sleeps very well,' said Caroline, leaning forward to peer at Thomas. 'Do you use quietness with him?'

'What do you mean?'

'My nursemaid would use Godfrey's Cordial for teething.'

'We use no such thing with Thomas.' It flashed across my mind that perhaps this was what the wet-nurse had given to Thomas, and why he had become so thin. A baby who is lulled into sleep with opiates would not feel his own hunger. 'I did not know that you had had a child.'

'One only,' said Caroline. 'She died before she was a year old.'

'I am sorry.'

She stretched her eyes again and said, 'It was a great sorrow, but time is a greater healer,' and she glanced sideways at Augustus, as if seeking his approval. But I noticed that her fingers gripped her cup tightly, and for the first time I felt a pang of sympathy for her. And then it came back to me, like sickness: dread, cramping my stomach again and sitting upon my tongue. Thomas, the warm sweet fire, the wrangling of Augustus and Caroline: all of that was far away and I no longer had the right to belong to it. I was divided from them, because I knew now that Lucie had not gone home to her family and died there from some complication of childbirth, but instead she rested in an unmarked grave in Clifton. Or so Diner had said to Madame Bisset. But he had said quite other things to me and I had believed them. Both stories flapped their dark wings inside my head. If Augustus had been alone ... But he was not alone.

'Where's Hannah?' I asked.

'Oh,' said Augustus, and a glance slid between him and Caroline. 'She has gone into Somerset already.'

'So soon!' I could not help myself: it came out as a cry.

'There were very particular circumstances,' said Caroline in her most condescending style.

'I know that she has gone to join Will Forrest, if that is what you mean.'

And has left the pair of you together, I did not say. It was comical to think of them in need of a chaperone. Caroline lifted my mother's tea-pot and carefully filled Augustus's cup before handing him the cream.

'You know how I like it,' he said, and smiled at her.

My heart was beating so fast that I was sick with it. 'Augustus,' I brought out, 'I have come because I need to speak to you urgently, on a family matter.'

'I think that Mr Gleeson may be allowed to drink his tea first, my dear Elizabeth,' broke in Caroline Farquhar, as if I were a tiresome child. But Augustus did not follow her lead. He put down his cup, unfolded his long legs and stood up, saying:

'You must excuse us, Caroline. Come, Lizzie, we will talk in the kitchen.'

As soon as the door was shut behind us, he put his hand on my shoulder and steered me to Hannah's chair. 'Sit down, Lizzie. You look very ill.'

'I am not well. I have come to ask you, Augustus, if you will take Thomas back for a while. I cannot care for him. He will be better with you.'

He stared at me but said nothing, although his face furrowed and tightened. Again I realised how much I had underestimated Augustus and taught myself to believe that my mother had married him almost out of pity.

'Is this your own wish, Lizzie, or your husband's?'

'It is my own.'

'But you were so strong against Thomas going to a wet-nurse.'

'I know. I am against it still. Philo will come to stay and take care of him, and I will continue to pay her wages. You will have no trouble at all. Thomas knows Philo and she will take good care of him. They can have Hannah's room. It will not be for long, Augustus. Only until I am better.'

'Have you seen a doctor, Lizzie? You are very pale.'

'No.' I hesitated, deliberately, before adding, 'It is not necessary. I know what is the matter with me.'

His face clouded with embarrassment, and I knew he would ask no more questions.

'When will Philo come?' he asked.

'I will leave Thomas here with you now and send her immediately, before the snow becomes too deep. Philo knows what to do. I shall visit every day.'

As I spoke I was untying the knot in my shawl behind me. I supported Thomas with my left hand and did not loosen the folds in case it woke him.

'There is everything he needs in the basket. Milk, clouts, his pap boat, his caps and dresses. Philo will bring more things with her and I will send a boy with the cradle.'

'Caroline is staying with her maid at Little George Street,' he said abruptly. 'She and I will go into Gloucestershire on Friday, unless the snow continues. I am to speak to the mill-workers at Nailsworth.'

'You need not worry about Thomas. You may safely leave him and Philo will do everything. Let me give him to you.'

I put shawl and baby into the arms that Augustus held out awkwardly. Thomas felt the change and began to squirm. 'He likes to be held firmly.' I took Augustus's hands and guided them. 'There, that's better.'

'Do they not bruise easily?'

'You won't bruise him. He likes to feel that you have him safe. He will probably sleep now until Philo arrives.'

'I suppose Caroline will know what to do, if he cries.'

'He must not have any cordials, no matter what.' I tried to soften my voice. 'He will do very well.'

Augustus was gazing down at the baby's face. 'At what age do they learn to speak, Lizzie?' He was imagining the conversations he would have with Thomas. Perhaps he thought Thomas would be another Émile.

'I am not quite sure,' I said. 'I am learning as Thomas learns.'

Augustus glanced up with a sudden, childlike smile. I had never seen him smile so before, but it came to me that this must be how he had looked at my mother in their most private moments. I wished I had mistrusted him less, while Mammie was alive. I could not break the habit now. And if I spoke, what could I say? I had defended Diner from the moment I met him. I had told everyone over and over again that they did not understand Diner as I did, who loved him. I had persuaded them out of all their criticisms. I had told them that they did not understand the world that Diner and I would build together, because it was not their world. But what was worse, I had told myself all these things. I had convinced myself that words were cheap, compared to stone. I had poured scorn in my heart on our little band, dismissing Augustus as a gullible idealist, Richard Sacks as a prosing bore and Caroline Farquhar as a rich hypocrite who posed as a radical. I had even blamed Mammie for her steadfast turning aside from what the world considered to be good. I saw now how they had humoured me. They must have talked long into the night, fearing for my future and hoping that I would find some happiness in my new situation.

How could I tell Augustus now that there were thoughts I did not dare to think? How could I reveal that if I was drawn and pale it was not because there was a child in my belly but because I was afraid?

Dread filled me again, like sickness. I had parted with Thomas. He had been my burden but my anchor too, and now I did not know what depths lay under me.

'Will you need your shawl, Lizzie?' asked Augustus. 'You must not be cold.'

'I have got my cloak.' I did not want to unwrap Thomas. At least he knew my old shawl and it would smell like home to him. He would wake and expect to see my face. He would bat the air with his fists, crying.

I must go home quickly, to send Philo on her way to him.

25

It is three days now since I took Thomas to Augustus, and still I have not been able to say a word to Diner of what I think and fear.

The snow has not melted, but every day it evaporates a little more into the winter sunlight. The temperature never rises above freezing. The ground is so hard that even if everything had been quite different, it would still be impossible to build.

Diner goes out each day, for three hours or four. While he is out of the house I brush and scrub and lift and scour. I empty our chamber pot and swill it round. I cook soup for us with bones and barley. I make bread and porridge. There is a five-pound bag of oats in the larder, and a stone of flour. Because I never leave the house there is very little fresh food: no milk or cream cheese or meat. There are carrots and onions enough to last us a few days longer, and a fat cabbage I bought from the market before the snow came. We have not touched it yet. Diner does not complain when I set another bowl of soup before him. Indeed, he praises me and says how savoury it is, and how delicious. He cannot break the habit of shaving a little sugar for himself from the loaf and holding it between his teeth while he drinks his glass of wine. There are two bottles left.

The house is as clean as it was when Philo was here. She was crying as she left with her basket and a bundle of Thomas's things. I tied her wages into a cloth and told her to give them to Augustus directly. I knew that I could trust her. She would fetch the milk for Thomas just as usual.

'If Thomas is ill,' I said to her, 'you must send for me immediately. And do not allow any medicine to be given to him without sending a note to me first.'

She stared. 'But you'll come and see us, miss?'

'Lizzie,' I said. 'Remember. Yes, I will come, Philo, but not immediately.' I kissed her and she clung to me until I put her away gently.

Three days. Diner goes out and returns. The French Ambassador has been expelled from London following the execution of the King. Pitt will not have it, Diner says. There will be war.

We go to bed soon after dark. We cannot keep a fire for longer and our stock of candles is dwindling. Diner forages for wood and comes home with a barrow-load. I think that he no longer goes to Grace's Buildings or to Corn Street where money is lent and repaid. I am not certain where else he goes and besides it does not matter much.

We fold into each other. He penetrates me and I penetrate him. We lie together for a long time, barely moving. If we cry out it is into each other's mouths and the sound does not escape. The room is cold but we burn. Sometimes we throw off the bedclothes and walk naked to the windows. The shutters are never closed. There is the Gorge, and the forest beyond. When the moon rises everything swims into being. The landscape lifts towards the light as if from the depths of the sea. They call the moon silver but I do not think it is. It is more alive than that. We stand and watch and then we plunge back into our bed.

Diner takes no precaution now. He enters me and he remains and I would not let him go even if he wished. I cannot remember what we were doing before this, or what I was thinking of: this is all there is. The King of France is dead and I am not sorry for it. I believe that he was a vain, luxurious man, as Mammie and Augustus believed, and that he was content if thousands starved. Or, at least, he was content to remain in ignorance.

But I cannot blame him too much. We are all content to remain ignorant, if it suits us. We know that we eat while other bellies cramp with hunger. Our houses are palaces to those who have none.

I am not sorry for the King's death but I cannot get the manner of it out of my mind. I wrestle with it while I scrub the floors and Diner hunts for wood. I have never seen a guillotine but I have seen an engraving and it is an exact contraption. It works very smoothly. We are ingenious in our cruelties. There is no need for an executioner to face his victim or huff with strain as he wields the axe. No more botched killings, because the machine will always be precise. I suppose it is better than a hanging but it works too well for me. They say the lips still move and the eyes open wide in terror when they see the trunk from which they have been severed.

I do not know whether they buried the King or poured quicklime over him so that it would be as if he never existed. Diner says that they would not want his bones to remain, for fear that royalists would make relics of them. In the news reports they write that people sprang forward to dip their handkerchieves in the blood of the King.

I try not to think of Thomas. He is with Philo and Augustus, and he is perfectly safe.

Sometimes dread rises in me when I am alone. I resolve that I will speak to Diner, and then he comes in. He lays his bundle of wood on the pile and says:

'How is my Lizzie?'

'I am well,' I answer.

'You are too pale,' he says. 'You must eat more.'

'I am very well.'

He lifts me into his arms and holds me tight. We rock from side to side, from side to side.

'My Lizzie,' he says. 'My girl.'

He kisses me all over my face, hot and quick. It is as if we have never touched each other before and that we must devour each other before we are devoured.

He says, 'We are at war, Lizzie. The French have declared war on us, and we shall not be slow to respond.'

I am not surprised by this. Everyone has been talking of it so long that it is almost a relief. War has come and we are ruined. Our world has not yet crumbled but it shivers on its foundations like a child's tower of bricks which cannot help but fall.

'No one will build now,' he says. 'No one will buy.'

That night, when we are asleep, there comes a banging and roaring outside. I do not hear it clearly at first. It weaves itself into my dream and I live through hours and days and years before I wake. The noise continues. It is not part of my dream, but real. Diner leaps out of bed and goes to the window.

'Stay there, Lizzie,' he says, but I do not. I go to the side of the window where I can see without being seen. Diner is at the other side. Our bodies gleam white although the moon is half hidden by a curd of cloud. The men are there below us, carrying torches. The flames go straight up because there is not a breath of wind. The men are muffled in rough clothes with caps drawn down over their faces. Two of them stand back, on the lookout, while the others thunder on our door. They shout for Diner; they call out vile names and kick the wood.

I look at Diner and see that he is smiling; or, at least, his lips are drawn back so that his teeth gleam.

'Will they burn us out?' I whisper.

'Stay still, Lizzie. They will go away.'

'Who are they?'

'Men who have worked for me. They want their money.'

'Will they break down the door?'

He shakes his head, judging, listening as they batter on the heavy panels. 'They will go away,' he says.

The torch plumes move. There is a crash and splinter of breaking glass. They have smashed the glass above the door. I start back, but Diner says, 'The shutters are barred. They will not come in, Lizzie. If they meant to do that they would have brought the mob with them.'

I cannot see the men clearly for they are hidden by their caps and those who are at the door are under the porch. I stand stock still while the cold sheathes me until I begin to shudder with it.

All at once they are gone. We see them tramp away along the high pavement, bearing their torches. Their shadows lengthen on the flattened snow. Five men. Only five men, although it sounded like many more.

'Will they come again?'

'I think that they will, but not tonight.'

It takes us a long time to grow warm. We huddle together but no heat catches from his body into mine. I am hungry and I want the chamber pot but I am too cold to get out of bed. We shiver. Diner begins to stroke back my hair.

'I am sorry that you were frightened, Lizzie.'

'I was afraid that they would break down the door and burst in on us.'

'Next time, they may. It is no use for us to hide in this house, Lizzie. They built it. They know every cranny of it.' He speaks almost triumphantly as if this is some-thing he has always foreseen. 'They see by the smoke rising from our chimney that we are still here, and it enrages them because we are living in comfort while they have nothing. Or so they believe.'

'Could we live without a fire?'

'You know we could not. We must go from here, Lizzie.'

'Hush,' I say, and I put my hands around his face and press his lips to mine. At last the heat comes. We are no longer cold and separate: we are one creature and we move together. It does not matter what happens now. There is no world: it has fallen away from us.

I wake again. It is dark of course; it is always dark, hour after hour. I think it must be the heart of the night now. I have been dreaming of Lucie. In my dream her back was turned to me. She was walking away, lifting the hem of her silk dress so that it would not be soiled. She walked quickly, lightly, and with purpose. In my dream I knew her destination and my body clenched with terror. I tried to call out to her: 'Don't go that way!' but my voice rasped and squeaked in my throat and no words emerged. She turned back as if she heard me but she looked through me, smiling at nothing. A breeze blew and the folds of her dress stirred, then rippled until she caught them down with her hands. My mouth opened and I said to her: 'Where are you going?'

'To see my husband, of course,' she replied, and as she spoke those words a chill of terror rippled over my skin like the wind lifting her skirts.

I am not dreaming now. I lie awake and think of Lucie and what took her from the house she shared with Diner to the grave not far from Mammie's. Diner did not want me to know that she was buried there. He lied to me.

I feel as if I am pushing back a weight, like a weight of earth that threatens to topple over me. I raise myself on my elbows and peer through the gloom at the hump of Diner's body, curled away from me. He sleeps on, breathing steadily and easily. He seems untroubled. We shall have to leave this house, and I shall have to go with him. I wonder where we shall go.

'Diner,' I say, but he does not stir. I am not speaking loudly enough. If I were braver I would lean over him and cry out his name. Or her name – it does not matter.

I sleep again. I dream again of Lucie. She has her back to me and she is walking away. She picks up her skirts and hurries, as if she is eager to get to a place I cannot see. In a moment she will be out of sight. Dread thickens in my throat and I try to call out but my voice will not come. I know that I must warn her but I cannot name her danger. She is wearing the silk dress and it ripples about her as she walks faster. Suddenly she turns and looks back, not at me but through me. She smiles and waves a greeting, her face warm with delight. Whoever she can see, the sight makes her glad.

'Lucie,' I say. The word drops from me like a stone in the freezing air and suddenly she knows that I am there. Her face does not change from its look of welcome but now she raises her left hand and beckons me on. She is not wearing gloves. I see the ring on her marriage finger and I know it. It is the same ring that I am wearing now. I understand that I must go to her but I cannot move, not even to turn around and discover who it is that she sees behind me.

Lucie isn't afraid. Her face glows like a summer day as she beckons me again. I must go with her, and then all will be well. I look down and see that my warm cloak has gone although I was dressed for winter. I am wearing silk, like Lucie. I run my bare hand over the folds of my dress and my ring catches the light. But already she is turning away. She is going and unless I follow quickly I will lose her forever, but I cannot move. I cannot go forward although my back prickles with terror, as if some beast that lies behind me has begun to pad forward on its sheathed claws.

I wake with a jolt, panting. I don't know where I have been, but something has flung me down on the bed, discarded.

There is Diner, still sleeping quietly as if he has passed all his nightmares to me and is at peace. I sit up, huddling the bedclothes around me. It is so cold. I find myself listening to catch Thomas's cries, but of course he is not here. I miss him not with my mind but in my body, as I miss Mammie. He is safe and warm, and if he wakes, Philo will cuddle him and give him her finger to suck until it is time for her to feed him.

Diner is a dark bulk, turned away from me. I shiver again. I feel as if I have woken not from one sleep but

341

from a thousand, and that I have come up through layer after layer until at last I am fully awake.

My mother would be ashamed of me. She never flinched, no matter how much she was vilified for what she wrote. She went on steadily, and shrugged when she was lampooned as a harridan in breeches. Anger was a torch to light her way, and she was never deflected. Mammie would not have rested until she had discovered why Lucie lay close by in her unmarked grave.

I should not be here. I know it for certain, as if a wave of knowledge has broken at last and is carrying me with it. I must get up, find my clothes by touch in the dark and put them on. I can move like a shadow when I want and he will not hear me. Listen to his breathing, so soft and steady. He will not wake. I will not wait to question him: that can come later. First I will take Philo and Thomas and all the money that remains to me and go south into Somerset to find Hannah and Will Forrest. We shall all be safe there.

I put my bare feet down on the cold floor. My clothes are on the wooden chair, which is all that is left of our fine bedroom furniture. I fumble on my shift and petticoat. There is no Philo to help me put on my stays, and I cannot do it myself in the dark. I leave them and feel across the floorboards as if I were fishing in a sea of wood, until my fingers snag my stockings.

The last of my money is wrapped in a cloth bag. Since Philo left I have kept it hidden deep in the flour jar.

'Go now,' says the beat in my head, 'go now,' but I cannot listen to it. I cannot feed Thomas, pay Philo her wages and buy food for the winter without money. I knot my loose hair back: it does not matter. It will be covered by the hood of my cloak.

I slip to the door. It opens noiselessly and I am round it and out of the room without looking back at the bed where he lies.

I feel my way down the dark staircase to the kitchen. There is the space under the stairs where Diner hoped to build his plunge-bath: that will not happen now. There is still heat in the stove because I banked it up with slack to keep the fire alive. I break the crust of the fire and push in a spill. It smoulders until light breaks out and flowers along its length. I light the candle on the table before my fingers burn.

The kitchen springs into light and shadow and there is a scuttle from the corner. I must set a mousetrap, I think, then remember that it is too late for this too. The fat-bellied flour jar gleams. I take up the candle from the table and crouch beside the jar. The lid is heavy and it knocks against the rim as I lift it. The clang makes my body stiffen. I set down the candle carefully, and plunge my hand into the cold silkiness of the flour. The bag is not there. It must have fallen deeper. I dig down, searching for an edge of cotton. I stretch my arm and feel as deep as I can, sifting down until my nails grate against the base. There is nothing.

'What are you looking for?' asks Diner behind me.

My hand clutches, and is still. Terror floods me. My

mind whips like a snake. 'I am measuring the flour for tomorrow's bread,' I say.

'A strange time of night to be baking.'

'The stove is still hot. I cannot waste fuel.'

'You are lying to me, Lizzie. Stand up. Look at me.' A glove of flour falls away as I take my hand from the jar. I stand up, slowly, to make time. 'You think I do not know you, Lizzie. What were you looking for?'

'Something of my own, that I had lost.'

'You have nothing of your own. You are my wife. All that you have belongs to me. All that you are belongs to me. You would be glad of it, Lizzie, if you loved me.'

'Why do you say that?'

'Do you think I do not watch you? I saw you tuck away your guineas where you thought I would not find them. I have given everything to you, Lizzie. I have held nothing back. I have trusted you entirely.'

His face is not clear behind the dazzle of candlelight. His voice is hoarse. I am more afraid of him than I have ever been of anyone and yet some other feeling pulses against the tide of fear. I am not sure whether it is pity or love.

'You have no reason not to trust me still,' I say.

'Then why are you dressed? Why are you not in my arms and naked to me? Why do you run from me, hide money from me and go walking alone?'

I begin to hope that he does not fully suspect me. He does not know that I have seen Lucie's grave and he has no idea of my intentions.

'I wanted to buy a dress,' I say. Grey silk glistens for an instant, and is gone.

'A dress,' he repeats. He is silent for a few moments, and when he speaks again his voice has changed. 'How can you be so simple? Do you still not understand our situation?'

I make my voice small and penitent. 'I am a married woman, and yet I have never had a silk dress.'

'Good God! Is this the liberty your mother preached to you? You want a silk dress while we are falling into ruin?' He makes a sound like a laugh but it is not a laugh. 'Never mind. What does it matter if we go to hell in one handcart or another? We shall go far away, Lizzie, to another town where I am not known. I can work. We are not likely to starve. Only I am not sure yet . . .' His voice dies. He stares ahead of him into the candlelight without blinking. 'I am so tired, Lizzie,' he says.

'Shall we go back to bed?'

His gaze flicks over me, suspicious. 'There is no time for that. Those men will be back again at daylight. The rest of my creditors will come for me more leisurely but they will surely come, and if I am not to end the day in a debtors' room in Newgate we must outpace them.'

'I will fetch my cloak,' I say, and begin to move towards the kitchen stairs, casually, as if this were any other day and any other outing. But his arm shoots out and seizes mine.

'We will get it together,' he says. 'From now on, Lizzie, we shall have no separation. We shall always go together.'

26

'We will eat now,' says Diner, 'since we have a long journey ahead of us.'

I stir the porridge round and round in the pan as it cooks. The bubbles rise to the surface, break and spit. Diner has lit all the candles in the kitchen and set them on the table and dresser. The kitchen has not been so bright for months. But I cannot relish the light. It means that Diner does not intend to return here. He is burning his boats. A saying of Mammie's goes round and round in my head: *You cannot have light without darkness.* I jump at the sound of Diner paring sugar from the loaf with a sharp knife.

'We may as well sweeten it,' he says as he takes the spoon out of my hand, drops the sugar into the porridge and stirs.

'We could bring the sugar with us, rather than waste it,' I say.

'Ever the housewife, Lizzie.' My body clenches at his

derision. I want to slap the spoon out of his hand but I subdue myself. I cannot anger him now.

He adds, as if explaining to a child: 'The sugar is too heavy for us to carry. We must travel light if we are to reach our destination.'

'We shall need food, wherever we go.'

He nods, but he is not listening to me. I will make a bundle of the oats and the heel of yesterday's bread, and whatever else I can pack into it. Probably not the cabbage, which is as big as a man's head. I find myself smiling, in spite of everything. And salt; we shall need salt. But when I start to prepare the bundle, Diner pushes it aside.

'It is not worth it,' he says.

'But we must eat.'

Diner's face contracts into a frown. After too long a pause he says, 'We have money enough to pay for our meals. Any cottager will be glad to share his meal in exchange for a few pence.'

It is clearly an afterthought and his lack of concern alarms me.

'We cannot walk into the woods and fields and expect to be fed,' I say, but he smiles at me, showing his teeth.

'You have no faith in me, Lizzie. I promise you that you will not be hungry.'

I turn away so as not to see his smile, and stir the pot again where the porridge is sticking. It is done. I ladle it into bowls, taking as long over it as I can, then I lift my spoon to my mouth, taste, swallow. Each spoonful takes a little more time. I look down into my bowl so that he will not see the calculations which race through my mind. As soon as we are in the street I will break and run. If I can delay us for long enough it will be morning before we leave the house, and there will be people about. This night cannot go on forever. *You cannot have darkness without light.*

'It is past five o'clock,' says Diner, consulting his watch. 'Eat up, Lizzie. We must be gone before daybreak.'

We swallow our porridge in silence. I am about to gather the bowls when Diner stops me. 'There is no need to do that.'

'I must put more wood on the stove.'

'For what?'

'Or at least make up a bundle of clothes. We won't find clean linen in a cottage.'

He looks at me, calculating. I cannot read the thoughts that thicken his gaze, but I give him back look for look: clearly, I hope, and without defiance. He must not believe that I fear to look at him.

'Very well,' he says. 'We shall pack up some things. I will come with you to choose them.'

We go up to our bedroom, each carrying a candle. My fingers shake as I pick out my warmest short gown, mittens and a quilted petticoat along with a change of linen. I roll them into a bundle and tie it tightly. I am about to choose some of his clothes when he stops me. 'No need for that,' he says, and I do not dare to question him. He keeps me always within reach of his arm. 'You are very slow today, Lizzie.'

'It is not yet morning. How can we travel in the dark?'

'We will take a candle lantern. The snow makes the ground light enough. Make haste or I shall begin to think that you are dawdling.'

He ushers me ahead of him out of our bedroom. Although he stays at my elbow, he does not touch me. He stops and looks back at our bed, the tall windows, the beautiful floor. He holds his candle high until the shadows leap and flicker. At last he lowers it and then he closes the door. I go downstairs ahead of him, into the hall, to fetch my cloak and boots. Still he is within an inch of me. He waits until I am done before he puts on his own coat and boots, and unbolts the door. A flood of freezing air comes in. Again he lifts the candle high to look at the trampled snow and the marks the men have made on the door with their boots and fists, and then he opens the candle lantern and sets light to it before putting his candlestick on the floor.

'You should blow it out,' I say.

'Why?'

'It might start a fire.'

'And if it does, it will save someone else the trouble of torching the place. Don't you think they will do that? It seems to me very possible. Put down your candlestick, Lizzie.'

The flame gutters and then steadies as I set down my candle beside Diner's.

'Should we not blow out these candles and take them with us for the lantern?'

'I have candles enough in my pocket.'

He takes my arm and draws me outside, and then he

pulls the door shut behind us. I hear him lock it with the long iron key, and then he turns away from the house until he is facing over the pavement, the grass beyond and then the Gorge. He raises his arm, lifts it high, stretches back and hurls the key as far as it can go. I do not hear it fall and I do not question him. I grip my bundle in my left hand. I have slipped some shavings of sugar into the pocket of my petticoat.

'Take care, there is ice here,' he says in his ordinary voice. We are arm in arm, as we have been so many times. I look back and there is our house, with a faint glow from the candles coming through the fanlight above the door. There is the black, jagged line of the terrace, unfinished, never to be finished now. The snow sends up its whiteness and the light from Diner's lantern is enough to make our shadows stretch and shrink. We reach the pavement but he does not turn towards the centre of Clifton. Instead we go down the steps to the track and then turn left towards the little winding path that zigzags steeply down through scrub and trees to the bottom of the Gorge. I pull back and dig the heels of my boots into the snow.

'Why are we going down here?'

'It is the quickest way to the water.'

'Yes, but we should go down through Clifton and the Hot Well. We can take the Rownham ferry at first light.'

'This will be quicker, Lizzie. Hold on to my arm. I will not let you fall.'

The path is steep and the snow here is not much trodden. I see movements out of the corner of my eye, as if creatures are whisking out of sight at our approach. There is no starlight down here, but our lantern shows the way. It is so cold that my jaw aches. It feels as if we are no longer walking on the earth, but into the bowels of it. I force myself to see the path as it is in daylight, winding coolly down. I have walked it many times. It is perfectly safe and soon there will be labourers tramping down here on their way to the ferry and the quarries on the other side of the Gorge.

A shriek makes me catch my breath.

'A rabbit,' says Diner. 'A fox has taken it.'

We walk on, slipping and sliding in spite of our boots. The way seems longer than I have ever known it, but at last we are down. The path widens, opens, and there is the river. Its muddy banks are almost covered: the tide is high. The water coils and twists in the starlight like a living thing.

'The tide will soon be on the turn,' says Diner. 'It will be hard to row at first, but then it will be easier.'

'The ferrymen are used to it, I suppose,' I say.

As if I had not spoken, Diner continues: 'But I will manage well enough.'

'Surely you will not row,' I say. 'It is madness in this dark.'

'Look there, Lizzie.' He takes my hand and guides it to the east, towards the distant Mendips. 'What do you see there?'

He is right. There is pallor in the sky, a smudge along the line of the horizon which spreads as I watch.

'Dawn is coming,' says Diner. 'We will have light enough for the crossing.'

I was afraid of the darkness but the day ahead makes me more fearful still. There is not a soul here but for the two of us: no traffic on the river, even. But the river is no longer quite black. It is changing colour as wan light spreads from the east.

'The ferry runs at daybreak,' I say.

'But the ferrymen will remember us. I have no wish to be pursued into Somerset by my creditors.'

Diner grips my arm and hurries us towards the Hot Well, or so I think until he stops some way off. There are stone steps leading down to where a boat sits, its oars shipped. She rocks on the sway of the water.

'Be careful on these steps, Lizzie. Hold tight to my hand.'

There are twelve steps. I go down carefully, with the smell of the river filling my head. I have always been so afraid of this water that no one can see into, thick as it is with silt. It is here now, just below me, roiling and sucking at the steps. If I fell, nobody would know. Diner holds me and guides me down to the step above the last.

'Stand well back, Lizzie.'

The boat has swum out a little way on the current, despite the rope that holds it. The gap is perhaps a yard. Diner pushes himself off from the steps and leaps into the bottom of the boat, which staggers under his weight. He pulls out one of the oars and holds it towards me. 'Lean back, Lizzie. Brace yourself and pull hard.'

I pull as hard as I can. The river sucks against me

and then gives way and the boat slides alongside the steps.

'Now, take my hand,' he says. 'Jump!'

In a moment I am over the side of the boat and on to the seat that lies athwart it. My skirts are tumbled and I am hot with the effort but I am safe and almost triumphant for an instant as the boat pitches under my weight. Diner grins at me. For a second we are at one, intimate, joined in our endeavour, and then he bends to untie the thick knot of rope at the bow.

I can see everything quite clearly in the grey light. There is no ice at the edges of the river, although the cold is numbing. It must be because the tide that swells up through the Gorge twice each day fills the river-water with salt and keeps it from freezing.

'Move to the middle, Lizzie, and sit tight there.'

I gather my skirts close. The knot is undone now, and Diner hurls the rope back over the steps. I think: This is not the way the ferrymen secure their ropes. They untie the knot from the bollard, pull the rope into the boat and coil it there. But I suppose there is more than one way to cast off a boat. I pull back my hood to scan the desolate stretch of water. How wide it is. There is a ship moored over by Rownham's Mead, waiting for the tide perhaps. But its sails are furled and it hangs so still it might have been moored there for years. I know it has not. I know it is no ghost ship. It is only the whiteness of the snow on the pastures that makes everything so queer and unlike itself.

Diner has taken both oars. He glances behind him,

digs deep into the water with his right oar to turn us, and we shoot out into the current. He is right: the tide has not yet turned. The water swirls and eddies as the surge of the river meets the surge coming up from the sea. A few weeks ago – years ago, it seems – I would have been chilled by the sight, but now I am indifferent. It is not the river that frightens me.

He is taking me across the river into Somerset, I tell myself. He wants us to go away where no one knows him.

I grip the sides of the boat and taste iron in my mouth. I am sitting still but my heart beats fast, as if I were running.

Diner ploughs the oars in deep to keep us steady as the water slaps and swills. I catch hold of the boat's sides, and cling to them. We are balanced now, with our bow pointing across the river. Other boats are putting out, scudding close to the banks or pushing against the current as we are. Muffled figures bend to their oars. They are rowing in another world and I know that if I cried out they would not turn.

There is a fine grit of ice in the air which thickens in the distance. Diner pulls hard and I find myself moving with him, as if I too am urging the boat onward with my body. I look back. There are the slopes of Clifton, marked here and there with trails of half-built houses. Diner says that they will never be finished now that the war has come with France. They will fall into ruin and sheep will graze over them as they did before. All the life we have had there will be as nothing.

All I have in my pockets is a little sugar. Diner has taken my money and now I must depend upon him entirely. Mammie taught me that a woman must not be weak, but instead learn to fend for herself. Her pen was enough to feed us in all the years before she married Augustus. I have the clothes I stand in, and my bundle. I can work and earn my bread, if I have to go as a servant. The snow-thick pasture is gliding nearer, and the forest. Diner glances behind him, judging the distance between us and the shore.

'Where shall we land?' I ask him.

'You will see when we come close.'

I look back again at the city. Scribbles of smoke lift from the houses huddled at the Hot Well, and below them steam coils from the surface of the river in the places where the hot springs rise. Everything is distinct, intense, as if I were seeing all through a reading glass. But I only want to look backwards. I want to see myself hurrying up the slopes to where Mammie's lodgings lie. There she sits up in bed with her writing-board propped against her knees. She's wrapped in her shawl and her spectacles are slipping down the bridge of her nose. She does not look up. She does not know that I am coming.

No, Lizzie. You cannot keep telling yourself the same story. Mammie has folded up her work. It's done, and she has gone. She has put down her pen, blotted her pages, shuffled them together as I have seen her do so many times, and then riffled the edges with her fingers as if to satisfy herself that she has done enough. She has risen and taken off her spectacles. There is a red groove cut into the bridge of her nose. She walks away, because her work is finished.

There is a bump. We have reached the other side. He has not brought me to the forest: the trees begin two fields away.

Diner has no rope to attach the boat to the landing-stage.

'Get out, Lizzie. Quickly.' I balance myself and jump on to the hard ground. 'Take hold of the bow, as I do. Pull, Lizzie, pull hard.'

I heave and struggle, as he does, until we have hauled the boat up on to the frozen bank. He says it will not shift now, for the tide is starting to fall and the boat will soon be ten feet above water.

It is lush here in summer, and the cows wade knee-deep in grass. It would be boggy now if the frost had not set in so hard.

'This way,' says Diner, as if he sees a high road before us instead of a cattle-track through sallow, frozen grass. The track leads to a stile, and beyond it fields stretch to the dark edge of the wood. 'We cut through this way, and if I have the direction right, it will bring us through the forest and out on to the road through Failand and then south.'

I am comforted a little. It seems that we have a journey ahead of us, and a purpose. He strides out surely, as if he does indeed know where we are going. My bundle is not heavy but my skirts slow me. I stop to kilt them up, for there is no one here to see me. Diner turns instantly.

'What are you doing?'

'I cannot walk freely.'

'Take my hand.'

There is scarcely room for us to walk abreast but he folds my hand in his and holds it so firmly that it would pain me if I did not keep up with him. I stumble once or twice on the frozen ruts and each time he pulls me upright before I have time to fall. I scramble over the stile and we follow the track across the second field. The trees are close. They are so thick that even now when the leaves have fallen, I cannot see the way ahead.

27

There are tracks everywhere in the snow. Rabbits, I think, and deer, and birds' triangular claw prints set lightly and then frozen. Rooks fly up, cawing. My wrist burns where Diner grasps it. The snow is deep here and untrodden by human feet. It comes over the top of my boots. It clogs the hem of my skirts as I wade through it.

'Come, Lizzie! You are dawdling again.'

Suddenly I am angry. It's well for him in his breeches and high boots.

'Stop,' I say, and he does stop, I think from pure surprise at hearing me order him. He turns round, still holding my left wrist, and takes my right hand too, causing me to drop my bundle. A spasm of something almost like laughter seizes me. We look as if we are about to dance away over the forest floor; only he is holding me too tightly. With a sudden movement, I chop my hands down and outwards. He lets go. We stand face-to-face, breathing hard.

'Do not drag me like a child,' I say. It was he who released me, not I who freed myself. But I will speak as if I did not know it. He is uncertain now – I see it. There is sweat on his forehead.

'I have not hurt you,' he says.

I strip off my gloves and hold out my wrists to show him the red marks where he has grasped me. They are deep on my left wrist: they will bruise. He says nothing. He bows his head; then he stoops down, picks up a handful of snow and rubs my wrist with it. The skin tingles.

'Is that better?' he asks.

I shake my head. He fetches up a sigh and a muscle jumps on his cheek.

'Let us go slowly,' he says.

'I will follow you.'

'Will you?'

'Of course.'

I would not dare to turn and run. He would overtake me in a moment and then he would have no trust in me and would not care what he did. He has my wrist in his hand still. Slowly, tenderly, he rubs in the snow.

'Put on your gloves,' he says. 'You will be cold.'

'I am very cold.'

'Follow me closely.'

We twist and turn and I keep my eyes on the ground so as not to stumble. We plough through a bewilderment of stumps, trees, snow, grabbing branches. We pass the ruin of an oak and plunge into a scrub of whitebeam. Branches join above our heads like ribs. Diner says, 'We will stop here, Lizzie.'

The path widens. Here is a little glade which must be pleasant enough in the summer. Now it is full of snow and blue shadows. High above us the rooks sail, still cawing.

'Why here?'

But Diner does not answer. He treads around the circumference of the glade, as if he is walking to some measure that is invisible to me. He glances up at the sky, at the trees and then he moves inward a little, clearing away snow with the sides of his boots.

'It is here,' he says.

'What is here? Diner, you said we must hurry. We have come no distance.' I hear the chatter of alarm in my voice, as I heard it from the birds that we disturbed.

'She is here.'

'Who?' I ask. The question leaves my mouth but I know the answer. Like a bat it unfolds its wings and blots out all other thought.

'My Lucie,' he says. He kneels down and feels along the half-cleared earth. 'This is the place, I am sure of it. She lies with her head to the east.'

I take a step back. Instantly he springs up from his crouch like a hare and I am within his grasp. He does not touch me.

'You are not well,' I say. 'Lucie does not lie here, but in St Andrew's churchyard.'

He stares at me in what looks like the purest amazement. 'Why do you say that?'

'You told the Frenchwoman she was buried there. Madame Bisset.'

'How do you know her name?'

'I heard it.'

'I had to tell her something,' says Diner, almost lightly, as if the whole thing were of no significance. 'But I must take you to task, Lizzie. It seems that you have been following in my footsteps all this while, spying on me as if you were my enemy and not my wife. Come here. Kneel down. Feel the earth here – No, you cannot feel it through those gloves. Do you not feel the contour, there, where the earth has sunk? I thought it should have risen, but now it falls away. This is the place. I am no grave-digger, Lizzie; it is not my trade.'

My scalp crawls as if ice is parting my hair. 'What are you telling me?'

'You know what I am telling you. This is the place. I cannot keep away from it. If you only knew how many times I have come here – But it makes no difference. Nothing changes. It is always the same.'

The earth is rough and cold. 'Tell me what happened,' I ask him, as I should have asked him long ago.

'You will not believe me, Lizzie. You will only pretend to do so. You will humbug me.'

'You must try me then,' I say. I know that I must keep him talking. He must remember that I am Lizzie and have done him no harm.

'Stand up. You must not kneel there in the snow. You are shivering.'

He reaches for me and I cannot stop myself flinching.

His hands grip, pulling me up. He beats the snow off my cloak.

'Tell me,' I say.

'It is true that I was angry with her. I had reason, Lizzie. She thought I did not know her tricks but I had her followed. She would smile at me when I left her, and say that she was going to her dressmaker. It is commonplace to praise a smiling woman for her amiable disposition. You do not smile, Lizzie. I like your grave face. I watched her dance with him in her bronze slippers that she thanked me for with a kiss. I watched her feet tap and turn, so fleet you would think she was not tied to the earth as we are. She smiled too much. There was to be another dance, and she intended to expose herself with him again.'

My chin aches, as it does when I am about to vomit. Another dance: the dress. There is a vile taste in my mouth. I breathe in deeply through my nose, and swallow.

'But this is no ballroom,' I say. 'How did she come here?'

'It was a fine evening and she wanted to hear the nightingales. She needed no more than her light wrap. She said that she had something to tell me but I knew what it was. I asked her about Hibbert. She pretended to know nothing. She thought she could humbug me as she had done before. God knows how many times she had deceived me. I took her by the shoulders. It was only to get the truth out of her – I would not have hurt her – but she twisted herself from me and ran.' He frowns, and puts out a hand as if to stop me. 'No. That was not it. I will tell you exactly. She twisted herself from me. I would not have thought she could run so fast, but she picked up her skirts and dodged through the trees until I thought I should have lost her.' He draws me to the edge of the glade, and points through the trees. 'There. Look there, Lizzie. That is where she fell.'

'Is there a drop?'

'I caught her there. I had hold of her skirts but I lost my balance and went down. She fell under me and struck her head. I did not see anything. I only felt that she did not move beneath me. I struggled to my feet but still she lay there. I did not dare to touch her. I was afraid to turn her over. I think she was not in her right mind to run so.' He stops, and heaves a breath before continuing. 'She had struck her head as she fell. Just here, at the temple. You see how the ground is full of stones. It was my weight coming down on her that made the blow harder. I did not understand. When I turned her at last her eyes were open, but they did not see me. I thought there was a spark in them when I lifted her and carried her into the light. I thought she would have spoken. There was no blood, Lizzie. Only a little from her nose. I took leaves and fanned her face.'

I see that he believes his story. It moves before his eyes and he follows it, this way and that. There is Lucie, dancing. There is the glade, full of sun. My skin crawls, no longer with terror but with a revulsion stronger than any feeling I have felt before. He believes it and there is no one living who can contradict him. Lucie is here beneath our feet, her mouth stopped with earth.

I have never wanted so much to remain alive. My flesh, my tongue, my lips all know what they must do.

'An accident of the most terrible nature,' I say. 'You must not blame yourself.'

He has steadied himself. He is seeing me now, not Lucie. His eyes search me with the old quickness, to discover if I am lying. I look back. I do not see him: I will not see him or Lucie or any of it. I look inward to where Thomas stretches out his arms for me, and Philo laughs, showing her gappy teeth. I feel the cold of the earth coming up through the soles of my boots.

'I cannot help feeling some blame,' he says. 'It is a heavy burden, Lizzie.'

I moisten my lips. 'And so you buried her here.'

'I had no choice.'

My thoughts burst within me, but I hold them down. There is a hazel bush at the edge of the glade and I go over to it. Diner does not stop me. I break off two twigs and shake away the snow. They are frail but hardy too, with some sap in them yet. I take out my handkerchief and bind the twigs into a cross, and then I push it deep into the snow where Diner says that Lucie lies. I did not think that Diner would let it stand, and he does not. He plucks it out of the snow and tucks it inside his coat. Then another thought comes to him. He unties the cross, shakes out the handkerchief and folds it into a bandage. Before I can guess his thought he is on me.

'Don't move, Lizzie.' I feel his breath on my cheek as he binds my eyes. I do not dare raise my hands to loosen it. 'Now,' he says, and he takes my shoulders and spins me around, once, twice, three times, until I stagger. I make a sound in my throat but I do not cry out. He takes my arm and leads me away.

28

We are on the river again before Diner unties my blind-fold. The sudden light dazzles me and I shut my eyes. When I open them there is Diner opposite me, unshipping his oars. The current has already pushed us sideways, but he rights us quickly and begins to row. The high cliffs of the Gorge press in on either side. We are moving downriver. But why the boat, if we are going into Somerset? We should have kept on walking.

'Are we crossing back to the Hot Well?'

'We may have too warm a welcome there. A band of my creditors gathered to meet me, ready to throw me into Newgate. We must press on, Lizzie.'

I stretch my cold fingers inside my gloves. I wish that I were rowing too, for it would keep me warm. Something is missing and I can't think what it is, until I remember my bundle. It is gone, and I have not noticed until this moment. It must have been lost after I put it down to make my cross for Lucie. I did not think of it then because once Diner bandaged my eyes I had no room for anything but fear. My bladder hurt and he let me squat down to relieve myself. I heard the sound of him doing the same. I thought he had blindfolded me because he meant to lead me to one of the drops which would kill me if I fell. Now I think he only did it so that I would not remember where Lucie lay.

Snow has a smell; I know that now. I have never smelled it before. And there was the sour, dry smell of the forest, too, before it changed when we went out into the meadow. He helped me over the stile. I did not realise at first what it was. All I knew was the climb and the fear of falling on the other side. I did not know how far down the drop might be. When my boot touched the earth, tears rushed to my eyes under the blindfold.

He made me help him haul the boat down to the water. The keel grated on the frozen edge of the bank, and then the angle of the boat tipped and I could hardly hold it. The tide had fallen. I pushed and the boat came to life as it felt water under it. For a second I thought of shoving it out as far as I could so that the current would take it away from us, but Diner held my arm fast. He turned me to him, lifted me by the elbows and set me down inside the boat. I thought that he meant to row me out and drown me and I shrank away from him, clutching at the seat. I did not dare to strip off my blindfold although my hands were free. I felt us push off from the bank and then the current came at us side-on, rocking us roughly until Diner turned the boat and we steadied.

Now I see that we are not the only boat on the river.

There is none close enough for me to hail, and anyway I would not take the risk. In an instant Diner could wrestle me over the edge into the water. He would say that I was insane and determined to destroy myself no matter how hard he struggled to hold me back. Women do throw themselves into the river. They fill their pockets with stones and plunge into the water to hide their shame. They leap from the Sea Walls. Sometimes their bodies are discovered on the slime of the mudbanks when the tide is out. Many are never found. I suppose that the tide takes them and hides them in the sea.

Diner ships his oars again and strips off his coat. He leans forward, rocking the boat, and places it around my shoulders. 'It will keep you warm, Lizzie.'

I cling to the hope his words give. If I am to be kept warm, then perhaps I am to live. He means us to moor downriver, and walk again until we find the road south.

He rows well, with long, smooth strokes that push us fast within the flow of the tide. We go past the Gunpowder House, where a ship is moored, canted sideways on the mud, waiting for the next tide. Suddenly I see a fox, more gold than red, padding in and out of the reeds. It lifts its head and gazes at me insouciantly. I have never seen a fox in such a light, as if it were my equal, looking at me over the water out of the business of its own life. I wish I were that fox.

Diner whistles through his teeth as he rows, and his hair ruffles in the wind of our passage. Behind him the river widens. I know this stretch well enough, from long walks along the towpath, but I never knew how the river changes when you are on it and part of it. It is wider. There is more light. We are more separate from the land than I have ever imagined.

A man on the towpath lifts his hand in greeting, and then plods on with his collar drawn up over his ears.

'Do you know that man, Lizzie?' asks Diner sharply.

'Of course not. He was merely wishing us good-day.'

'He may keep his wishes to himself. What is that?'

There are two men on horseback, riding out from the city. They have fine strong horses: their flanks steam in the winter air. It puzzles me that gentlemen should have taken out such splendid animals when the earth is hard as iron. If they should stumble on the frozen ruts they will be ruined.

The breath of men and horses smokes. They are looking across at us, shading their eyes against the glare of the snow.

'Who are those men? Do you know them, Lizzie?'

'No.'

'Then tell me why they are looking at you.'

'They are merely curious. They are surprised to see a woman out on the river in such weather.'

'Be damned to them and to their curiosity. Draw your cloak over your head, Lizzie, so it hides your face. Bring my coat close around you.'

The horses have stopped. They fling up their heads and the men gentle them. I think I can hear the snorts of the horses across the water, but I have to look over my shoulder to see them now. The men are conferring. A wild hope leaps in me that they are uneasy about me: that they are asking each other how they may help me. Diner bends to the oars and rows faster. I look back again and the horses have turned. The riders are going back to the city. They have seen the heavy yellow cloud ahead of them over Wales, and they are uneasy about the weather. They have not thought of me at all.

'Why do you look back, Lizzie?'

'I was looking at the horses. The sky is growing very dark ahead of us. I think we shall have more snow.'

He does not answer. It is less easy now to see the detail of the bare trees, the reeds and the grey heron that each stand their territory along the bank. The air is growing thicker and more grainy.

'We must find shelter,' I say.

'Do you think I should build you another house?' he asks, and gives a bark of laughter. We are almost at the Horseshoe Bend. I would never have thought we should have got here so fast, but with the falling tide and the strength of the current, Diner's rowing is more a matter of keeping us on course than of making way. He has judged it all well.

I see nothing ahead of me but whiteness as the river widens. We will come out into the sea, with its eddying channels and banks of mud and sand to trap us. Whatever Diner intends, it will make no difference. We will be caught there. The boat will overturn. Our boots will fill with water and our sodden clothes will drag us down. I suppose we will struggle but I cannot think of that. We will both drown and no one will know what has happened. If they ever find us our faces will be so mauled that they will be unrecognisable. And it will be so cold.

Thomas will not even remember me. Philo will believe that I have taken my money with me, and abandoned them.

If only I had not always defended Diner. I persuaded Mammie and Augustus that I could imagine no better husband. I bristled like a cat when Hannah sniffed and criticised. I kept from them all the signs that troubled me.

Thomas. My arms imagine his hot, damp weight. For an instant I smell his baby scent of milk, urine and new bread. I feel the quick pulse of his heart. If Thomas were here, I would do anything to protect him. If he were here, I would act.

I hear the clack and creak of oars in the distance. Another boat, not ours. When I glance behind, I see it, slowly coming clear out of the fog. A longboat, three times the size of ours. Now I can pick out the figures at the oars but I cannot yet see their faces. There are three pairs of oarsmen – no, four. The oars rise and fall in perfect rhythm as the boat glides towards me. I wonder that Diner does not see it gaining on us. He looks up, and then bends to his oars again without giving the least sign of alarm.

They are coming close. They are going to pass alongside us within yards, and still Diner does not see them. They are muffled in their cloaks, but then, as they come alongside, their hoods slip back from their faces.

I see them all. There is Augustus in the bows, rowing in the first rank with Caroline Farquhar beside him. She rows hard, as if she were born to it. Behind them Susannah, paired with Richard Sacks. And there's Hannah! Who would have thought she still had the strength to pull an oar? But there she is, paired with Will Forrest, whose red hair glows like a beacon through the icy fog. I see Philo too, and the dressmaker who made Lucie's silk dress. I know that they will have Thomas with them. Philo would never leave him behind. He'll be snug in his cradle at the bottom of the boat, wrapped up like a caterpillar against the cold.

Their faces turn to me. Their eyes search for mine, although they do not break the rhythm of their rowing. Now I hear their breathing, hard and deep with effort. All at once they lift their oars and drops of water fall from the blades as their boat shoots alongside. They are smiling with relief because they have caught up with me. They have come for me, I know it, and I know they are waiting for me to come to them. I stretch my arm as far as I can, hoping to touch one of their oars. In perfect symmetry, the oars fall. The last of them sweeps through my outstretched hand but I do not feel it and it makes no mark.

As the boat passes I see her, sitting in the stern. She has her writing-board on her knee and she is scribbling down notes. She looks up as she sometimes does, pondering, and then she sees me. Her gaze sweeps over me like the beam of a lighthouse, illuminating everything, and then it returns to settle on my face. As their boat surges on she looks back, leaning on her elbow, watching me. She continues to hold my gaze until the boat vanishes into the white curtain of snow and mist ahead of us.

I am so cold. Soon I will be too cold to think. I must think now, while I can. That is why they came. I must act.

I shift on the seat, watching Diner closely. At once his eyes are on me like a cat's. I cannot wrestle him to take control of the boat. He has the oar and he can batter me with it. He does not stop rowing but his eyes never leave my face.

I remember the sugar in my pocket. My fingers are clumsy in my gloves, so I strip them off and burrow deep into my petticoats. I come on a sugar-shaving, sharp as glass. I take it out.

'What are you doing, Lizzie?'

'Lean towards me. Open your mouth. I have something for you.'

'What do you mean?'

'Close your eyes and open your mouth.'

'What is this, a game?'

'A good game.'

He will not close his eyes. I show him the sugar on my palm, and then I bend forward until I feel his breath on my fingers.

'Open your mouth.'

And he does. I slip the sugar between his teeth.

'Swallow it. I have more.' I take another splinter of sugar and feed it to him. 'It will give you strength.'

'Strength!' His face crumples oddly, as Thomas's does before he cries. He stops rowing, and his right hand drops from the oar. It tilts up sharply and I just save it as it begins to slide towards the river. I drag it back into the boat. Diner does not move or attempt to touch me. He is still holding the other oar, but loosely, as if he has forgotten what to do with it. I pull it into the boat too. We turn slowly, drifting sideways.

I fetch another piece of sugar out of my pocket. It is not the last, thank God: I have put in more than I thought.

'I wish I had the wine for you as well.'

'I wish you had.'

I look down, and as I do so I glance sideways. We are being pushed towards the elbow of the bend. I put another piece of sugar between his lips.

'You are not afraid that I will bite?'

'I am not afraid of you, any more than I am afraid of myself. You are too much part of me.'

'Ah, Lizzie,' he says, as if my words pain him, 'if you knew me, you would want no part of me.'

'I know you,' I say, and I do. A fierce light has burned all the foolishness out of my heart. He has deluded me but I have also deluded myself, and willingly. I have wanted him to be what he never was.

'I did not mean to kill her. It was my weight that bore down on her. If it had not been for the stone when she fell she would not have died. Do you believe me, Lizzie?'

I stroke his cheek with my right hand, and one by one I offer him the last shavings of sweetness. We are coming into the bend fast. The mud glistens where the tide has sluiced it down. Black seaweed clings to the bank. I dare not take the oar to guide us in.

'I have visited her many times,' says Diner. 'You did not know, Lizzie. You thought I was at Grace's Buildings. I was unfaithful to you.'

'You were never unfaithful,' I say quickly, for I do not like this direction of thought. 'Lucie is dead.'

'That makes no difference,' he says, and sighs. 'You said once that to kill was to cross a river and that there was no way to return. How did you know that?'

'I spoke without knowing.'

'Is there more sugar?'

'I think it is all gone now. But there is still sweetness on my fingers.'

I put them into his mouth. I feel him suck them, as Thomas used to do, until all the sweetness is gone. With a soft bump, we graze the bank, float off and then come in again. Diner stares around like one waking.

'Why have we stopped here?'

'The river has brought us here.' I do not stop stroking his cheek as I gather my skirts around me. 'It is too cold for us on the river, Diner. We must come ashore here. We must find shelter or we will die of the cold, out on the water.'

The boat is lodged. Soon it will be stranded, as the tide continues to fall. Diner glances at the bank and then the water, and knowledge returns to him. I get up, slowly, holding his hand. I make myself move simply although I am in a fever of calculation. Slowly, steadily, so that there is no clear moment when I can be stopped, I step out on to the suck of the mud. I know it cannot be too deep here, with the reeds growing so thick. It will not hold me fast.

'You must help me a little,' I say as I let go of his hand.

He too stands, and steps out of the boat, but he is heavier than I am and sinks deeper.

'Step quickly,' I say. 'Do not let your weight rest on the mud.'

The mud wants to hold us but I will not let it. At each step I cling to the reeds and pull myself up by them. The mud is harder now. On the last step I tug my boot free and the mud releases it with a gross squelch. I am on solid ground, sweating.

A half-hour later I could not have done it. The water would have sunk too far and there would have been too much mud. I wipe my hands with a bunch of dead grass, and then I scrub them with snow. Diner watches but does not attempt to clean himself.

'My Lizzie,' he says. Our breath comes in gouts of white between us. He does not try to touch me but he stands too near. My body quivers with awareness of his. 'Where will you go now?'

Surely he is teasing me. He cannot mean to let me go. Or he is testing me, waiting to see if I will run?

'We must follow the towpath,' I say, as if I have never dreamed of separating myself from him. 'We must find shelter before the snow comes.'

'You know that I cannot come with you.'

'What do you mean?'

'You must go alone.'

'Without you?'

'I have another engagement, Lizzie. Isn't that what they say?' He smiles, as if at his own absurdity.

'Yes.' I know I must agree, I must please him, I must not go against him now. Against my will my hand creeps out and lays itself on his sleeve. My body has not caught up with what my mind knows. It remembers his body and mine, conjoined, not to be parted. One flesh. My hand presses his sleeve.

He does not respond. He was one flesh long before I knew him, and not with me. I look at my own hand and hate it: I am a slavish thing to myself. I snatch my hand away from him.

'You understand me very well, Lizzie,' he says. 'You say that she is dead but I cannot help myself. Wherever she is, I must visit her.'

He steps back. He glances behind him, measuring the distance, and then he turns to me again. 'You must keep my coat, Lizzie,' he says, and he fastens it more securely over my cloak. He nods, as if he is satisfied, and then he turns away again, lifts his boots high, as I did, and climbs down the bank. The mud sucks but it cannot hold him. He shoves the boat hard and as it begins to move he throws himself into it.

He takes the oars again with the old mastery. The drugged, dreaming look has gone. He is the same man who strode out of his house each morning, to oversee the building of the terrace. It was his own vision, and nobody else saw it. It would be realised despite every-thing. He always knew that.

He lifts his hand to me for a moment.

He will turn the boat. He will fight his way upriver, back to the meadow and the landing-place. He will return to Lucie.

I watch, shading my eyes, as he rows out to the middle of the river. But he does not turn. He does not fight the current. He steers until the boat points west and when the current takes him he digs in his oars and rows strongly, as if he wants to go even faster. He is going with the flow of the tide towards the sea. He is at the next bend, rowing hard. I cannot see him well. I blink to clear my eyes, and then I understand that it has begun to snow, and that it is the thickening flakes which hide him from me. I blink again, and he is gone.

29

The old woman puts me on a stool by her fire and clatters her kettle on to the trivet. Pictures appear and bloom in my brain, more real than the tongues of flame in the fire. I have been drugged with cold but I did not know it. I think she understands it for she takes off Diner's coat but not my cloak, and wraps a blanket around me. It stinks of onions but it is warm. The coat collapses to the floor, sodden with mud, and she picks it up, chirruping, and hangs it on a hook beside the fireplace.

The kettle clatters. Heat stuns me: I cannot stir. After a while she puts into my hands a tin mug of hot spiced ale. I lift it to my lips and scald myself gladly. The ale goes down and spreads out to my fingertips.

'I have not got a halfpenny,' I say.

She nods. She knew as much, and it does not matter. I remember that I have a handkerchief in one of my pockets. I will give it to her when I can move my fingers. There are chickens in the corner of the room, bunched together and clucking to themselves. A cot in the corner; a deal table; two stools. Strings of onions and bunches of herbs hang from the ceiling. I begin to see it all as the ale warms me until my feet tingle with returning blood.

She found me on the towpath. She had a bundle of firewood on her back, but she stopped for me. There were not many words between us, or I don't remember them. I think she believed that I had tried to throw myself into the river, and thought better of it, and that was why I stood so shocked and shaken with the cold. She tugged at my sleeve, nodding to me as if I was simple. She would not let go of me until I understood that I was to come with her.

I would never have found the place on my own. She led me over a stile, across a field and into a copse, and there it was: a stone hut – a single room, black with smoke, thick with a brew of smells. The warmth hit me like strong drink and I staggered. She put me down on the stool and I have not moved since. If it were not for the old woman I would still be on the towpath now. I would be picked up in the morning, frozen.

The old woman is busy at the table. I turn my head and watch her cut a chunk off a black loaf, which she hands to me, showing me that I should dip it in the ale and swallow it. The bread is very hard. She has no teeth so I think she must always take her food like this. I thank her, and swallow the sweet, stale bread. It goes down into me like life itself.

'Iss ee ungray?' she mutters, in a voice so thick and toothless that I can barely make out the words.

'Yes.'

She stands, reaches to a stone shelf and fetches down an egg, which she coddles tenderly in her hand. In this cold weather there will not be many eggs. She breaks the egg into a bowl and whisks it hard with a little whisk made of twigs; then, nodding at me, she places the bowl in my hands. I must swallow it. I lift the bowl to my lips, tip it, and make myself swallow the egg. After that I hand back the bowl and take another drink of ale. The bread is gone. The old woman strokes my head as if I am a child, and I thank her. If I had my bundle I could give her some linen. I reach into my pocket but there is no handkerchief. I remember the blindfold and shudder all over.

She fetches a chicken and brings it to me in her arms, holding it close to me as if to make us acquainted, and then she sets herself down on the other stool next to me, with the chicken in her lap, stroking it. The firelight plays on her face, which is seamed with dirt and wrinkles into patterns which look like the crazing of a field after drought. She stares into the fire and croons to the chicken, or to me, or to herself. She smells sour, gamey, like a creature of the woods and not a woman.

There is a pile of wood built high along the wall. A barrel of water stands in the corner, and a crock which must hold oats or flour, for there is a wooden measure on its lid. A couple of blackened pans hang on hooks above the fireplace. Everything is almost within reach because the place is so small.

We sit for a long time and then she says something about a babby, but I cannot make out the rest of her words. I am startled for a moment, thinking that somehow she knows about Thomas, but that cannot be the case. She must mean a grandchild of her own, or more likely a great-grandchild. But she sees that I do not understand and she points to my belly. Of course, she believes me to be a girl in trouble who has come here to throw herself into the river and end it all, as others have done before her.

'No,' I say, 'no, there is no babby.'

She takes no notice of my words. She reaches to stroke my belly through the blanket and she chuckles as she does to the birds. The chicken does not like it. It sets up a flurry of jealous squawks until she smooths it again.

I sleep there for two nights. I tell the old woman my name, but she does not tell me hers and she never uses mine. Perhaps she cannot hear me, although she is quick enough whenever one of the chickens stirs. The day turns on them. She feeds them grain by hand, or the peelings from our vegetables. If she has nothing else to give them, they peck on a heel of black bread. Each morning she sweeps out the bed of dried reeds and rushes she makes for them in the corner of the room. I go out and scavenge for wood, taking care not to be seen. I skin and joint a rabbit that the old woman has caught in her trap.

I sleep on Diner's coat, on the floor beside the old woman's cot, and I relieve myself in the lean-to privy. Her eyes are not good enough for sewing, although she has needle and thread in a box on her shelf, so I mend her cloak where it has ripped as she foraged in the woods. She does not light candles, although she possesses three. Once the brief daylight has gone, we sit by the fire. I hold a chicken in my lap and smooth down its feathers, as she does. Sleep overwhelms me: I have never been so tired. The past is hidden. There is only this room, the chickens, the rankness of living and the old woman's face. I sleep more than I have slept since I was a child.

On the third morning I wake and know that it is time to leave. I am strong again and I am afraid to take too much food out of the old woman's mouth. I promise myself that I will return and pay her when I can, but I know that it is not with money that I can repay such a debt. She is as unconcerned by my leaving as she was by my arrival. She watches me wrap myself in my cloak and she lifts Diner's coat to me, but I shake my head. I shall not take it. She looks at it, pinching the broad-cloth between her fingers. She knows how good the cloth is. I push it into her arms, for I don't believe it will bring her the bad luck that it would bring to me. She may lay it over her cot on the coldest nights or if she wants she may sell it.

The frost still holds but there has been no more snow. The air is so bright and sharp that it makes me gasp. I am over the threshold and she is already closing the door to keep in the warmth. She will forget me soon enough. No doubt she is already crooning to her chickens, rummaging in their nesting-places in the hope of finding an egg.

For three days I have been hidden from my own thoughts, but it seems now that Diner walks beside me. A woman may die from a fall, if the heavy weight of a man bears down on her. It is credible.

I see her run and stumble. I see her brought down.

30

June 1789

Lucie chooses her silk. There are four bolts laid out on the counter, each a different variation on the theme of grey. They range from silver to pewter. She takes off her gloves to feel the quality of each. The best way is to hold the silk to your cheek and caress it, because the skin of the face is so much more sensitive than the skin of the hands. However, she has found that people in England are ignorant about such matters. They look askance when you pinch fruit, smell fish or press a cheese to be sure that it is ripe. They say, 'You can do that once you've paid for it,' which she did not understand when she first came.

She is not going to hurry this. Mr Gilliam has shown her several silks which she would not even call grey. There is too much blue in them. She will ask him to take each bolt to the shop door again, because she needs to see how the silk responds to the light. Of course she

will be wearing it by candlelight, in the Assembly
Rooms, and that light cannot be reproduced in such a
small space as this shop. But she will try her best.

Mr Gilliam suggests that if he brings the silk to the
window, that will give her a very fair impression of
its quality, but she shakes her head. She knows that
he prefers not to be seen holding a bolt of cloth in the
doorway, but if he wants the sale, then that is what
he must do.

The pewter is, after all, a little too dark. It will set
off her hair and skin but it will be passed over. People
who have no taste will think it dull. She does not want
a dress which needs to be furbished with touches of
colour; she wants a silk which will speak for itself.

Papa would approve of her carefulness. He has
worked hard all his life, from the age of eleven, and he
is among the best tailors in Bordeaux. Or he was, before
he fell ill. He continues to work, but he is very slow
now. Thank God, he has always saved and lived frugally.
It used to annoy her when she was younger. She could
not understand why they continued to live in two
rooms, when they might have afforded a small house
as long as they went a little outside the city. He
dressed plainly. The cut was good but each coat had to
last. He said that people did not want to see a tailor
growing rich at their expense. It made them think that
he charged too much.

Papa salted away his money. She never knew how
much he possessed but she believed it had become a
handsome sum over the years. He was able to give her

a dowry, very much to John's surprise. He had thought that she was a poor girl, a little milliner without resources or background. Lucie supposes that if he had wanted her less, he might have calculated more.

This silk is a gift from Papa. She did not ask for it or expect it. She is married now and far from France. She wants him to take care of himself, not to indulge her. He sent the money in a letter.

'Spend it at once, and on yourself,' he wrote. 'Write and tell me what you have bought, and how you look.' She had to read it over twice to believe it. Her careful, frugal father who never wanted to spoil her, who told her to dress modestly without making herself conspicuous. She was a milliner, not a woman of fashion, and her clients would prefer to see her dressed in decent black.

She will surprise John. He will have no idea, until he sees her on the night of the ball at the Assembly Rooms. He does not much care for dancing but he will dance with her in this dress. He has not been himself lately. It is because he is always working too hard. He becomes angry with her for no reason, and questions her over where she has been and what she has done. One has to take such things lightly. She laughs and tells him that her life is very much less interesting than he thinks. She goes to the shops, she sews, she tries to read a little of the newspaper that he brings home in order to improve her English. He works long hours, which she understands and respects. That is necessary, if a man is ever to build up his business. It is how she grew up with Papa. As soon as she was old enough she began her own training and she too worked assiduously to master her craft. She can call herself a milliner. It is not nothing.

These silks. She hesitates between two of them. Although she has not said so to Mr Gilliam, she has already dismissed the other two from her mind. She is thinking of how the silk will fall. She will not make the dress herself, because there is enough money for her to take the silk to Mrs Iles, who will do it better.

Mr Gilliam holds a bolt of silk to the light. It is the most silvery of all, and yet the sheen is subtle. He turns it this way and that. He unwraps a yard to show her how it falls. She feels it between her fingers. Suddenly, daring, she lifts the silk to her cheek and rubs it, just a little, a caress. He looks askance but he has no need. She never powders.

'This one,' she says.

The silk is wrapped in tissue paper and then made up into a parcel. Should he send it? asks Mr Gilliam, but she says no, she will take it with her. She has decided to go straight to Mrs Iles.

The discussion is delicious, in the little room beside the surgeon's at Jacob's Well. Lucie has respect for Mrs Iles, who knows what she is about. The room is modest but Mrs Iles has the latest patterns and quickly understands what Lucie wants. There is a great art in making a dress which moves with the body perfectly, and although Lucie is not sure that Mrs Iles possesses this art, she knows her silk. She knows how to show its beauty to the best advantage. She measures Lucie with great care, asking her to lift her arms, hold out her arms, bend from the waist. She even asks Lucie if she will dance a few steps across the room. Lucie does so, swaying through the small space in her stays.

Mrs Iles will cut out the dress. They fix a date for a second fitting, but in spite of herself, Lucie appears doubtful about this. Mrs Iles assures her that it is no matter if Lucie cannot manage it. She has taken the measurements most exactly.

Lucie does not explain that it is hard for her to go out alone: John does not like it. The dress will certainly be ready for the Assembly Ball. The fee is set and she decides that she will pay it now, for otherwise John may see that she has money. Mrs Iles is to be trusted.

The afternoon is balm to Lucie. She is safe here. There are no misunderstandings between her and Mrs Iles. This is Lucie's world, and she understands it. No one will question her here. She is a very good milliner who has served her apprenticeship and gone on to build up an excellent clientèle. She has always worked hard. John did not want her to start up a little business here in Bristol. He said that there was no need for it. She was a married woman now, and he was able to provide for them both. But sometimes she wonders if this was the beginning of the difficulty between them. When they first met, she did not depend upon him as she does now. She did not watch his frowns and smiles with an anxious heart. If he smiled, she was smiling too. If he frowned, she asked him what was the matter. She went home each evening, took off her dress and washed herself and then she put on a plain cotton gown to do the housework and prepare the evening meal for Papa and herself. She was content.

Ah God, what is she saying? John is a good husband to her. She has left her home and France, her clients and the little streets where she is known and her custom is familiar. She has done all this and it was the right decision.

He is nervous. He works too hard. These things lead to misunderstandings between them. He imagines things that are not real. He ponders over them as if he wants to madden himself. One day he is cold with her; the next he grasps her to him so fiercely she cannot breathe.

Or perhaps it is the language. Lucie speaks English poorly. When she does not know what to say, she smiles.

He says that he will take her to hear the nightingales. She does not want to go into the thick dark mass of forest on the other side of the water, but she will not refuse him. Things have been bad lately. Once he tore up a letter from her father before she was able to read it.

'Your life is with me. Why do you cling to the past as if you prefer it?'

She thinks how his face will change when she tells him her news. He has not guessed, even though he watches her body like a hawk. Men are not as good at counting as women are. There's a new taste in her mouth and a sour twist in her stomach each morning.

They cross the water. It is a perfect evening, warm and still. She lets her hand drift in the current as he rows. He looks young today, as he used to look in France when he came to her father's house. She could almost persuade herself that he is that same man.

'John,' she says.

He looks up. A row of drops shivers on the blades of his oars.

'I have something to tell you,' she says.

'What is it?'

'Not now. Later, when we are listening to the nightingale.'

'I wish you would not smile like that!' he says violently, and she drops her head. This water is endless. What are they doing here? She cannot imagine. He loves her; this is why she came to England. This is why she finds herself in a wooden boat on a dirty river with a man who tells her not to smile.

They land. They follow the track through the meadows and he helps her over the stile. Now they are among the trees. Light filters through and flies buzz in her hair. The wood is rank with nettles, ivy and clinging vines. It smells of meat that is rotting. She thinks there must be an animal here which has hidden itself away to die. A deer perhaps. She puts her hand on his arm.

'I should like to go back,' she says.

'You have not heard the nightingale.'

She nods dumbly. There is no point in saying

anything. Misunderstanding is so thick between them that it has become a third language which neither of them speaks.

'Here is the glade,' he says, and they stop. She can hear nothing.

'Of course you can. Listen.'

He catches hold of her, turns her to face him. He does not know his own strength. He is not looking at her even though his eyes are on her face. She makes a sound in her throat.

'Listen!' he says and he shakes her hard. She bites her tongue and tastes blood. He is still shaking her, jerking her head this way and that so she cannot properly see anything. She feels something hot spurt out of her. She has wet herself. He holds her so hard that she cannot pull away from him. She twists in his grip, forward and then back. She ducks and her mouth gets to his hand and bites, as hard as she can. He cries out. For a second his grip slackens. She claws and bites and now she is free of him. She runs, stumbling over the rough ground. He is after her at once. Her skirts catch on brambles but she rips herself free and scuttles into the undergrowth where she will be smaller and faster than he. She is not thinking now. Her mind jags with terror and she plunges on. Her shoes fall off. A branch knocks her head and she whips herself under it and runs on.

He brings her down. She smashes headlong on the stony ground and he is on her. She hears his breath in her ear. She hears the night—

31

July 1793

Six months have passed since I lay on the hen-woman's floor. It is late July. Stock-doves purr from the woods on these warm and sleepy days. We eat cabbages, carrots and early potatoes from our vegetable garden. It is Philo who harvests them. She likes to shake soil off roots, and slash through cabbage stalks. The chickens are hers too. We keep our own goat and it provides more than enough milk for Thomas. He is crawling everywhere now.

There is a letter from Susannah. It has not come through the post, but has been brought first to London from Paris by a friend, and then onward. It was sewn into the lining of his cloak, which is the way with such letters. Susannah ought not to have returned to Paris, Augustus says, but it was impossible to persuade her not to go. She shares a room with a teacher of music, a Girondist like herself. They live quietly. They do not speak at meetings or draw attention to themselves. They are witnesses, Susannah says.

Augustus has tramped from Bristol to bring the letter. He will spend some days with us now, talking late into the night with Will. I hear their voices through the open window, and smell the smoke from Augustus's pipe. I go out to join them.

Charlotte Corday has been guillotined. She chose to kill one man in order to save a hundred thousand: or so she said. The question has been debated endlessly between us since Augustus first read Susannah's letter aloud last night. Augustus is for the Gironde, but even so he cannot approve of the assassination of Marat. Mademoiselle Corday said at her trial that Marat was perverting the Revolution, and this is why she killed him. Whichever way one looks, there is blood.

Susannah stood at the Place de la Révolution for the execution of Mademoiselle Corday. She waited for hours in the rain and so was close enough to see the event clearly.

'Read her account again, Augustus,' says Will. Augustus unfolds the letter, clears his throat, adjusts his spectacles and begins:

'You cannot imagine the crowds, my dear friends.
The guard had to draw their sabres to prevent
Mlle Corday being torn to pieces before they
could get her to the guillotine. She remained
composed. The noise all along the Rue Royale
and in the Place was indescribable, but when she

394

laid her head under the blade there was silence. You cannot imagine how steadfast she was. Her shift was soaked through with rain and her hair was in spikes where they had cut it short. The head fell. It was very quick: she stood, she knelt, she was no more. There was an instant of confusion, and then something happened which I have never seen or imagined possible. The assistant of the executioner – a carpenter, they say, whose duty is the correct functioning of the whole apparatus – seized the head, lifted it by the hair high for all to view it and then slapped the face hard. Her cheek flamed red where the blow was struck. The crowd gasped. They cried out in shock, as if at an abomination. Even those who had been ready to kill Mlle Corday with their own hands called for the blow to be punished.'

We too are silent. Augustus folds the letter carefully. At length he says, 'Charlotte Corday sacrificed her life, as I suppose, for the sake of her ideals. We may disagree with her, but such firmness of purpose demands our respect.'

He looks from one of us to the other. In the old days I might have thought him pompous but now I perceive – or think that I perceive – a deeper uncertainty.

'On that logic, any man may kill if he does it firmly enough,' says Will.

Mademoiselle Corday's cheek reddened under the blow, as if she were still alive. It was not enough for the executioner's assistant that she was dead. He slapped her to insult her. There must be more punishment. To kill someone is satisfying but then they are dead. They have got away. A body may be mauled and dragged about the streets but the spirit has escaped. If the man who slapped Charlotte Corday had been able to do so, he would have taken up her lifeless body, stitched her head back on to her shoulders, returned her to prison, tried her again, convicted her, jolted her through the streets on a tumbril, waited for her to kneel, signalled for the blade to drop—

'Did Susannah know Charlotte Corday?' I ask, and Augustus shakes his head.

'No. Mademoiselle Corday was not part of any circle in Paris. She lived in Normandy, and came to Paris only for the purpose of killing Marat. This will be a disaster for the Girondists, Lizzie, among whose number I count myself.'

But you are not in Paris, Augustus, I think.

'You must convince Susannah to come home,' I say. 'What purpose can it serve to watch such horrors?'

'She is determined.'

'They are all determined, it seems to me. What ideals are these? Charlotte Corday had a kitchen knife and her opponents had a guillotine blade. The result was the same.'

'Sometimes blood must be shed for the greater good,' says Augustus.

'I might kill for Thomas, if anyone threatened him. But I would not shed blood for words,' I say.

'Do not distress yourself, Lizzie,' says Will. He flaps out his handkerchief and offers it to me. It's only then that I realise I am crying. Tears run over my jaw and into my ears. My nose fills with mucus. I bury my face in Will's handkerchief and blow hard.

'In your condition, Lizzie . . .' says Augustus, patting my shoulder awkwardly.

Charlotte Corday is dead and Susannah will not leave Paris. *I have killed one man so that a hundred thousand may live.* That is what Mademoiselle Corday said at her trial. It sounds very fine. I suppose that she believed it and so she went to her death with a composure that was admired by all. She set her teeth to endure the jolt of the cart over the cobbles, the cold, the rain that plastered her shift to her breasts. *I have killed one man so that a hundred thousand may live.* But can that be true? Can any death be so justified? I believe not.

Perhaps I have not got enough philosophy to believe it. I think that one death leads to another, like sickness. *On that logic, any man may kill if he does it firmly enough.* My mind sheers off from the thought of it. I see Lucie in a light dress with her summer wrap around her, stepping out of the boat. She thought that she was going to hear the nightingale. But without Diner I would never find her grave, and even if I did, how would it comfort those poor bones to see Diner wag at the end of a rope? And my child would be branded the child of a murderer. Surely Lucie would not ask for that.

He is gone, I tell myself each morning. He will never

come again. I hope that the boat drifted in the snow-storm and was rammed on to a mudbank. He had no coat, and if the cold had not already put him to sleep then he would have gone down into the dark without a soul to know it. I hope so.

Will is watching me narrowly. He knows that these are more tears than I would ever shed for Charlotte Corday. He suspects that I have a secret and believes that one day he will get it out of me. He is very good with Thomas, far better than Augustus. He glances at me sideways sometimes, out of his light quick eyes, when he is playing with Thomas, and I know what I am meant to see. Even so, I can't help smiling at the crow of laughter from Thomas.

Will said to me one day, 'Sometimes I have to wait a year or more to find the right line to end a poem. Sometimes it comes all in one breath.'

'I would not have thought you were a patient man,' I answered.

'You are wrong. I know how to wait.'

Now there is a rich slant of light outside the window. I stand, breathing shallowly. 'I will go and see if there are any eggs,' I say.

'I will come with you, Lizzie,' says Will, and Augustus gives us an approving look.

We are rather too elegant for cottagers. Will was telling the truth when he said that there would be money. On the flagged floor there is a Turkey carpet, and we have lamps and copper pans that glisten in the firelight.

Hannah says with her old dryness that we are very luxurious, but Will only laughs at her. It seems that Hannah likes to be laughed at: I would never have guessed it.

He writes in a little room over the stairs. The walls are whitewashed and there is a deal chair and table, looking out over the garden and the hills beyond. 'Will is up in his room,' we say, and no one interrupts him.

I share a room with Thomas. I do not want to be parted from him again, even by Philo. He snuffles in his cradle like a little pig, and then I can sleep. Philo has her slip of a room above the kitchen and she is content. The warm days pass quietly. Philo has learned to plant and tend the vegetable garden and milk the goat. We have an orchard of four apple trees and an old plum tree propped with wooden stakes. Will says that he intends to construct a bower, although what it will look like I cannot imagine.

It is an idyll, I suppose.

The roar and rumour of the city reach us sometimes. Augustus comes often, as he did today, tramping the thirty miles from Bristol and thinking nothing of it. He does not bring Caroline, although I would not mind her presence now. His face is creased with anxiety over our friends in France. These are dark days, he says, but the true spirit of the Revolution is steadfast and it will triumph.

I think of how blood smells, and fear. They make much of Charlotte Corday's composure, but I would not be composed. I would kick and spit and struggle to the last second. I would use my nails and teeth to cling to life. I would not willingly play a part in their theatre of death.

Augustus paraphrases Shakespeare: 'Out of this nettle, danger, we pluck this flower, liberty.'

The old woman was right. There is a child in my belly, lodged under my heart, dug in deep. At night it pounds me with fists and heels. I can see that Augustus is fearful for me. He cannot help thinking of my mother's death. He said to me once, 'You are made very like your mother, Lizzie. You must eat well, and rest. Do not exert yourself.'

The balance of my body is changing. Sometimes I stagger when I get out of bed too quickly. I do not expect my weight to be where it is. My feet are swollen and there are thick blue veins on my breasts and belly.

No one speaks about Diner. They know a little; not much. They know that he is ruined, has gone away and will not return. Perhaps he has sailed to the north of Scotland, as Will once meant to do. But I think not. Be truthful, Lizzie: I *know* not.

Augustus says that the great terraces of Clifton stand arrested, as if the clock has stopped. It looks like the ruin of some ancient city. No one believes that the building will ever be completed. Builders and speculators are bankrupt, and there have been suicides. Diner is only one of many who have died or disappeared, and so he will be forgotten all the more quickly in the general wreck. It was a folly, Augustus says. They ought to have left the green fields to flourish, and not treated land and property as if it were a sure gateway to wealth.

I think Augustus, in his heart, is satisfied by the ruin, even though he would not wish ill to anyone. He did not want to see those splendid terraces slung above the Gorge, triumphant, dominating. He saw nothing but greed in Diner's vision.

We do not see one another clearly, any of us. When Thomas is tired by his bold adventures across the floor he crawls to me and clings to my skirts. In spite of his weight I lift him on to my hip and hold him there. I bury my face in the nape of his neck and kiss the hollow. He twists to face me. He regards me solemnly, pats my cheeks with his soft hands, laughs when I shake my head like a bear and growl. Thomas has no fear. I promise him that all's well and for now it is. I cannot promise more: I have learned better than that. I have so deceived myself. I have loved, with every fibre of my being, a man who lied to me from the instant that we met. A criminal: a murderer, I believe, although it will never be proved. His hands roused me to ecstasy in spite of what they had done before I knew him. I try not to think of Diner's hands on my body, but I feel them still, just as I feel the movements of the child he has seeded in me.

Will is a child, a boy. He jumps over the cabbage patch for sheer delight. He catches me in his arms and says, 'Marry me, Lizzie!' and I laugh and disengage myself. And yet when he goes up to his whitewashed cell he is another man. I would not dare to open the door and I am almost afraid of what he will bring down with him, on those pages crossed with his leaping hand-writing.

I will write my witness too. I want to write about Lucie, and how she died. I should like Augustus to understand what Diner was. He killed Lucie and sometimes I believe that he has killed me, too, but there must be something that can be salvaged from this wreck.

I see our house rise again, even though sometimes I hated it. The vaults; the wide, beautiful floors; the lovely set of the windows and the curve of the banisters, rising up and up in rhythm. I see those things now, because Diner saw them. I cannot stop seeing them. I cannot pull Diner out of my life, like a thorn from my flesh. He is within me. There were times when I did not know the difference between his body and mine. He inhabits my dreams.

I go too fast. I must learn to be patient. The baby pounds me, fists and heels. It is impatient too. I think: You would not be so eager, if you knew the world into which you are coming. But then my heart quickens and I am ashamed of fearing that I will not find in myself any love for this child. There must be love, even if it destroys us.

I think I will see Mammie again, when this child is born. I long to press myself against her, and warm my icy feet on her thighs. Her heat will be mine and there will be no more division between us. She'll stroke my hair back from my forehead. I'll smell the ink on her hands.

'My girl,' she will say, and I'll hear the sea-rush of her heart.

Afterword

As you go through Birdcage Walk you will see the gravestones deep in a tide of green. Some inscriptions are legible, others worn away. The undergrowth rustles with birds and squirrels. I have been walking through here since I was a girl and now I think of the inhabitants of those graves with fellow feeling. Once they were eagerly alive; once they were mourned. Now they have become part of the endless silence which surrounds our brief lives.

In this novel I am writing not only about a particular period of history but also about the ways in which the individual vanishes from historical record. This is something which has preoccupied me for many years. In my novel *The Siege* I wrote about a key historical event, the Siege of Leningrad, from the point of view of a small group of people, friends and family, trapped within the city. They lived through experiences which were at the most profound level a resistance to Hitler's intention to tighten the vice around Leningrad until its population was utterly defeated, and they lived 'from below', without privilege, without power or any sense of control over these huge events. But at the same time their actions and their very survival transformed history by contributing to the endurance of the city and to the turning of the tide against invading German forces. In *Exposure* I wrote about the Cold War, spying and deception from the viewpoints both of the spy and of the family which is ripped apart by the fallout of his betrayals. The voices of those who are cheated, imprisoned, stripped of jobs and homes tell the story.

In *Birdcage Walk* I was drawn to a period of great political upheaval and social change. It's the time of the French Revolution, when the fear of popular uprising haunted monarchs and politicians throughout Europe. British radicals followed the progress of events in France with passionate enthusiasm, but in some cases, as the Revolution unfolded, doubt was already growing. Wordsworth might write that 'Bliss was it in that dawn to be alive / But to be young was very heaven!'; however, very soon the streets of France were all too clearly full of complex and bloody rivalry, dissent and the growth of terror. Again, I wanted to write about people whose voices have not echoed through time and whose struggles and passions have been hidden from history.

Julia Fawkes is a British writer, renowned in late-eighteenth-century radical circles. She writes with the confidence of one who knows that an eager readership is waiting for her. Her voice is original, persuasive and disturbing, for she is writing about equality, the rights of women and the poor, and about the damage to society caused by hereditary privilege.

But the Prelude makes it clear that not one word of Julia's writing survives. Her work has not been preserved and all that is left is speculation about who she was and what she might have written. Even within the novel itself, there is none of Julia's writing apart from a fragment kept by her old friend Hannah, and shown to her daughter Lizzie. Julia's flesh has long since dissolved into the earth.

It seems to me that this was the common fate of so many of our ancestors, and as such it fascinates me. Only a very few people leave traces in history, or even bequeath family documents to their descendants. Most have no money to memorialise themselves, and lack even a gravestone to mark their existence. Women's lives, in particular, remain largely unrecorded. But even so, did they not shape the future? Through their existences, through their words and acts, their gestures, jokes, caresses, strength and courage – and through the harms they did as well – they changed the lives around them and formed the lives of their descendants. I wanted to show in the character of Lizzie Fawkes the profound influence of her mother Julia. It's an influence which Lizzie resists, much as she loves her mother, but still it colours her life.

The question of what is left behind by a life haunts the novel. While I finished and edited it I was already seriously ill, but not yet aware of this. I suppose that a writer's creative self must have access to knowledge of which the conscious mind and the emotions are still ignorant, and that a novel written at such a time, under such a growing shadow, cannot help being full of a sharper light, rather as a landscape becomes brilliantly distinct in the last sunlight before a storm. I have rarely felt the existence of characters more clearly, or understood them more deeply – or enjoyed writing about them more. I loved writing about the minor characters: Augustus, with his blend of absurdity and integrity; Hannah, so deep in the habit of devotion that she must find a new object for it once she can no longer serve Julia; and the ridiculous Caroline Farquhar, who rides in her carriage accompanied by her maid to view the conditions of the workers.

John Diner Tredevant is one of the most disturbing characters I have ever written. He is builder and destroyer at once, a clever and capable man, a man of vision defeated by a tide of events which he cannot control; and he is a murderer. I wanted to write about what murder does to the killer and how it destroys from within.

Throughout the novel, the fear is that Lizzie Fawkes too will be destroyed. Even in an Afterword, it's not for the author to say 'what really happens'. What happens is what happens inside the reader's imagination. But Lizzie – tough, observant, passionate but at times frighteningly innocent Lizzie – must change, harden and learn the way down to the underworld and back again if she is to survive.

I want to end as I began, with Birdcage Walk itself.

Time has taken away the church which was once attached to the graveyard: it was bombed to rubble in the Second World War. Rosebay willowherb grows so tall that the graves are all but hidden. No one lays flowers here; no one mourns. It is a beautiful place and also, on a winter night when rain thrashes down and light flickers through the cage of iron and lime branches, a place to make the living catch their breath, and hurry on.

Helen Dunmore
September 2016